The End.

Daaafuq?

The old way...

A blank page to reflect...

hands like it's the first TIME. Hug as if your LIFE depends on it. LOOK at them... like you're about to lose your eyesight. LISTEN... as if you're about to hear a secret. Sleep as if a big CHANGE is coming. LOVE them... as if they are YOU. Be TRUTHFUL to each other. Only allow PURE thoughts... that are worthy of YOU. KISS... like you'll never see them again. Hold hands like it's the first TIME. Hug as if your LIFE depends on it. LOOK at them... like you're about to lose your eyesight. LISTEN... as if you're about to hear a secret. Sleep as if a big CHANGE is coming. LOVE them... as if they are YOU. Be TRUTHFUL to each other. Only allow PURE thoughts... that are worthy of YOU. KISS... like you'll never see them again. Hold hands like it's the first TIME. Hug as if your LIFE depends on it. LOOK at them... like you're about to lose your eyesight. LISTEN...

THE WISDOM OF THE PENIS

WoTP

S.O.S.

MANUAL

DISCLAIMER

I wrote this *book* a certain way, so teens have the chance to take back what they thought was lost (altered, changed). For those of us no longer a teen, the freedom (*relief*) to go back and re-visit what we did, how we saw things, what we interpreted it to mean (let that be our road MAP) and be cleared of all misconceptions we had (*have*) about ourselves.

It's truthful, authentic to the core—a young adult's life. Their voice, emotion and temperament. It's written as if I'm one of them, stepping in and out of the role of a Fairy Goddess, who offers wisdom and insight about their life, love and self. All my personal stories and the stories told to me by teens, ranging from 14 to 23 years of age, are actual events that happened. I quote them verbatim. Their names have been changed to keep their identities private. I talk a lot about things that are never spoken of. I feel strongly that if we don't, they will continue to reign over us. Each generation stagnant, advanced and regressed (at the same time). Most importantly the silent cries... never heard. The language and content of this book is not meant to offend anyone. Its sole purpose is to be genuine and preserve the truth and emotional coloring of what's been shared. As with my experiences as a teen, how I felt and reacted to them.

My prayer...

To remove each blemish of bad experience you had (without scarring). Just as to my great surprise... it did for me while re-reading this book. Erasing marks (stains) I had no idea I was hiding. All experiences rewashed and recycled. ALL Fresh! I wish to plant a seed of hope and light in every teen (adult) so that the Fairy Goddess in *every* girl is no longer waiting to be BORN. The inner warrior in every guy, no longer stifled, smothered or asleep, waiting to claim HIS world.

Relationship Issues

From an Athletic Point of View.

LIFE - LOVE
YOU

If you REFUSE to ACCEPT anything but the very best...

YOU very often get just that.

Dedicated to you...

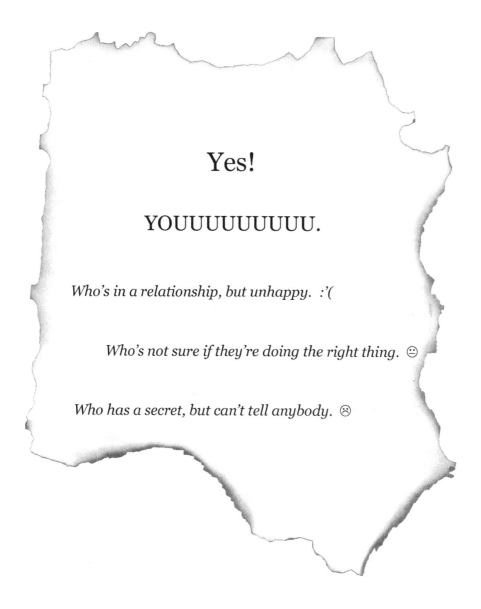

Yes!

YOUUUUUUUUU.

Who's in a relationship, but unhappy. :'(

Who's not sure if they're doing the right thing. 😐

Who has a secret, but can't tell anybody. ☹

Printed edition December 2016

Published by Gébo X Productions Inc. 10271 Yonge Street, Suite 100 Richmond Hill, ON L4C 3B5

inquiries@thewisdomofthepenis.com

Design by Nichole Kolman, Graphic Artist Christian Mauricio Wilde - A labor of love.

ISBN 978-0991673513

This book is cryptic...

If you don't get it now I assure you, LATER... you will.

Peace out. ☺

Feed her heart before you feed your hard-on

Love divided by nothing equals UNITY!

The Wisdom of the Penis - S.O.S. Manual

$$\text{WoTP} = \frac{<3}{0} = \underline{1}$$

Einstein would be proud. LOL

This book will speak to YOU...

What if...

You could **never** communicate how you feel?

Communication is a *gift*...

Everything in this world communicates *something*...

The birds, trees... ocean. Even the sky in its strength of *silence* is speaking. A building too makes a statement. *CAN'T TOUCH THIS!!* :D In LOVE... there is such an enormous loss when the soul is left, alone (connecting only physically) while its very core is ignored... unheard.

Communicating is a SURVIVAL skill...

Emotional Intelligence: Is it taught in your school?

My Promise...

I promise to keep YOU close...

So no one can hurt you.

Reminder!

SLANG !

This glossary is designed for the unaware (the unconscious) and the adult world. The terms and slang used in this book are explicitly in sync with the Y generation (young adults of today). Generation Y is also known as the Millennial Generation. FYI Generation Next and the Net Generation also belong to us. :=) If this was Monopoly we'd own the board. LOL The slang and phrases used in this book were obtained from the guys and girls I met while writing and a couple I created on my own (desperately needed). ☺

- **AF** (as fuck e.g. confusing AF)
- **Amnesty** (granting pardon for committing some specific crime, getting off the hook)
- **Bae** (oddly, a Danish word for poop, but used for someone's sweetheart, an upgrade to babe)
- **BFD** (big fucken deal)
- **Baked** (someone very high from smoking pot, stoned)
- **Bitching** (complaining like, "She wouldn't stop bitching about her boyfriend.")
- **Booked** (caught)
- **Boss** (something or *someone* that is so awesome or unique, they stand out)
- **Bootyism** (like a religion, but all about ass)
- **Brutal** (intensely bad)
- **Bum douche** (the lowest grade douche)
- **Butter Face** (everything's hot, but her face)
- **Cam-toe** (when a girl's pants are too high and tight in the front, showing the crease between her labia majora a.k.a camel toe)
- **Chated** (when someone rips you off, lies to cover it up or scams you)
- **Chirped** (being given shit in public, being made fun of them)
- **Chlorophyll** (a green pigment, that's in all green plants and has the responsibility of absorbing light so it provides energy through photosynthesis, since we humans and animals get our food supply by eating plants, well most of us... photosynthesis can be said to be the source of our life also. Look up benefits!)
- **Cock blocker** (when a girl tries to get in the way of YOU and the guy you're trying to hook up with)
- **Cray** (crazy)
- **Crib notes** (cheat notes to make up for, lack of studying)
- **Cyclops** (a member of a giant one-eyed species)
- **Daft** (stupid)
- **Dafuq** (what the fuck - short form)
- **Dang** (another word for damn)
- **Dip Shit** (person who says stupid things, annoying)
- **Ditto** (same thing)
- **DL** ('down low' something that is a secret and needs to be kept quiet... hidden, on the DL)
- **Dope** (signifying amazing like, "That's dope!")

- **Douche bag** (someone who takes advantage of people, puts people down to make themselves look better, acts like a know it all, annoys you to no end)
- **Drum driving** (drumming on your steering wheel to a song while driving)
- **Dutty** (person who's dirty, used, gutter mentality)
- **Dweeb** (someone who doesn't fit in or acts like a loser)
- **Enigma** (a person or thing that is mysterious, puzzling, or difficult to understand... me lol)
- **Erotica Jones** (my way of saying erogenous zones)
- **Family 'jewels'** (a guy's most valued commodity: His balls)
- **Fleek** (way up there near perfection)
- **For reals** (means for real, in actuality)
- **GED** (General Education Degree)
- **Ghosted** (when someone disappears on you, leaves you stranded)
- **Ho** (person who has zero self-esteem, no morals, and sleeps around for any reason, basically a slut)
- **Horn-dog** (guy who just wants SEX and is extremely horny)
- **Hundo p** (an abbreviation for a hundred percent)
- **I'm cryin'** (laughing so hard)
- **Imprinting** (a werewolf type thing, falling in love—at first sight. So strong happens instantly... very powerful force of UNCONDITIONAL love, not necessarily romantic—a permanent BOND)
- **Junk** (used to describe a guy or girl's sexual assets)
- **Killed it** (victorious)
- **Leaking** (crying)
- **LMAO** (laughing my ass off)
- **Mack** (make out with someone)
- **Magic stick** (penis)
- **Mains** (your close group of friends)
- **Manscaping** (when a guy shaves off superfluous fur, especially down south)
- **Man-up** (be a Man)
- **Manwhore** (guy who sleeps with anything that moves)
- **Mofos** (mother-fuckers)
- **Murk** (beat or defeat someone, something fiercely)
- **My bad** (admitting you've done something wrong)
- **NGL** (not gonna lie)
- **Nosferatu** (first film about Dracula)

- **Numb-nuts** (a very stupid person with the IQ of a pebble)
- **Obvi** (short form for obvious or obviously)
- **OMG** (oh my God)
- **One-eyed beast, joystick, mini-me** (some nicknames guys give their penis)
- **On point** (when something is of exceptional quality)
- **Orifice** (an opening in the body)
- **Pen15** (word with number attached to it, to disguise 'penis')
- **Plea bargain** (agreement in which a defendant pleads guilty to a lesser charge and the prosecutor drops the other more 'serious' charge)
- **Piss worthy** (hilarious)
- **Plox** (please)
- **Propagate** (to spread, re-produce, breed)
- **Pubic wig** (full, very bushy vagina)
- **Landing strip** (shaved clean *except* for one thin line of hair, like a landing strip for a plane)
- **Rainbow Party** (a party where girls wear different color lipsticks and then give a guy a blowjob, resulting in different colors on their penis)
- **Ratchet** (someone who is or looks trashy, ghetto, slutty, a mess)
- **Roasted** (being mocked, made fun of)
- **ROFL** (rolling on the floor laughing)
- **ROFLMFAO** (rolling on the floor laughing my fucking ass off)
- **Sesame** (taken from Ali Baba and the Forty Thieves... "Open Sesame!" Secret word used to open a door concealed among the bush. How fitting) :P
- **Sexting** (texting dirty shit, verbal foreplay, being really graphic and praying they'll be lured to sleep with YOU)
  Sick (insanely good, awesome, SUPER COOL)
- **Shade** (when someone gives you an underhanded comment)
- **Shag** (to screw a girl, have intercourse with her)
- **Ship** (short form for relationship)
- **Shittles** (cute version of shit)
- **Skank** (girl who sleeps with anyone)
- **Sketch bag** (root word – sketch (y) someone who looks like they're up to no good. Questionable, weird. You can tell they'd take advantage of you if they thought they could)
- **Slay** (tops killing it—MAJOR triumph. Victory)

- **Slu** (slut—sleeps with anyone, a short form of slut)
- **Solace** (comfort in a time of serious distress)
- **Spazzing** (out of control, freaking, tripping on someone)
- **Steeze** (combination of style and ease)
- **Stoked** (excited)
- **Swagger** (a person's walk, attitude... of confidence)
- **Ta-Ta's** (boobies)
- **TBD** (to be decided)
- **TBH** (to be honest)
- **Tdot** (slang for Toronto)
- **Till** (how many guys you've slept with)
- **Tool** (idiot, loser, someone who's gullible)
- **TTYN** (talk to you never)
- **Twat** (person who is ignorant, annoying or just unbearable)
- **Uber** (a German word meaning 'above'. Americans have translated it to mean super, the best, greatest)
- **Vag** (vagina)
- **Va-jay jay** (vagina)
- **Vas Deferens** (Latin term: Known as the 'carrying away vessel'. Narrow tube of the male reproductive system that carries sperm from the epididymis into the body to prepare for lift off. During ejaculation the smooth muscle in the wall of the vas deferens contracts, pushing the sperm toward the penis. My term: ONLY once we're satisfied does your jizz pipe contract and shoot your load)
- **Wheeling n' Dealing** (a prep before dating for a guy, pursuing someone he wants, a total balancing act between flirting and dating)
- **White noise** (crap that interferes with hearing, your mind talking shit, other people talking shit)
- **Without prejudice** (law term that means, without implying an admission of liability... guilt)
- **WTH** (what the hell)
- **WTF** (what the fuck)
- **Wuss** (zero balls, no guts, not a real man—pussy)
- **WWJT** (what would Jesus text, texting etiquette)
- **Zero chill** (uncool on so many levels)
- **11:11** (when you notice by *chance* it's eleven minutes after eleven o'clock... a MAGICAL time and you make a wish)

Call Me...

An Intellectual

Badass

This book's made from recycled paper cuz its *recycled* knowledge...

(The rules of grammar have been emotionally upgraded)

OUR LANGUAGE

THE WISDOM OF THE PENIS

^_^	Constipated-type smile
☺	Smiley face
☹	Unhappy
(=_=)	Tired
>.<	Confused or in pain
;_;	Crying a lot
:-|	Bored
(^_*)	Kiss my butt
(~_~;)	Sweating
_	Dazed
@_@	Eyes popping out
-_-	Eyes closed (sad/scared)
o_0	Scared (thanks Kristen!)
;_+;	Eyes swollen from crying

;<>	Big juicy kiss
:D	Smiley face with teeth (big happiness)
;)	Smiley face with wink/sneaky
;P	Smile with tongue out (stupid funny)
;P	Only kidding (maybe not)
:S	Don't understand (confused)
☺	Not happy/hopeless
:O	Shock
:-7	Smirk
:-E	Vampire
:')	Happy crying (relief)
>:o	Screaming!
:-~~	Drooling
]:|[	Robot

:*)	Kiss (quick peck)
8-)	Nerd
Q:-)	Graduate
O:-)	Innocent (halo effect)
-.-	Watching you
:-&	Tongue tied
:(	Crying
:-}	Embarrassed smile
:||	Pathetically sad
:-}	Smug
}:}	Loves trouble
<3	Heart (signifying love)
^.^	Wondering/confused
:#	Lips are sealed

A Note to Adults...

This book's designed for young adults (in slang) so you can understand what they go through, struggle with, their thoughts (fears) what gets them stoked. What they're CAPABLE of...

(when truly inspired)

...to bridge the GAP (if possible) between you. And to re-introduce innocence to those of you who have FORGOTTEN (don't feel worthy), to trade-in guilt (old model) for freedom... new model.

(So YOU too can be pain free) ☺

Key point...

It's THROUGH the eyes of a young adult (k, before they drove you insane, even after) that you'll see life REFRESHED (re-connect). Guilt can't touch YOU.

YOU feel entitled.

Light...

Energized... loved.

"Out of the mouths of babes Thou perfected praise." Psalms 8:2

Young adults learn more from what you ARE... than what you teach (preach/force/threaten). They understand and see a LOT more than we think. When you say... "Do what I say NOT what I do." Honestly...

That's being hypocritical.

A quick shout out to all my people. *Jokes*

Longgg.

Hugs n' Kisses

<3 <3 <3

To all the young adults over the past ten years who openly talked to me about what was going on in their life, as a means to reach those too scared to talk, too timid to come forward, too afraid to admit... Those I got to *know*... who enthusiastically talked to their friends, students and brought important material to my attention (issues) assisted and supported me, were inspired to CHANGE... I'm so proud of YOU. All the random people daily that encouraged me <u>not</u> to quit—NO MATTER HOW MANY BALD SPOTS I HAD ON MY HEAD. LOL Whether you were in my life two days, two weeks, two months, or two years... I love you allllll!

Your VOICE *has* been heard. <3

In addition, I'd like to thank these people for being BORN.

My Mom... Irreplaceable (for lack of a better word) <3 Unique... my gem. And that includes alllll you moms (in case, no one's mentioned it). My mom, no matter what pain I was in ALWAYS put it in its proper place... in the *light*. Inspiring me. I will never let you go... mom. <3 I extend her spirit to YOU (since she's dead) continue where she left off (through *this* book). ☺

My Dad... Worked so hard I never got a chance to know him. He gave me a special gift just before he died. He said... "If a man has YOU he doesn't *need* oxygen... (to breathe). If he ever lets you go, it's like losing something in the *ocean*... He'll have to wait ANOTHER hundred years to find it again." A Father gives his daughter the final imprint of *how a man will see her*... I'm so grateful to have known his heart. All the rest of YOU (Dads) pleeeeze SPEAK UP. We need you...

Michael R. Monteroso... A forever-love thing. Confirming... it absolutely exists. I had to move from LA to New York for school, all he said... "Another place... another time. I mean it Nichole I'm not just saying it." With an extensive celebrity clientele, he was known as the Trainer to the Rock Stars. He created the Workout Warehouse in Beverly Hills, where the ultra famous would go (unbothered). LOL I remember asking, "What'd you drink when you laid out the floor—it's UNEVEN." "A couple beers."

Michael died. Unexpectedly.

What really freaked me out? While preparing *this* page and re-searching archive articles I discovered, Michael was about to focus on a certain demographic. Young Adults. LOL He planned on helping them through communicating about fitness in his videos with his connections (music industry). He never told me. Odd, how the *idea* for this book came a few days after he died. Years later... while completing this book (fluke or not) I find out, we were headed the same way. Only he *knew* it before I did. Another *place*... another *time*. THAT'S WHAT HE SAID! Through this book we ARE joined—death can't touch us! (*Sniff... Sniff*) When it is magical... it always LIVES (no matter what). A mystical component does not abide by the rules of this world. Love YOU forever... Michael. ;_;

Frank Agueci... My Mechanic (my ROCK). Refused to let me STOP—no matter what I went through. Even when I was really DARK. I'm like, "I want... to DIE. Come back... Start allll over." He's like, "You're ALREADY dead. Now you're BACK!" And I'd snap out of it. TURN my whole world around. ☺ Make things happen. He sparked me in a way that gave me the *power* to CHANGE everything. He BELIEVED in me. He knew my strengths before I did (never gave up on me). He'd be like, "I feel like I'm supposed to help YOU do something very IMPORTANT." Frank... you will always be a sacred blessing. ;<> Promise to check my oil REGULARLY. ^_^

Frank Tito... A guy sent from the *heavens*... Who in my most desperate times, when he didn't even know me (without hesitation) LENT me money to continue the book. A man of true insight, business savvy, HEART (a rare mix). Without YOU Frank, I don't know what I would have done. ;_; Thank you for believing in me and standing the test of time (with your MOOLA). Lol A regal Knight, you remain in my heart... saved this damsel's ass. BIG time! Hugs...

Don Harben... A retired teacher who gave me the COURAGE to push 'my message'. Who unified (in my mind) what I was trying to DO, so it was clear, solid... Inspired. Who crystallized for me the *truth* of my book. WHY it was needed. He remains my dove, arriving only when there's *a message* for da' book. LOL Unforgettable...

Michael Landsberg... A man I was fortunate to meet when I was invited to be on his Talk Show. When YOU have a man like this in the wings, who responds to allll your emails (never too busy) it gives YOU a great sense of 'certainty'. Michael inspires you... Go BOLD (or go home). A visionary. He's capable of seeing things not yet *formed*... luckily for me. LOL When it comes to creative endeavors he has the innate ability to see it from the *eyes of the world* (both present and future). My 'Carte Blanche'. You're the best Michael!

Michael A. Levine... A rare breed of a man, so accomplished it's ridiculous. With a passion for law and the entertainment world, he dedicates himself SO much it's hard to believe it's just 'one' person. When you know a man like this, even if you don't see him, (much) knowing he'll always give you his opinion, point YOU in the right direction and most valuable lesson of all... When he says things like, "NO, is the first step to saying YES!" Works like a charm. His perfect faith in *himself* assures perfect faith in others giving him, what he WANTS (insanely brilliant). He carves a forceful mind in YOU. You have to succeed. There is no other way. Michael... A *silent* gift to me (and many others, I'm sure).

Gord I. Kirke... Practices entertainment and sports law in Toronto. As well as teaching law at a couple Universities in Toronto, he is a guest speaker at many Canadian and United States Law Schools. All the students look up to him. Hesitant at first, to show him my book (he's SO smart) I quickly saw (with him on my case) it was *meant* for him to read. He's like, "Nichole, where's my book?!" Waiting... for the verdict (*haaard*). Finally to hear... "I LEARNED a lot." Gave me value (equals 'winning'). Thanks!

Paul Lewis... President & General Manager of Discovery Channel. A man loaded with responsibility and yet... *hilaaarious* you'll piss yourself. It never mattered how busy he was when I had a question, idea... frustration. He'd be THERE. Replying with his no nonsense approach, humor tactics, precise strategy—a KILLER attitude. A man who constantly encouraged me to rise to the TOP. A powerful Ace. In a land where time works in twenty four hour blocks, this man carved out mini-blocks *'just for me'*. :D So I could climb my way up, have sure footing (be locked on target). Still to this day, he has no IDEA the strength and confidence HE gave me. A big present is what YOU are Paul. Thank you... Hope this book makes YOU laugh so hard!!

James A. Carmichael... Produced and arranged the hits of The Commodores, then teamed up with Lionel Richie to co-produce 'Missing You' for Diana Ross. His incredible talent led him to work with the Jackson Five and many other artists on Motown. Fortunately, he was referred to me to train. Never one to speak without purpose, he just looked at me one day and says, "One day Nichole... YOU will write." I'm like, "Me...? Write? HAAAA! I don't know *big* words." He's like, "YOU will write 'simple' to the masses, like Jesus did." "Uhh... yup. *Surrre. right.*" He saw so much in me. He made me feel like whatever I'd do, would be 'significant'. Always in my heart, James (hugzzzz) Signed, The Spirit of the Dancer.

Charles Glass... Considered the Guru of Training, not just in the fitness industry for bodybuilders but world class athletes too. I remember the first time Charles approached me. He was watching me workout. He's like, "YOU train a hundred percent. A hundred percent of the time! You're very WILLFUL." I'm like, OMG I can do *whatever* I put my mind to. *Sweet.* Three weeks prior to competition, depleted as hell I'm like, "Charles... I'm starting to get TIRED." (~_~;) He's like, "You CAN'T get tired." I'm like, "Oh..." And like magic! I wasn't. Not then... not 'ever'. No matter how taxing my life was, how hard I'd NEVER stop. I never quit. I kept hearing his voice in my head (YOU can't get tired). It wasn't a request. It was the LAW. A torpedo—is what YOU created, man. Timeless... is what you are.

Daniel Roopnarine... I ACTUALLY had to fight this dude, just to 'acknowledge' him. Such, is the humble character of this man. Like an invisible warrior silently (without my knowledge) he secured my domain name, held it in secret for years. I'm pissed searching for it, cuz someone's claimed it! It was him. Daniel kept it for me (safe n' sound) for so many years. ☺ Your HEART must have been chiseled in different time, dude... A time lost in the void. Mmmmwwwah! God Bless YOU.

To the guys I silently admire from a distance...

Whose words and actions have inspired me. The world's billionaires, their determination and amazing ability to remain undeterred (during HUGE lawsuits) CEOs of large software companies, businessmen with incredible tenacity, creative geniuses with BIG balls, who have strengthened me (in my times of need). I'm so grateful to all these men who never knew the impact they had on one girl's dream (in spite of her fears). They provided for me the perfect mold (an exact fit) through which I can plough through *sooo* many things. Some people have close family. Some... close *friends*. I have powerful men, quietly by my side (in my mind). Lol Resourceful.

The 17 yr. old guy... Who started it all... A random named Chris who walks by me at the gym, with this huge pimple on his forehead. I'm like, "Whoa... *That's* a girlfriend issue, pimple if I ever saw one." He freaks. He's like, "WHY do girls always expect guys to read their mind (know what they're thinking) allll the time? I give him an answer. He put both hands on his head, slowly shook his head side to side, he's like, "Omg! IF YOU TALKED... A THOUSAND GUYS WOULD COME! Which inspired seminars and the demand for a book. A whole hearted thanks... dude.

My Girls!

Anna Stambolic... At the time, Director of Outdoor Life Network (OLN). While hosting their TV Show, Anna asked to meet with me. I was so nervous. She said, "Nichole, I had my nephews and nieces over the weekend while you were on TV—they could NOT take their eyes off you. They just sat there. Literally *frozen* while you talked. YOU have something... and it's special. You're meant to do GREAT things." A powerful woman says that to you, you *don't* stay the same. It acts like a shield, protects and guides you. Fuels your ass, man. You Anna, remain the lighthouse in my seas of adventures. Priceless... You'll ALWAYS be for me. <3

Tracy Gray... CEO of Aradia Fitness, Fitness Pole Dancing. A self-made woman whose razor-edge business sense and shrewd insight is hard to duplicate. Tracy became my client and good friend. Believing in every girl's right to shoot for the moon (*give to herself*) SHINE, she created a platform (with heels) in which they can. After I answer a question about a guy she was seeing Tracy demanded, "Where's the BOOK? Nichole start writing! The WORLD'S waiting for your *wisdom*." Which pushed me forward—fear and all. Never stopped since. Love you girl!

Christina Koutrouliotis... We all have a special little angel... Patiently watching us, ready to kick-ass (for us) reminding us... Baby STEPS (forcing us to take a break). Over the last 7 years mine has been a Montessori Teacher named, Christina Koutrouliotis. Every time I'd be like, "What IF... no one likes it?" She'd be like, "THERE'S NO IF!! THERE'S NO IF!! Give me shit, every time I had doubt. Stayed by my side till it was DONE. Still freaking—there's no more re-dos!! LOL A true gem and huge blessing to anyone who knows her.

Driven by Spirit...

Had I not been granted the *connection* to an unstoppable force shielding me from conventional thought—this book would NOT have happened (it'd be missed).

Learning to see...

Through the eyes of the body

It gave me an internal compass to be RAW—tell it like it is. Own it. Navigating me through the corridors of hellll, I was steered to closure. Fueled by spirit... my safety was secured (arriving where I needed to) *in your hands*.

No fear, no doubt, no question.

And if YOU don't think there is a Spirit, just GO visit your friendly neighborhood morgue. Take a look at the eyes of a dead man (*no spirit*) vacant. Morbid... maybe, but just gotta make my point.

To Everyone...

I'm SO grateful that people I met took it upon themselves to tell me, show me, convince me, I had something important to say. Don't know what I woulda done if your MOM and DAD didn't meet. LOL Just goes to show, no matter what you're going through (forced to give up) have to *LEAVE*...

You <u>are</u> being RE-ROUTED.

It all leads you to the right person (people) who've been set up for you. Including those ugly experiences... when seen in their true light, will enhance YOU (if you understand their function). <3

To win the game of LIFE...

P.S.

To the guy I was so fortunate to meet who encouraged me to finish this book. Who continues to be informed, responsive, direct-to-the-core on any input towards this book. Thank YOU Steven Zuccaro.

THE

PURPOSE OF THIS BOOK...

To extract the hero, hunter and prince...

from EACH ~~asshole~~ *Oops! I mean guy. LOL*

If only each guy GOT this book... as a birthday present. LOL

Essentials...

1. Tissue box (for tears piss worthy & sad)

2. Pen or pencil to do assignments

3. Markers to circle important shit

MENU

WoTP

Substance & Insight

Desserts

Real Yummy

Mints

<u>WARNING</u>

The statements in this book have not been FDA approved. You may have difficulty absorbing, assimilating, digesting (and or burping) the substance in one sitting. LOL Take your time, a meal rushed is never savored. I'm serious. It's deep.

$$wotp = \frac{<3}{0} = 1$$

An Empty Cup...

If YOU start with an empty cup—you can only gain. Free your mind of everything you *thought* you knew... wanted to KNOW. Had to know.

And you'll receive it.

CAN'T receive if you already *think* you know (no room to enter). ;P

The Message...

Take this book and close your eyes.

ASK...

What am I in the dark about? What do I need to see that I'm NOT seeing?

OPEN to a page...

(Start on your left)

Your Fairy Goddess has spoken!

Your Inner Warrior (for you dude). LOL

I DARE YOU...

YOU WON'T BE
THE SAME...

AFTER YOU READ
THIS BOOK.

The 4 Lessons

You're gonna need a highlighter!

I believe there's a certain cooking process to alllll things. After all... we are cookin' man. (All *hot n' bothered*) LOL Seriously. We take jabs at you guys all the time then complain you're not tender *enough*. We poke and prod and stick it to YOU—right where it hurts. Then wonder why you need SPACE... (to heal). My bad. When we're really pissed... we let you soak in it. Give you the *silent* treatment.

Life HAS a system...

If we adhere to that system, we'll not only get to the top of our game— we'll CHANGE the game. :D Everything we thought we knew... feared to say, felt we knew... afraid no one would listen, wondered why this... why *that*—we'd DECODE it. It's the *reason* you picked up this book.

(Or someone gave it to you)

CLASS PREP

The world is INCOMPLETE... without YOU.

—I'm not kidding!

The time is *now... TAKE IT.*

The power is YOU... <u>Own</u> it!

This BOOK brings to you allll you would know... (could *know*) might know, in the future (*if you're aware*). Q:-)

Imagine...

Your best friend gets transported to the **future** becomes a worldly adult—has allll these relationships (drama n' life shit) comes BACK. To tell all the girls... Why you guys do all the DUMB shit you do. Tells all the boys... Why we girls do allll the crazy-ass-bitch things we do.I MEAN... There are **reasons** why we do what we DO. And the life signals we *miss*... till (sadly) it's TOO late. ;'| It gives YOU hindsight in *advance*...

It's your destiny CARD...

Will YOU play? Will you fold? Will you put it in your back pocket (use it as your secret weapon)? Probably. If it meant you gettin' ahead... gettin' what you WANT (for yourself, your life, your love)?

(I would)

Life is 'learning' HERE...

Biggest crash Course YOU'LL ever take. Lmfaoo

Maybe that's why *creating* feels like Heaven... singing, acting, dancing coding, writing... K sex (that's obvious). You guys see a hot babe you're like... "*OMG. I think I'm in heaven.*" Your voice drops... can't speak. Can't think, can't function (thank GOD your part works automatically) and there are no crib notes (cheat sheets) on *Earth*.

No one you can pay off (previews) and the bags won't show under your eyes (if you passed/struggled/failed) you'll feel it in your SOUL. Agents of fear (your demons) follow you wherever you go, if you've done something you can't live with.

Second chances don't come often.

But a hall pass'll set YOU free! That would be doing your favorite thing (singing, sports, cheer-leading, martial arts, writing, acting, graphics). It's your escape man... your *heaven*. It's the one truth NO one can challenge in you, ya know it's real. YOU know it's a part of you.

You feel complete when you DO IT.

It's your TRUTH (so your reality) doesn't matter what people think *truth* don't make no decisions, so nothing to decide between... just YOU and your sport (music, dancing, acting, writing, coding) ...pure bliss.

AND NOTHIN' AND NO ONE CAN SEPARATE
YOU.

(God help them if they try)

The following stories are true. The names have been changed to protect the innocent, unconscious (wasted) and clueless. Scenarios, peculiar hysterical circumstances and *personal* stories have been taken from my experiences with great resistance on my part. Four DAYS crying by the lake. Like! Do I REALLY need the whole world knowing allll this shit?

FINE!!!

Bringggg it!!

I've also included observations I've made as a professional trainer, (competitive athlete) from all my years in the gym (spyin' on people) a.k.a. PEOPLE watching. Seeing what makes a guy go to a girl, what does he need to ensure 'safe passage', how girls respond, what makes them doubt a guy (move to or AWAY from him) body behavior (patterns) key indicators that come up allll the time, when a girl *makes* the first move, a guy (his *friend*... for him). Getting awesome feedback and encouragement from everybody. Young adults talking 'bout all their issues, slang, struggles and personal stories (what really

PISSES guys and girls off) my clients (both male and female) *fo shur* my life... And the <u>hard</u>-earned facts I was awarded.

After graduating the University of Adversity. LOL

EARNED that friggin' degree *fo* shur. #!!*!@&#?%!!@#!*

A thesis is born!

Relationship Issues from an Athletic Point of View...

I like!

It took me *forever* to see how my competitive spirit RULED when it came to a guy. And even though it really drove me... in terms of what I wanted in life I found out (fairly quickly) how it DIDN'T— when it came to my relationships. Ugh. And how I stuck to my ways, even though there was a better way (*smarter* way) easier way. Why COULDN'T I stop? Something 'inside' wouldn't let me.

<u>LESSON ONE:</u>

The warrior is always in search of a battle...

(There was SO MUCH to think about)

It was like a chess game. I was going crazy trying to figure it all out. *_* Every time I'd pass my King (he's pissed) the bishop (his *friend*) would make a move. Trying to advance, he'd be blocked. And like a pawn (limited mobility fo shur) he'd be captured. (Booked) But that still did *nothing*. ;'| King and I... stale-mate(s). NOT going anywhere. Game over. So Done. Couldn't even call my Knight... gave him up to have my King. ;_;

What I saw as strength (totally off) and what I *thought* was weak-ness... FLAWED. Just the thought of being vulnerable made me break out in hives. I HATE being weak. *Eewww*. Then one day...

A light bulb moment. :D

The power of a little girl...

I lived with this family, they had a two year old little girl. One day, I took her in my car (on my lap) we drove in circles in front of her house. Ever since then... EVERY friggin' day, "Kiko I want CAR." Missing two front teeth so can't say *nnni*... I'm like, "No sweetheart, not now. I CAN'T. Big rush. When I get back—promise." She's like, "Kiko... I want CAR." (BIG smile) Like she's gone deaf. Like, she never heard me the first time. I'm like, "Noooo baby girl... I can't. I am SO dead if I show up late for work. Gotta run!" I'm tryin' to put my shoe on, hopping downstairs. She's at the top of the stairs lookin' down. She like, "Kiiiko. I WANT car!" o_o (Holds her stare) I call work. "Heyyyy it's me. I'm coming—just caught in this HUMONGOUS traffic jam. Or maybe, the President's in town! It's sooo messed up. YOU know what. It's gonna take me a good THIRTY minutes *extra* for sure." How did a little girl totally rearrange my whole day?

She always gets her way...

Was she really weak (vulnerable) or was she powerful? The MOST powerful thing in the world... the one thing (K, maybe two) that doesn't even have an IQ (really) but makes anything you're pissed about (upset or sad) *disappear* in like, a nanosecond?

Nano: Something extremely small. Taken from the Greek word 'nanos' which means dwarf. So yeah, by all means use where appropriate with your guy. ;D

The TWO things that can make anger disappear instantly—that's NOT a drug? Animals AND babies. At least while you're looking at 'em... For instance, if a little puppy peaked his head from behind this book, what state of mind do you think you'd be in? Smiling already...

If it was sitting on your lap staring at you? Even though you just broke up with someone (parents got divorced) someone close to you moved (super stressed) your heart would be *open*... not shut with anger.

(Closed cuz no one cares)

Vulnerability... (placed in safe hands) is very *powerful*. It brings YOU in... *keeps* you there (as long as it wants). Just like puppies! Kittens, a girl's tears (gets you every time). In the same way, your absolute BELIEF in yourself, lures people into your orbit. YOU are irresistible...

It took me so long to challenge what I thought was *weak*... crying in front of a guy (asking for help) accepting a compliment, having a guy do ANYTHING for me, really. Then I'd analyze what I saw as *strength*... Making him totally DEPENDENT (he'd die without me) staying with a complete asshole, telling myself I could change HIM. Compromising... Like, *fuuuck me!*

(I hear YOU)

LESSON TWO:

We always teach what we MOST need to learn...

This book's friggin' proof! LMAO

It only sinks in once you've *taught* it to someone else. It HAS to go through you first (KNOW you **got it**) lol so you're calm inside (in your approach) cuz you know you've nailed it. And that's why words never teach... just *experience*. Doesn't matter how well they talk the TALK, if you don't feel moved—it didn't hit your GUT. That's cuz it's pure animal—doesn't respond to wordiness, just what's already THERE... experience. This could also be why parents freak out (most of them) at the things they never truly mastered themselves (so CAN'T reach you) or it always fucked them up, so they think it's gonna fuck YOU up. The more they freak, the more it's a familiar zone. Sometimes it seems like they're silently screaming at *themselves* while looking at YOU.

6.

Maybe next time we'll show some sympathy. LOL

When someone's being preachy, tellin' you how to BE (or not be) repetitively. Doubting you'll get it (do it). Chances are... Somewhere they've struggled with it (or still do). Whether someone's givin' you a compliment, speaking against YOU, making fun of YOU—the root of it (literally) is inside *them*. YOU can't recognize something you're not familiar with... (to comment on). If they feel good about themselves (they see recognize they're special) they'll see that in YOU.

Or the opposite...

Although they're criticizing you, somewhere they're suffering from it (in a different way). Either cuz of themselves (*in their head*) or another person (usually someone close). Harsh on YOU (someone's being *harsh* on them). A bully... they've been bullied. Hurtful... they've been hurt. An insensitive ASSHOLE... they're desensitized to their own PAIN.

You can only DO what you've experienced...

It's easy to *learn* bad shit... Secretly, it's pain without a mouth to CRY. So it needs to be LOUD (noticeable) communicates through behavior, cuz you never learned to ASK. Repeat after me... 'help me'. Again... That's a start. <3

(Don't worry you'll get used to it)

When you no longer feel help-*less* you'll realize... you're supporting **yourself**. It's like asking for money (when you don't have). Sucks. When you know you have, just need some to get by (but can pay it back) it's not so HARD... (to ask). If you have confidence in yourself, that you'll get it (cuz you know you're good for it) you'll get it. Your behavior alone... feelin' good about yourself *makes* people feel good about givin' it to YOU.

My Acting teacher always confirmed this in class. He'd be like, "If you're truly feeling pain (in your scene) people will feel it too. It must *travel* through you." So obviously, it needs to be felt internally first. Then it can be delivered... message received. Experience *felt*. In reverse, it also works. Someone accusing YOU of something (you're sneaky, selfish, showing off, manipulative) wouldn't be able to identify *that* without first **experiencing** that. There'd be no reference point. They'd be neutral about it. If they saw it, they wouldn't really know what to label it. Haven't formed an opinion (judgment) on it... (yet). I'd listen very carefully next time your friend's pickin' on someone (accusing or criticizing them). It TELLS YOU how they are... literally. Or could be (when you're not around).

Yeah, I can be sneaky. :P

REVIEW:

To teach... or have others feel anything (love, hate, humor, pain, sadness, inspiration) has to be inside YOU first. You need to feel *that* (be that). That's why girls who love life are always HAPPY. They love themselves... it's a *positive* vibe (NOT a selfish one). They feel good about their shit. And YOU guys are so pulled to that.

You wanna feel the love. (Ditto) A guy who's confident KNOWS he can make a girl happy. If inspired. No one can top him, he excels in HAPPY 101. Like, after a date. He doesn't attempt a seat-HUG (in the car) he *gets* out of the car, goes allll the way around, opens the door. Hugs HER. *Impressive*... Seriously, it's hard enough to know *how* to hug a guy, so it's best they lead the WAY. Real life example. I hook up with a guy, he tries to hug me while we were walking. I'm like, "I don't DO hugs... Not into 'huggy-shmugy'." We get back to his car and he drives me home. I'm about to step out and he's thinkin'... 'So she doesn't do hugs, huh? We'll see about *that*. I'm gonna get out of the car, go all the way around, open the DOOR—*give* her a hug.' He wouldn't give up on the hug! The going to the door... was INTERCEPTION. Full throttle. LOL It worked. Course, I found all this out after we were official. :=) One thing fo shur. We girls DON'T like lazy and we don't like giver-uppers. The kind of guy that thinks of a girl morning - noon - night, watches her in class, at work (if they're working together) the gym (NOT a creep) for real (totally into her) analyzes her every move. Wants to know who her friends are, how to bypass the snobby bitch closest to her. A lot of work. LOL He'll figure a way. Cuz he'll study her closely. What she likes (don't

8.

like). What gets her STOKED (upset). And he'll wait for the *perfect* time... to step in. Be there for her. He's on a MISSION. That's hot. He knows he can make a girl happy... so he's very picky. Like, a good *boss* is.

Stay in groups till he's fully identified HIMSELF.

> What you *feel* inside... is what people **pick up** on.

Even though they might not know how to read it, they'll respond to it (cuz they'll feel it). So if you feel worthless (no one wants me, I'm unattractive, there's nothing's special about me) EASY prey. A guy or girl can feel *that* be pulled to you (use you). In a sense... you really are transparent. If you feel like shit, people feel it. If you feel like a winner—people are more careful with you (they don't want to lose out). ;D Just like a person who really inspires YOU. They can ONLY make you feel that way if they're truly *inspirational*. Somewhere... they've conquered something powerful (personal) a true warrior. Need an emoticon that bows here. I know what you're thinking... Some people can fake it—and then what? *I'm fuuucked.* (Not so)

E.g. Some actors cry technically on 'cue' (really well) that's why when you watch them in a movie (see *tears*) you don't feel much. And you're NOT insensitive dude. K. Maybe you are. When you pulled out *waay* too soon. Careful... I may send The Testicle Fairy to go n' collect—YOU don't like to pay your dues.

My boyfriend's like, "Testicle Fairy, huh? What does she leave behind?" The *other* testicle. LOL

Crying for real, is always a struggle when it's authentic. Actors LEARN to cry at designated times (it's what they're trained to do) but that doesn't mean you'd respond to it. Emotion *responds* to emotion... it's the only world it knows. That's why seeing a girl cry, is so hard (especially if she's yours). If there's no rich inner life (real sad feelings) stimulating your body into 'action' your body won't be stimulated (when you watch it). That's why it's so easy to be into someone who's *already* into you... you can feel it. (Only they haven't told you) It's feeding your attraction to them, even if you're unaware. And yes... you can totally be hot for someone who doesn't know you're alive (yet). Sadly.

Sometimes seeds take a little longer to sprout... and *grow*. LOL

The boo fuckin' hoo game...

(You'll wanna pay attention to this part)

You guys could be cryin' your head off trying to make a girl BELIEVE you—still won't do much. Unless... She's real gullible. Or you're an actor. But when you're actually *choking* on your words, when it's uber difficult to even SAY it, then she'll pay attention. Cuz she can feel your *struggle* (pain, embarrassment) cuz it's **real**. And don't even *think* of pretending to choke. This book will be EVERYWHERE!!

I remember one summer, a really cute guy in the gym was tryin' to hook up with me. But he had this EX thing going on—so nooo THANKS! He kept telling me it was over. *Right...* I skip the gym for a week... just to clear my head. I come back. While I'm parking I see his friend. But he's walking funny. Super bow-legged. Maybe, he pissed himself. :P It looked painful... Maybe he hurt himself in the gym. I go to ask. "Hey Charles. YOU okay? Why are you walking like that?" He's like, "*Sticky* luggage." Looks *down...* between his legs. O_O Dafuq? You guys can be seriously disgusting. He's like, "There's nothin' more *grossss* on a hot humid day than wearing boxers and hearing them slap against your LEG." (Ewwww) "Uh... There is. You havin' to peel them off." Regardless of Mister disgusting and his *baggage*... it made me realize that we <u>do</u> feel things (when it's real). And we don't even *have* balls! So glad I'm a GIRL. We don't have that problem, we don't have things flappin' (*slappin*) in the wind. LMAO Except, maybe when we TALK. ☺ We can feel you... makes up for all the times, you feelin' us. LOL

(Payback's a BITCH)

I walk into the gym and see the guy (pursuing me) by the entrance. Looks, like he hasn't SLEPT in weeks. Huge dark circles around his eyes. You'd think it was stage make-up. Omigosh!! Maybe it is. Guys can be so creative (you just never know). Seriously, he was so down he actually LOOKED sick. I walk up to him I'm like, "Are you alright?" He's like, "I thought you left. Moved AWAY." I'm like, "No, I took a break (lie) you look TERRIBLE." He smiles. But only half a smile... you know the one you guys do when you're relieved—don't know what to say next (in a daze) type. ...A *crooked smile.* THAT'S sooo sexy.

Just so you know.

Still... he's got an EX hanging (like a hangnail) its gotta go! But it's gonna hurt. Too bad! It takes TWO... or there'd be nothing to hang on to. Not impressed. He must be holding on *somehow.* Maybe he's waiting for someone new before he lets go. THAT'S so wrong. Cuz trust me, when you least expect it someone's gonna leave YOU.

Exception: YOU have a psycho bitch on your hands (scary). That's <u>not</u> normal.

So, he's reaching into his gym bag he's like, "I got these... for YOU (t-shirts) in EVERY color. I had them the whole week." Coulda sworn I heard violins playin'. :D Cautiously... I start dating him. When a guy looks all emo on you (cuz he hasn't seen you in a WEEK) that I pay attention to. @_@

Like I said the body doesn't lie... it *responds* (or doesn't) when something *makes* it (love, sadness, emotions). I loved how he made me feel. Like I could be myself. :=) That REALLY showed on our first date. He was so excited to see me! Counted all the smiley faces he sent. Fifteen. Right after class he picks me up in his car—one HUGE *mother fuk—er* bright red TRUCK! It felt like a *dreammm* sittin' in there. I felt like Barbie in her big badass car. We go to a café. He gets a table and I go to the bathroom. But I peek from *behind the hallway...*

Right... like YOU'VE never done that.

You just never know when we're watching YOU guys. So keep eyes respectively 'in check' it really impresses us when we see OTHER girls tryin' to make a move, and you be *immune.* You got our love-bug. ☺ Not to mention, that girl'll be even hotter for YOU—she's ready to SPILL it. She's so turned on by the FACT that your only focus is your girl (potential). So, staying true blue secures YOU won't be that shade *later.* (Blue balls) Or, if you're scum... You've lined up empty vessels (*skanks*) for your next jizz load—rainbow party fo shur.

I'm watching him...

11.

He's sitting at the table with a vase of daisies on it. And what's he doing? Picking off the petals **one** by **one**... "She loves me... She loves me NOT. She LOVES me. She loves me NOT." *I RUSH* over to the table. I'm like, "Stop!! You're running out of petals! And you're killing the flower. Why you doin' this to your-self?" "Cuz... *I'm really into YOU.*" "Fine—then go to the source, man! Like, I'm right HERE." "Much easier to ask the flower."

(Feeling all gooey inside)

What really won me over? We're talkin' about family n' stuff and I tell him how I don't have anybody. I'm like, "It's cool. When I'm lonely and afraid I do like *this*..." I wrap *both* arms around myself (to hold me) his eyes water.

That completely blew me AWAY. <3

Caught this badass mermaid—tail, fins, hair n' breasts.

Note:

Mermaids don't have legs that open—if he wants her he has to capture her... *all of her.* <3

He was so *sensitive* to my pain, even though I wasn't showing (true sensitivity). Then there's you guys... who cry so fucken easy it's SAD. Cuz it's mostly about your shit. The second we talk about our stuff you whine about how bad it is at home. So... we say nothing. Try to be there for YOU. Meanwhile we have no one (to be there for us). A guy like this, is used to accessing his emotions (actor, singer, writer, gamer, graphic artist) or... is truly in love with you (at a **breaking point**) even then, it's hard to let it all hang out like that. It's like, he's *giving up* a part of himself, putting it in front of your feet. NOT knowing if you'll step on it. Fart on it. Pick it up... BIG risk on his part.

(Fair)

Still... When we have a fight and you guys are like, 'sorry.' It's all about YOU. Cuz you're *not* sorry about how you treated us (neglected us). }:< You're sorry, about what you lost, what it looks like (to *others*). Not havin' something you can count on. And mostly, what everyone's sayin'. LOOOOSER. You made a **big** mistake.

You know it's true...

One more thing about the little girl in the car...

(We'll get to your point *soon*... promise dude) LOL

She gets what she WANTS... Why?

Check List: (Little Girl)

   ☐ *Sweet*   ☐ *Adorable*   ☐ *Confident*
   ☐ *Happy*   ☐ *Loveable*   ☐ *Princess No. 1*

How do you match up to that? All six need to be present. It's not a coincidence, that six in numerology is the number for LOVE.

Unleashing our power comin' up!

I thought about it. How one little girl could get away with SO much. I thought about it a lot. Then I started *obsessing* about my whole entire life. Like, how I ran my life. More like, how it ran me. Right into the ground! FACE first—*majjjor* nose burn. Not pleasant.

Sacrificing my security and my future (**bitter**) giving away money (**angry**) ignoring my career (totally **miserable**) and sport (mega **frustrated**) stopping school (feeling like a LOSER) cuz of family.

Putting myself last...

NOT getting what I want.

So I can tell myself... I'M A GOOD PERSON.

It kept smacking me in the face. And I saw how it affected everything I did. Every connection I had with a guy or girl. Like! I can't believe I let this one *bi-atch* get away with SO much. We'd go to a club. And just cuz one time I ACTUALLY wore make-up (to match her three foot paint job) she gets pissed. She's like, "Those guys that just passed, looked at YOU." She's throwing some shade. Fine. Whatever. I'm like, "K... Maybe they looked at me *first*—but then they looked at YOU. So you're the one they're gonna REMEMBER." Down playin' myself so my BFF could feel good. So she wouldn't feel like she had competition. Putting myself down so she could feel up. She's the type to walk down the hall, while I'm talking to a guy I LIKE... start a conversation with him. Zero chill. (Cock blocker) I was mad AF. Said nothing...

Don't you hate it when they come into class and they're like... "Hey! Look at my new bra." Says it out loud. Pulls a strap out so her whole boob is practically showing. Then she's like, "*Oooh*... my boobs are itchy." scratches it for the WHOLE universe to see. Takes a selfie. Just cuz she needs so much attention. Ratchet ass bitch. I felt like I didn't have the right to be beautiful (if it meant someone I cared for would feel less). I KNOWWWW IT'S INSANE.

(It's how I felt)

Everything I thought I knew about relationships (guys/life/self) was OFF. That same boss-ass attitude (athletic mind-set) I had about life, made me painfully aware of just how *easily* it was used against me. My strength was pinnin' me down, man!

LESSON THREE:

A sword can save a life just as quickly as it can take one.

My life and its intensity (obstacles, injustices, severity) all prepped me so I COULD be a champion. I <u>had</u> to WIN. It delivered me *back* to the world... whole. It showed me.

Like coal... being pressed into a diamond

the more pressure the more you SHINE.

Just like watching TV Specials on MMA fighters (love YOU guys). They say the best fighters come from Brazil. Why? Cuz they train in the most dangerous neighborhoods. You need a drug lord's permission just to interview them. LOL And just like that, my experiences geared my mind *a certain way*... My competition (training) was never about ANOTHER human being, it was about me—and the war I was having with life. WHO would win?

No matter what the odds...

I was already equipped with a do or die mentality. So everything I'd go after, I'd get. Career - guy - job - sport. I'd WIN... Cuz I HAD to. All the shit and constant struggle, was okay. Cuz just like training with weights, the way you guys do when you're thinkin' of your enemies (to push you) **same** thing. It's all about the stuff that's happening to you. All you're thinking is... *YOU'RE NOT TAKING ME!! Grrrr*... All that resistance puts you way ahead of the competition (life or sport) cuz the overspill is just <u>guaranteed.</u>

GO HARD OR DON'T GO!!

And you find yourself doin' things you never *thought* you could. So when you <u>do</u> tackle the GAME of life... You WIN. On your terms (it's a given). Not just cuz your technique is uber hot—cuz you've eaten enough dirt to KNOW...

<u>LESSON FOUR:</u>

Strength *comes* from **no choice**... That's where it lives.

That's how it's BORN.

The **secret** to life...

It boils down to one thing. Who'll get tired first... YOU

Or your obstacles? Whether you're striving for a championship, dream come true, a GIRL—that's right I said 'girl'. You don't strive for a guy (they'll sniff that shit out). YOU *inspire* a guy (...*meow*). It takes guts (and not the kind you think) it takes *skill*... (self mastery) and along the way there are lessons to be *learned*...

Pens out!

(On second thought markers)

CLASS IN SESSION!

Announcements first...

All throughout the development and *birth* of this book (MAJOR C section) *ahead of time*... so loads of rebuttals, blocked attempts, fear.

A dangerous passage...

(Heartache)

Giving up... STOPPING.

S T U C K

(A lot of tissues)

They say, everything you DO or THINK will affect the next *seven* generations (stagnation versus renewal). Standstill... Rebirth. Holy crap! And you don't think YOU matter? You're **IRREPLACEABLE**. You've been *brought* here do something significant. That little feeling always tellin' you that... I'm confirming it.

(Fairy power) LOL

If you don't do it... It'll be LOST.

Something that you and only YOU can do.

(Don't fuck with that)

YOU will have an effect on every person you meet, what you say... (message YOU give) even your special brand of wackiness is gonna be important. It'll make them DO something... go somewhere, trigger an event, set things in motion cuz YOU my friend... *Are a time keeper.*

Synchronicity is waiting for YOU... to happen.

If you're feeling stuck and *block* yourself—you could be blocking generations to come.

K... PUSHING FUCKEN THROUGH!!

(Contractions...)

Do I **release** this book now? Is it too soon? WILL they accept it?

HUGE conflict with name... LOL

Isn't that just like humans? Judging a book by its COVER. Blacks, whites, gays, lesbians... Jew, Christian, Muslim, Atheist... emo (cops, guys from the hood, rich girls).

WHAT THE ACTUAL FUCK?!

Sorry... There's no way, *what the fuck* is anywhere *near* adequate to describe the largeness of the situation. It's about LOVE y'all! When something's different our need to unify with it is *threatened*... we perceive incompatibility (exclude it). Our guilt... wanna connect but can't (creates doubt) makes us feel *weaker* when not whole (solidified as one). Lack of recognition to what we know to be safe makes attack mode feel *normal*. Hate... always follows fear.

Division...

Haters. Bullies. Racists.

I'M TALKING TO YOU!!

$$wotp = \frac{<3}{0} = 1$$

Love divided by nothing equals UNITY.

Aaay-men...

Everything different, when in sync, produces harmony (unity) as it blends together. For there to be harmony there must be... *difference*. And then like magic! Total *unexplainable* beauty. A symphony. It's almost like, we need all of us to achieve that perfect pitch, sound... love. Each brings in their own frequency, tone, depth...

Like a necklace with all the different colored beads. ☺

All powerful businessmen know when discussing BIG BUCKS—order the same drink! Mirror body behavior. Just like monkeys... They cross leg, you cross leg. Lmao Unison can be beautiful. There's no disruption, like a calm lake—no waves.

B-O-R-I-N-G... ☹

(Nothing brought to the mix)

Too much of the same thing, can be stale. En-RICH is to make 'more'. Maybe through this book, we can show... that when you judge a book by its 'cover' the gem too... stays *covered*. Darkness is scary.

LABOR PAIN!!!

AAAAAH!! Humongous amounts of *HOURRRS*—tension, exhaustion, false starts (ton of tears) shocks like, is there an epidural for a BOOK? >.< Delivery...

A finished product!

(There were *complications*)

I was TOLD...

"What makes you think you can have this *baby* (write a book for young adults) what qualifies YOU? The parents are gonna think you're putting concepts into their kid's head."

Yeah... Like DON'T fuck—what a CONCEPT.

Why, doesn't it occur to anybody that the way bullying, sex and drugs are being handled (in the schools) is NOT effective? Crazy... doin' the same thing over and over again. Definition; Crazy. Not in one's right mind. Who's got the right mind? Maybe young adults should have some input here (since it's THEIR issue). Cuz it isn't going away. I know I'm going off topic. Girls go off on tangents (it's what we do).

And the sooner you realize that, the better off you'll be. Seriously. I need to vent. How many *more* girls and guys have to be terrorized, isolated, commit fucken suicide—before someone pays attention? Realizes, there's a need for a CHANGE? And yet there's concern about material being too raw, honest, truthful (blogs, songs, books) tellin' it like it is. God forbid they should see (have to admit) a non-traditional approach could actually work. Well I'm sorry. I'm gonna give it... RAW. I'm gonna give it sweet.

I'm gonna give it HARD.

(Just the way you like it) ;P

Truth be told... It's our FORMULA. It's **real**...

And real has no fear—*it's not afraid to be.*

(No defense necessary)

I second the motion! Can I second my own motion? ^'.^

My book! My rules.

*Words from the heart touch the **heart**...*

(That's why)

To all those who said this book's too raw (deep) young adults won't get it—too many f-bombs, I'm not a psychologist. What right do I have to write this book? CHANGE the title. It's too shocking. It's causing too much shit. (**Let it die**) For all those who walked away—*after* admitting how MUCH value it had for them, sayin' "This book REALLY helps people." Here's what I got to say...

I VALUE what I have to say. I value the truth of my convictions. And I *value*... young adults (their pain). What they go through (their stifled cry for help) quest for TRUTH and direction—they're worth it.

As well...

Jesus was the son of a carpenter. What qualified him... to reach out and express a truth he *knew* was vital? What about Moses? Wasn't he a slave (with a speech impediment)? And still he led his people to FREEDOM. Mother Teresa. Did she EVEN have credentials? She was home schooled. What *qualified* her, except for her intense desire to give LOVE? Martin Luther King...

...That man walked down a road that was never WALKED.

One man—BIG CHANGE.

Cuz he believed...

I'm a Girl...

I love...

THOSE are my qualifications.

And I have a special connection with young adults. Bite me.

CAUTION

You'll miss vital information if you attempt to read this book fast.

Your call...

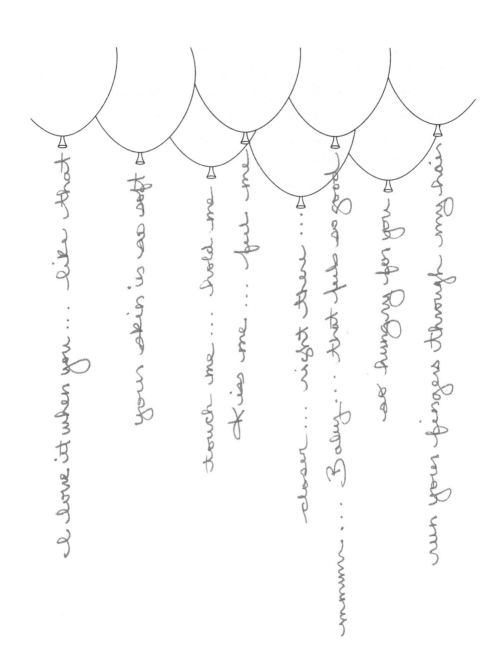

I love it when you ... like that

your skin is so soft

touch me ... hold me
kiss me ... feel me

closer ... right there ...

Baby... that feels so good

so hungry for you

mm my body is craving every inch of you

YOU can't fight love...

It doesn't know that language.

The Relationship Bible
Love 101

K... Love is **love**. It's like, a twenty-four hour surveillance system... its *ongoing*. Once the passcode has been entered (your heart uber happy) the program begins. *You can't pretend the* pass *code wasn't entered.* It's been activated.

Example;

"I love YOU... I HATE your guts."

"K, I love you..."

"We're so DONE."

The heart *still* feels the same, you can't change the heart. It doesn't pump in reverse. LOL You CAN change your mind. Truth be told, you needed them. They made you look good. They completed a part of you (you thought was missing). You got something with the package (friends... popularity, confidence).

My dentist keeps arguing this part (technical aspects of a heart) he's got a real scientific brain. Not an ounce of metaphoric ability whatsoever. LOL But, he's got the DRILL. (Ugh) On my *next* visit... he's like, "Nichole. I've started working out." I'm like, "So... Are you saying the book *inspired* YOU?" He's like, "After meeting with you, I had to work out my frustrations. I benched the WHOLE rack." I'm like, "Really? How much was on it?" He's like... "Just the bar." Haa!

Speaking of the HEART...

Do you notice, it's the only organ (other than the obvious one) linked to LOVE. We never link love to any *other* organ. I mean... Are we ever gonna say, "I love YOU... with all my intestines (all twenty five feet of them)." No wonder I get acid reflux when you try and kiss me. LOL "You BROKE my rectum. It hurts to love you, man." LOL "I CRIED my liver out." ...Always thought you were TOXIC. "I really want this with all my bladder." BUSTED. Why's it only related to the *heart*...?

Tweet me your answer! #nonprofitorgan

29.

The heart... How you feel about *them* doesn't really change (even though they messed up). Unless you realize, they've hacked into your system—deleted your **valued** files (download stash) had remote access to your hard drive (TOTAL control) forced you to drop your wall—virus protection disabled. *AAAAHH!* Now you're *susceptible*...

Then you shut it down.

They weren't MEANT to be in your system.

(They never had your password)

They were *sneaky* about it. }:< So you disconnect them. Or they get blown off course, find someone else to hack into (*use*). Thank GOD... Cuz that's the last thing you need, someone tapping into your network—use up all your memory (no room for anyone else) screw with your *software*... Seen as a threat, it puts you in freeze mode. NO ONE can reach you. That's serious. The 'blue' screen of death... **not** a good place to be. YOU feel nothing (can't do nothing) can't move, can't undo. Once your soul's LOCKED—*fuck* any creative work (you usually love to do). CAN'T. Feel dead. You've CRASHED (nothin' works). Unless you re-boot(y). LOL Someone exciting, someone un-expected... TOTALLY captivating. You're lit UP fo shur.

And when you're with someone cuz of *reasons*... instead of just how they make you feel. It COMPLICATES things. Cuz all of a sudden, YOU feel for this *new* guy (girl. You see them and you're in a complete daze. You're havin' trouble with your current guy (girl) but you've been together for a while so loyalty, insecurity (will the new one be any different) and foreign territory... (fear of the unknown) all play into the equation (manscaped/not). Pubic wig, landing strip? @_@ (HAD too)

So you break it off. But they start texting you. You're like, "Why are YOU texting me?" They're like, "I think we got into things too fast. We should start OVER. Re-build our relationship." You're like... "*Shuuuut up.*" And they're erased from your memory. Just like the SECOND exams are over!

Doesn't matter how much studying you did. How you made formulas out of your notes (just to memorize them) created songs, used acronyms, made up stupid nonsensical phrases (just to help you remember the 'exact' order) it's GONE.

When it comes to a guy or girl...

*We **do**... without doing (knowing) and everything gets done (handled).*

Whether your guy (girl) messed up (fesses up) or does all this good stuff (cuz they really like YOU) if you coast for a bit and just **watch**... true shades (hopefully not the throwin' kind) <u>will</u> be revealed. It's hard I know... and scary. Cuz sometimes they seem SO perfect, you wanna dive right in—tell everybody! It's OFFICIAL. We're a couple. It's nerve wracking waiting to see if they 'screw up'. Or even more intense... If THEY'RE the one. So now, what? Omigosh... This is IT!! The *moment* you've been waiting for. Like, forever. It's here. There's a reason Mother Nature gives us *seasons*... A reminder that we have them ALSO.

(Disclosed knowledge from another place!) .)

Watching a guy or girl in all their *seasons* before committing is crucial. They may have some dark spots—mother's a witch (thinks all girls are evil) dad' s never there so all guys must suffer. Or they may appear spotless (dirt, well hidden). Problem is... Most of us get hooked on other people's *reactions* which makes us STAY or leave (no matter what it's like). In our mind it grades us on how we're doin', with that person (what kind of person we <u>are</u>). TOTAL bull... Btw. Why do we pick on bull's manure so much? How come it's never rabbit shit, ostrich shit or zebra poop?

Every relationship *talks* to us...

I was looking for a new place to rent. I found it. Exactly what I wanted. The lady of this new place was really happy with me. She had a daughter (in her late teens). I let my landlord know I found the most *perfect* place. We had grown close, he was selling his house—I needed to leave. I would miss this place. The old man next door, who always cleaned the snow off my car. I'd watch him from my window every morning, I never had a Grandfather. But! I was sooo EXCITED. So I met with the lady and her daughter. The minute I saw her... I knew, we'd be friends for LIFE. It was crazy. Her daughter's like, "I know... *you were sent* to me." WTH Her only sister was a real fuck up. I felt so tight with her. It was ridiculous. We were SO connected it was sick, although she loved her mother, not the same. She even offered to sleep on the COUCH till my room was ready.

Her mom then changes her mind... ☹

She was used to being her daughter's *everythinggg*.

Yeah... one of *those*.

I woulda been the sister she could RELY on. She never had that... I text my landlord. "It's gonna take a little while longer, she changed her mind." He texts me back. "BUMMER." And I'm lookin' at his text, feelin' like SHIT. Like, oh poor Nichole she didn't make the grade.

At least, that's how it played out in my mind.

When you don't get something you really want, you usually see things in a negative way (towards *yourself*). Even if someone tells you something in a neutral way or they're like, "It's not **meant** to be." Most of the time you see it as a strike against you. Just like NOT making the team. You tell your dad, he's like, "Better luck next time." You feel dumb.

So I text him back.

"YO! Just like Columbus when he saw it WASN'T land, his crew could have said... "*Bummer*" (in Spanish). His response to that? "We MOVE forward!" There's only *sadness* when what you think is TOTALLY it... is no longer a possibility. Like, the girl whose mother was jealous of how tight her daughter and I were. Which means... excitement! It means what you want is *close*. How do I know? Cuz Columbus didn't just wake up one morning and see LAND. He saw twigs floatin' on the water (a sign land's comin') birds... that PROBABLY shit on his head, which told him—he was close! My place was coming! And it was going to be AWESOME. It's just life's way of showing you it's *near*... almost there, cuz it's in line with the same *frequency* of what you're looking for. YOU'VE just experienced a tremor of what's comin' (on the way). Or you wouldn't have seen it. It's a hint of what's approaching, you're just at a distance so you can't see it yet. ☺

Like, when there's a couple making out in front of YOU. ☹

Happens all the time no matter where you ARE. It's coming! Be happy, cuz that tells life YOU want it! Don't be sad, life takes it as a **rejection** (think you don't want it, it makes you sad). MORE mixed messages. Seems to be Earth's tag line. LOL

You're not forgotten... It's just being *wrapped* in the prettiest way possible (they're super HOT) perfect environment (where you'll meet) best-case scenario (trusted circumstance) for YOU. Count on it. If you respond negatively (feel like shit) when you see a couple you'll be indirectly saying... *Fuuuck that* (to life). Push it AWAY (without knowing). You wouldn't have seen that... if it wasn't on route to you aligned with your *path*. The whole universe is constantly setting you up with people to bump into (that connect you to what or who you want) show you something (you read by chance) prompting you to act, overhear something (to secure you) see something on the net (*movie*) radio... that CONFIRMS. It's a go!

You already know this to be true...

Look at the *last* good thing that happened to YOU... trace your steps *back* to what happened (apparently negative at times) to get YOU where you are now. (Do your homework) You'll see. So be happy when you see something you want (that's been on your mind) cuz you're NEXT. Or that energy wouldn't have come (to you) now. Love comes... when it's welcome. Seriously. See the same awesome ride (all the time) be *happy*! It's showing you where you're going...

In style!

If there's anything YOU want.

You've got the PLAN (inside you).

The vibration you feel... when you're near it (YOU gettin' excited) is your first CLUE. Just like your first date! That *energy* sustains YOU carries you to the next step. (Scary one) You asking for another date All those close calls... *almost* got it! Thought it was IT... is your second clue. The continual pull you'll have towards it (no matter what shit you're going through) people sayin' it's NOT time (parents, friends, coaches telling you NOT now) is when you know it's **here**. Cuz it's pulling YOU. And what *pulls* you is like a rubber band... at times, it can LET GO! Someone got scared. Unexpected opportunity lands— but you're NOT ready! They finally CALL... but you just moved. You'll never see them again.

...AND IT SNAPS!!

(Right in your face) o_O

Stings like *hellll*. But it doesn't mean it's over. Sometimes you cut them off, cancel a gig (too nervous) rubber band breaks—you LOSE that person, job, *opportunity*...

One day I couldn't believe the top acting agency in NYC calls me for an audition. I had sent my pics (along with a thousand other actors). LOL I was starting out, so I knew they'd never call. I had like, ZERO credits, nothin' on my resume, except my photo and hobbies. But they DID call! And I'm like, 'Omg! I can't go. I'm SO fat. They'll never take me.'

(My gymnastic coach always told me I was FAT)

That's SO rude. My boyfriend couldn't believe my coach said that. He's like, "What a LOSER." Regardless, I decided to wear my baggiest sweats (XXX) and just let them know I was at a sports commercial audition, prior. I get there...

It's in one of these tall, tall buildings with chrome this n' marble that. I was afraid to touch the door KNOB. LOL Felt so underdressed for the tiles. But sticking to PLAN! I'm riding the elevator... a little nervous cuz of the body thing, but in sweats! They CAN'T see me. (Yaaay!) Someone greets me and takes me into this huge room with a long boardroom table. *Hmmm...* Not one coffee stain? (Impressive) But there's allll these boxes all over the place. Maybe they're moving. I sat there, waited. Made good use of my time too. Bit off all my nails and chewed all my cuticles simultaneously. Gifted! I'm expecting one of the agents to come in through the door.

But that's NOT what happened...

A very important lookin' man (in a suit) holding a suede folder comes in. It's the PRESIDENT. Freaking! (In silence) I do the only thing I can, on such short notice (to calm down). Take myself *AHEAD* of time, to when I'm a grandmother... Grandmothers AREN'T scared of shit! They look you in the eye—cop, criminal, security (it don't matter) tell YOU what they think. It's like, they've got this super-natural power or somethin' (at least, it feels like they do). You're always scared they'll put a hex on you or somethin'... you never wanna piss them off. Even if their face looks like an old straw broom, doesn't faze them. EACH wrinkle is like a medal etched by life. They've earned it. It's like, allll their love shows through all those lines... and ANGER. O_O If I were you I'd go hug my grandma. Like NOW. Some of you guys be like, "Damn my grandma's got alotta *those*—better go hug her!!" ROFL And don't leave out your grandfathers EITHER. They can be SO adorable.

My boyfriend and I were having a video chat with his boyfriend's grandfather, on his birthday. We call him Tata, hardly speaks a word... of English. Strong as an OX. And hilarious. Whenever I see him, I tell him he looks great. He's like, "YOU... Liar." Every time I try to teach him English he's like, "I... *donkeyyy*." Like... he's slow. I laugh my head off whenever I visit, cuz he's always doin' funny things. Like! The last time he was all happy n' shit, I'm like "Tata what happened?" He's like, "¡Dejé arriba el asiento de la taza del baño y tu abuela se cayó de poto al agua!"

Translated: "I left the toilet seat up and Grandma fell all the way in... hit the water."

Not nice. Especially, cuz she was sleepy. I'm like, "You know... When your grandson pulls that shit on me at my house, I charge him twenty dollars. EACH time. We're up to three hundred and seventy dollars. I get paid at the end of the month." I snuggle up to my boyfriend... we're kissing in front of Tata he's like, "*Come on*... don't count money in front of the *poor*..." (in Spanish) I'm like, "Huh?" My boyfriend's like, "At 65 years old he doesn't get much *bizz-ness*..." LOL

I remember riding our bikes over to see him. Tata comes out to greet us. We park our bikes against the tree and he stares at our bikes, for a long time. I'm like, "Tata. Come ride with us!" He's like, "I... ninety years old." I'm like, "Enough with the ninety years old CRAP. Do you *think* your legs know how old you are?" He smiles... all the way back into the house. Grandfathers need to feel 'useful' always include them in things. Give them stuff to DO. Grandmothers need to feel important. Ask them for advice! TEACH them how to get on forums, where they can be helpful to other kids (who are depressed) who don't have a grandmother (so they stay connected). Share what's happening with you, so they can ride your youth wave. They don't nag or condemn like parents do. With them, we get wisdom WITHOUT attitude. Since they're closer to seein' God... I'd listen, if I were YOU. They may have an important *message*...

OMG... My story!!

So, the President walks in with this lady (female agent) has this really nice tan. It's freezing in New York for at least eight months but all important people have tans. A nice smile too with really white teeth, probably cuz of the tan. He sits and *stares* at me... I stare back. Grandmothers can do that. Speaking of stares... I JUST HAVE TO TELL YOU! One of my clients from Argentina looks at me one day. She's like, "Neecole, if people look at YOU—look back at BOTH eyes." I'm like, "*How* do you do that?" She's like, "Look in between their eyes." I'm like, "But that'll look stupid like, I'm lookin' in the middle of their HEAD." She's like, "Na nah, it won't. Do like this." (She demonstrates) "K! YOU look deranged." She's like, "I look strong and confident. And they know they can't mess with me." "Yeah, cuz you look deranged." She's like, "Just look at their *third* eye." She points to a SPOT on her forehead. I'm like, "What if they don't have one—don't you need to be spiritual n' stuff for that?" She's like, "It doesn't matter just look in between their eyes, a little above. And their eyes won't be able to influence you." "*Ooooh... sweet.* K. Next time I have to—*I'LL BURN THE SHIT OUT OF* their third, fourth and FIFTH eye (if necessary)." Overkill... (ma middle name). Haaaa!

With this in mind, I stare at the President tryin' as hard as I can, to look at *both* eyes (third eye) but I think I got it confused. Probably ended up with one eye *lookin'* for his third eye... *Wherrre* is it?! CAN'T find it. The other eye's zigzagging—*ACROSS HIS FACE* tryin' to remember, where it's *supposed* to be. He can cast me as a Martian! I'm just prayin', I remembered to cover this one LARGE zit I had on my *third* eye. Cuz if he's doing the same thing it'll totally over-power my third eye. Hey, that might not be a bad thing. ☺ I try to divert his attention I'm like, "I'm sorry, I'm not properly dressed. I came from a third CALL BACK for a sports commercial (big smile). Or I would look totally different for you." He interrupts me. "Nichole... Do you know how many photos I get DAILY?" He picks up one of the boxes, flips it on the floor. There's like, hundreds and hundreds of pics on the floor. He opens his brown suede folder *carefully* lays out my photo. If I was a ROCKET I'd blast *off* my chair—through the ceiling, through the clouds *through* the stratosphere. But I'm a GIRL.

I just sat there... percolating.

He points to the picture. He's like, "Your picture JUMPED out at me, Nichole. That's rare. It doesn't happen often. It's your *smile*... There's *magic* in it." OMG! He knows I'm not from here. My cover's compromised!! K. I was born on a full moon—wonder if that's how he knows? *Careful*... I may put you under my spell.

(Too late)

Abracadabra...

YOU lovvvve me!!

I couldn't help thinking. Dannng! My mom was right. All I have to do is *smile*... ANYTHING is possible. Remember that girls! Our smile is a very *powerful* tool... I was talkin' with my friend Tony. He's like, "It's the one thing we look at Nichole. It sets everything right there and then. We're like, 'Omg! I'm so *drawn in*... or Oh... my God Tony you're an idiot. You didn't get a name! You didn't get a NUMBER. What's the matter with you?' That's when I *knew* smiling is the thing." Wow... They should teach THAT at schools.

Rule No. 1 SMILE

Equivalent to Rule No. 1 for Guys. OPEN the damn door. For anyone! Then we're like, "He's sooo NICE."

Listening to Moms is so hard sometimes even if they're RIGHT. We figure, they're just biased so they'll say anything. And they're hysterical, contort the simplest things. Like, my mom and I are joking around. She's annoyed so she's like, "Why don't you shovel it." "Uh. Mom... LOSE the 'L'. You're butchering the word." I'm cryin'. Dads, we love YOU too. Just do us a favor. If you're texting a response (you wanna let us know it's funny) it's LMAO <u>not</u> LIMA. We're not into lima beans. And FYI it's not 'lots of love' (LOL) either. Cute...

(Queen of Tangents... is what I AM)

So the President looks at the female agent he's like, "I want to put Nichole in a couple of Prime Time Soaps with a couple of lines, to start." I freeze. @_@ She's like, "With all due respect sir, I would feel better if she came back and read 'first'." Why you gotta be so technical (BITCH)? I thawed out pretty quickly after that. OMG! I have to wear real CLOTHES! We schedule another appointment and I ask for the longest stretch of time possible— I SOOOO GOTTA TRAIN!!! I have to show him I can look really look good. o_o I have TWO weeks to lose 25lbs.

I keep telling myself...

I'm NOT fat. I'm just off season!

Who am I kidding? There's NO WAY I can do it in such a short time. I call one day before I'm supposed to be there. I'm like, "Hey! I'm in AFRICA. I'm up for this 'big' part." :D They totally understand. Whaaat...? It's totally possible—I just borrowed that 'possibility'.

Besides, I give good phone. Luckily, they aren't aware of my gym, one block away from them. Can't imagine what would have happen if I'd see him there. I'd have to be a TWIN. Course, if we both get hired... that would be an issue. Regardless, by the time I see him and he sees I LOST all this weight he won't mind it so much, that I stretched it a bit. ☺

THREE MONTHS...

It TOOK me. We're talking lean, mega-mean sexy as shit, machine. I trained every single day. I just kept remembering what he said, how he picked my picture out of everybody else's! It made me feel so special.

I trained like a *BEAST*...

And whenever you do that, there's always 'one' shithead who tries to undermine you. I asked this one guy to hand me a weight, he's grunting to showing me how taxing it is for *him*. I get it. I get it, wuss. He hands it to me (music's blasting in my EAR) mind's clear (amount of reps I'm goin' for) and WHAT does he say?

"Careful..."

Tell the WEIGHT to be **careful!!!**

I KILL IT! ☺

If your girl (guy) is about to do their sport; track, gymnastics, swimming, wrestling, cheerleading, snowboarding... weights, DON'T ever make them *think* they can't do it (don't undermine them) as long as you do, you'll undermine *yourself*... (too).

We only teach what we know... lol

That's why the best opportunity for you is when someone really needs your HELP. And you (for real) have to put yourself in their shoes—think of a way out. Just sayin' to them, "That sucks... Don't worry things will turn out." automatically like that (haaate that) doesn't inspire, is annoying (like waiting for the LAST minute on a download) useless. You're not in the *guts* of it... with *them*. You're not feelin' what they're feelin'. Cuz when you do you *think* of something they can't, see something they couldn't, cuz at the time they're immobile (but you're not). You're going back there (with *them*) only you're not stunned, so you can see (hear or feel) things—catch things they weren't able to... cuz they were SHOCKED.

THAT'S being *there*... for someone.

Not... "That's too bad man. Wish I could do something." Cuz when they don't invest in you—YOU feel unvalued. Not worth much (pathetic, for even mentioning it). Basically, you're on your own. When they ACTUALLY inspire... you don't feel alone (anymore). And *they* will find... that they gain strength in their life.

Cuz before you can persuade anyone of anything you gotta *feel* it's **possible**.

THEY gotta see it happening (for YOU) you can't feel the conviction of what they're sayin' till THEY do. And that way...

The student teaches the TEACHER.

The person who needs your help... HELPS you. And when you receive a lot of training (helping others) you are *awesome* for yourself man, cuz your mind's already conditioned to look and <u>find</u> a way out. Or in. LOL If you're strong, you'll teach *strength*. Scared... you'll teach *fear*.

Unsure... doubt.

What do YOU teach?

I teach Drive & Victory!

When spotting someone in the gym make sure you're *thinking*... yesssss! YOU CAN TOTALLY DO THIS. You don't have to scream it in their ear (like a lot of you guys do). LOL You need only **think it** and they'll feel it—cuz of the intensity of your thoughts. YOU focused on them... they'll feel THAT. It's just like when someone across the room (down the hall) at a party, is lookin' right at YOU. You're not aware of it (*at first*) but something makes YOU look right at them. Course it's always hysterical to see a guy spotting his friend *YELLING IN HIS EAR*...

"C'MON ASS WIPE LIFT IT!!"

Now I get why you guys have a blank look on your face when we spaz out—*YOU'VE GONE DEAF!* Lmao Or, you'll push yourself in the gym. Your face is so strained, you'd think there's a HIPPO sittin' on your nuts. Relax! Your face's *not* working ! LOL At least, it's better than the face you have when a hot girl *passes* YOU... ridiculous. Lmao.

Sport... is like LIFE.

When you set a goal and make sure your form (plan) is precise— *YOU JUST FUCKEN GO!!* You're programmed to <u>win</u>. The way to get hurt (let down) is when you *hesitate* (get scared mid-way) back out of a move, catch... leap. Can you imagine your Coach saying? "There's a whole lot that could go WRONG. You could take a spill... get seriously injured. There's always a possibility you could die." Or your dad. "Well son, you're going out into the world, there's a lot of people tryin' to do what you're doing. It'll be HARD." Why can't it be FUN? "The chances of YOU succeeding is real low." I get Dad wants you to be 'aware' but why can't he be like, "You've picked a HIGH goal—you have everything it TAKES (to win)." Why are you basing it on *statistics* instead of WHO your son is? What he's bringing in. Success is not based on external opinions but an internal compass. That gives you a reading—what you are, what you've GOT, where you're GOING. It doesn't matter what anyone says (comments). When you feel like a winner, you ARE. It's <u>that</u> simple. And what do *winners* do... rise to the TOP. Cuz they're not full of shit (that stuff'll weigh you down).

Our mind will go wherever it's directed...

If it's put in our head it has to be TOUGH—it has to be hard, it will be (wherever we go). I'm not sayin' there's no *effort* involved. It doesn't have to be difficult. Especially, if we keep the canvas of our mind clean—let the colors of the *experience* FILL IT IN (for us). Not react (judge) what has not taken form yet (circumstance) cuz in your heart you *know* you're a shape shifter... YOU have the power to mold things to your WILL. As long as...

- You do not judge it 'as if' it's *final* (cuz then it will be).
- You continue to STUBBORNLY hang on to your vision (no matter what).

If it's your destiny (your cards) *it'll be played out.* How do you know it's your destiny? It's a fierce CALLING... YOU can't stop it (doesn't take holidays). It's relentless (you can't live without it). It GIVES you tremendous energy just thinkin' about it. Since our mind can be told what to do—like a dog it's gonna find *that* bone. And if it's being told it's hard—it'll never think of lookin' for it where it's *easy*... It'll look for it where it's difficult. After tremendous effort, frustration, disbelief AND struggle, it'll find that bone—in a tough spot (dive, bad situation, sketchy people) cuz it was thrown out (no one wanted it). Our mind WILL go wherever it's *directed*...

I was so excited when I finally decided what I WANTED in life.

My Dream...

When I told a close friend of my parents she's like, "We allll have dreams Nichole." Huh? So does that mean I CAN'T? Fuck *that*... is what I was thinking. And cuz she said it like *that* made me feel like I didn't even deserve to *have* a dream. Like, what right do I have to have a dream? (Just cuz hers never came true) I felt stupid... That I would even *DARE* to have a dream. ☺

So I said to her...

"I'm prepared to pay the COST of my dream!"

And what have I been doing allll this time? PAYING... with agony, heartache, suffering, struggles (isolation). Cuz one person put it in my mind—I DON'T have a right to have a DREAM. Like, I'd be *stealing* from other people (who tried, couldn't get there) ...still *waiting*. ☺ So while in jail... YOU pay for it. I've appealed THAT verdict.

Amnesty granted! Yaay!

I remember tellin' my parents...

"Dad. Mom. I'm MOVING to L.A. I'm gonna dance in music videos and movies. Have my own Production Company." My Dad's response. "Are YOU craaazy!! You don't even *have* a GREEN card." I'm like, "Green card, purple card... whatever! I'll get it." I kiss them both, go to my room. Did not give my dad a *chance* to say anything—made up my MIND. At the time I had no idea WHAT a green card was, how *tough* it was to get one. Or... What the chances were of getting one. Had I known, I would have never gone for it. After announcing my plan, my best friend asks me to check out this new Club. I go. I'm dancing on the floor throwin' moves, having a great time and a cocktail waitress walks right up to me. She's like "Are you gonna DO anything with *that* dancing?!" I'm like, "Hell yeah! I'm going to L.A." She's like, "SO am I, with my friend. I'm an actress." *"Saweeet."* We form a friendship. They move there ahead of me. I go on vacay to check it out. They have a party and I meet this *man*...

Who becomes my boss and ends up sponsoring me.

CASE CLOSED.

DON'T FRIGGIN' PUT A CEILING ON OUR DREAMS!

(*Pahleeeze*)

Some of us are giraffes in *spirit*... we can't have ceilings! Or ostriches. My sister always called me ostrich-neck. I have a long neck. LOL All ballerinas have one. :D

CLOSING STATEMENT:

If there's nothing on your mind except what you WANT and you **GO AFTER IT**—soon after life starts conjuring up allll kinds of interesting connections, surprise hook ups, situations (circumstances) for YOU...

...the moment you step up your game.

(Follow your yellow brick road)

Just friggin' DECIDE!

And that way you won't be like them, all those telling YOU it can't be done (still waiting).

Back to the Agency!

(LAST time)

I'm training non-stop (TWICE a day) strict diet, exercising in the gym (bed) push-ups till I DROP (right into my pillow) almost passed out. It was time... needed to test it. Maximum impact is what I was looking for. I wear something snug to the gym. OMG! A guy wasn't paying attention did a double take - triple take and—WHACK!! Right into the pole. His face went 5D—felt *nothing* (state of bliss). LOL It's okay. His nose needed an adjustment. What?! That's TOTALLY funny.

K... That's bitch with a capital B for you (dude).

The day ARRIVES. I put something sexy on, seriously on fleek. Short summer dress (*strapless*) sandals, hair loose, tousled so the President can see—I'm a GIRL. Boobs, legs, a waist... the whole *sheeebang*. LOL

I go there. I don't bother calling cuz I know I'm gonna make an *entrance*. And he's gonna be so happy I lost all that weight. I couldn't wait to surprise him. Now he can see the choice he made was a good one. I walk in...

ALL EYES ON ME...

So far, so good.

I ask politely to see him and am told to have a seat. I sit and cross my legs (major *shine*) thanks vanilla and coconut lotion! *Fan those fumes.* :D A male assistant comes out and I'm sittin' on the sofa like Queen of Sheba... waiting for her subjects. He's looks at me... He's like,

"I'm sorry Nichole he DOESN'T want to see you."

"WHAAAAAAAAAAAAAAAT?! But does he know it's me?! I was the one he met three months ago. When I was FAT." "He knows." "Oh." (Guess he doesn't like waiting) I can't believe we bonded with our third eye n' shit and he *still* won't see me. I don't know if I wanna do this ANYMORE. I'm so pissed. Major STING...

(That one left a burn mark)

And you're *thinkin'*... "What the hell? I thought I was **meant** to do this?" You ARE! Or with a girl (or guy) you like, "I thought they liked me." They DO.

MY point...

It's always a *push n' pull* infuriating fucken feeling, cuz you're thinkin' one way... then they do something (something happens) and YOU pull away. It's just the way we respond to things (each *other*) me thinking I was FAT. It's the dynamics of a situation <u>needed</u> to bring about a certain experience to *TEACH* you...

You ALREADY are...

'The way you need to be'

(I was already approved) :(

And this way...

NO one leaves their mark on you. :-E Tells you you're too fat (bad coach) too short, it's too late, you can't afford it, odds are against you. *And you have no doubt...* YOU are ONE of a kind. So barriers, self-imposed thoughts (usually) between you and your career (guy, girl) are *broken...* and you know it's real. Cuz nothing's *changed...* YOU still wanna do it (you still want *them*) it's meant to bring YOU together... after allllll the bullshit. In love... your strength is *their* weakness (SO appealing) you feel like you're on top of your world (*deserving*) their weakness *softens* you. You see where you can assist, hard to resist since you're such a hard-ass (*not trusting*) been hurt so much. Each helps the other FIT into the criteria of *love...*

I DESERVE...

I TRUST.

The cycle of life...

Harmony... (love's favorite melody)

The push n' pull thing will continue (want them, don't want them, want THEM) till it can go the distance (*come back*) with more give (leniency) annoying but necessary. Any rejection (person, place, thing) you CAN'T change (disappointment... shock) is a complete severance of *that* rubber band. Which means, not 'poor you'. It means you do not have a *bond* with them, career (job). YOU thought you did but it was *not* your rubber band (though it looked that way, felt that way) yours would not break. It's you. It sustains YOU. You can't lose the part of yourself that is YOU.

You are being **RE-ROUTED**.

And although when THAT happens it almost feels like, you're walkin' through the *Valley of Death* (every inch of you empty) do not confuse the valley with being your HOME. You'll know you do, when you feel

46.

like dying or you feel like you *can't* go on (they're gone) it's *gone*... some part of YOU is dying. THAT part is walkin' through... Since it's attached to you, you're *there*. You can't separate what you're going through and what you're feeling.

Just REMEMBER...

Once there is a loss, there <u>will</u> be a gain. There *has* to... that HOLE (inside you) is callin' to be *filled*... And it WILL be filled. You've been stretched (although painful) it's made room for 'more'... *different*. Somethin' you weren't receptive to (before). Hugs...

Shit! Forgot about my landlord!

Fess up! You forgot too. Haaa!

It was annoying to receive this negative text from him. Just cuz for *him*... it'd be a bummer (not gettin' a place he went after). For me, it was a signal... I was CLOSE! After I text him back 'bout Columbus he had a different *attitude*. He's like, "Nichole. You're definitely in the zone, a champion 'mindset'." I'm like,

I AM THE ZONE.

And that's what I mean! Don't let people creep you out with *their* fucked up way of seeing things (lousy remarks) cuz it'll make you feel like SHIT (even if they think they're trying to help). It's inferior. It does not help. When you have a busted rib does a good coach say— "Omigosh!! You're hurt! What a horrible thing to happen." No. He's like, "Holy FUCK! You killed it out there!!" When people feel bad for you, it does not do *anything* for you—UNLESS it's an immediate release. Cuz you're venting (crying, screaming) to a person who actually cares. And they're absorbing alllll that shit—sucking it out of you. Like a good vampire. LOL It really helps if they can make you see it from *another* angle.

That would take skill.

And you'll know right away by the energy you feel inside your *body*. 'Up', amazing. Down or neutral? Sorry to say, useless. We don't need anyone to regurgitate how fucked up we are now and to narrate all that's happened, just so we can hear it in another voice. We already feel <u>so</u> drained and helpless.

Especially us girls we NEED to cry!

The ancient animal cry we make in our tears...

signals our soul's strength to come.

And **nothing** can match that.

You will see... Although there's an *illusion* of pain (cuz it's happening now 'live') it's not permanent, it's transitory... like a BAD dream. You *feel*... there's snakes allll around you, someone's runnin' after YOU. You're so outta breath—you're freakin'!! You feel the *fearrr*...

Then you WAKE UP. And you gotta pee. :P

Well I'M WAKING YOU UP!!

Sorry, can't pee for you.

I'm letting you know that 'every' disappointment (so-called failure) break-up, letdown, devastation (in your mind) rubber band breaking, is YOU being **re-routed**. To meet 'someone', see *something*... do something else that sets you on your true course—*to fly to your island!* (Real destination) A journey YOU were meant to have.

That creates a story YOU were meant to tell...

Dang... I love it when you smile.

(Just got bigger) .)

48.

Look at your best friend (girl/guy) hobby, career, sport, an opportunity that's happening now... backtrack to what happened that got you there, I meant it, when I told you to do it. So, the next time MAJOR shit happens you can ask...

WHERE AM I BEING RE-ROUTED TO?

And say!

I'm TOTALLY willing to go there. Show me!! Who... What, where I'm *supposed* to be. Bring it!! I'm not afraid. And do not JUDGE what hasn't fully materialized (yet). Expect something good, something exciting. Cuz it's *there*... it just needs YOU to access it.

Secret pass code: **A. S. K.** (*Appreciation of Sequence Knowingly*)

Once you ask it'll make an appearance—show its ass *sooner* than years later. And you'll be spared all the pain, disappointment, feelings of 'change'. Your new motto? Change is GOOD.

Repeat after me... CHANGE is good!

(I CAN'T hear you!)

Fine... I'm far away. But I feel you! <3 The harder it is to separate from a person (thing or situation) the bigger and **better** the change (your reward for no longer putting up with SHIT).

And ANOTHER thing about a girl's tears.

K. Call me a tangent ADDICT. I accept...

Right after I wrote the part about a girl's tears summoning up her *strength*—very next DAY. I'm talking to a girl and she's telling me how much she suffered when she had Mono. She's like, "It was crazy. For two whole MONTHS I laid in bed (weak as shit) couldn't go to class, out with friends—just felt useless. My friends tried to help, even a naturopath came over (put her on some stuff) NOTHING worked. I kept getting weaker and *weaker*. Finally I got so fed up. I'm like, That's it! No more!! I decided... **That's it**. Through my tears I cried, "I'm through with you!! You're LEAVING!!"

She CRIED all night...

Next day it was all over.

She wasn't sick anymore.

That's why sometimes when we're upset it seems *strange*... to you guys. It's like we've COMPLETELY fallen apart, you did your best, but nothing you said or did helped. When you left we were a mess... YOU feel bad but it's like nothing worked.

NEXT TIME YOU SEE YOUR GIRL...

She's a whole new animal.

She's the same but different... you're even a bit scared. Something happened. She's changed (*in some way*) she seems stronger some-how.

You don't have to get it dude.

The best THING you guys can do when we're LEAKING... crying. Tell us it's okay to cry. Just be like, "Cry... Cry as much as you want, I'm here." Fucken powerful words. My Dentist is like, "It took me *seventeen* years to learn that." Wow... That's like, a whole lifetime! Shame they don't teach important things like, HOW to understand each other, in school. We don't even have the 'same' brain. A girl's brain is much different than a guy's brain. :-7 Aaaa-men... LOL

And YOU guys are thinking...

50.

Aaahh... that's WHY. Makes so much sense. I knew YOU were weird.

It's CALLED... A challenge guys.

It stretches your brain...

It's not just about stretchin' *that* part you know. So, we're gonna think different, feel different, communicate (*fo shur*) different. And that's key to any relationship (including, any job situation). Understand the *person* and you understand how to give them what they want... Which opens the door to *other* things. Like, do I have to *SPELLL* everything out?

W I D E OPEN...

(Ya feelin' me, dude?)

THEY feel like you know them (deep inside). You read them. The heart's on the *inside*... no matter what sex. IF it's a guy or a girl thing, they'll be anticipating that first cosmic *kiss* (cuz they feel *so* close). A career or job thing (you being so in tune) is like your personal stamp, mastering relationships, it confirms to the other person you're best for the JOB. You're in sync with them. YOU have their *formula* (a way that ensures you'll reach them). YOU stand out. That to me, is kinda important. Then again, I'm sure somewhere in my life knowing a quadratic equation, polynomials and how to dissect a 'frog' is gonna come in handy. LOL Or that Iroquois Indians have a ritual that initiates guys into manhood. Basically, they stand around a pole, where ropes hang with hooks attached—piercing their nipple. FIRST guy to pull *back*... rip his nipple off is da man.

(S&M right there in our history books!)

K. This is uber important guys.

DON'T...

Tell us **not** to cry (just cuz it makes you feel bad) cuz you feel helpless, it's not about YOU. Us laughing is GREAT (and will help) if you have a sense of timing or human nature... My boyfriend walking into a DOOR is hilarious. Makes me laugh all the time. Except... When he walked into the corner of a WALL—almost split his head open. I balled so bad. He wobbles over, hand over his eye he's like, "It's okaaay. I'm not bleeding." I throw my arms around his neck. Squeeze SO tight, our chests are mashed together... I sniffle, say "*I love you..*" He's like, "I love YOU... with all *our* heart." It makes us feel BETTER to cry. Call it... the 'ninth' wonder of the world. LOL

Guy Logistics...

(Breaking it down)

Crying removes *emotional* thorns. Like, if there's a thorn up your ass it would hurt, right? Same thing. It makes us uncomfortable. Cuz to us it stands for <u>any</u> and all events causing PAIN (that we're aware or unaware of) which is why when you try and help and you're like, "What's wrong?" *WE WANNA TEAR OFF YOUR FACE!!* And we freak out cuz we don't know 'exactly'. And we don't know how to talk it *through* or even—where to BEGIN (at this point). It's waaay beyond that. We just need to be like a river and cry it ALL OUT. K!

Crying carries shit out of our system.

And presto! We're like... it never happened. The *power's* in the tears... dude. It carries stuff out. We even look *better* (more refreshed). Just we're usually too drained from crying to notice. And it's interesting, cuz right after we cry our friends are like, "YOU look good. Did you take a nap?" Lmao Which is NOT to be confused with gut-wrenching crying (alotta shit still left inside) eyes bloodshot and BULGING (bug-eyed) nostrils red and flaring, that's an **incomplete** jammed up waiting-to-happen *in the process...* crying.

I was getting some copies at the printers one day, I had just finished crying for three straight DAYS (cut off my ex) and the guy behind the counter is like, "Your skin *looks* awesome." I'm like, "Yeah? Well... just go get your heart **SMASHED**—*TILL THERE'S NOTHIN' BUT JUICE* and you too can have fabulous skin!" But he was right... I pass by a

52.

mirror, I'm like—daaang! YOU do look better. Just love it when pain can be productive. No credit to the asshole (assholette) of course.

It's hard when your PAIN isn't noticed...

Especially when it's so OBVIOUS. You feel unimportant and stupid for havin' it affect you. Basically, you feel like you're from another planet (if you agree twitch nose 'once'). Who knows, there could be *another* person reading the same **exact** part, across the room. Omg! What if they come right over? THAT would be sick! Let me know if that happens. So my boyfriend's like, "K. If I was twitching my nose— I'd be looking around the room to see if anyone saw me. So yeah... that way, I might notice if someone else is reading the same book." Guys are sooo self-conscious. Except! When it has to do with taking off their pants. They want you to notice then. O_O No stage fright THERE. In front of other guys, yes. Lmao

I remember for the longest time, something bad would happen and I'd be walking down the hall (school) or gym I'd see a guy... It's *clear* I'm MAD. He's like, "Hey... How you doin'?"

LIKE—IS MY PAIN INVISIBLE?!

Next time it happens...

I'm super pissed, guy walks by he's like, "Hey, wuss-up?" I'm like... "*CAN'T YOU SEE WHAT'S UP?!?* It's written alll over my face." The *next* guy walks by, "How are you?" (NO expression) I'm like, "Is that a rhetorical question? Or are you actually ASKING? Whereby, it would require an *actual* answer." (No response) I'm like, "Ask me what I NEED. Cuz then I can tell you... I need to cry. I need to talk—for like, hours and hours and *hours*. I need some air... I need CASH. I need help with my assignment. And then... YOU can direct me in the best way possible. THAT would be helpful. Not this... how are you crap— don't really wanna be there for you, got my own shit to deal with, but wanna make it LOOK like I care." I rest my balls.

Next time I see Mr. Deadpan he's like, "I'M THE HUG TROLL... You can't pass without hugging."

Not much into how are you—how are *shmooos*. But, perhaps some conversational stimulation is in order to help the recipient. 8-) When people say, "How are you?" depending on their tone, you can usually tell they don't want a (true) answer. Half of the time they're not even lookin' at you. ☺

My picks of the Week...

How are you?

- I'm *interesting*... If they're not really paying attention.

- I'm a lottta things... If overwhelmed.

- I work on a need-to-know basis—do YOU need to know? If full of shit.

- Ask me what I NEED—get rid of the middle man! If annoyed.

- Can't be defined by a single syllable, like 'FINE'... If feel good about my shit)

- I'm *aware*... If it's a border-line enemy.

- I'm moving at *sonic* speed... If they're jealous.

- I'm PURPLE... If they don't really care.

When our life is in suck mode, we end up (unconsciously) associating the **'how are you'** question with a feeling of isolation, when it's done like that. We think they either don't wanna hear it or there must be something off about us (for feeling like that). TBH. They may actually wanna know how you are, but if you say how you're feeling (without being authentic, blow it off) if they care, they may feel helpless and frustrated they CAN'T help you. And the whole cycle continues. YOU feel they don't really wanna know (misinterpret that as not caring) and you're like, "Fine."

Using the variables from the picks on the last page, separates the fluff from the *shaft*—boyfriend's laughing. Says it sounds like a guy shaving his pubes. I sit corrected—wheat from the *chaff*. Lmfao

When you're aware of the people who just *ask* vs. people who actually wanna *know* it breaks the conditioning that makes you think no one gives a shit. And cuz you're affirming you're pushing *through* (validating yourself along the way) and it doesn't seem hopeless to those trying to assist you, they're encouraged to help you get there. Just like... Let's say you're drowning and someone's tryin' to help you, but you're not even *trying* to swim (life sucks so bad) waaay too difficult to help (you). Interestingly! People always help *those*... who help themselves. They're encouraged by your belief. It sways them... they're always following your lead, man. They love the hero (heroine) 'underdog'. They want to be THERE... for the fighter (in you). That tiny little light *inside* that **refuses** to die. And...

There is so much *power* in the spoken word. DON'T friggin' strangle yourself. In taking this authentic guided approach you're cementing in their skull—YOU WILL WIN. You believe in yourself. So they DO too (no matter what). It's up to you... only YOU.

I say this...

No matter what you're going through (people ask) acknowledge the pain (if there) but <u>also</u> acknowledge you're swimming!! The picks are guide posts. So get friggin' creative. Create your own special brand!

(I salute your AUTHENTICITY in advance!)

Most people...

Don't realize they do THEMSELVES a huge injustice when they try and *think* of what to say... to start a convo. Or go online, get top so-called conversation starters. LOL Here's WHY... Usually, you're standing in line waiting to get food (drinks) club, whatever... YOU see someone and right away there's something about *them* you LIKE. Their nose, hat, hair, eyes... (k boobs but don't SAY that) the sound of their voice, what they just *said*. But seldom... do you say anything. You just watch (silently) *think it*... there's all this excitement BUILD-

ING—you say nothing. It dies. I can't tell you how many times I've seen someone and *commented...* on something that **really** made me feel good. That I lovvved about them—LED ME RIGHT TO WHAT I WANTED (needed). It was awesome! As I continued talking with them they would say something that was s̲o̲ important for me to hear (WITHOUT me asking for it). You see... The person that *inspires* you (catches your eye) IS your secret access to WHATEVER you want. You being inspired... acts as a 'vibe key', actin' on it (tellin' them) triggers the energy lock. You'll see their emotion go UP almost right away cuz you're tellin' them (for real) what you love about them. Or if it's a girl towards a guy what you LIKE. Chances are it's somethin' they've been having an *issue* with (debating about) wondering about. And don't be surprised if they're like, "OMG! I was just thinking about that—YOU'RE my angel! I've been looking for a sign. Or... funny you should say THAT (a popular one) I've been praying on this."

Since it's something they needed to hear they'll be very excited at you mentioning it which... TURNS the lock. As you converse on *other* things (due to real rapport) the lock OPENS. And they inadvertently tell you the perfect place, person or idea you've been looking for! They ARE... your pass code. And you will be sooo fulfilled. :D So liberated! When humans TRULY connect—it's always a very *powerful* experience. It doesn't have to be limited to the one you love, sometimes you meet someone (never forget them) never see them again. What we needed from *them* was delivered. Makes sense, since the missing component to getting *what you want* lies in... connecting (noticeable in love fo shur) otherwise key's dropped (not received) life's more challenging, isolated... disconnected. Being inspired (moved) to say something to someone opens the floodgates to so many things you didn't even *know* you needed. Which is why when you automatically say, "How are you?" without first taking them in (at the very least) to see *where* they're at, YOU short circuit your ability to receive impressions, feelings, insight or any message (warning) that may be coming in to you from them. Like... They're in pain and feel it's inappropriate to show it (conditioned to hide it) make light of it (joke about it) so operating from a compulsory position. Which leaves very little (if any) room for spontaneous impulses... SPARKS. Cutting off your ability to *connect* with the person (truly). Pain always screams on the inside first. I only *talk...* once inspired.

(Like my moans) LOL

And cuz you're not artificial (impersonal) deceptively polite, empty or flat, it's always stimulating—and what's stimulating is *alive*... REAL. Memorable. Refreshing. Almost extinct, cuz so few of us do it. This is not so much an issue between *close* friends cuz they're like family, with them it'd be weird to be that formal. You're NOT gonna see your brother (sister) first thing, be like, "How are you?" More like, "Why did you take my............ give it back!" LOL This is more of an issue for those of us that have been thrown into the work world, mixed into the lamb stew of society. *Baaaa...d LOL*

Imagine NOT having to think of what you're gonna say to someone, (you'd *like* to know) not needing to fill empty spaces with empty words (so much WORK) just let it *happen* (genuinely) working it moment to moment. Looking at each other like animals do... till words *have to be* born. Smiling... cuz you just sooo get each other. That's probably how aliens do it. We've so deviated on this human plane.

A REAL connection...

(Organic meets programmed) LOL

An ingenious plan set up to **release** our divine goodies, only once we allow our inner guidance to LEAD—reach out (connect) when *inspired* to... give. Makin' us dependent on a real connection (genuine communication) so we have to acknowledge... we're meant to be JOINED.

I was trying to think of how I was gonna break into radio. I was buying a ticket for a movie and commented on the tellers *voice*. I lovvved it... It was sexy, low and brassy. I told her I thought she should do RADIO.

(Inspired for real, and mentioning it)

She FREAKS. She's like, "Omg! I've been trying to decide allll month. Do I finish school or go for that that radio opportunity? I've been praying on it! Thank YOU (very heightened energy). We talk some more (established rapport) and I find out on this radio opportunity, they're looking for SPEAKERS. Hellllo! Another time I'm waiting in line tryin' to think of a good slogan for my t-shirt series. I'm paying for my food and I notice a guy behind me. He's got this giant CUP CAKE (allll these colorful sprinkles on it). It's obvious. I'm like, "Fight... With your girl?" He's like. "Yuuup." I'm like, "Feed her heart... before you feed your hard-on, huh?". He's like, "I would TOTALLY buy that! Put it on a t-shirt." So, 'cupcake man' helped me (without knowing it) create something... Just cuz I commented on what got my attention. Whatever you talk about, has to be something that **pulls** you (guaranteed) it's something they need to talk *about* (or hear).

It's like, the person you're **inspired** to TALK TO is your magical vault (to gettin' you what you want). To open it... YOU need to tell them what inspires you (about THEM) without hoping or needing anything. Simply stating... a TRUTH. In other words... *don't* tell a girl you've never seen blue eyes like THAT and ask, if she wants to sleep with you. Lmao This accessing your secret map, works best when you're sayin' something you REALLY like about the person. And are happy cuz you're telling them something you're stoked about. It doesn't matter what mood they're in, if they even seem like they wanna talk (or not) in a bad mood. If you see something you LIKE... and it truly *pulls* you... tell them.

And FYI...

If you ask a girl for her number and she doesn't want to give it to you (now) there's a *reason*... Smile. Say, "K!" Upbeat. Walk... Let her remember your confidence. You were not deterred by a 'no'. You will move on, till the tide turns... and it will TURN. Or the one who tops her will show up (the *other* was a stand-in). And don't be surprised when you do hook up with the right one and the *other* one... is now interested. Happens alllll the time. Once you feel like you have it **inside** (cuz you actually do, or something *close*...) it will come. That's why it seems like life gives you what you no longer need. It was MATCHING what you *felt*... (you deserved). If your body's ecstatic cuz of one girl (guy) you're crazy about, even if it doesn't work... BAM!! You get an upgrade. Out of nowhere—it happens. But ONLY if you sustain *that* feeling—sheer stokefullness. ☺

Girls...

It's best to compliment a guy on something you admire he DOES (not his looks). Or you'll feel really dumb if he *already* has someone. Or he'll think you're running after *him*. So... will act differently than if he *had* spoken to you first (cuz he's interested). Just picture yourself as a Queen... YOU are merely complimenting one of your (manyyy) knights. LOL

There's ONE more question (besides, how are you) that can be self-serving, highly judgmental... limiting.

How old are YOU?

"I'M OLD ENOUGH TO KNOW WHAT I'M DOING."

I would let them know! I'm not an age... I'm pure ENERGY (if questioning my ability). I'm not defined by NUMBERS (if they think what I'm goin' after I don't have the experience for).

THE AGE COMPLEX...

An INVISIBLE curse.

A ritual instilled, so we can cast a spell on ourself—the perfect crime! :P Making us BELIEVE our days are numbered (right from the start) so too late for *this*... too early goin' after *that* (limiting us from using all our potential NOW). Putting us on a never ending, fearful mind-set that discourages us from being all we CAN BE, doin' all we want to DO, in order to have the life we WANT. That then, deliberately over-flows to what we have (*don't* have) skin color, status, education, experience... looks. Embarrassing us if we *don't* accomplish (collect) enough (by a certain TIME). Giving us a 'time's up' card, when we've reached (*passed*) a certain number. Training us... to dismiss celebrating our **birth** (who we are, what we've done, what we're made of, what we're ABOUT) only to focus on... How much time we *served* on this planet. Lmfaoo

David's deep serene nature, when he goes to the zoo the apes blow him *kisses*, his amazing ability to make <u>any</u> girl laugh (while mimicking her) not afraid of speaking up on any injustice (no matter what the cost) has a such a reverence for creation (won't even step on a ANT) an uncanny ability to make elderly people feel... like they've gone back in time (*with him*) he listens so intently, says the wisest thing to anyone in pain (they call 'psychic surgeon') has an extremely poetic heart, you'd think him and Shakespeare were bros, can figure out how to fix anything mechanical, without any instructions.

THAT'S fucken worth celebrating!

Instead, we 'celebrate' the number (stigma that comes with *that*) MISS the person. The *person* is not the NUMBER. We celebrate their life only after they die (fucken hysterical). While we're alive we celebrate *death*... with each number COUNTED. Not the lives we've affected (altered) CHANGED cuz we were **born**. We don't pay homage to (celebrate) our mission... (stamped in our soul) what we're *born* to do (carried out in its own timing). It's hardly ever rejoiced (or heard). We pretend our birthday is a great thing and for a while... it is. But then it's NOT. It becomes a waiting game... *borrowed* time, as the numbers pile up and we get further and further from our initial 'vibe'. Then all we feel is an *echooo* of what we once used to be. Unfair.

Why...? Cuz we went upstairs to where our number *lives* (kept it company) forgot allll about living in our body (where our *vibe* lives). It's no wonder as we turn into an adult, we're less excitable. Unless we're so far up (number) we don't care anymore (expecting to leave ANY day) so live back in the body, get happy over ANYTHING. It's understandable why our vibe is *vibrant* as a child (excitable by all things) then slowly disappears when we become more and more aware of *time* (our number) and what does time do? It *passes*...

So at times, we act reckless just cuz our time's running out—call it mid-life crisis. At times we waste it cuz we feel we have sooo much of it. Countdown...

(Till you *expire*)

60.

And the weight of *that* (especially for women) is **unbelievable**. It's so severe a lot of young adults feel old. WTF?! Women don't have a chance to *BREATHE*. It's a mad rush to accomplish everrrything. Cuz after a certain *time*... They feel wilted (not useful) or in demand, except for chores. Some women FIGHT IT. Go to *extreme* lengths... to look 'young' errr... Some, decide to develop their brains (get smarter) since their looks are of no use (so they tell themselves). And some... totally pretend (to the world) it doesn't MATTER to them. They love being 38, 52, 65, then drink a lot of red wine to deal with their secret *loss*...

The beauty of a girl... woman IS COMPLETELY TIMELESS.

If she's healthy in her love of SELF. Fulfilled, expressing her *passions*... (career, hobby, cause, family... Man). Solid in her OWN eyes. Women would never need to try to look young (instantly) if they didn't have the preconceived notion they were *looking* old... to begin with. And they didn't feel they had a time LIMIT to doooo so much. Like, I'm sorry. I have no elation (whatsoever) celebrating the number I turn into, as it climbs into mortality heaven. Putting focus *there*... on how much time we've put in (here) makes us slip into invisibility (eventually) our identity lost (or in jeopardy). Especially, when the picture of each person (their *message*) is hidden (obscured) by the frame (number). Is it showing signs of deterioration, collecting dust... Chipped? Not able to sustain itself (anymore) is the value even there? The message is always waiting (*eager to be noticed)* even though encumbered by the frame. When we focus on the frame we will *lose* sight of the picture. The picture can present itself *without* the frame... The frame is useless without the picture.

WHY are we focusing on the thing that doesn't matter?

Maybe this is why Fairies don't age. ;P Somehow, we've adopted this mentality that takes away our power, ability to heal, create miracles, do **anything**... that's hard to imagine (at any given AGE). Except for certain people who refuse to be plagued by attaching a number to their butt... it eludes most of us. I believe it manipulates our expiration date. Our mind starts creating *conditions* associated with it. And once we think it, so it is.

A.G.E.

(Atrophying Genetics Erroneously)

The next time someone asks, I'd be like, "I'm one thousand, two hundred and thirty four—a ZOMBIE with a really good makeover." It's different if it's someone who loves YOU. They see the inside of you... the whole you, no judgments, no stigma, no aligning you up to society's expectation bullshit.

My Tribe...

WILL NOT be defined by numbers (things). My tribe CELEBRATES the person... beauty, uniqueness, talent and purpose of *that* person. How many lives they've affected... altered (influenced) cuz they were born. Not the CLOCK ticking. So we don't lose (ever) the magnificence of their *picture*... its message (NOT framework) nor the condition of the frame, when its sole purpose is to support not camouflage. When we go up in space there is NO aging! There's no sense of TIME there... I think things just got warped in *time*... cuz if time was designed to document how long we are somewhere, why's the burden of that 'time spent' (usage) reflected on us? Why's it not neutral? If we come from another planet and land here, report in our journal from time to time, it'd be like, "It's been 105 years today, since I set foot on this strange place." LOL

(...the way it was meant to be)

When logic rules YOU...

Magic can't find you.

K... All YOU guys, boyfriends (close guy friends) WRAP your earlobe around this one! Next time your girl's upset (any reason) don't say...

"You should have sex, it'll make you feel better."

That's the LAST thing on our mind when we're scared, confused or worried. Unless you're into *fucking* girl... remedy or poison, you'll know, by the side effects. YOU... wondering who the hell you slept with (too hung over to remember) no energy, desensitized, a little more cynical, actin' real happy (crackin' jokes) cuz you're NOT.

CLASSIC DEFLECTION...

We don't work like you guys! You're upset, you have sex—you feel *better*. You're bored, you have sex—you feel stimulated. You're anxious, you have sex—you feel *relaxed*. YOU'RE stressed... you have sex, you feel refreshed! I call my buddy... I'm really upset, right away he's like, "Do you wanna go get a room?" I'm like, "WHY are you talking about a ROOM? I'm upset!" "I know, but you'll feel better." (Grrrr!) I'm like, "I'm UPSET and you wanna fuck me?" He's like, "I'm just sayin'. We can lie next to each other. We don't have to do anything. I can just massage your breasts." "MASSAGE my breasts?" He's like, "Yeah, just think of me as your slave." "First of all! I don't see you massaging my breasts, as slave thing—maybe in your warped sexual fantasy! And Secondly. You're not massaging my breasts!" He's like, "K. Well, I've had a really bad day, do you want to massage *my* breasts?" I dunno which is worse *this* or when you guys are fighting with us, cuz all of a sudden you're like, "Knock... Knock..." Don't friggin' make knock-knock jokes!

That's NOT how you listen.

}:< *You think that's funny huh?* He who laughs now will cry *later*— when his balls are ABOUT to explode. Cuz she's goin' down on YOU and something you say (or do) makes her STOP (right in the middle of it) cuz you've tempted the winds of fate dude NOT to blow... (you).

And another thing that's really ANNOYING!

Whenever you guys are *pissed* and don't get your way (we show no interest) you think you're Mister 'cock-of-the-block'. So you're like, "YOU couldn't handle it." Omg!! I gotta tell you. This guy in my math class was tellin' me how I *wasn't* his type (can you be any MORE obvious). He's like, "So... Are you into girls?" I'm like, "No, I'm not into girls." Guess, if I wasn't into HIM I had to be into girls. Can we say... *IN–FLA–TED*. Douche bag. Every time I saw him he kept sayin' that. He'd be like, "YOU into girls? You into *girls?*" Finally, I'm like... "No. I'm into SQUIRRELS." He's like, "You couldn't HANDLE it." (Really?) "Listen up! I don't *need* to handle it. I'm NOT in competition with you... I need to *receive* you. And if that's the case the only question is do I WANT to?" I hope I pierced both his nuts.

(Loser)

There are sooo many tricks you guys play on us! Bottom line. If you want *down*... BE down. Some of you are like, "I bet you couldn't do it, for twenty minutes STRAIGHT." Personally... I'd be like, I have gag reflexes—I CAN'T.

Take the TIME to figure us out!!

Cuz the type of guy that *does* (no doubt) is gonna get what he wants. Cuz he's smart enough to give a girl what she wants... *first*. Water the plant THEN it blooms (not the other way around) tool. Unless... it's spoiled, uncared for, petals sprawled all over the place, all kinds of nasty shit crawlin' in that one. Guaranteed.

When it comes to SEX...

One thing you guys don't get. When we're upset... It's like we're held *hostage* in our mind. Seriously. It's brutal. When we're like this... the only thoughts we have are BAD ones. Ones that scare us (worst case scenario types). We can't think clearly and we can't think logically (that one for sure). You guys can be pissed put it aside (for the most part) I'm talkin' dumb shit NOT like when we break up. That's MAJOR. But YOU can put it on the side and go watch a Game, return to it *later*... We can't do that.

HOW can you do that?

—Lucky bastards. LOL

It totally consumes us! We can't move, we can't eat, we can't function (properly). Unless, we have an animal to focus on (and I'm not talkin' squirrel). Like... a fish named goosey! A dog, cat, pony. K. For all those who are in to it... Snakes, reptiles. (Happy?) You dooo understand they eat ROACHES. And let me tell you how those things can *crawl* into very tiny open spaces. Eeeew. Can you believe there's a fish named GOOSEY? Nemo, I understand but Goosey?! My girl friend's like, "What should I NAME my fish?" I'm like, "I dunno, name it after your favorite THING." "K. I'll call it GOOSEY." "*Awh...* that's so cute, you wanna name your fish after a bird." "Yeah. I have one in the freezer." "YOU HAVE A GOOSE IN THE FREEZER?!" "Not that kind, the Vodka. It's my fave." "K... YOU wanna name your fish after an alcoholic beverage?" "Yeah."

Back to...

How YOU guys handle anger differently...

Maybe it has something to do with your part...? I mean, when we're upset it just spills out kinda like *our* part. But you... like your dick, can move it this way (that way) put it aside for now, *hold it...* YOU can put it away. We can't tuck anything away!

Unless, it's a secret. And that's never for long, you'll find out sooner or *later* cuz everything spills out of us eventually... Otherwise, like our bladder it hurts to keep it in. We like, literally explode (at some point). And that's NOT pretty. Seriously, we're kinda stuck till we get through our shit. We try and act normal (not think about it) but that just looks like we're there... *but not.* ☺ And that's cuz our endocrine glands secrete more estrogen (a feeling hormone) so we feel *everrrything* under the sun and every other planet LOL Even things that don't make sense, we feel. We CAN'T just put it away when it's bothering us (*although we try*). Our body will respond to it—even if we don't want to (it does).

It's obvious to EVERYBODY just before our period.

We're a little bit more... *intense.*

I remember I had this roommate. He knew to stay away at LEAST, fifty feet when I had my period. It went evil on me last month! Flat lined two whole days. But this month... I felt nothing! I was so happy. ☺ I look at him... I'm like, "Hey! I just got my period." He's like, "It's not my fault! I didn't do it." *Jumpppy...* (Fair) And when, he'd get on my nerves I'd be like,

DON'T MESS WITH ME—I'M OVULATING!!

Having a period can be a powerful experience. Seriously, just cuz of how guys *respond* to it. For instance, I'm rushing to class, I get there and there's this jerk sitting next to me (*drooling*) :~~~ Disgusting. He starts talkin to me and he's being gross. I interrupt him! "Oh... Wait! I think... YES. I *just* got my period." He's like, "YOU just got your period?" I'm like, "Yup... And it's GUSHING." He takes off!! Haaaa! When I told my boyfriend he's like, "Hmm? Well, when we're in that state transporting sperm (havin' sex) don't mess with us either! Cuz we're SPERMULATING! Ahaaaa!" I wanted to puncture him with my claw clip... venus fly trap (as he calls it). LOL

And they say *we're* always looking for equality. LOL

So I look up venus fly trap (plant) just to see the similarities. Scaaary! He *does* have reason to fear. LMAO I show him my findings. He's like, "I actually have seeds for those." I'm like, "You might wanna get rid of those, don't want those seeds in the *wrong* hands... (*hehe*) Who knows what she'll feed that venus 'fly trap' when she's PISSED." LOL He's like, "K, now I understand what you mean when you're like... "Don't mess with me, I'm OVULATING. Deal." I love having a BOYFRIEND. xD

They're so much fun.

I was training this university girl and I had her warming up on the treadmill. All of a sudden, she's like *"Just so you know,* I'm bleeding profusely through my uterus." I'm like, "Right NOW?" She's like, "PROFUSELY." "Well, it's leg 'day' and you're doin' squats! I'll go get a bucket."

68.

Wouldn't that be an awesome way to get rid of a guy you don't like? LOL Interestingly, she's complaining 'bout girls havin' a hard time gettin' over a guy. How wimpy they are. "Ditch the tissues and grab your running shoes!" She bellows. I start... ripping her *apart* (stretching her). She's like, "K... where's the tissues? *You're not human...* (boo hoo)." Whatever gave you that first clue? Lmao

My girl friend's like...

"If a guy approaches me and doesn't seem to wanna leave I make this FACE and hold it." (Wtf?) She shows me. Apocalypse III. LOL That'll work. My mom always said, like, "If you make a *face*—it'll stay that way." FACT or FICTION? I dunno. I see a lot people looking very constipated, these days. Still, I'd rather talk about my period, not into premature wrinkles.

Guys, during *these* times we are completely OUT OF CONTROL. And yeah, some girls act real nasty towards you guys. Call it... Boyfriend ABUSE. Cuff 'em and put in solitare (with LOADS of ice cream). LOL K. I was just told solitare is a card game. I meant solitary. My English! (Not so good)

Seriously. It's an issue cuz our hormones DO rule us. And they're controlling how we FEEL. And if that's the case, we need to give them more *time* (credit and seriousness) definitely more listening to! Cuz they HAVE something to say. If you're feeling drained or sad, need pampering—TAKE IT. And pass on going out. Still... When we're on our period, cuz there's so many emotions, it's hard to access our inner *knowing.* Don't confuse listening to the body under the influence (booze or blood) LOL with going against what you know is right. Like, sayin' shit like, "He's so beautiful... Look at him, he's GOT swag. I know he's bad news but I really WANT him—I should go get him." Cuz it's the same girl, who's used to doin' *that* (ignoring her feelings telling her he's bad) that will ALSO not stand up for herself when he or anyone *else* mistreats her, neglects her, takes advantage of her. Makes her feel uncomfortable. She's *not* accustomed to listening... just **responding** to her body's 'impulses'. Which are triggered when she's *off* balance (or body in this case, is cycling). This is why I feel we sometimes fall sooo hard for a guy, stay in a lousy situation (put up with it) fix him for the *next* bitch...

The FACTS...

69.

Estrogen for those not aware, is a hormone that's made out of a bunch of compounds like, estrone, estradiol and estriol. It's the <u>main</u> sex hormone in a girl and is mandatory for our menstrual cycle (period). :P It's <u>also</u> responsible for secondary sex characteristics like; breasts, hips, increased amounts of body fat in our butt (real pain but guys lovvvve it) *thighs*... Can we talk. Sooo strong, can crush YOU (athletic, dance types fo shur). It's also the main reason we DON'T have facial hair (well most of us lol) and have smoother skin than guys. Yaay for that. It also ensures that we process and *absorb* feelings allll day long which means, if we're stranded—ditched by our best friend cuz now she *has* a boyfriend (girlfriend if it's a guy) so no one to talk to about our PAIN, the only thing we'll hear in our head at this moment... YOU'RE so stupid. (Lame) Can't you do anything RIGHT? No one wants YOU. You're a fuck up. When our body (*feeling* dominant) starts to feel *down* the energy in it starts to go down too (cuz we feel like shit). We CAN'T feel sad without it <u>also</u> affecting our body. This is significant...

Being UNHAPPY is not an option girls!!

It fucks with our CHEMISTRY.

Once our mind is *down* our body will follow... It's *so* easy to stay depressed when our life force is leaking (body crying). It's difficult to push through all that shit, when there's no energy to do it with (or it's blocked). It's like... You CAN'T move. Your *spirit* is not supported with the body it came in. A now... very run down house. And everything just piles up (against YOU) so you think.

OVVVVERWHELMED...

(Even more depressing)

Releasing endorphins naturally by moving our body (dancing, skating, jogging, swimming... training) becomes essential. It DOES the one thing we need—gets us the fuck out of that place (our head) and gets us into the *senses* of the BODY. Now before you guys are like, "Let's fuck then." We're not looking to be emotionally bankrupt (either) alligator BREATH. Always a smart ass in the crowd. (_*_)

We're talking the *senses* of the body like smell, touch, sight, sound, taste. We can get into *those* and feel happier. Just look at us when we eat a CUPCAKE (with a ton of sprinkles on it). LOL Hundreds of balloons released in the sky (always puts a smile on our face). Something that smells like, coconut, vanilla, strawberry, melon. Holdin' a baby chick in our *hands*... distracts us nicely. (:V) Doin' our nails (different COLORS) taking a hot bath (with bubbles and our favorite music) great smelling lotion... puts our <u>body</u> (then our mind) in a *goood* place.

My guy was trying to surprise me when I was in a shitty mood (SO stressed). He invites me over to his place. Parents are gone the *whole* weekend. ☺ I open the DOOR... There's like, a million rose petals on the FLOOR. I'm like, "WTF? I coulda slipped and broken my neck! It's supposed to be scattered alllll over the place NOT bunched up like this. That's *such* a health HAZARD."

Whatta bitch... (there I said it for you).

Whether you're putting on make-up, gettin' your hair done, havin' a facial, snugglin' with your warm comforter... hearin' (seeing) the ocean, havin' HOT chocolate! With like, ten feet of whip cream. Allll of that will make your spirit feel 'different'. And that's cuz, you're feeding the heart of the body (*its feelings*) bringing your spirit up!

THROUGH MAKING YOURSELF FEEL GOOD...

Where there is spirit... there is life!

WRITE that somewhere.

Bet you didn't know CHOCOLATE has a chemical in it that boosts your endorphins (an I'm so-friggin'-happy-hormone) and serotonin levels, a chemical produced in the brain (functions as a neuro-transmitter). Kinda like, when one nerve cell *talks* to another... lets them know if something's off or on. Probably text each other *cell to cell*. LOL Low levels of serotonin are linked to mood disorders. Like, hellllo DEPRESSION. Who in their right mind would give up chocolate?! Not me. And... There's a certain ingredient in chocolate that *stimulates* our sex drive—as if we need it to. LOL

Got your attention! :P It's an amino acid called, phenethylamine which is ALSO released in the brain when we fall in *love*... Hence, known as the love DRUG. A chemical that mimics the brain's chemistry of a person *in love*. Major mood elevator! A chemical that acts as a 'love drug' in a chocolate bar? We're being controlled by the chocolate FACTORY! AAAAAH!

Now it makes sense WHY they link chocolate to LOVE all these years. They didn't link it to licorice or jujubes! Dude, if you remember any of this about your girl YOU won't be walkin' around wondering, (*duh...*) and you won't be paranoid doin' the *wrong* thing. You'll know you're on top of it, in control, content... *SAT-IS-FIED*. Cuz you'll learn how she functions, juggle her moods (expertly) be a true magician... LOL

Earn that magic stick. ;D

And that will make YOU extremely valuable.

Every girl likes to believe in MAGIC. It's where love is *born*... And you'll be on your game, unlike most guys (fucken clueless) who wonder why their girl's walkin' all over them. One minute she's nice, next (literally) she's Medusa—with hair extensions. Loves you to death—then hates you. YOU have all answers. Maybe this part should be called...

HOW TO MANAGE YOUR GIRL!

(How to diffuse da' bomb—*pms*)

It's allll in the details.

Girls want and need DETAILS. Aaaay-men (to that). LOL That's why when we're lyin' next to you and you're like, "You're so precious..." We're like, "What do you MEAN?" You're like, 'Is this a trick QUESTION?' Same thing when we have a fight and YOU apologize. :| "I'm sorry about last night." "Yeah... Which part?" We don't like skimmers we need to know that you know exactly why we're pissed... So be specific (pleeeeze). And we won't keep bringing it up.

Guy: "K. I'm sorry for the WHOLE thing. Can we fuck now?" ☺

Girl: "No." (Not effective)

If we feel happiness (on the inside) it will *OVERRULE* our mind (bad thoughts) but our body has to produce it (initially) it can't be manufactured by YOU dude (can't be 'man-made'). LOL So it can't just be sex (when we're upset) cuz we'll feel like we're being *taken* from. Remember, you've got the wand. We've got the crystal... and it's buried deep. LOL As you know... the wand is not complete without the crystal. If you wanna end up with just the *stick* in your hand, be my guest. LOL We need something just for us (affection, snuggling, your full attention) so the power in our crystal can light up! Then once touched by YOU dude... *FIREWORKS!!* (Of the most high) <3

For those that are slow...

Where our focus is <u>will</u> dictate how we feel. If we feel taken from (*sex*) which is not the same as cuddling (that's *gooood*) we may act like we enjoy it (or even enjoy it) but we'll resent it. Cuz in our head (when we're upset) we're a prisoner of Worryville. THAT part's being ignored. };<

Which translates (to us) that our PAIN is being ignored (no one cares) cuz it hasn't been dealt with, cuz it's still in question, cuz no plan B has been worked out (just in case what we're worried about *does* happen). Unless we're doin' something just for us that's making us HAPPY. Something that rebuilds our confidence (in ourself) gives us a welcome diversion (from our issue), a commercial break from our intense EPIC. So we can *give* to our self... strengthen our crystal. :D

And NO you cannot be our commercial break.

(Commercials don't reach out and grab YOU)

We'll know right away (as well as YOU) by the energy we feel in our body, if what we're doin' is enhancing our well-being... and soon enough, your 'being'. :D When we focus on *that* (well-being) seeing how our vagina's on the inside (*inside* job) you focus on your 'being', seeing how your penis is on the outside (*outside* job) then it makes perfect sense that YOUR bridge to happiness is through your dick (a well known fact) ours... an *inside* job. SELF.

...My crystal is glowing. :D

It's tough when our issue is with YOU dude. Still, if we control our focus (good thoughts, healthy distractions) we'll *control* our emotions, not have *them* control us (make us feel like shit). A task for only a true female *warrior*... a very passionate being.

Just makin' sure you girls are *fool-proof!* LOL

All Female warriors hands up!!

Like NOW!!

Love you.

The world needs YOU! We're the light that leads guys to *heaven* (on earth). LOL What we focus on will establish how we FEEL. You control your mind (not the other way around)!

Depression SQUISHER comin' up!

Takes you out of your mind, when it's holding you there (against your will) in a crappy setting. ☺

Must haves!

DEPRESSION TOOLKIT:

Smells... Lavender, strawberry, cotton candy, peach lotions, vanilla lip gloss, coconut body scrub, a guy's cologne. *Warm* apple or pumpkin pie... FRESH baked bread (see how you smile).

Sounds... Music, ocean waves, leaves blowing, the wind. Loud LIGHTNING (scary and exhilarating) birds whistling, raindrops tap dancing on your window, seagulls calling each other, dolphins squeaking... a great song (you can hear over and over and *over* again). LOUD. Sometimes you can listen to a song in a different language—not get it, still makes you feel good. See! Love is a universal language. ☺

Touch... *Soft* things, wooly things, silky things, feathers, rose petals (just not bunched up on the floor). LOL Your toes deep in the sand or water. *Hard* things don't appeal to us right now, sorry dude. But definitely! Check back. Timing is everything. LOL

Seeing... Big firecrackers, a sunrise, sunsets, rainbows. BRIGHT flowers, colorful desserts, puppy, kitten, hot guy (always does it if you're single) a NEW dress! Magazines, haircut, make-up. And depending on the severity of where your mind is, a necklace or a ring given to YOU (or created by someone you love) makes you feel GOOD.

Taste... A popular one. Anyyything with sugar! LOL Ice cream, chocolate, black licorice (usually if your adrenals are shot) butterscotch, salty things (since they energize you) potato chips (fried stuff, not healthy but works) sushi... a great choice. Salmon and avocado help the brain feel happy. Almonds, another good fat (actually gets rid of headaches due to its magnesium content, key for headache prevention and its ability to relax blood vessels) watermelon, figs or bananas for potassium. Critical, when you're down and especially hung over, since alcohol is a diuretic. And doesn't only cause dehydration but electrolyte loss (like potassium). Then you're draggin' your ass and don't know why. My favorite... ROASTED marshmallows!! Yogurt (very calming) warm rice or almond milk (with honey) makes you feel like everything's going to be alright. The TASTE sense dominates mostly (at times) highly abused. Sadly...

Guys...

Rip the last page OUT! (Keep in your locker)

Just sayin'...

Girls all of these are essential, so bad feelings *have* to exit when you have thoughts that are not worthy of YOU.

So you're able... *to receive.* <3

Cuz you feel SECURE, solid (not scattered or torn) *connected*... So things can reach you (nourish you). Once you lose your sense of 'self', it's **through** your senses (touch, taste, smell, sounds and sight) that you're able to come *back* (join the world). Except, when they're on STRIKE. You can't *see* right in front of you or hear what's being said (feel anything) cuz you're numb. But, if you get out of your head, (dive into your *senses*) there's no interruption from your mind (now, in a very shitty place). Once the focus is purely on *them*... they'll slowly gather your broken pieces, one by one. Glue them back with *spirit.*

You'll feel GOOD...

And when you feel good... *mysteriously* you're inspired! And when you feel inspired (cuz you feel good) it acts like a MAGNET yelling!! **"I deserve good shit happening! Like NOW."** Since you're made primarily of estrogen your value *system* is tied to your feelings (not intellect). And yes, it's *goood* to be smart (always) but if it's not balanced, with the intelligence of your body (namely your feelings) major detention IS to be expected. As in... You'll be held up—all over the place (in your life). Misery equals attracting *more* crap into your life (cuz you feel bad). So it's like sayin', something about me deserves this (and you accept it). And when your body sees that you've NEGLECTED assignments on a daily basis (taking care of YOU) your punishment... BODY in exile.

(Unwilling to co-operate)

So you're down (depressed) no energy, get sick a lot, never in the mood to do anything. Have fun (what's *that*)? You'd rather be alone (not true) do five term papers that aren't due, CLEAN up your room (only if your computer's broken). LOL It's always surprising to hear (when bad stuff happens) "Nichole... Why you letting this shit get to you? (Oh I dunno, it's making me question *EVERYTHING* about my-self) Why you trippin?" And the *worst*... "But you're so smart, don't let it bother you." Makes me feel like an even BIGGER idiot cuz I can't figure out how to hold it all together.

Your mind's *strength* will make sure you don't deviate. And if you were a ROBOT that'd be fine (I suppose). But you're a humanoid... with boobs. A girl... way more complex. I'd toss self CARE, neglect my body, health, eat shit, not sleep, forget about working out, dance, treating myself. Which btw only makes you feel YOU need to suffer (*more*). Kinda like reverse psychology! Weird how that works. LOL Just for the record. I painted my NAILS today. And I swear! I was so friggin' tired I'm like, holy crap! There's NINE fingernails left...

I'll never make it. :'(

I had no energy LEFT. My body was starving for a break (something different) but then my mind's like, 'NOOOO. You stop when you're done.' I couldn't believe by the time I finished my nails my energy was UP. ☺ It was so fundamentally absurd. That little joy... I felt seeing my nails PAINTED (shiny) made me feel stronger (*in my body*). I was totally refreshed. Like, I had a nap for hourrrs. So neglecting (postponing) enjoyment... due to dedication to a cause, guy (family, friend) anything you feel guilty about means... YOU'VE set up camp in your brain (abandoned body n' feelings) except for a means to an end (peeing when you absolutely have to). Guess what I learned! YOU ignore it and it will ignore you. You give it just enough to get by, it'll do the same...

(It's into equality) LOL

What I didn't get, mostly living in my head did NOT fuel my body, givin' energy to my body *gave* me good thoughts (drowning out voices tellin' me bad shit). So I know it's impossible to feel *good* in your body and think bad THOUGHTS. There's no room! LOL Too much good stuff flooding it all at once! LOL

77.

When we jog, dance, workout, skateboard, fly, leap, snowboard, gymnastics, swim THERE'S NO WAY we have a bad thought.

LOOK AT THIS LIST...

One of these sentences (thoughts) will jump OUT at YOU. It's the one... *sucking* your skull. Identify first. Smash into bits second. If you get emotional lookin' at ONE... That's the maggot that's been eating away at your *insides*. Circle the bastard!

No one understands me.
There's something wrong with me.
I'm worthless.
My life is supposed to be hard.
I'm meant to be alone.
I'm supposed to suffer.
I'm a monster.
I'm a loser.
I always fuck things up.
I'm weird.
Who would want me? (*I DOOOOOOOOOOO!*)
I'm an idiot.
Bad things always happen to me.
It's my fault.
I'm disgusting.
I'm stupid.
I'm not important...

Now that it's out of hiding... *DROWN THE FUCKER!!*

Get the body's voice **louder**.

It's not easy emptying your head! Ya think all that meditation shit is EASY? Our mind is SO filled with crap it just overcrowds space. (Hoarder!) Standing room ONLY please (thoughts that last two seconds). And you wonder why you have a short attention span. LOL

Meditation has *never* been my thing. It's very difficult for a hardcore athlete to sit STILL (anywhere). Unless they're exhausted or makin' out. :P Passively waiting... is never a natural byproduct of being an athlete. We like to run, train, swim and dance it out of our system! When I was almost finished with this book, I herniated a disc in my lower back. Pure hell. Couldn't do a thing. Hard enough needing my boyfriend to walk me to the bathroom... help me pee. And YOU guys know **nothing** about wiping. It's tap, tap—not try and remove the whole top layer of the vagina with a tissue! I couldn't go any-where. Once my spine supported my body *sitting* I decided to put on my favorite chill music (nature sounds, spa) a foreign song (I don't understand) so my brain wasn't tempted to WORK reluctantly. I put my cell timer on HALF an hour. I'm like, Noooo way! I can't sit THAT long.

But soon after it was like, VACAY. I got to be *somewhere* other than my bedroom. I closed my eyes... to my surprise, it felt like I was giving a **present** to myself. My only JOB—listen and enjoy. First thing! Tears start fallin'... no clue why. I realized I was seeing (*in my mind*) all these fears I had, things I was worried about, things that bothered me (I never spoke about). All this toxic GUCK crammed up in my heart. A heart *cleanse*! LOL Very emotional. But strangely, my tears didn't fall *cuz of the bad shit* cuz all of a sudden I felt SO happy! My mind's showing me stuff like... How *lucky* I am with my back injury (I can walk!) How much my boyfriend loves me, all the people supporting me (cheering me on) and I'm OVERWHELMED with gratitude. It's like... There's buckets of tears for all these things I'm grateful for. After a few minutes, the tears stop... but understand! I wasn't TRYING to be grateful, like I was tryin' to score points with GOD. I just felt so light. So cared for by life, wrapped in this fuzzy blanket of Love. It was such a spacious feeling, probably cuz the shit was cleared and it made ROOM. LOL A sure sign my body's storage of massive waste has been emptied (good stuff comin' in). The corners of my mouth start going UP. I begin to focus on everything I *want* to happen. What I'm aiming for. I saw it... I felt it. I went THERE. And pretty soon! It was taking me on this wild ride. Allll this amazing shit was happening right in front of my eyes!! Like, I was looking into a magical vortex! It was EPIC. It wasn't meditation—it was medi(expec)tation! A spiritual SPORT. :D Going after what I WANT... with my mind, body, feelings. I'm COMING!!

I start to feel amaaazing!!

I get an *itch*... then my hair falls across my face, there's a dull ache in my back. I'm like no—not NOW!! I just bought my own island! Just like when you're daydreaming in class! Your elbow slips over the edge of the desk or someone startles YOU (Teacher) and you lose the whole picture!! I DIDN'T move. I paid attention to the itch... stayed with it, observed it. Didn't react to it (scratch it). It was so *haaard*. But HOLY crap! It went AWAY. I couldn't believe it. How could an itch go without me scratching it? Where would it go? The ache, the itch, everything (physical) left... once I *observed* it. Let it have its day. LOL Just needed my attention. ☺ Now when I do my vacay thing and there's an *itch*... I'm like. *Ahhh*... There you are! *Wait for it*... Poof!! GONE. I feel so masterful. Next I'll be moving objects (with my mind). Lmao

The *itch*... is a part of YOU and if you push it away (not let it happen) you'll be pushing it further into you. Just like an emotion you *resist* (not used to feeling) works the same way. If YOU feel an emotion and automatically wanna snuff IT (choke it) so you can avoid it, it will come back... It never GOT your attention. Little did I know the suffering happens in the *resisting*... in not being okay with it (shame, guilt) refusing to address it (not in the actual *emotion*). It's kinda like... Once you tell your best friend your deepest darkest (most embarrassing) secret and they're **okay** with it—doesn't have the same effect on you. The emotion (...*itch*) has a beginning and an end... like everything else, nothing's permanent. It *changes*...

As soon as I'd see a certain emotion come, I'd see it like a nose bleed... needing my attention. If I wanted to see the end of it, I'd need to look at it... pay attention to it (acknowledge it) see how long it needs me for. Not put it off, set a reminder... Later! If I refused, I'd never see the end of it (*ever*).

It became MY template for relationships!

(Since I AM the type to react *first*—ask questions later) LOL

The meditation also balanced my tendency to be too aggressive with my boyfriend, since it filled me with a much needed CALM... brought out a whole new essence—call it MAGNETIC passivity! LOL A way to pull my guy in... (*close*) without any effort (the way it was meant to be). ;D And now, when something comes up (unplanned or nasty feeling) I pay attention to it, stay with it... receive its message. When you get an itch your body's trying to tell you something (authentic). It's *communicating* to you. If you react automatically and scratch it the communication has been cut. You may think that itch (bad feeling) will never go away *without* scratching it, blocking it (getting drunk, baked) but its message to you is... PAY ATTENTION. Find out what's going on. It needs to know you *know* it's there. And as you get familiar with it (see it as *okay*... to feel that) not tell yourself it's stupid or lame it won't be threatening. And this way, you're living life on *purpose*... not just reacting to it. LOL Now... You're powerful.

And even if it *peeks* back into your life... needs more attention, not finished givin' you notes on yourself (not as threatening, you've already met). LOL

As I trained myself to excel in this spiritual *sport* (lol) trained myself to *observe*... it'd overspill to people and circumstances. If something came up—I wouldn't grow seven heads out of each ARMPIT. Freak. I wouldn't **react**. That word alone... suggests re-acting a scenario. That's totally what we're doing! We're re-enacting something that happened a long time ago (in the past) with someone else... in the *present*. LOL What an unfair way to kidnap TIME (or it wouldn't upset us so much). Kinda like, someone accusing you for the *first* time of something, you're more baffled (confused) than anything else, not MAD (unless it's been *done* many times before in the past). I observed myself *not* reacting (not telling myself what I *thought* it meant). Half the time... it didn't even go anywhere *near* where I thought it would go. LOL I'd stay with it, be okay with it (not have my head INTERROGATE the shit out of it) let it happen... It got my attention. And I conquered... Owned its ass. If I would keep re-acting (try and stop emotions, protest, stifle, blame) I'd be IGNORING the deepest part of me...

The things that come up (emotions) are *yours*... never someone else's.

This is a hard one to get (even after you read it a hundred times). ;P And cuz they're *yours*... if you diss them, abandon them—you won't feel *supported*. As I continued emptying my mind there's no added pressure to an already air-tight bag of CRAP. So I can afford... to observe. Be a spectator. And I'm *spared* of sooo much pain (and energy loss). Do YOU know how much **energy** it takes to maintain 'angry status'? A LOT. Holding a grudge is like holding your breath, best to DUMP that shit, not carry it around. Most important... If you don't react cuz you're supported inside and secure (know the truth of where things are comin' from) catch the person off guard, they're expecting you to FIGHT. When you **don't**, their words (accusations) bounce off YOU—and goes back to its original owner (*them*) since there's no fuel to keep the fire (their bullshit) going. It dies. And cuz there's no resistance from YOU (**reaction**) there's nothing to make it bigger (no explosion) it's a misguided missile that returns, once the destination is not reached.. and *that's* when they feel it.

Why didn't I know about this BEFORE?! Lmao

When we girls are upset our thoughts are attached to *emotional* weight—that's HEAVY. We need to empty those. It doesn't matter how *smart* people think you are you could be hurting yourself—and no one would see why. That's cuz when you ignore yourself you're like a teeter totter (no balance) unstable.

When you least expect it...

Yeah. That's a GOOD idea. Get your Mom (big sis) or best friend to READ it. :D

I had made myself work INDOORS for yearrs... Missed every sunset, watched guys and girls make out through the window, lose bright sunny days (wishing I HAD a boyfriend). I felt like I was working in a CLOSET. Each holiday (sad, no family) even New Years Eve (no biggie, don't have a boyfriend). It didn't matter if I was ordered to go write outside. I made myself sit in a corner where it's dark and quiet, so I could focus. A girl would bring me my drink, look around at all the empty tables and chairs and be like, "You're not a fucken DEAD animal! Go outside and write."

Finally... I'm like, fuck it she's right. I decide to train again. See a movie. Get a facial... go to the lake! Play my Spanish music (fave) and lay on the grass... K, so I pass out right away. And I don't even know how many hours passed, when I woke up I just cried. I felt... like I woke up from a *HUNDRED YEAR BATTLE!!!* Every part of me was thoroughly spent (neglected, forgotten... dead). LIKE... a friggin' dead animal. LOL I took off my shoes, walked on the rocks bare foot, just having my toes grip the rock felt incredible. I sat there... looked at the water. A *smile* came on my face—but nooo YOU don't understand!! I didn't wanna smile (still pretty grumpy). It just came. Like, there was another person inside me JUMPING UP and DOWN screaming!!

FINALLY YOU DO WHAT I WANT

(What took YOU so fucken long?)

Instantly, I had more *energy*. A smile will appear on your face (or tear) when you finally allow yourself to do... 'be' *have* what you truly want (but are too responsible to ask, too disciplined to break away from, too focused to take time out for). As soon as I did that (take three WHOLE days off) allll the things I worried about, felt bad about (doubted) all the what 'ifs', went AWAY... (for real). It was so simple. Strange... When you go on vacation or know you're moving away (to a different place) NOW that person calls! That job opportunity opens up, YOU get into that *group*. Somebody *notices* you... You're accepted to that SCHOOL. It all happens right before you LEAVE (especially when you're looking forward to it) either way you're 'happy'. ☺

SYNOPSIS:

1) It doesn't matter how smart you are, if you're *upset*... you'll feel like shit (your body is *linked* to how YOU feel girl).

2) It doesn't matter how smart you are dude, if you're filled to the brim with FRUSTRATIONS and don't get it out of your system, you'll be tempted to do it in a *destructive* way.

YOUR body <u>needs</u> to find an escape route **to release pain**. K. I'll SPELL it out *one mo' time...*

DRUGS, BOOZE, SKETCH BAGS...

Is what you'll be pulled to (when filled with toxic pressure). Or you take it out on your girl (someone you love) mom, grandparents.

Especially if you're smart and know how to manipulate them.

(I have to say it, cuz it's true)

Then they think it's their fault, feel guilty (like they're to blame). Not cool. When you feel good inside it makes you *receptive* to the good stuff in life, cuz your soil's fertilized... so good things can grow (you're happy). Then you're focused on alll these good vibes comin' in. Like when you move to a new PLACE (unless you're leaving friends behind) there's no history, no memories... or great memories (it's a familiar spot) YOU feel great!

You feel entitled...

That's why star athletes have a sense of entitlement on and off the field. They feel HIGH...

What's that?

Yeah sure, you can feel high *that* way. Just keep in mind every decision you make has a COST. Sometimes the cost is so minimal you hardly feel it (at *first*) till it collects *interest*—you needing to do it more and more and now the pressure's on. You've got collectors up your ass—in your face, at your locker. Scary... Sometimes you leave a large down payment (thought you could handle it) but took on more than you could chew (swallow). Weekly installments seemed 'safe' but soon totally took over your life. Sucks. Every single decision you *ever* make will have a PRICE. Make sure you can afford it.

Once in debt... it leaves a life-long stain.

You can try and cover it up but when people get close *enough*... they'll know.

Back to my *sistas!!*

If you feel bad about something in your life girl, you'll feel tired (drained) cuz your body's *connected* to your emotions (though you may try not to show it). And when you feel DRAINED (cuz of a guy, girl, obligation, too many things at once) you won't feel *worthy* of anything good cuz you *feel* bad... Which indirectly tells you you're *bad* without you knowing it.

(Yes... deep breath is needed) LOL

So, without meaning to, your body will be attracted to guys (situations) that <u>are</u> bad (*make you suffer*) cuz inside you feel *bad*... And when you feel bad you secretly feel guilty (like somethin's wrong with you) you must have done something to cause this (even though you know you didn't). When you feel **guilty** a part of you will look for a way to make you pay for it—losin' the fact that, it wasn't your fault to begin with! *Grrrr!* It won't matter *what* happened... If someone did something to YOU or you did something to somebody, you feel bad (so *body* feels bad) and is attracted to what it already *know*... more BAD (shit). And that way it feels like it's taking up in the same residency—your Sorority Shit house. Union RULES. LOL And you wonder why you pick the **same** guys? Lmao Think about it for a MINUTE.

No, seriously put the book down. Think about it...

When you feel bad you will pick badly! I believe, the key to releasing yourself from this imprisoned maze lies in the *senses* of the body (smell, touch, taste, sound, sight) body's BLUEPRINT. When we make our body feel good, by doing something we love our body's in a constant good kick-ass feeling. Which then shouts to the WORLD!

Damnnn... I'M GOOD. Totally WORTH IT!

Like an invisible neon sign above your head!

The mind can and will hold us *captive*. Time... can free us (true) but it can also keep us *locked* up (long time) cuz we're <u>still</u> thinking about that asshole (skank) all the bad shit that happened (what we lost). Then we feel hopeless (like it never ends) disconnected from what's going on NOW cuz we're back *there*... in shitsville (trapped).

Selective amnesia (if only).

Love keeps us **present** (that's why it's a 'gift'). This is why parents love it when we're small (secretly wish we'd stay that way, a little *longer*). Hate drags us to our past, shoves it down our throat till we UP-CHUCK it so many times we feel sick (of everything). If that happens? Straight up! Smell some LEMONS. Totally works. Love IS the only thing that *escapes* time... cuz you're completely untouched by anything around YOU. Like, you're in some enchanted bubble. There's *no time* there... that's why when you do something you love six hours FLY and you're like, WTF? Doing something or being with someone you **don't** like—2 MINUTES... feels like an eternity. Can be excruciating.

IT'S SO IMPORTATNT TO LOVE OR DO SOMETHING YOU

LOVE...

Otherwise, it's easy to go into a depression...

(Depression = expression... stuck)

FACT:

YOU can get yourself out of where you are NOW. Seriously! You <u>do</u> have the KEY. It's buried in the body's senses... need to unlock *those*. K, just to pound it in your skull guys—that's why sex DOESN'T work (when we're upset). Don't know *why* you don't get that. LOL Logic has no say when the spirit's trapped DOWN under (isolated). It's during these moments... a girl craves a guy who *has* the endurance (smarts) to understand her... continue digging, cuz literally at times, we feel like we're being buried ALIVE. You find out all about us, what others *don't* see. This is NOT for the feeble, insecure or I-don't-really-care-I-just-wanna-fuck-her 'type'. Middle finger—flipped, right at YOU dude.

WANTED!

- Guys who'll look out for their girl!
- Guys who we can look up to!
- Guys who'll direct a searchlight over our emotional seas.

86.

...So the mermaid can come home.

Show him all the magic *she's* about.

Cuz when we're upset and ejected out of our mind (*wheeeee)* land in our BODY... we're distracted from our mind (temporarily). Once we feel good inside, good thoughts follow...

(Circle so you don't forget)

It's amazing how powerful anyone can feel when they're high ABOVE ground. Who doesn't have a smile on their face when they're FLYING!! Unless they're scared shitless. Sitting on top of a high platform like a cliff or building, all of a sudden your problems *don't* seem so BIG. They're *smaller* (not as severe). Nothing changed, just the altitude (*attitude*). Serves as a reminder! We can always be (any given time) BIGGER, than our issues. Depends *where* we see it from, what angle (and whose). Taking a hawk's eye view of things works wonders. A hawk... would never freak over issues. It'd just WATCH. The eyes have great patience... *when anticipating a change...* Once it sees it (like a hawk) it strikes. SOARS! Frankly... I just gotta say one thing to my guys. There's *SUCH* a tremendous amount of pressure for YOU doin' the right thing. ALWAYS. Seriously. I don't know how YOU manage.

DUNNO HOW YOU DO IT!

Except to say... in *this* lifetime, you took the greatest challenge of all.

GIRLS! GIRLS! GIRLS!

:-& (Tongue tied) LOL

Girls... Stand up wherever YOU are. Get UP! Join hands. Form a group and SHOUT it to the world! THREE times.

In this body beats the heart of a GIRL!!
In this body beats the heart of a GIRL!!

(1 more time!)

Know it, <u>own</u> it and *occasionally*... rub it in their faces. LOL

And guess what guys...

Since we're feeling oriented, once we feel good we'll feel HAPPY! And your job just got a WHOLE lot simpler! Cuz when we're happy we feel like everything's OKAY. Which makes YOU feel like everything's *perrrfect*—cuz as much as you guys can compartmentalize your shit, when it comes to us feeling *bad* your whole world just got WORSE. You know it, I know it, everyone knows it. Such are the perks of living in Pussyville. We all know when your girlfriend's bitchin' and in a crappy mood—how NOT good you feel (dude). When her inner strength and confidence *returns*... it's a turn on for YOU. Nothing you guys find more *sexxxy* than a girl who shows confidence in HERSELF. Cuz that makes YOU look good (dude).

In your eyes...

SHE KNOWS HER VALUE.

(Can't fuck with this one)

A real Challenge...

And when she *tames* YOU (horn-dog) you'll love her to no end—cuz she broke YOU. No one ever did that before (they gave in). And that fills you with awe. Like, how the fuck did she do that?! She did it 'on her terms' (that's how).

She's SPECIAL...

You know it. I know it. And now EVERYONE knows it.

(YOU done good, dude)

88.

Sorry.

I don't casually exchange body fluids...

MR - CONCEPTOR
(PART 2)

S.O.P.

Standard - Operating - Procedure

A MUST!

(What to do when SHIT happens)

1. If someone like a friend, girlfriend or boyfriend is hurt and you acknowledge their feelings (it's fucked what happened) *that's* cool (if you totally get them). Just don't make the mistake of making them feel like a victim. Cuz then they'll (feel bad) and like established in previous chapter, they will deep down feel like they're to blame. Expect *more* (of the same). They're a victim of life remember?

2. Help them by FOCUSING not on the situation at hand—**BUT WHO THEY ARE!** What their strengths are. ☺ What they're ABOUT. Their track record, how they came through *before*. How they were victorious! How they turned everrrything around! Not... "Oh, man. That sucks. But you've been through worse." Technically correct, it doesn't *inspire*. And depending where they are emotionally it can make them feel *stupid* for even bringing it up (MORE strikes against them). Anything with guilt *attached*... like, you've put up with more dude, children in Africa are starving (although true) and your assistance backfires into a helpless feeling (for them). Like, this is just another SMACK in the face (they're supposed to take) since most of their life they've been a punching bag (anyway). Guess it's just their FATE. ☹ Hell no.

3. It's very effective when you put a person's *focus* on what they did before (to get on top of it) with a LOT of conviction, followed by... "You can DO this! Remember that TIME...?" Recounting accurately and in an explicit manner details of the scenario (every little item—how they succeeded) gets their senses back *there* and feelings of triumph in their blood— PUMPED. Puts them back in winning-mode.

4. If it's a GIRL dude (as mentioned) distractions help us find our *path* back to the body's senses (drives our energy up) makes us feel GOOD. Which puts YOU back on an unbeatable track— to succeed in love, life (that you deserve) cuz YOU feel successful. Once you guys master a girl and her emotions (a very slippery slope) you can make ANYTHING happen. Cuz it primes you to switch tactics at a moment's notice! Be SUPER creative with nothing—no prep time. Solve a maze of thoughts that have *nothing* to do with one another. A girl's favorite fortress. ☺ HER psyche... one of the (if not the *most*) complex things to work out. You will always do well in life when you *master* your emotions... influencing people is very easy when you can master the TOUGHEST critic (yourself). Command your *fate*—or have it dictate yours. You **decide**. Cuz what you want all will be taken care of, in the most unexpected totally flawless WAY... if you just *decide*.

(I promise) <3

EXAMPLE:

Your guy or girl (that you love) ends it... on TEXT. Simple! Real love's a comin' (they were just prepping... YOU). ☺ So next time, you're not too trusting right away, so the next one... *works for it*. So the next guy, you're sooo gonna take your TIME with (here's crossing both fingers and toes). So the **next** one... you're not gonna make the CENTER of your whole world (so fast). And so, the next ONE, you don't so easily *accuse* (till all the facts are in). My bad. LOL

AND YOU'RE NOT AN IDIOT IF YOU STILL LOVE THEM!

Cuz that loving feeling... is gonna *take you* places. It's gonna get YOU where you need to go... Final destination. <3 Pit stops can be so annoying, I know. You just need to understand... you haven't had a lot of earthly experience to know, all the things you loved about *them* are traits you *will* find in another. So you need to clearly separate (and see) it's not so much JOE, MICHAEL, ANDREW, DANIEL... ALEXIS, ELIZABETH, ASHLEY, MICHELLE that you're crazy about. It's certain 'aspects' of their personality. And of course, the fact that you're fiercely attracted—like the scar on his chin, the birthmark on her shoulder) thick animal-like eyebrows. *Sighhh...* (I feel you)

It's the things they did. How they carried themselves (MAJOR swagmanship) how they thought, made you laugh, reacted and responded to YOU... Oh! And it's this one other tiny *thing*... another time (promise). That's why it FEELS like you're *stuck* on them, can't rip yourself apart. They filled your prescription—many *repeats*. But some of you OD, some got addicted and *some*... don't believe in alternative medicine—until you got a BAD reaction. You never suspected it'd be poison. :'(Took so much out of YOU just to heal. Then of course... you feel like they took all your love with *them*...

THEY WERE YOUR DRUG MAN!

(They made you HIGH)

No other feeling like it! Withdrawal... can be SUCH a bitch. You try to ride it out like a bad flu—passion fever peaks! It HURTS to want them. A hellll... only those who have lived through it can talk about. Exhausted, you can't cry anymore. THAT part is actually welcoming. And slowly, it's like the anesthesia starts to wear off—*YOU COME TO YOUR SENSES!!* They didn't take your 'love' with them.

It's with YOU...

Just be aware, when you break up with someone and all you want, is for *them* to want you back (then you can LET GO) see it for what it is (other than a very fucked scenario) in truth... It's not what it seems (at all). THAT happened to me...

I worked in sales. I had the biggest *CRUSH* on this guy. He was my boss. He was from the Middle East. And I thought it was *soo* adorable that he was raised on a farm, up in the hills. How he tended to his flock of goats. *Awh...* Something inside *him* was pullin' me like crazy. I mean, I couldn't think of anything but HIM.

Memory hog!

He's all I saw *inside* my eyes... It was innn-sane. All he'd do was SHOCK me (let me down) turn his back on me—*after* telling me I was right. Guess, he didn't have the balls to stand up for me (in front of his staff). Privately, he'd tell me he agreed with me, I was the *most* important person, working for him. In front of everyone... he acted differently. It RIPPED my heart out—squished it between its fingers. I suffered... quietly. I was in so much PAIN (over his betrayal) couldn't even *pick* up a phone. It was like, my body died. All I wanted was to please him, make him happy.

(Am I the only one that's FUCKED?)

I wanted him to be proud of me (my sales). I hated what he did to me... Make me believe—we were a TEAM. Then leave me for target practice for everyone (say nothin'). After, tell me I was right. MIXED signals... Ya think?! I could never take him seriously cuz apart from seeing he couldn't stand up for me, he was moody (insensitive) at times rude, major communication 'issues' and he hid behind his work. Relationships were just too much for him—it'd make him face his 'hot one minute - cold the next' exterior. Can we say... BIPOLAR!?!

Still, I realized he was *exactly* like my father. Who also never stood up for me (never around). He was the exact *interior* of a man I deeply loved... that I never felt love back from. So it wasn't gonna happen— cuz he was a duplicate of that *exact* equation (never happening) that's why the *pull*... It communicated (inside) as the same thing—so it kept calling me over...

To rectify... retrieve (*what never came*). ☹ ☹ ☹

When you want someone, you know is FUCKED—who's not nice to you, acts nice then mean, *know*... it's a powerful dynamic (someone else) they represent. An exact chemistry match (inside) which is why you're gravitating *towards* them... It's not only familiar—it's PRECISE. They not only remind you of the person, they start doing things the other person never did (*that you wanted*) and it so FUCKEN lures YOU in. I'd have a private meeting, I'd put on my ugly glasses. I'm like, "Don't look at me with my glasses." He's like, "Let's go buy you GLASSES." That *shocked* me cuz he's such a tight-ass with his money. You couldn't hammer a PIN into his butt-hole. Seriously. All the secretaries have to buy their OWN sticky pads. Or he'd give them old ones (used) with notes from old employees in them. I cross my leg... and he's looking at my running shoe (which

I have to admit is gundgy) he's like, "Do you wanna come with me to the store?" I'm like, "Why, do we need to pick up supplies?" He's like, "I wanna buy you a new pair of running shoes." AHHHHH!!

I'm sooo fucked. <3

And I'm thinkin'... KEEP talking and put all emotions on hold—till you figure out what the fuck's going on! W*hyyyy* is he DOING this? He's never asked me out before (k that would really mess me up). When I'm alone with a guy I'm like, completely *STUPID*. My brain slips outta my uterus on the way out the DOOR. I couldn't figure out why he was acting like he was interested! When he first hired me, he told me he hoped this job would change my life. I'm thinkin'... Whaaat...? He doesn't even know me. So I'm like, "Yup. When I can go to MONTE CARLO on vacation I'll know it changed my life." He's like, "I speak French. Maybe we'll go together?" Whaaat a charmer. Then again, there's always a truth in every joke. My mom always said I was SLOW. I'd never get it... right away (if a guy's into me or not). Doesn't dawn on me unless he's direct. And TELLS me.

Like, how many guys do that? LOL

I remember this *reeeeal* hot guy, he's like, "What are you doing *tonight?*" I'm like, "Well... First I have to wash my hair. Then I have to clean my dishes, repaint the bathroom, vacuum, work on my project THEN—I always do my leg raises, right before I go to sleep." Every time I saw him, he was like, "Hey! What are you doin' TONIGHT?" I give my 'list'. Finally we hook up at a party and I start to talk to him (only I'm about to leave the country) how brave of me. LOL We end up confessing our feelings, which is ALWAYS easiest to do when you're about to MOVE. So I'm like, "But you never asked me out?!" He's like, "I asked you out THREE times! I usually ask just 'once'." K. Just to give YOU guys the heads up! Ask 'in advance' for a date—so there's no confusion. And actually ask us out on a DATE. Don't just ask a question. We hate it when you beat around the bush—if YOU like a girl just say it.

She may be literal, like me!

And don't treat her like a LAST minute thing. She could dump you last minute (when you're not expecting it). What goes around—bites you up the ass when you're not ready. So, next day I'm working in my office and there's a *knock* on my door. I open the door... No one's there. I look down and see a brand new pair of running shoes. ☺ *Whoa...* These shoes are on point! *Yaaasssss.* My boss is hiding in the hallway...

(Tempting) ;D

I go to him...

I'm like, "WHO do these belong to?" I just *couldn't* believe in the middle of the day, when he's so busy—he'd go shopping for my SHOES. He's like, "I got them for YOU." I'm like, "I DON'T believe you. Where's the BILL?" He shows me the bill. Puts his thumb over the price (sooo cute). I'm like, "I *lovvvve* them." I turn them over ...only they're not my size. I'm like, "I'm an 8 not a 7 and a half. Broke my big toe. It's bigger now." He grabs the shoes and takes off! I figure, in a few days, I'll have my shoes. ☺ Twenty minutes LATER. I walk into my office and the shoes are on my chair (size 8). Life is *beeeeautiful!*

It was allll this special attention that killed me. It was hilarious, he couldn't talk to me *without* putting his hand on my shoulder. So I'd just flick it off. I'm like, "MUST you touch me every time we TALK? I mean... Do I *look* like a BASKET of fruit?" Half the time, I don't think he even *realized* he was doin' it. He'd just have a need to *connect.* When I'd be frustrated and we'd talk, he'd put his hand on my shoulder *reeeal* lightly (in slow motion) cuz he never KNEW if I'd whip it off or let it stay! LMFAO It bugged me when he'd *touch me,* made me feel so weak. Like a flower without water for months (flimsy inside). I'd tell him my office chair was smelly, he'd BUY me a new one (next day). Then he'd get pissed, take it back. I'd complain about the lighting he'd be like, "Do YOU wanna go down the street and get new lights?" We'd go. I was sooo nervous walking alone with him. Then he takes off! Walks like—*A HUNDRED YARDS AHEAD OF ME!* I'm like, "YOU must have me confused with one of your goats. Shepherd boy. (Sooo insulting) Like, why are you asking me to walk with you when you're NOT walking with me?" My dad used to do that (with my mom). Needless to say he got pissed and changed his mind about the lights too. Course, there are times when I'd get pissed and he'd just LAUGH. He thought it was funny the way I'd get allll worked up. Such a guy thing. Omg. I couldn't believe after the first week he was like, "If you make me money—seriously I will DIE for you. I'll take a BULLET for you." (Doooo say?) Two weeks later I break all records (even though personally, I didn't hit my quota) he was SO happy. I'm like, "K. Just so we're CLEAR. If you say—you're gonna die for me, take a bullet for me—you'd better be prepared to do just that. Don't be saying things and THINK I'm gonna forget— cuz I will not FORGET. Cuz we don't forget (anyyyything). We just file it away for safe keeping." Bring it all up (and yup things from two years ago too) when we're mad at YOU. Cuz we take your words seriously—and DON'T talk shit like that, it stresses us out. Straight up. We don't like it. It's lame. You'd be A LOT more useful, if you stayed around. :P

He looks at me...

Nervously laughs, then stares (a long time). And it's *such* a turn on... He's like, "I mean what I say, Nichole." I'm like, "What do you mean?" He's like, "I mean... I *know* you didn't make your quota. (OMG! He remembered) I'll just give you the money. So you won't be short." "But, that's like a **thousand dollars**." "I'll bring it tomorrow." I just looked at HIM. o_o He was scared, didn't know if he made the right move (or the wrong one). I looked *away*... then back. I'm like, "REALLY?!!" He takes his hand and *caresses* my face with the back of his hand... then stops. THEN kisses me! (On the cheek) But it wasn't like, a little peck. It was a good 4.2 second kiss. *His kiss said...* I **really** like YOU. K... This is so awkward, what now? He's my boss and he's acting like he's on a first date with me? His face is BEET RED. It's okay. I like beets!

The fact remains!

He went for it...

And when a guy takes a risk (like that) it says A LOT to me. I was so HIGH... it took allll my strength not to whizz around the room. Calmly (as if not affected) I'm like, "K.. Just take it out of my next paycheck." He's like, "Give it to me when you have, whenever you need money just text me how much."

OMIGOSH!! I have my very OWN bank.

I couldn't believe how he wanted to take care of me (like that). It really got to me. Even if I *was* short... I'd never call him on it, it was enough he offered. Still, my female client is like, "Test him. ASK him for money. Then do it again and *again* and see if he'll do it." Stupid bitch!

DON'T trifle with a man's heart... it's a precious commodity.

Guys aren't stupid (well... most of them). They don't offer to girls who take advantage of them. He TRUSTED me. I offer my hand to shake on it, he takes it... turns it over. Kisses it (like a *perfect* gentleman). Our eyes never separated. Even though we were in the office when he kissed my hand it was like... we were transported to another PLACE. Everything around us disintegrated as we travelled through time— INSTANTLY! Almost as if, looking into each other's eyes opened a secret portal... and we were *taken* to a Ball. A very elegant Ball. Where guys bow to you and shit. My trance was *broken* when I reached for him and he turned into a piece of plywood—didn't hug back. No pumpkins... no warning!

Days later I still couldn't understand why he reacted like that. Maybe, he has a girlfriend and wants to be loyal? Fair. Two weeks later we're in his office talking, one of his staff (total JERK) went Godzilla on me—no reason. And my boss is telling me I should overlook it. That the guy's just being immature. I get up...

Right in his face I'm like—"*I DON'T TAKE SHIT FROM ANYBODY!!*" Certainly not something you *usually* say... to a BOSS who just hired you. But to my surprise he's like, "*Oooh!* I like THAT. Are you like that with your boyfriend?" *Daaang...* He's fishin'. I didn't have a boyfriend at the time—but didn't wanna let him know. I already felt vulnerable. I turn away and look at the *WALL*... And it's so hard to make a wall *look* like it's got something to say. LOL He repeats his question. I cave and tell him, I don't have a boyfriend. (Right this second) We keep talking and I notice this woman walk by... I just caught a glimpse, she was wearing a red jacket. He's like, "That's my girlfriend." CHOKE!! I don't look. I don't acknowledge, I just keep talking. He gets texted, takes off. And all I gotta *say*...

As *soon* as he left...

My heart sank right into my left ANKLE. I felt like someone SCOOPED my insides out. I died (right there). Omg! He's GOT a girlfriend. For real?! I *couldn't* move... My heart snapped in TWO ☹. I barely know this guy! WTF? Why was my body RESPONDING as if she already *knew* him? She was already attached (bizarre). And SO pissed me off. I couldn't EXPLAIN why everything felt one way—while in my mind, I was just getting to know him (so nothing recognizable there) just inside.

(Sooo unfair)

I kept telling myself... it's okay he's got a girlfriend. Don't have to worry about anything happening (*sooo* stressful). I need a guy, like a boil on my butt. Time goes by and he's still saying things like, "I need to go pick up (*whatever*) why don't we get it together?" And I'm like, "Are you kidding? Do you know how many phone calls I have to make?!" Cute... he's trying to get 'alone' time. Didn't see it at the time. (Slow remember?) He starts calling daily to see what supplies I need. What color I want, what type. One time I'm like, "Hey! I was just thinking of YOU." He's like, "YOU were thinking of me?" (Silence) He was like *a little boy*... from a different time (in a man's body) with a GREAT ass. Just stating the facts. He continued dropping hints at things to do (*together*). I'm like, "I don't think your *girlfriend* would like that." He's like, "WHAT girlfriend?" I'm like, "Your girlfriend. The one that walked by while we were talking the other day."

"She's SEVENTY FIVE YEARS OLD."

Sneaky bastard!!

Once we were at a store and the guy behind the counter asked me what brings me to Toronto here from Los Angeles?" I'm like, "Destiny..." My boss is like,

"She came for me."

Yup, he just escalates 'cocky' to a whole new level.

Little did he know...

He was right. But then! He'd turn into Dr. Jekyll/Mr. Jackass. Completely turn against me. I'd ask for clarification on something and he's like, *"I DON'T HAVE TIME FOR THIS!* I don't like repeating myself. If you wanna talk to me—talk numbers!" Zeroooo chill. And like, fuck *offff.* Seriously. I couldn't take it ANYMORE. How can something *sooo* right—be so hurtful? It made no sense. I had so many panic attacks, I was scared comin' into work (havin' him scream at me). I couldn't sleep at night. It's like... you know you've found your *home* (in this monster) same time there's fear. I couldn't concentrate on my work. I'd get spasms in my heart—don't blame her for freaking! The spasms got more and more intense. Like, it literally felt like a ELEPHANT sat on it. It felt *bruised...* I went to the doctor. She made me do a bunch of tests. She told me...

I HAD to quit. ☹

For some reason HE had a profound effect on me. Cuz ANY other guy, I'd definitely tell him where to go. And it's not that I didn't put up a fight. I did. But conflict between him and I <u>paralyzed</u> me. I cried for a WEEK. It was gonna be hard to leave him. Like, trying to rip a scab off your knee the skin *tearrring...* all that gushy part. He made me so HAPPY (without even trying).

Weird, when he first hired me I told him, I'd be moving back to LA (in a year). His face went white. His mouth DROPPED he's like, "You *think* I'm gonna let you go?" Scary but ooooh so *romantic.* I'm like, "What do you mean?" He's like, "I mean... I feel bad. You'll do a LOT here then you LEAVE?" (Nice cover!) I'm like, "That's okay, you can send checks to LA. They do accept checks there." He's like, "YOU won't leave me."

He's right, in my heart... *I never left.*

Still... NEVER underestimate a GIRL.

Before it escalated to allll that DRAMA I confirmed to him that although I'd be leaving while I was here I'd make him a lot of money. He was *sooo* sad. I'm like, "Don't worry. I SAID, I'll make you a lot of money." He's like, "But I want you to be *happy.*" I'm like, "What's the difference? I'm STILL making you money." He hesitates. He's like,

"—I care." All these things not only brought up my experiences with my dad... it gave me 'hope' that this time round—I'd get to *feel* the love.

It's a hole... that's hard to bury (or fill up). ☹ ☹ ☹

I ask my current boyfriend if he thinks my story is 'understandable' cuz it's deep, man. He's like... "It's a bit CRYPTIC. But don't worry, before people learned to speak languages with their mouths, they understood the language of symbols. The amoeba will understand." I'm like, "Are you trying to be funny? What's an amoeba?" He's like, "It's a single cell organism." "What's THAT have to do with this?" He's like, "God *speaks* the language of symbols. It speaks to the *soul*. As far as I understand, the little critters of nature can communicate with GOD. We have a little more trouble with that, so sometimes we don't get it." I'm sooo relieved. Cuz I know most of you have a little tiny beast in YOU somewhere... *Prrrrr*

Back to my point!

Let's say... you're *stuck* on someone and can't get past it. Especially, if you know it's wrong (or become *obsessed* with them). And you don't even *like* them—they don't pay attention to YOU. They're mean to you. They don't really care... they act the opposite of what they 'say'. Know... He (or she) is an exact duplicate (in chemistry) personality, feel or demeanor of someone *familiar* to you, a person you know (or used to) and has drawn YOU in... by doing SOMETHING you always wanted the *other* person to do (but never did). So feels real. It's a hunger you can never satisfy, cuz you never ate in the first place.

You're rehearsing (Act: 3 Scene: 22) of father, brother, mother, sister, first *love*... or crush (what you never HAD). Way too many takes, plot's too thick (jealousy, possessiveness, envy, intensity, chaos, conflict) out of frame (feeling like a standby) too many sound effects... ☹ That's why you were 'pulled' in the first place. They were perfect for the part.

Sniff... Sniff...

Whaaat...? You never laugh and cry same time? Where I come from we mix n' match (emotions) so sadness no longer feels like pain... Laughter's no longer taken for granted.

Everything can TURN in an eye blink!

It's hard to imagine that a strong intense relationship you can't let go of (with a guy or girl) is not searching for a *fantasy*... of re-playing the past (with mom... dad) a chance to reclaim yourself whole. (Unscarred) Since you can't see how precious you ARE... you've made *this* relationship the **replacement** for it. That's WHY they mean the world to you. They're giving you yourself *back*... the part that's been lost (hidden from you). Only through them, are you able to realize how amazing and awesome you are, cuz they give you *that* feeling... If it's someone you've never hooked up with (mack) and there's a persistent *strong* feeling... two souls **eager** to harmonize, cuz they recognize each other's frequency (*as the same*) the pull's **intense**. And as far as I'm concerned, you've known them ALREADY. Just remember. EVERY decision you make will bring you *closer* to being happy or farther from it. It's a real easy way to tell. People on this planet, don't DO easy. Lmao

When I hear...

"He broke up with me and took all my love." I have to ask... What the is THAT? And *how* is that even possible (truly)? First of all, there's no guy or girl that can give, unless first they *have* (it). Agreed? YOU giving is proof... of having. So how can a guy (or girl) *take* everything you have? TBH It was you that gave, which means it's you that has (always will *have*) love always stays close to its *home* base... That's why you guys are always *trying* to slide into it. :P

K. That was hard not to.

If you wanna be exact—it's only when you give, that reinforces to your *brain* how much you 'do' have. It's like taking a head count. So you know how much you have. So you're actually *giving* to yourself cuz when you do do *that*... it acknowledges YOU have (so much). You're able to deliver. YOU cannot lose what you possess.

(I would go back and highlight that)

Then YOU won't be pulled into HELLLL (thousand times a day) over what happened *suffering*... Since the **thought** of suffering has been removed (trashed) Along with the crippling thoughts that flash with it. (Total *indecent* exposure)

Like...

~~No one understands me~~. The right person <u>will</u> understand me.

~~There's something wrong with me~~. There's something <u>special</u> about me.

~~I'm worthless.~~ I'm SO valuable.

~~My life's supposed to be hard.~~ My life's supposed to be fun and happy!

~~I'm meant to be alone.~~ I'm meant to be with people who LOVE me.

~~I'm supposed to suffer.~~ I'm supposed to have JOY...

~~I'm a loser.~~ I'm a winner—willing to risk for what I WANT.

~~I always fuck things up.~~ I'm not afraid of making mistakes.

~~I'm weird.~~ I'm unique!

~~Who would want me?~~ ANYONE who would really know me.

~~I'm an idiot.~~ I'm smart, even though I don't know *everything*...

~~I deserve bad things to always happen.~~ Only good things come to me NOW.

~~It's always my fault.~~ I'm ALWAYS learning! :P

~~I'm disgusting.~~ I'm an incredible being!

~~I'm stupid.~~ I see and learn things in a *special* way.

~~I'm not important.~~ I have tremendous VALUE even though I don't always see it.

~~I'm a monster.~~ I'm a sexy beast!

ONLY BLESSINGS COME TO ME!!

Is the thought that shreds these thoughts to pieces.

It's why you're *here...*

(with me) <3

~~DRUGS~~?

I'm ALREADY high.

YOU catch up to me!

BEST drug in the world... LOVE.

Why is this book Urgent?

We girls have CHANGED.

We're not the little damsel in distress...

Anymore. We're confident. We're independent. We call YOU on your bullshit. It's NOT a secret anymore (sex). We're up front about it. It's not mysterious anymore. Stop tryin' to hide things, we know you wanna get in our PANTS. Don't sugar coat it. Just say it. We're open. We're into sports and we're ambitious. We wanna kiss YOU so we do! *Saweeet.* But then we change. Something really upsets us and we cry. After all... We're still a girl.

THAT TOTALLY THROWS YOU A CURVE BALL!

Guy...

Now I have to redesign all my plans. Why couldn't she just show this part all along? I have no idea what to do. I ask a friend and (sadly) get some real bad advice. It seems like she could handle anything.

So YOU guys are more confused than *ev-errrrr.* (Fair)

You're self-conscious about things ALSO. Especially when it comes to something simple, like opening the car door. Cuz you're thinking, "Should I be the MAN... Chivalrous? But if I open the car door, is she gonna think that *I think*... she's weak? Cuz she just KILLED a 10k, she's a mixed martial artist, she heads the debate team and works out FIVE days a week. She could even hurt me!" While we're thinking, "Why are they so *slow?* What's their PROBLEM?" And you guys are like, "Did I mention she's a total BITCH (when acts like that)." We get it. "Did I MENTION she bench presses more than me?! Understood.

One of the managers at a café I was writing at, is like... "To be a MAN iz not easy, YOU have to deal with their *moods.* Everything iz big deal. For us, it's yes yes—no, no iz fine. We don't want to argue and YOU know what? Even if we *don't* want to argue iz BIG deal. So we just accept it. In Venezuela, iz same thing."

Girls...

107.

We wanna take the lead, ask him out, make plans, fix his issues (an aggressive energy) then we want *him* to make plans (surprise us) take us out, buy us things... like flowers (a passive energy). Btw guys, that shit does not get old. *Just sayin'*.

Honestly girls, when we go back and *forth* like that it's very confusing for them. If we're consistent (aggressive OR passive energy) at least, in the very beginning so he knows *how* to be with us. It'll be a lot easier. Cuz understand, our aggressive actions (ass-grabbing him in public, texting him non-stop) may not come *across* as we want it to. Then we wonder why he's backed OFF.

RULE #1 Girl

Be his dream girl—NOT a pit bull with lipstick.

(That could actually HURT)

Being sarcastic with a guy (in front of your friends) givin' him shit over every little thing, making him feel like a bag of CRAP de-masculinizes him (in a big way). YOU know you do. Instead of... inspiring him, cuz you're such a 'mystery'. LOL Especially to yourself. LOL Half the things you do baffle you. Still... You abide by no law but your OWN. Some girls... Bow down to trends, worship social media, (peer pressure) when they could be serving their *truth* (instincts) follow their path (what makes them happy) obey only LOVE... somethin' they know is **real**.

For *those*... pure at heart.

You know what YOU want. You're not into leftovers. (*Barrf*) You'd never sell yourself short and you'd never sell out. You've got way too much going for you. You'd never hook up with a LOSER, cuz you can pierce a guy's heart with just one LOOK. (God help him) You're not afraid to look a guy (that you like) in the eye and SMILE.

Requirement: Big balls (even if they are invisible).

108.

Then...

He knows he's found YOU.

He feels like a Boss when he's with YOU cuz he's got everything (in YOU). He can't take his eyes off you. He can't take your *face* out of his HEAD (it lives there...). You're allll he sees, thinks and breathes. That's why he FORGETS to pack important stuff for his trip, misses the off ramp on the freeway, leaves his wallet at the ATM machine. When we go back and forth like that girls (tough, soft, tough 'repeat') it's like a BROKEN traffic light. Guys go mental! They can't figure out what to do. Move forward... take charge (hold back). We wanna lead. No you do it! We want you to make plans—be in charge! But don't want you to take over. Eventually you guys are just sitting there (not sure what to do). Might explain that dumb look you have on your face. Not always their fault. The *beast* in a guy... don't do well with SHOCKS.

This way—no *this* way! Oops! (No warning) *THIS* way... Shift gears *grrrind!* Nothin' more embarrassing for a guy than grinding his gears in front of anyone (really shrinks his dick). It means he can't manage his machine. LOL No wonder they feel *stripped* of their manhood.

Whenever there's experiments on animals (real kind, not man) LOL and they get zapped (shocked) they always end up docile (passive). I bet... Even if we put a guerilla in a cage (bitch YOU spelt it wrong) Oops. I meant gorilla... ma' eeenglish. :P Even if we zap a powerful animal every time it *tries* to leave, after a while it won't even try (doesn't matter if the door's OPEN) no killer instinct left. The beast in him... *dead*. It becomes passive (yielding to control).

Animal cruelty NOT ALLOWED!!

(Four or two legged animals) :P

Tell me you're gonna **trust** a guy you can control (no mind of his own). Be *honest*...

We shock and confuse guys when we take charge—then wanna be tender (loving) feel their arms around us, especially when there's a storm. One minute we're tellin' 'em what to do, how to do it (as if they don't know) next on an emotional day, we're mad when they *don't* take charge. Help us! In the way that we need it, goddamn it! My bad. And every time we freak (cuz they're not *getting* it) it messes them up. Not that we can't tell them our feelings... we can (totally necessary) but when they're not used to hearin' it, cuz we hold it in, takes them off guard. They're not used to us *telling* them. TELL THEM from the get-go! Cuz when you trust a guy to handle your shit, he'll do his best NOT to let you down. Honest. Sadly, some guys have no clue what 'manly' is anymore. Especially, since we're doin' it mostly (actin' like a 'guy'). Lol

(Oh... *poooor guys*)

But we've also gotten fucked up (fathers not being around) feeling isolated (left out) not being cared for—it scares us! And when we're scared (haven't had anyone we can depend on) we don't trust anyone will be. And even when someone is there, we still don't trust that. So everything gets stuck inside (feelings) and NO ONE knows shit. We feel like we have to be strong (act like a guy) cuz we're not used to it *being* there. But then we crave alllll that guy stuff you do... (for us) and secretly we just wanna be your 'girl'.

WE... Just both REALLY need each other.

RULE #1 Guys

Be more romantic, protective—like a true vampire. LOL :-E

We *sooo* need that (even if we don't say it) 'we' do. We don't like to come out and say things... it's NOT the same. And this way we can *feel* like an 'actual' princess... alluring, magnetic, 'special'. And hopefully, not pull any TOADS into our pond (warts are so unpleasant). Check his fingers. You just never know.

You guys could have a sore under your penis (not tell us). Then we ask you why you have a bandage on it. You're like, "I cut my dick shaving." (Booked!) YOU wanna shag us and we feel like a complete tool (we believed you).

Tip:

If you have a wart on your finger (or toe) soak it in apple cider vinegar for at least 30 minutes, till surface skin thickens and turns white. Carefully remove the callus till you see the root(s) of the wart (little dark dots). Cover with apple cider vinegar soaked cotton ball. Put bandage on it. Keep it like that for several hours. Air out and let dry. Repeat. Till dead and gone. Do NOT put your dick in apple cider vinegar!!! LOL

Go see your doctor!

FYI Most warts are due to a potassium deficiency, not enuf bananas! LOL

The PROBLEM...

There's is no indicator for guys of when they *should* man-up—when not to. So it's hard to *know*. It might look like they're trying to take over our life. And they don't want that. It's like playin' a game of ping pong with *yourself*... it's frustrating. She's on *this* side (need to take care of her). Oh! Now she's flying over to *that* side. K! I need to back *off*. She's mad. Oops! She's back on *this* side—I need to stand up for HER. Can't hesitate! (He who hesitates loses one or BOTH balls) Hold up! She's rolling (coasting...) can't tell? Does she want me to *step in* or not? K... She's on *this* side again—she wants me to hold her. Fuck!! Now she wants to be da' boss (telling me what to do). Five minutes later. *Dammn...* she's in my arms, makin' all these love noises. K, guess I'm the MAN now. Just wishin' I could text...

S.O.S - Girl CAN'T make up her mind!

Soon...

(Real soon)

Girls, I'm not siding with them. As long as they don't know how to BE we're gonna be in hellll. After all, as far as we're concerned...

"IF YOU LOVE ME YOU'D KNOW!"

Right?

But they have NO idea when to take action! OR IS IT GONNA PISS US OFF? And if they hold back cuz they've tried *so much* (did nothing) we'll be pissed. We'll just think they don't care. All this constant swinging back n' forth is not getting us anywhere—spider man at least LANDS. LOL Changing our mind, no warning (classic) taking the lead then refusing to, is not only tiring they get DIZZY just dealing with us. So to them... We're being 'bitchy'.

THE DOMINO EFFECT...

When one thing *leads* to another thing... tilts on that thing, makes it do something and how that continues. Somehow, somewhere we lost *our* game. Relationship line *blurred*... with all this grey matter. HAA! I meant grey area not talkin' brain tissue. :P I'm referring to, allll this wheeling dealing, hooking up (real vs. one night stands) fucked. Tell me something, by the time we're actually dating are we supposed to feel relieved, happy? Kinda nervous (what)? Cuz I need to know.

Answer: _____

Here's how it lays out. LOL I'm gonna *wheel* Andrew (communicate, text msg) then Andrew's gonna tell everyone we're dealing (going out/last minute calls/mack but no emotion, test run). And I get that... YOU guys just wanna test run your dick—see how well it goes with our vagina. Is it a match. Then eventually (hopefully) we can work our way to actually going on a DATE (if that ever happens).

How come this *feels* like being in the Army? You start out as a Cadet. It's the battle of the SEXES (you can take it). You wanna work up to 'private' (special privileges fo shur) but how many hits do you have to take? And will you *survive*? Or will you permanently be *wounded* (scarred for life) LAST thing you want. Or will there just be marks... for *EVERYYYYYONE* to see!! Hate it when that happens.

CUZ... GUYS JUST DON'T WANNA DATE.

They have this wheeling-dealing hook up shit going on, where they can *have* their cake and stuff their faces in it too. Just *love* our ta-ta's! So now BFD we're finally dating. Or... As some of you guys put it, "She *suckered* me into dating her." K. All the excitement and suspense of getting to know a person... gone. (Or not) YOU tell ME.

☐ Yes ☐ No ☐ Maybe

Other than seeing someone's social media profile thinkin' "Oh *he's* cute..." Asking your girl friend (who knows him) is he PROPER? There's just no way of <u>really</u> knowing (these days). We buy into all the teen magazines (read all this shit) try and catch things online (try to keep up) latest trends, books; 100 Shades of red, green and purple. WTF? Raunchy shit... like, radio shows that instruct a guy to CALL a girl (he likes) ask 3 questions... The last one: "Do YOU wanna fuck?" If she says yes, he wins a PRIZE. She wins... Embarrassment. Sounds like a dating reality show I saw once. Guess, runners up don't receive herpes complex 1, 2 and 3. FYI This book's gonna be the antidote to all those trying to fuck with a girl's head (body) turn a guy's mind into silly putty. Sorry! We won't be infected. We've been injected with The Wisdom of the Penis. LOL Finally— a vaccine with GOOD side effects!

Let the TRANSFORMATION begin.

TBH... You guys can be deflated asses

(ass-holes) *AHAHAHA!!*

YOU call us fat all through grade nine, then we get BOOBS you're like, "Whoa... You're HOT." Like... we're gonna forget. Sometimes you guys'll joke (*so you say*) when you take us out, pay for a movie, then you're like, "Next time you PAY—only kidding!" We're like, "What a dick. Shame." Cuz now it's in our mind. And there's no way we won't remember (or let you forget). You've been sentenced, tried and executed (not necessarily in that order). I HAVE to tell it like it is. Of course we took your words seriously. Cuz we took you seriously, dude. And now we hate your guts forever (and never tell you why). It's different if we 'offer'. Still, I don't know why a girl would accept a date (meaning, she really *likes* a guy) then offer to make it 'platonic' by paying for herself. Oh *yeah*... so she wouldn't feel obligated to do anything *afterwards*. Does that actually work?

(Yeahhh, right)

If a guy is asking you out, it's cuz he likes YOU, wants to get to know you. Guys aren't like us. They're not gonna have lunch with you to be 'nice' (like we do). Then our mother (or friend) is like, "Give him a chance, he's a real nice guy AND he likes you." (Bonus) Why would I go out with a guy so I could get used to him and he can grow on me (LIKE a fungus disease). If I don't feel anything while I'm out with a guy, you'll notice my latte cup will *slowly* be shredded into a million pieces (by my very OWN hands). Bored! My gut is not vibing with him. No REFILL. I don't go out to be *nice* I'm not a missionary. I go out to be real... cuz that's where the 'unreal' happens. For it to be *that* unbelievable it would need to be real... And besides, my Fairy Goddess ethics wouldn't allow it. Bringing just my outer SHELL (body) while my heart is left behind, skipping the interaction... is inhumane. Kinda defeats the whole PURPOSE. Like, why are we even getting together?! Your real essence (*soft* spots) are needed, so the person knows alll the fragile 'handle-with-care' places. It pumps their blood, connecting. Otherwise we could be hemorrhaging (heart crushed) and they'd never know it (not in tune). Emotional transfusions are hard to come by. Needs to be 'exact'.

To go out with a guy just cuz he asked... all Fairy Goddesses *know*... Study the species (a while) admire from afar (two aisles over) cuz to go just cuz you wanna be polite... and you could start feeling a hollowness in your gut (reminding you) your heart's NOT there. It's challenging to remember, you need do NOTHING except enjoy yourself (with HIM). Hard to do when you're in 'how can I improve his life' mode. *Fuuuuck!* The bitch is right! (HAD to)

TBH

A guy who likes you WANTS you to enjoy yourself. That's his goal. Money is the one thing guys place incredible *value* on (a known fact) it's also the toughest thing for them to let go of... It *has* to be worth-while (that's why he picked YOU). Course. If the guy knows you're paying for yourself and he's got *nothing* better to do he's NOT as picky. That's when you usually experience the 'sound board' effect HIM talkin' 'bout his ex, parents, other bullshit. Feels more like a therapy session than a date. If he's rich then image is what he values... something rare that no one else *has*... he VALUES.

Guys, when you joke about having us pay for it 'next time', we don't like it. We see it as you valuing money over US. And you just go try n' feel up your dollar bill, dude. Not quite the same thing, huh? It makes us feel unvalued. We don't like to feel we owe you anyyything. So the very next time you see us (in class, hallway or street) we will pay you back (just to get the whole thing over with). When you make it seem like we owe YOU—it's highly insulting! You failed to *notice* you're getting us for the whole entire evening!

And we have cut off the rest of the population to be with

YOU.

Enhancing your whole entire immune system (just sitting next to you). So maybe... We should send YOU a bill.

What's that?

What if you're giving up the whole population too?

You forget...

In this world the egg *doesn't* chase the sperm...

So sorry! Don't see it that way since in the entire history of testicles it's been girls, who *inspire* guys (NOT the other way around). Don't just sit there feeling like a dumbass, cuz you made a mistake. Make it up to her! Take action. It always BREAKS fear in half. Stop wondering what woulda, coulda, shoulda happened. YOU have a penis... It *points* for a reason.

GO GET THE FRIGGIN' GIRL!!

The sperm CHASES the egg!

And this is also for allll those guys who invite a girl out, tell her to order *whatever* she wants—then go overboard (on your beer). Now you wanna go halfsies in order to lower your half of the bill. And still wanna try and kiss her good night? WTH? Unless, she's too stunned to tell you she'll be in no rush to see you again. YOU just put yourself in the 'friend' zone, dude. You know... that little space between boy and FRIEND? So many fallen brothers in that *zone*...

A moment of silence, please.

Now you have no manship over her. You're not a man in her eyes (you're a friend). So don't even *think* of crossing the border (fugitive). Having a guy ask YOU out cuz he's interested and wants to get to know you, so wants to plan an awesome evening (pay for it) see if he can get (*earn*) more time with YOU eliminates the halfsies BULLSHIT. And don't worry guys... I've outlined a specific chapter on how to **un-do** what now appears to be SO done. It'll take precision (require patience) and plenty of cupid arrows. To pierce hardened smiles (locked up hearts) attitude of steel. Doable...

(When innocent *on your part*)

On the other hand us girls can be so unaware...

Girl-on-girl hate. What's up with thaaat? Picking on a GIRL cuz your boyfriend's hittin' on her (cheat on you) welcome to TWATVILLE. Meanwhile, your guy gets away with it... Don't think so. And has he learned anything?

Yup...

That you will be aggressive and protect him (like a guy) and he can be like a girl (magnetic) keep *pullin'* you (other girls) in. No matter how pissed you are—you can't resist. And you wonder why he doesn't man-up? YOU just grew a dick! Congrats. A guy doesn't mind letting you do allll the work, he's hardwired for *logic*. And if you wanna do all the work, why would he stop you? Every time you think you've figured it allll out (how to BE) it changes... The media's like, 'Stand up for your GUY (Why has he been abducted by aliens?) GO to *him*... He's shy. No wait! Count 3 seconds. Then... Say hi! Encourage his feelings. (Why, do I REALLY wanna sit and listen to him whine allll day?) It boosts his self-esteem.' We've got PLENTY other ways of boosting his self esteem. Then they're like, *"You hurt my feelings."* (He's soo sensitive)

...OHHH CRY ME A RIVER. (- _-)

I was living with this roommate once. When I had told him I don't have feelings for him he's like, "You hurt my feelings." I'm like, "WHY you actin' like a girl dude—I'm the GIRL. You're the guy. All this vagina envy is NOT gonna get you anywhere." He's like "So, when are you taking me out, anyway?" I'm like, "Again—I'M the girl. You're the guy. You have the *balls*... you can take me out. So hurry up and find your masculinity there's a great concert on FRIDAY." ☺ He's like, "Are you sure you don't have my balls?"

(Good question)

SPEAKING of vagina envy!

Omigosh. Cray cray! Yesterday, my boyfriend's like, "I had a dream I had BREASTS." Femininity overdrive. LOL Creative types! Haaa! He's like, "I was in the shower and I knew I was dreaming, I had these BIG breasts. So I thought well... before this dream *ends* I need to take advantage of this! I JUMP up and down. (*Ooouch*) Take both of them. Raise one, lower the other—squish 'em!! (AAAAH! They're not BALLOONS) Shake my body *side to side*—REALLY fast!!" Scar tissue on the rise. "Grab *both* nipples—shake 'em up and down." STOP! I **can't** take it. Calling alllll CARS. Calling allll CARS. Man abusing breasts (in dream) armed... and potentially threatening to his connective tissues! Lmfao Now we know why *we* have the breasts THEY don't like to be man-handled. I'm like... "If I could I'd hang you by your testicles and puncture them with a tooth pick. Make you drink a TON of water!" It's the least I could do after what he did to my boobs. He's like, "But they're mine. Temporarily. Every guy at some point wishes he HAD breasts—JUST for a day." So I'm like, "Bae, you'd be disappointed. It only feels good when you *give* 'em. It's like, me sayin' I wish I had *balls* for a DAY." Had to compare it to a pair of round things that hang. He's like, "Are you kidding? Do you know what it's like every time you sit on your bed and have to **reach** and pull your nuts out from under your stinky BUTT HOLE? My friend's like, 'What's wrong with YOU?' You're like... 'Sat on my nuts.'" Nope don't know what it's like. LOL

We don't *have* balls... that you can see, anyway.

Back to da' sensitive dude.

"You HURT my feelings."

Reeeally...?

I'd be like, "YOU must have me confused with your shrink. Cuz yeah... If you wanna pay me a hundred dollars an hour to listen to your feelings, I will." Seriously, when a guy's like, "You *hurt* my feelings." after telling him YOUR feelings, it tells your brain a few things.

1. Don't be honest about *your* feelings, change the conversation (lie).

2. It's not NICE to say things that although true, may hurt someone else. Suck it up (don't tell).

3. Put up with shit. Endure... maybe things will change. Try to block your discomfort in *other* ways. Food! Alcohol... drugs.

4. YOU... don't really have a RIGHT to feel what you're feeling... if it hurts *him*. Get it together!

As soon as you get a guy like this? Count on one thing. HIS feelings will be in competition with yours. As in... yours will have to WAIT (be put on hold) indefinitely. Or, he could just say... "GET over it."

Woww... how profound. Would have never thought of <u>that</u> one. Can't imagine life without YOU... dude. Allll that support. Kiss my butt. (_*_)

I was doing cardio in the gym, this cute guy gets on the bike *next* to me. We start talking he's like, "I'm a *sensitive* guy…"

ALARM!! ALARM!!

Quick—emergency **eject!!**

Eject and get the fuck off that BIKE. Get away from *that* guy! But not before I reply, "That's SUCH a shame. How did it happen? Never mind—gotta go!" Guys like that, think it's a plus… and to a girl (unaware) maybe in *her* mind (it is) cuz she thinks that means he'll be extra thoughtful and considerate. Yeah to his own ass. A guy who's sensitive to a girl's feelings doesn't make it known (so she can step all over him). *Smaaart.* It's not something he shouts out to the WORLD… "Hey! You've got the upper hand—soon as I see a tear."

When a guy announces he's sensitive—it's a WARNING.

…HIGH MAINTENANCE! LOL

Which makes you more sensitive to *his* feelings (less to your own) cuz he's the focus now. Not so bad, yours can come a close second. (Ugh!!) Your first clue… Everything he says (especially towards YOU) starts with, "*I feel…*" And I'm not saying all guys like this are bad, just sensitive (delicate) usually a dominant mother, strong female figure, absent father and perhaps unknowingly (or not) gets you to cater to his feelings. The downside of that? YOU let him… cuz somewhere, somehow, a key figure (*protector*) someone who could handle your fears (worries, doubts) a Father… wasn't around (gone or abusive). Result: YOU don't feel it's natural to show your fears to a guy (when you're scared or vulnerable) and especially be a FOCUS… have all that attention. So you *become*… the protector (towards everyone else) put the focus on your guy, so he won't see how you really are. :*(

That's why it's <u>such</u> a fit.

You're independent, self-sufficient, highly capable (strong) and sacrificial (if you need to be) he's dependent, not so capable, needy (emotional). And it always feels so right (natural) to give... what you *never* received (in these circumstances). Not sure why. Course, some of you girls LIKE guys who are mostly a feminine energy. My boyfriend was at this party. Two girls show up and everyone knew they're into sensitive guys (lot of gay friends) they like their manner and temperament. They walk through the DOOR they're like, "Hiiiiii! We're the resident faghags!" K... I'm cryin'. For those girls who <u>aren't</u> into guys like that—HEAD'S UP!! When a guy's used to saying, "I feel..." while talking to you, he'll usually ask YOU what you *think*. Two feeling types wouldn't usually pair up (too emotional, pure mush) no conviction, no direction. Two thinking types *clash* since they don't pay a lot of attention to feelings (both wanna be in charge) both wanna be 'right'. Each wanna be da' Boss. LOL This is why... opposites *attract*. One is always in charge, leading, protective, territorial (decisive). The other is more emotional, nurturing, pampered, patient, seductive (hard to let go of). These energies apply to any couple relationship that is official (same sex or otherwise). We all have our own mix (masculine, feminine) inside us. Those of YOU adamantly against what I'm sayin' cuz you're like, "I'm perfectly happy the way I AM." The only thing I can say...

Just cuz you're *comfortable* (being a certain way) doesn't mean there isn't *more* you can be (have) explore, find out about... inside YOU. For those of you that are afraid you'll lose *that* (what you've earned) and are highly attached to it—nothing gets lost, cut off (deleted) diluted, just *enhanced*. If you're up for the CHALLENGE.

(If you're curious)

Speaking of... masculine and feminine energy. We *know* everybody comes from a mother AND father—CAN'T AVOID THAT. So since we didn't come out of rock—except for some (waaay better relating to things than people) I'm just sayin'... Let's maximize! You get to say when you feel balanced. It's not *about* fifty-fifty... everyone has a different center. You'll know when you've hit your *sweet* spot when things that used to intimidate YOU no longer do. At first, it's gonna feel awkward (little frightening) to bring that energy up front (you put it away for a *reason*). Once you bring it OUT and experience it... it won't just amplify you, it'll give you added dimension you never know you HAD. *A strength*... misportrayed as a weakness.

120.

An example of how energies COLLIDE... come to a screeching halt. Get bumped off then merge (come back into sync). I meet up with a close guy friend in my dance class, Tom (a street dancer). He's like, "*Wusss-up?*" "Chillin." He's like, "I'm writing a term paper on; The PERFECT guy. For my psych class." "For reals?" He's like, "Yeah... Why don't we hook up and do something together! Since you're writing about relationships?" "Cool!" Seemed like such an awesome idea!

Fuck no...

When we got together after showing him my book, tellin' him that it's about to be released he's like, "**You should read this *other* book**. The guy writes just like YOU." It's like, he deflated my whole entire being (in a SECOND). *Brah*... ☹ I worked so long on it, it's about to be released and he's telling me SOMEONE writes just like me? Yup... just wanna go race and read *that* book. Like never. What if... I'm like, "Yo! Tom awesome performance, man. You should go check this *other* B-boy, he's got mad skills. Dances JUST like you. So I'm like, "Nahhh... Don't wanna read *another* book that talks about what I TALK about. Don't wanna be influenced. Wanna keep it organic." (Dumbass) He's like... "Whoa. Why you gotta be so strong? I'm being generous making a suggestion. And you don't wanna listen!"

Generosity... doesn't come with a price tag, *fool*.

So I'm like, "IT'S NOT SOMETHING I WANNA DO." (Two Bosses) It's so intense, my heart's back pedalin' into my throat. I can't believe he's going all ORANGUTAN on me. Maybe he should read his *own* term paper. Rolf Even though he just dropped into my frenemy pile... I wanted to take the opportunity to work my book... *on him*. Walk my TALK. Completely disarm him. (Hehe) Make him human again. LOL

We can call it...

Field Research: 101

Like a BOSS...

My voice goes *soft*... I talk openly about my fears. Maybe if I look at this *other* book, I'll feel like SHIT (about my book). Maybe...

everything I WROTE has already been done! Then I'd feel like my book's *worthless*. Almost a decade WASTED!!! O_O Life amounting to NOTHIN'. Ugh!! I let it all hang. Talk about all my insecurities. Then I'm like, "Tom I feel like I can't talk about anything you suggest... cuz then you freak—if I don't like it. We're supposed to be tight." I got totally vulnerable... just spoke my bare bones, my eyes got teary (it captured him). He couldn't MOVE. He looked at my big blue eyes staring *right* at him—CHANGED into the most caring guy ever! He's like, "You know, when I see someone like *this* I just wanna give them all my strength. I wanna hold them. I wanna be there for THEM." (Protective) Mission ACCOMPLISHED!

Next time walk YOUR talk, man!

That's... the perfect guy?

Maybe, if she's had a lobotomy.

And even though I explored my fears (deep down) they'd NEVER stop me. But it was a GOOD experiment. LOL So he's like... "But you seem so strong Nichole. I'm in shock to see you vulnerable like this. You're so CONFIDENT." True... and only a confident girl can *explore* the possibilities of deep seated fears, look at them, stare 'em down— CHEW 'EM LIKE CEREAL!!

This is precisely why I say summoning up *both* energies is not only useful and practical but very handy! LOL As long as they come up for air they won't be stifled (suppressed) come out ass-backwards (mini monster) they've been concealed so long. You'd think this guy was made of CELLOPHANE he's so see-through. Human beings are hystericallll (and unique) in the sense that *except* towards themselves, they can see STRAIGHT through each other, even if they don't know what it is they're looking at exactly. They know when something's off, just don't always say it.

Once Tom felt needed (valuable) he forgot about his self-inflicted rejection wound (his suggestion). Still, it'd be far too uncomfortable and intense to work with a guy like that. I ONLY walk on hot coals for 6 ft. 7 gurus with husky voices, who live in castles. LOL Had Tom balanced and anchored himself with his *logic* (masculine energy) he would have seen it for what it was... a *suggestion* (not 'attach' himself to it). He would have shrugged it off. Fully knowing, a girl's very capable of *changing* her mind. LOL

(Quite often)

As much as he was in touch with his feminine side, he was DROWNIN' IN IT. Gulping for air. When a simple suggestion wasn't taken, personalizing it... a cognitive distortion a lot of people suffer from. Allowing a *negative* thought pattern to affect them. And it's NOT even true. LOL Hmm? Maybe, since the North and South pole are so far away from each OTHER (*longing* for each other) there's an internal storm, and the friction's altering our electromagnetic field Totally affecting our behavior. LOL We can listen to someone talk, then go BLANK. Like! Someone's snatched our memory. We CAN'T even tell if a vibe belongs to *us* or not (are we sad) or are we picking up a sad feeling, depression (cuz someone *close* is depressed). Might explain why we're down and don't even *know* why... I was never like this till I woke up on this PLANET. Omigosh! I just thought of something. Since there's all this talk about pole shifting, the north and south pole *swapping*—I think it happened with us!! The male and female axis on Earth has totally TURNED on its head.

Thaaat's why we're givin' so much head! LMAO

Back to guys and sensitivity!

A lot of you guys brag about being sensitive. Like I said... Problem with that, it's not towards your girl's sensitivities it's towards *yours*. Everything's UPSIDE down. LOL Which means when both feelings are at stake (now, two feminine energies competing for center stage) YOURS will bud in dude.

It wasn't till I showed Tom my vulnerability (feminine energy peaking) that his masculine *energy* came to the front lines, ready to defend, protect... serve (both in practicality and purpose) be there... for a girl (*her* feelings). Girls, if you release all your femininity *finesse* (sweetness, softness, gentleness, cuteness) you'll bring HIM in... He'll be grounded (anchored in confidence) you'll be *high*... (cherished and valued). Didn't have to do a thing.

Maybe I should write a paper on...

How to *maneuver* a GUY.

Bring the best *out of him*...

When I told my boyfriend what happened with Tom. He's like, "YOU totally steered him... You *drove* him. Did you know steering wheel in Spanish is manubrio (man-u-vrio) like maneuver." LOL He's such a wordologist. LOL

The mechanics of energies...

Something we need to watch. <3

Cuz they will *sneak up* on us (girl or guy) while they're playing us. (Aware or not) The dynamics of these energies on the job are a lot more concise and easier to deal with. Bosses (men or women) are usually a masculine energy. Complimenting them, goes far. They're usually starved for that, since they push themselves non-stop, can be hard on themselves and are more concerned with results than how they're feeling. Letting them know how <u>good</u> they are (as a boss) or even one notch further... tellin' them how awesome they are—they can handle SO much and not break. Even if they think you're sucking up to them, be like, "I look up to YOU man!" If it's a relationship there's one goal... to score (secure your place in *their* heart) touchdown (manyyy places) both team (mates) WIN.

Just make sure you're playin' for the *home* team (your guy, girl) or you could be benched (neglected) traded... (cheated) called foul (*f!!*#!%!!#*kk*) dropped... and dumped.

When guys continually say...

"What do you think?" It puts us girls (and keeps us) in our head. Alienates our feelings cuz they're not brought into focus (often enough). Then we never hear from *them* when we need them (most).

And now we don't know HOW to feel. With our career or sport we all have to have BALLS (we're driven) so it rolls a lot easier there. LOL Unlike having, one too many *balls* in our relationship—WAY too much drama—AMP-HI-THEATRE. Lmao Bouncing off the friggin walls! Both, your job and your training are the two places that demand action - goals - competition. We *need* to stay in our HEAD—focused (no distractions). Keeping on course. It's not a fairytale, it's a different reality. We want the TOP position (increased salary, prestige) at all times. We're a little more flexible in the bedroom. LOL

(Well, some of us)

In companies where creativity is essential, we need a mix of feelers (highly intuitive, sensitive souls) <u>and</u> thinkers (rule breakers, ball-busters, warriors) for BEST results. When a guy is constantly forcing you into your *head* (at times a critical place) it forces you out of your <u>inherited</u> kingdom linked to feelings (feminine *essence*). Makes you check in with your BRAIN—ask it what it thinks. Rationalize your feelings (if they even surface). And even if they do... to give you the heads up something's coming (you didn't think of) it'll be missed. o_O

OPPOSITE (energies)

Attract...

If you're with someone who says, "I feel..." and you're like, "But I feel..." It won't go anywhere. If one says, I **think** the other will say I **feel** unless you're fighting. Which usually goes like, "I think... You're wrong." "Well I THINK... you're fucked." If you let your guy know how you're feeling by starting the sentence with, "I *feel*..." it won't be in opposition to his 'communicative' structure. Unless he's used to sayin' "I feel..." (A LOT) And this way he'll be inclined to say, "I was thinkin'..." Which will put him in his masculine domain (logic) you in your feminine homeland (feelings) so it'll be easier for YOU to deal with them (naturally) and he'll be leading you there. And you can let him know, how you're feeling (without sounding bitchy, bossy) leave a clear communication trail, nobody getting hurt, lost (mixed messages) ignored... If he's not strong enough to pull you out of your shit (when you're really upset) can't stomach seeing you like *that* (so leaves). Makes an excuse as to 'why' he can't be there for YOU then he's not accustomed to being there for a girl (no inner strength). He's broken... (Out of order) He could have a strong mother that's usually strong *for* him (used to taking care of HIM). And since she's strong (keeps her pain to herself) no need on his part to develop *that* (emotional) muscle. He's being taken care of so a) can't do it on his own b) definitely can't do it for someone he cares about. He never did it before. No need. No practice.

Moms...

Be aware when your son is used to having his emotions taken care of (a priority) and you can hate me for this—just *waaay* too much pampering on your son. When you treat him like a flower then totally ignore your girl (yourself) cuz what the hell, she's *responsible*—she can handle herself. She doesn't 'need' you. Sooo wrong.

She DOES. ☹

When you love her...

YOU love yourself—but you can't do that, can you? Cuz YOU don't feel you deserve it (to be happy). So you keep yourself from giving to *yourself* by focusing on what you **need** to do (be *strong*) blinding yourself to the fact—you're HURTING. So your girl *can't* feel your love—you're working so hard to keep it away from you (the little girl inside who's never earned it...).

Whoa...

I was living with another roommate. Honestly, this book should be called; *ROOMATES FROM PLUTO!!* His name was Gerald. What a fucken LOSER. He was a lot older than me. For the life of me, I couldn't figure out why being from the Military (so real strong guy) did he act the way he did, when I told him how devastated I was when a guy I trusted **deceived** me. I'm balling so hard I'm *shaking*... Gerald stands there, doesn't say a word. I could tell it was hard for him to see me like that. I'm like hiccupping as I talk. "Will you (hiccup) read something I (hiccup) *wrote*..." I SO needed to feel good about something, but he's like, "Gotta go!" When he first told me he was in the Military I remember feeling so safe. Like, nothin' bad was gonna happen to me. He'd be like, "We should chill more. You need a TRUE friend." But here, I tell him to read something I wrote so I can feel better while I'm crying my eyes out—he ghosts me! I literally drop to the floor. Cry uncontrollably looking at the ceiling... till it stops. Then I'm like, *I HATE ALLLLL GUYS!!* It happens. When a girl's been severely disappointed (and hurt) by a guy. Kinda like, a twenty-four hour virus. LOL Then it disappears (hopefully). Some girls stay sick a longgg time. Hate-bug never leaves them. Vaccination is only covered by *love*.

But I noticed something...

When it's the *worst*... and no one there for you, YOU toughen up. Like instantly! It just happens. There's no one there, so you don't have the luxury to immerse yourself in alllll that shit (pain) sink into it, do back flips in it. No audience so life span shortens considerably. LOL My conclusion... Anger somehow *strengthens* you. Acts like a sunscreen—against the sun (*of a bitch*) who did this to you. All of a sudden, you just don't care. And that feels good, cuz the pain has stopped. YOU feel nothing...

And that's peaceful.

Days later...

It *still* bothered me how dweeb (Gerald) could do something like THAT. Leave a girl (he thought was really cool) crushed... crying so hard. Only now, it was more scientific (emotional part killed off). Amazing how once *that's* gone you're so productive. I HAD to figure out why, it was too weird. So... in the lab of my analytical mind, I was busy workin' it—mixin' his thoughts and actions (what he did, didn't do, say, how he operated) a pinch of insight *here*... dash of data there! Voila. A <u>formula</u>. I just needed to TEST it. He was in the Military for God's sake! They fight wars! Why was he acting like that? BUM DOUCHE. He had the spine of a jelly fish. I dunno... Do they have an Army for jelly fish? (*Jokes*) As I worked my spirit back up and focused on my goals (what I'm capable of) seeing the whole guy thing (deceived) as a carrot dangled by life. TEASE. I rapidly regain my composure and we start talking. He admitted to being a total wuss.

Just so you know guys, it's 'rarely' comforting... after the fact. So he's like, "I disappointed you. Didn't I?" Uhh... YEAH. He's like, "I hated seeing you in so much PAIN." So YOU left!! Jerkola? I'm like, "That's why I don't need someone to *just* hang with (chill) take up all my energy (not meet my criteria) not be there for me, when I really need him." Makes no sense. Especially to the emotional accountant in me—not balancing my books!! I'd rather hold out for a guy 'designed' for me (with inner strength). Who would NEVER leave me (or any girl) in pain... a real guy. So I'm like, "Are you an only child?" (Spoiled... a possibility?) He's like, "No." "The youngest?" (Overly protected... maybe?) He's like, "No. I'm the middle." K. Insufficient evidence (inconclusive) can't prove my theory. Really thought I was on to something. ☹ I keep at it...

"Were you and your mom... *close?*" "Yeah. She always said I shoulda been a girl." *HELLLO!!!* But the military *part* still made no sense. Those guys are ruthless. Love YOU guys! So I'm like, "I can't believe you were in the Military, that's so cool. Was it scary?" He's like, "Well... I was in the Air Force." I'm like, "Yeah, what was your rank?" "I worked in administration." *Kaaay!!* Very close to mom (maybe a little *too* close) which acted like an umbrella (always sheltered). Never hardened his shell. Poor boy—lucky his dick gets hard on its own. Hmm... wonder? TTYN. Moms, when you pamper your boy and make things really easy for him, protect him, *spoil* him... shelter him, hold *your* feelings in...

6 Things that can happen... (to your BOY)

- It gets him accustomed to THAT. So his girlfriend has to do the *same* thing.

- It stops him from developing his emotional muscle (handling emotional things on his own) so by default he doesn't get a chance to *practice* using logic, to address turbulent situations (caused by life, circumstances, girlfriend).

- He attracts a modern-day mother figure. Someone who's in charge, responsible, meticulous, overburdened (sacrificial). That takes care of him (and his feelings at her expense). *Just like you...*

- Cuz of all the work needed (on him) a girlfriend will demand a 'hefty' price. As in... he won't have much say (in anything) since she's used to running everything in the relationship. Which will piss YOU off.

- The manly part in him will crumble (sadly) as with most things not in use (or fed). His sense of *self*... will always be in question (so doubt, depression) can't face himself. Possible substance abuse, POT, food, alcohol addiction or other careless acts with money (property) to make someone *step* in and 'take care'.

- He lives with silent fears (that are stifled) cuz his stick shift has been stuck in *neutral*—can't get past it. (Not used to initiating for himself)

6 Things that can happen... (to your GIRL)

- She feels she isn't *entitled* to being taken care of, she needs to be strong (capable) like YOU even when she's not feeling well. Assistance in any way (for sure with money) is NOT an option. She'll find a way... even if it kills her.

- She will have a challenging time with anyone being 'gentle' (with her) since she's never *experienced* that. She'll see it (or interpret it) as her being *weak* or it'll feel weird. Unless she's drunk or on her period. We know hormones rule. LOL

- She sees it as her responsibility to take care of her guy. Like, he's her child (cuz that's what she saw). She'll never run to him for help, she wouldn't want to OVERWHELM him. Besides, she can take care of herself. Sound *familiar*?

- Romantic gestures and *gifts* (from him) may be seen as a waste of time (money, an overkill) since that side of her (*receiving*) has been paralyzed. So serves no purpose, in her mind.

- She'll cry in silence, doesn't feel she deserves to cry out *loud* (not worth all that attention) since you Mom were too busy with her brother, who really 'needed' it. LOL

Yes, I'm talking directly to YOU.

I met a mother from El Salvador named Anna. She's like "I treat my daughter and son equally. I don't want to *repeat* what my mother did. I say to them, the only difference between you **two**? One has something that *hangs* and the other has a *CUT*." Lmfao Maybe crude, but she's right! Good for YOU! The daughters around the world that feel left OUT... thank you! <3 Moms... Don't over-protect your *sperm* it's meant to be *FEARLESS* (courageous) and sure of itself. It's the only way it'll get the egg... His goals, girl. What he deserves in this world.

Protect your egg... it's meant to be protected.

So she can feel *safe* to blossom.

...Be all that she CAN be. Dads connect here. YOUR daughter needs to feel **treasured** and cherished by YOU (so badly). So she'll *expect* it (from a guy) and see any mistreatment as strange (and not normal) WALK (immediately). Most likely, she'll never be lured there cuz the deepest part of her, is searching for something she *knows*... a place she recognizes as **home**. Opposed to staying in a bad situation waitin' to receive the *love* (she never got). Figuring if she'll just endure, she'll get it (be entitled to it).

LOVE DOESN'T HAVE TO BE EARNED!!

She *deserves* it just cuz she IS your daughter.

Girls... UNITE!

So that each girl may know love, attract 'it' (instead of a loser). Extend your friendship to include the outcast (you know, the weird one sitting by the window). She'll have *more* to offer YOU than you know. You have no idea the rush you'll feel (true high) when you do something like this (my sacred goddess) especially since, you're not forced or manipulated (feel guilty). You will be in shock firstly, at the *power* of transformation taking place... **you'll feel it in your bones**. Secondly. This chick 'ugly duckling' who sees herself as unwanted will make you see something about *yourself* you woulda never seen. She has fresh eyes—*tells it like it is.* Your friends won't (they're used to YOU). LOL She has strength that's not *familiar* to you (something you never needed to develop). She'll show you... the <u>one</u> part of you, YOU were too scared to look at. The one that's *still* haunting you... The one you CAN'T stand. Cuz she's *not* scared. She faces that every day. You see, the 'ugly duckling' on the outside, is YOU on the inside (in the dark) somewhere... (YOU don't like yourself). Can't stand yourself. When you two *connect* you'll cancel out each other's ugly. ☺ By embracing one... the other one (in you) is *embraced* (transformed). NGL you need her more than she needs you. You can't get to that part (without her). Love's opposite is ugly (a place where no love is found) she knows the *way*...

BREAK the spell!

And you'd better write and tell me about it!

Wouldn't it be cool if it turned into a WORLDWIDE thing? Students taking the pledge. Uniting with allll those separate from us. Hmm? What schools would be most successful? What country? Why...? Realize now, a weak link in our bracelet *means* it can disconnect (fall and break) we lose the *value* of that bracelet (us). It affects all of us (eventually). When one girl is isolated, alone (hurt) it WEAKENS us all.

Whoever saves one life saves the world...

Talmud

Let NO girl go un-loved: COMMANDMENT # **11**

(They left that one out)

When a girl who's been ignored (by a parent) picks a guy who's been the FOCUS (protected and shielded) and is let down by him, she'll have two choices.

- To handle her <u>own</u> shit, learning he CAN'T so not really bonding to him emotionally, not feeling truly fulfilled.

- She can only be with him a *certain* way.

What does this mean for YOU? Holding off on true thoughts, fears... doubts... (he doesn't wanna hear 'em) which makes you feel weak for even having them. So now, you need to prove that you're not. So you suck it up. Tell yourself 'FUCK MY FEELINGS'. But oh, fo shur be there for *him*. Just to prove how **strong** you are. K. Now I'm MAD. Hold off—gotta go bang my head against a wall. *There...*

There's a dent, I'm good.

So, strong for him—weak for YOU. There's definitely something in our water we're drinking. And since you're used to taking care of your guy (making sure he's happy) when you try to take care of YOU (do things that make you happy) he's like, "Why you being so SELFISH?"

And YOU cry...

Why do you cry?

Cuz in your *heart*... putting self first is a *BAD* thing. A real Fairy Goddess (btw) has no problem putting herself first, she's okay with it. She'll be the first to say... "Uh. If you want head—GIVE head. Waiting..."

That *word*... Selfish (I see as being there for **yourself**) you see as a bad thing or it wouldn't have affected you. And it wouldn't have affected you so MUCH if you weren't already sooo sacrificial (obviously a god you worship). The only time we sacrifice ourself (do things we don't wanna do, give time we don't have, energy, money, favors) is when we feel guilty *somewhere*... in our life (about something). So we're just paying our dues (in our mind). Since it's seen as a *negative* (being there for yourself) so conflicted. So we KEEP doing shit we don't wanna do (with friends, family, boyfriend, girlfriend, parents, coach).

Make a LIST...

132.

What you feel <u>bad</u> about. Doesn't even have to be about you (parents, siblings, friends) but definitely something you did (or someone did to YOU). Either way you feel **bad**. Feeling bad means you feel guilty (in some way) see yourself as the cause, somehow. And unless you see it, squish it (bury it) discard it cuz it's not true so *DOESN'T BELONG TO YOU*—you're still farmer Joe (Josephina) picking up other people's shit. Which is why you CAN'T stand yourself. Or see yourself as disgusting.

Two conflicting opposites...

Sacrifice vs. Self

(Which one will you *serve*?)

When one *calls* the other fears... one has to lose out.

<u>Example:</u>

- They'll feel bad if I *don't* do it. **They'll feel good cuz they found ANOTHER way.**

- He'll think I'm playing hard to get. **Yeah... And SO?**

- She'll be *sooo* let down if I don't do what she wants. **She'll respect YOU for not doing what you don't want to do.**

- What if they leave me? **That'll clear up the BLOCK for the real one to come in.**

- They're depending on me. **They will learn to be dependent on themselves.**

So if someone wants you to do something YOU don't wanna do chances are your *self* will be afraid to voice its feelings (if you're used to sacrificing them). It feels good, 'natural' to do for others at your expense, instead of standing up for yourself (thoughts or feelings).

Letting people know it's NOT what you want to do at *allll*. Like I mentioned earlier and definitely worth mentioning TWICE. We usually respond strongly to something we have a personal *issue* with... If you're sacrificial and they tell you you're being selfish (difficult or sensitive) cuz in your mind it's **not** okay to be that way, and has been associated with bad feelings (thanks to parent, sibling, teacher, relative or society) you <u>will</u> respond to it in a BIG way (feel bad) defend against it (be MORE sacrificial). And it will hurt.

If you want *power* over it...

YOU need to have power *over* yourself.

As in, let yourself know it's **okay** to be that way... self-focused, (my word for selfish) preoccupied, sensitive or difficult. Cuz you're different... you're not a stereotypical human. You're exceptional! So some unique angles have been formed, takes *skill* to handle you. ☺ Once your MIND accepts, it no longer bothers you, you don't see it as BAD... It'll be like, a bullhorn to allll those out there!! THIS NO LONGER APPLIES.

STOP! GO READ THAT AGAIN.

YOU...

Teach people how to react to you (handle you) be with YOU.

Educate them! LOL

My boyfriend's like, "Gold... *is like a girl*." (Here we go...) lol "Its value is in its softness (purity). If it gets diluted (mixed with other metals) it loses its value, gets harder and *cheaper*. If it's authentic electricity passes easily through it. Like a girl on top of her game. Electrifying. It's a precious metal cuz it's uncontaminated. Like a girl who holds out. Expensive cuz it's worth more (loads of time, energy and many dates) cuz it's the ONE. Delicate, so it needs to be *protected* so it stands the test of time. It doesn't tarnish. Like a girl who doesn't stain her reputation. It's a beautiful, *beautiful* metal, there's something about it that sets it *apart*. Like the one that YOU can't forget. And where's it found? In a *vein* that comes from the heart of the earth (you know it's real)." And guys know you're not fool's gold (fake) you're genuine... and that *costs*. :P We're talking gifts, magical moments, making plans. You don't come cheap! There is no sampling your goods.

Then they treat YOU a certain way...

As established, since people are transparent to other people's *senses,* they'll always act toward YOU the way the inside part of you is speaking to yourself (quietly). Fascinating SHIT. So remember... IN HOUSE is best. Inform yourself. Which will inform others. New rules! New playing FIELD. Since people always sense what *bothers* you ('bout yourself) even when you don't tell them, they'll be feeling your vibe that says, "Attack me... I know this part of me is bad." Their senses are *listening* to your lack of sense. LOL

Re-wire the head, man!

Strangely... We accuse *others* of where we fall short and others accuse *us* of where they fall short—can't accuse someone of something you don't *recognize*... haven't experienced. Guess we're designed in a way that helps us understand each other by what bothers us 'most' about the *other* person (given WE see that, of course). LOL Don't BLAME the other person. :P We actually need the other person to show us what we *can't* stand about **ourself**. Hillllarious!!

Back to male AND female energies!

It's SO apparent that masculine and feminine energies have been dissed (ignored) and completely overlooked. It's such a MAJOR issue. It causes sooo many conflicts. These energies completely change the way we see and *react* to each other, in our relationships (here on earth). Which is why it's necessary to integrate BOTH (energies) to make sure we're guaranteed love AND success. After all, we have to deal with both sexes *everywhere*. Especially in a world, where you monopolize one side (it dominates) abandon the other, fail to draw *strength* from it. Anything that dominates *has* control... over YOU. That's so universal. There has to be harmony (a special bond) mystical marriage... between your inner male and female energies *first* (before it's duplicated in your outer world) so you can ATTRACT the one you're meant for, not designed for (by circumstance).

Example:

A girl needing to learn to be tough (takes the lead) attracts a guy too criticized to feel secure to approach her. She goes to him, makes him feel comfortable. They hook up. YOU must be familiar with your WHOLE self or you'll be slanted... so *pulled* to someone that's the opposite of what you really **want**. Have a lottt of conflict. Which is cool... cuz in the end, you're far too spent to do a THING for a guy. SO now attract a giver. And you dude, fed up with being de-masculinized by a girl, making all the decisions, feeling like you're with your *mom*. So it all works out in the END. But at what price? You vow never to fall in love *again*... but you suffer cuz you have so *much* to give. That's why even though in the beginning they seem like a fit! Something was off. The broken part of you *fit* into their broken part (jagged edges) brought about by fear, intimidation. They **never** really fit... the whole YOU. Just appeared to sustain you. Truth is, you kinda needed each other to keep the fragmented pieces together (feed each other's empty spaces, keep it filled, stay miserable) so you can tell yourself it's better than nothing.

Once you equalize and balance BOTH sides (masculine and feminine) you bring in the part that *couldn't* keep up (languished behind) to join YOU (complete you). That's why after a lottt of pain (YOU holding back on giving so much) you finally attract someone who truly is in sync with the true you. (heals YOU) instead of hijacking each other's strengths to make up for what's missing. Now your *inner* world is whole, so you meet the SAME. And it feels WEIRD—at first. No drama, no upheavals, no work just gliding. And you feel different... but you also feel free, with added strength you didn't know you had. It's like, YOU do less... and get so much MORE. It's a bit *strange* (at first). Take it from me...

Strange... *has* its advantages. LOL

136.

Masculine Energy...

Love's a challenge! Is logical, practical, direct, strong in business (decisive) takes action, competitive, a leader (doesn't give up) ruthless, responsible, fiercely protective (if guy, *LIKES* to pick you—not have some girl pick *him*). Masculine energy initiates your career or sport. Strikes like a match! It's an aggressive, sure of itself—relentless energy. BIG balls. Ahllo! We all need it at work.

Feminine Energy...

Is playful, receptive, listens well, lovvves to TALK, affectionate, emotional, nurturing, passively *magnetic*, inspires, doesn't CHASE, mysterious... Walks AWAY from anything uncomfortable. Does NOT look back. Self worth, extremely high. How you say... a reeeal *biatch*.

Feminine energy is healing... beautiful, gentle, loving. It's highly magnetic (charm <u>plus</u>) dripping with seduction. Doesn't like vulgarity, conflict or discord. As a guy, it's his gut instinct that helps him sniff out when a girl, guy or situation stinks. And LEAVES. Selective with his battles. High moral code.

(K. Reflect on why I put Masculine Energy off to the left and Feminine Energy, in the middle of the page.)

Without ample masculine energy in a guy, he can become too passive (waiting for things to happen, procrastinating, girls need to come to *him*) insecure, lacks drive (a.k.a lazy) lacks the confidence to strike out in the world! Goes on substances to help him *cope* with all his overwhelming emotions. Since logic is rusty, not used to working properly so can't depend on it. Without sufficient feminine energy in a girl, she can become too bossy, bitchy, hard-ass, difficult to get close to (speak her feelings) ask for help, receive *compliments*... do things just for HER. (Right here!) LOL She's mostly comfortable in executive mode (in charge) in control. Since she has trouble standing up for her feelings and waits too long to voice them, she no longer relies on them to tell her if she's happy (safe).

When we're too much on one side, we're restricted, have to depend (twofold) on that side to support us, so it's going to be off. Law of Balance. Just like having a weak (injured) side you now have to overcompensate with the other side. Then the weak side (hardly used) gradually gets weaker, the stronger side gets injured (over use) misalignment of the body, chronic constant pain, you get HURT. It feels odd for us to address the *other* side which is now stale, left unattended—so pissed off, doesn't even wanna TALK to you. *Both* energies are here to serve the male and female 'genders'. Ha! Just HAD to say that word... *gender*. Masculine minded girls who abandon their feminine energy will be very TIME oriented and time will ALWAYS win. So hard to take *baths* (unless sensual, like pole dancing, cheerleading, yoga, hip hop dancing types) difficult to buy pretty things, experiment with hair, makeup, open up (about feelings) hear good things about themselves. One exception; injured athlete who has no choice but to chill. Unless this type of girl really **cares** about her appearance but conceals it (sees it negative) so quick to call others VAIN (conceited). Though they seem strong on the outside, trust me they're NOT when it comes to standing up for *their* feelings. (Fragile inside) Which is why they need to be so *tough* on the outside (but no one knows it) especially since they put out great efforts to run after a guy (on his terms) while he doesn't really pay much attention to her. They live on logic's turf, feelings make too many waves, so bumped off.

Like my friend Cassandra! She's like, "Nichole. This guy I'm really into I text him. Like, five HOURS have gone by and he still hasn't text me back. It makes me *craazy*! I'm the type of GIRL that gets what she goes after!"

(Nice masculine type)

YOU can't go after a guy's HEART.

It's a gift when he gives it...

So she's like, "I text him again. 'Hi ugly.' He's like, 'Why you being like that?' I'm like, 'Hi *bae*... is THAT better?' Guess I hurt him." So I'm like, "Kkkk... Why are you acting like a GUY trying to please a girl? Why are you acting like some huge girl who uses her weight to bully people and *HAAAS TO RUN AFTER A GUY*?" She's like, "Omigosh! You're right. I don't wanna be a guy." I'm like, "K... Pretend you don't come from your parents. Sometimes that can set us back. Pretend you live in a CASTLE with like, seventy servants and everyone's getting YOU whatever you want. #happy! You wouldn't feel like *running* after a GUY." Course, if you're used to having all that money it might not make a difference. When you feel you have A LOT you don't give so fast (so much) or rush to give. Cuz you know you have *a lot* (to offer). Unless of course, you're pissed off at your parents and tryin' to get back at 'em. Like it works. Or be like, fuck the world (punish yourself type shit).

Sometimes, it takes a while till we actually feel incredible *just* being us. Usually, it's linked to something we can DO (really, really well). Until then... we can PRETEND. And you will see when you practice your fairy tale type existence, that you will observe *more...* act less (towards a guy) smile more (bring him to you) not chase HIM. Cuz you know you're the prize—NOT booby prize. :P Seriously, when you feel it deep inside. Like, you've got servants n' shit, you'll act a *certain* way. Which draws guys and people to you, cuz people always wanna be part of something GREAT. Which YOU are (just don't know it yet).

But you WILL...

And remember!

What you're used to is what you'll get, cuz you'll always get what you expect (deep down) *Awww... you smiled.*

Dimples!!

So you need to get used to a different world. And to get that, your inner world has to be there (first) then the outer world *comes...* to **match** it—it's a love thing. LOL *They're drawn to each other.*

Cassandra got bulldozed by her masculine side taking charge (doin' all the work) pursuing. So not happy when she didn't accomplish her GOAL (getting him to call back). Which then got her anxious, made her *doubt* herself (so going crazy as we speak). You can't force a guy to like you. Buttttt... you can release your magic (*bring him in*). Then YOU decide (if he's a keeper).

To all my mystical mermaids!

Repeat after me!

I promise... Cross my heart (**do it**) to not let anyone in *there*... Unless he's WORTHY. For I know if I do... I'll never be the same.

I'll be HUMAN. Ahahah!

So sorry! Don't casually exchange body fluids.

He'll be looking at you thinking, "Where's she from?" You'll be looking at him, thinking... a *very distant star.* " Back to my Earth girls...

Earthbound... heaven born (*fo shur*). ☺

This part's CRITICAL

There absolutely needs to be a commitment between the two parts of YOU (masculine and feminine) till death do you part. LOL YOU split? Nasty repercussions ahead. Great IDEA. GO give this to your sister. Just don't tell her it's for her. Tell her you want her *opinion.* LOL

I had this one friend, she was a tough girl (hardly ever smiled) we were working on an assignment together. We had a DEADLINE. Everything's cool till one day I text her, we gotta talk about our assignment and she texts me back, she's not answering calls and closing her cell. There's a person she wants to avoid. Tells me to email her. Email her?!! How do you email hours worth of stuff to discuss? We have a deadline. That's so fucken immature. At the very least say, "I'll call you back on my house line." Needless to say that and many other so-called, 'I never got your text.' when I tried to get a hold of her and she'd text me last minute ENDED our relationship. I felt supremely chated. #pissed. A prime example! A very strong minded girl, who could not SPEAK UP for her feelings. To one 'idiot' that called her. So everyone *else* had to suffer and find some OTHER way of getting a hold of her.

140.

The opposite of that...

Feminine minded girls who live exclusively in FEELING land and have a hard time focusing on one thing. Scattered... at all times.

Need to talk A LOT.

Change their mind (quite often) difficult to make decisions (take action) make things happen (without constantly changing it over and over and over again). Since, they're connected to their feelings, they also have the ability to tell YOU where they stand. And that you SUCK. Aren't scared of turning their back, cuz it feels bad to THEM.

Let me put it to you this way dude.

Just like your unit *fits* into our unit, releases tremendous power (physically AND emotionally) we need to be brought 'together' (masculine & feminine) instead of being a '*part*'... which is why you guys feel like a *dick* (when you put your feelings ahead of your girl's) insensitive. A pussy... when you let a girl step allll over you (no backbone... too soft). Or with YOU girl... a piece of ass (when you let a guy have you SO QUICK) don't want to wait till he's made it clear... YOU'RE THE ONE.

Did you figure it out?

Why did I put masculine to the left... feminine middle of the page?

Answer:

Structure *verses* center of attention. ;P

Age of Role Reversals

A masculine minded girl (competitive, ambitious, protective, aggressive) who *forgets* to leave her balls (present company included) on court, at the gym, job... brings it home to her guy—last she checked *was* a masculine energy will clash, causing an 'It's complicated' status to turn *off* and on—more than a strobe light. And that's cuz, similar energies **repel** (Physics remember) creating conflict. Forcing the guy into a *passive* state... just to keep the peace. Opposites attract. Mother Nature makes no mistakes. Two *pairs* of BALLS... a lottta scrambled messages. LOL

Just when I was looking for confirmation of my theory I meet two guys at a café. One of them... I can't even. He was *so* hot. How was his body *like*?

...Like doctor recommended. LOL

He was one of those guys you felt instant warmth with. And his English *accent*—SICK! He was *so* stoked about what I was writing. When I saw how excited he was—glued my ass right to HIM. You know how... someone freaks over something you SAY, you wanna just be around them. Their reaction feeds your soul, man. I'd tell my mom something exciting. A guy thing, opportunity, news she's like, "That's good." ☺ I'm like, "Uh... Mom, aren't you excited?" "Yeah. Do you want me to stand on my head?" "Yeah! I need a visual. Some sort of proof that you 'got it.'" The worst feeling in the WORLD. You're *sooo* excited... tell somebody, they're like, "K..." Or with a parent (adult) "*That's* nice..." Translated: "Don't give a fuck." Buzz kill. Goes right through your cuh-hone-ays. Translated: Emotional diarrhea. ☹

I'm sitting there, trying to look like I'm **not** that interested. Like, I just want to jump HIM! Land in his lap, and stay there forever. You could just tell this guy *takes in* a girl's feelings. He's strong enough on the inside, not to let it FLOOD him (huge relief). He'd be the lighthouse in my stormy seas... *Purrr*. I know what you GUYS are thinking. Every guy acts that way in the beginning. Like they're *so* perfect they can handle life n' shit. But nooo! I'm telling you this guy, would NOT collapse when a girl's having a bad hair day. Seriously. He wouldn't be gulping for air, when she's talking a million miles a minute—reciting her recent happenings. HE COULD TAKE IT.

His is name...

CYRUS.

We start talking 'bout how *UNCLEAR* the roles have become lately (between guys AND girls). He's like, "You know, there used to be a time when it was Ma and Pa—now it's *BLAAAH*. It's so **unclear**. You can't even be manly today, it's threatens so many girls."

Our nature dictates itself...

When you look at a female polar bear and a male polar bear, you can tell who's WHO. With us, you're not so sure. Most of us keep (unconsciously) engaging in different roles all the time, vacillating back and forth (especially in the beginning) which sets us up for a fall, each time. Cuz we're pulling in a guy we don't *really* want—but don't see it till later (once we're comfortable with him). It's all messed up. When we move away from our (true) nature we lose power. Like, a flabby muscle that's unused... it gets weak. And cuz we're unstable we compensate with *other* parts.

(...to feel strong)

Girls actin' like guys (overly aggressive) askin' *them* out, protecting their feelings (acting territorial and shit). Guys actin' like girls, waitin' to be asked so they can feel secure, sensitive, passive (seducing a girl without initiating). Each tryin' to be *half* of something they can never (*completely*) be... losing all of what they can *powerfully* be. Making them feel insecure (ungrounded) weakened... limited. When one part of our nature is either *ignored* all together in favor of the other or diluted (so weakened) half the strength lost in the conversion, a hidden part is *abandoned*.

When a guy's in touch with his femininity (not a girl's) as I said... push comes to shove, his feelings come FIRST (can't deal with hers). Girl-on-girl hate. Being possessive with our guy, taking care of him, being his watch dog, trying not to hurt his feelings (so he'll stay) all serve to give us a pseudo sense of security and control. By *not* standing up for our feelings, following logic... it wins by default (cuz we think they show weakness). Whatever leads... wins.

Yo! Take it like a Man... by standing up for the Woman in

YOU.

Same with media n' shit...

We're losing strength in our feminine *essence* cuz it's either porno-sized (degraded to less than) or stupid pretty, takes a hundred selfies a minute (IQ of a turnip) not much for convo. No substance, no intensity... no **real** woman.

Interesting...

In places like Europe and South America, where feminine and masculine roles are more pronounced, they have language with male and female nouns. Gender is *attached* to each thing. In English speaking countries we're neutral about it. LOL Gender neutrality, but a lot more (gender) confusion. :P More and more girls are acting like guys *wondering* why their boyfriend's accusing them of acting like a guy ('dude' is now interchangeable, used for guy or girl). Seriously? WTH? Girls are opting not to have a boyfriend cuz they're too much work (don't want the DRAMA). There's no distinction between masculine and feminine energies (in our language). Guys are losing their ground (initiative) drive... so paralyzed by rejection. Languages with gender assigned to them appear to preserve the essence of both sexes, encouraging a complementary relationship *not* a neutral (competitive) one. Conflicted. More about *this* later (fo shur). Where people grow up with a broader concept of masculinity and femininity in language, they practice it. They're innately aware of a softer and tougher nature without assigning weakness or superiority to it so naturally, it's carried over to their *relationships*. Since it's repetitive it's strengthened (defined) *more*... Making us recognize each time, the delicate complexity of a woman's nature, the clear simplicity and strength of man's nature. Then, there's places where roles have been blown so out of PROPORTION it's top heavy. ☺

Talk about cauterizing the flow of love.

Our perception of where it's at (peers, society, social media) leads us to make decisions we're not necessarily happy with. Like this one girl I know who sees everyone's into fucking and one night stands and cuz she's hardly approached, feels there's something *wrong* with her (not really pretty). No one 'wanted' her. So makes herself available. and gets into that whole scene. One day we're talking and she's like, "What does it mean... When a guy puts his finger in and outta your mouth?" I'm like, "Uh. BACTERIA?" She's like, "I'm serious. Let's say you're doing it and he puts his fingers in your mouth, really stretches your lips so your gums are showin'. Are you supposed to enjoy it? Cuz I told a girl friend she's like, 'THAT'S just rough sex.' I felt so dumb." I'm like, "Sounds like this guy's confusing you with a horse—and who the fuck does *that* to a HORSE? If he's stretching your lips like that? I'd report him to the animal protection authorities." Sicko... Mishandling horses.

Then there's YOU girls...

Who enjoy doin' weird shit for the sake of sayin' you did it. BFD The same with givin' head, you do it cuz it makes you feel powerful... *doing*. Wonder if you feel the same power him pleasing YOU? *Receiving*... I'd question that if I were you. Cuz you **do** have a vagina— it HAS an opening. LOL It's meant to receive. K... *then* give back (but only once you're HAPPY). So my girl friend's like, "I thought I was supposed to LIKE it." I'm like, "I dunno... some guy stickin' his fingers in my mouth, stretching it like that—I'd feel like *A PIG BEING FITTED FOR AN APPLE*. He's the pig. What else did he do? Spit in your vagina." "OMG!! How did you KNOW?" "Cuz he's into porn. He's a porn FREAK doin' everything he's learned online."

Porn is sooo fucked.

It's sad that some girls feel they don't *have* a choice. Some of them actually look like they've been drugged. It's like, they're not even there. Like, they're oblivious (desperate for cash). Then there's these university girls who SELL their virginity to the highest bidder. That shit never leaves YOU!! It's like doing a crazy tattoo when you're drunk. Next day.... Whaaat did I do?!? Only WORSE. As far as I'm concerned, porn is an abomination of what sex is *supposed* to be (between two people). My boyfriend's like, "You know... The part that's really fucked for me 'bout porn? There's ZERO amount of love present." Like... Why would anybody watch it to *learn* about sex? Sex is about *connecting*... porn's completely devoid of love. And the part that really grosses me out (more than anything they DO that's *gross*) is how you can see in their face the TOTAL disconnect (from themselves). Just hopelessness, what-the-fuckness and fear. Not that you've seen much of it." Can't say that I have. Not into eye sores or genital sores.

Guys, if you wanna know what a girl likes, ask her! When it's a true bond NOTHING matches it. Just so you know. And I DO mean 'nothing'. It is... from *another* world. No drug HERE is gonna take you there. It can't be had artificially or synthetically. And... you don't need to do a thing.

Love is a 'present'... a gift from Life to YOU.

In a special package...

You'll know it's for you cuz you'll be in a sorta *trance*... when you see it. And you won't be able to take the person out of your mind (for like days, weeks). It'll feel like they already *belong* to you inside YOU. There'll be a strong PULL. Just one condition. You need to feel good enough about yourself to *accept* it. Or it won't open. And you'll never get to see it. Guaranteed. You'll think about it the rest of your life. Sad.

So I tell my girl friend what I think about this douche bag. She's like, "That makes SO much sense cuz I felt like we weren't even connecting." Duh... there is <u>no</u> connection. It's NOT a real relation... *ship* with you. It's a shagging session made for sheep... sheep follow. There's no **relation**-ship (relating) someone who gets your exclusive **ship** (to paradise). Just isolation (feeling alone) tryin' to pretend it is what it's not. I'm like, "Sex is ABOUT connection, it's meant to be enjoyable. There's a 'joy' element present so that doesn't even qualify. That's not rough sex—that's no sex. LOL Stretching my lips over my face?! Like, I'm not GUMBY." And for the record guys... Spit is NOT lube. And lube's a short cut anyway. Do you know how many chemicals are in THAT? I've never had a boyfriend use any of that crap on me. He'd just go pick up some condoms. Ask where they are. Sales girl be like, "YOU looking for extra lubrication?" He be like,

"Nope. Don't need that." She's like... '*Oooh.*' I know cuz he bragged about it all night. Guys and their bragging rights! LOL Course, seeing a huge purple hickey on his neck was probably a dead giveaway. Guys... When you're really *into* a girl, get her going cuz you *know* her (so know what to DO) she'll be more into you emotionally (your security deposit). LOL It's not *just* about touchin' her here and there— SHE'S NOT A CALCULATOR. It won't add up.

Every girl's got her own code... *that YOU need to discover.*

A thief that knows how to get in may get away with stealing some, but he'll never <u>own</u> it. It's marked. Waiting for you to decode your woman dude (in Braille).

And ANOTHER thing. When you're finished having sex with us, don't be doin' strange shit. One girl I know is like, "If <u>one</u> more **guy** takes his *thing* and slaps it on my forehead or stomach after we're done— I'm gonna take it and I'm gonna *BREAK IT*—till it bleeeds!" I'm like, "Omigosh... you're going to break it? You're not gonna bend it?" She's like, "Yeah. What's bending gonna do? It won't do shit. Breaking IT... that'll teach him what's good." "K.. I'm down." We're not your ashtray guys. DON'T be tapping that thing on us!

When a guy does all this weird shit and it feels odd to YOU... Stop. Tell him you're not comfortable with it, it doesn't feel good to you (it's degrading) *teach him...* some guys need a tutor. Even a guy who loves you (and it's not a random) may get this idea cuz of his friends, try all this stupid shit. In his mind it's supposed to make you feel good. Go to the woman dude. LMFAOO

I remember one boyfriend... we broke up, when we got back *together* and slept together, I could not believe the shit he was doing. I loved the way we had sex, why'd he have to go and RUIN it? Now he was doin' shit like... We'd be doin' it and he'd flip me on my front (do it some more) then my side, back to my FRONT. Then my back! I'm like, "Bae! I'm feeling like a PANCAKE. Can you make up your mind?

Aahhhouch! You're on my HAIR!!!"

I stop him...

I'm like, "What are you doing? We used to have sex—it was *HARD* it was *fast*—it was in! Then I'd go to sleep. Now you're doin' all this *slowww* shit. And it's driving me insane." He's like, "But baby, when we broke up I read all this stuff about sex online and they said go SLOW. I just wanted our first time to be perfect." I laughed *so* hard... my jaw cramped. (K, another reason too) ;P So I'm like, "Bae, the way we did it—*was* perfect NOT into this delay shit. I want it hard I want it *FAST*—and I want it *sooo* fucken in–**when I wannit!** And if you wanna go slow—THINK manual labor. Hands *down*... ultra effective." Want my man's imprint. Demanding bitch... Yup.

And as for YOU dude, who disconnects a girl's head from her body— just fuck just that, so she doesn't *really* exist. You're never really plugged into *her* (although your part is plugged in quite nicely) what else do you do? Ask her to go *down* (on you) right after a fight? So you're like, all made up and cuddling you're like, "Do you wanna go down on me?" :D She's like, "I'm still mad at YOU." You're like, "*Awhh*... come on you're better than that." Like, where do you guys get all this psychological (yet super effective) bullshit? Lmfao Personally. I'd be like, "I'd love to, but my gums are sensitive. YOU first!" But hey, if it's suction you want I got a vacuum outlet in my room—you can stick your dick in there. I'm sooo resourceful.

At the risk of sounding redundant...

Sex is about connecting... for a truly EPIC feeling. Who you are, your body, the soulful-type of bonding you feel when you're with THEM (and nothin' matters) equals fulfillment... inner strength. YOU don't feel alone in the world anymore. To break one stick, is a lot easier than two sticks... *tied* together. <3

(YOU can protect her from being broken)

<3 <3 <3

The connection *between* male and female is their true *nature*, whether in a relationship or within themselves. When this balance is broken it shifts (overcompensation) we become vulnerable to out-side influence (relationship pollution) suffer.

Same thing with land and medicine. We affect our earth in a negative way—it kicks back! (We suffer) It retaliates... shifts. Just like a girl. YOU ignore her, she'll let you know about it. Might not happen right away, but it'll happen. And allll this deforestation!! *WHAT ARE WE DOING?!* Why are plucking out our TREES it's how we breathe! Besides, where will our aliens land? LOL So now, we have all these massive worldwide weather changes we have to deal with. Like, do I seriously wanna take a winter coat for my summer vacay? And that's not all! Increased levels of carbon dioxide in the AIR cuz we're SUCH a dumbass for cutting down our trees, which naturally filter and consume carbon dioxide, interrupting the whole water cycle. Not to mention! Extinction of plants (even *poisonous* plants give OXYGEN) and animals. Now... Mother Earth is *pissed*. We need to be gentle with her. She's a *lady*.

We take drugs to fix one problem there's side effects (we suffer). In the olden days the biggest side effects was a BAD taste. Course, back then it was a mixture of plants, strange herbs and prayers. So we KEPT the plant. Lmao Use it to get *high*... Trouble is, although it can sharpen our senses, make us motivated (temporarily) eliminate fear, make us witty... you can't get high without getting LOW. Nobody talks about *that*. After a while, you're slow... reaction time nil. It's dangerous to drive. And you look STUPID. Wasted. Long term effects equal personality disorders. We already have sooo many! LOL We begin to disassociate. We no longer take part in life (to any great extent) no motivation. We are permafried. Then need more and more to reach that *high*... Our connection to getting that (naturally) LOST.

You can't stand yourself without it. YOU look in the mirror—see a POT HEAD. And everyone knows it, you can't function without it. Paranoia drapes your personality and you slip into—never never LAND. Now you're scared of *evvverything*. How you sound, how you look, how you smell. Good LUCK *ever* finding your Tinker Bell, Peter Pan. Just as well, you've been on pot so long forget about your rod shootin' anything but blanks (gonna need that ONE day). Sperm quality, speed and swimming com-promised. They're *high*... can't swim properly. LOL

Your sperm's not CAPABLE dude.

Doesn't that bother you? Only one in five know where they're going. The others are chasing their tail and the rest... treading water askin', "Wherrre are we? WHAAA-happened? What is this place?" o_O Maybe, they're waiting for the egg to come to *them*? (Wouldn't be surprised) Not much of an investment for immortalizing yourself in another human. Just think of the legacy 'dees nutz' could have for generations to *come*...

Bragging rights! :P

Bad enough sperm has been on the decline (for years) due to all the environmental pollutants, plastics and lifestyle. It's all over the net. Omigosh! Can YOU imagine if there was worldwide male INFERTILITY? Then what? We girls already have bigger balls. We'll have no use for you guys. You'll be like our SLAVE (some of you already are).]:} It'll be ATLANTIS all over again! *AHHHH!!!* Please guys. We need YOU and your balls. Still... our smile will always bring you to your knees. (Genetics)

Doin' drugs purposely that fuck us up, so we can get a *buzz*, where we can't even tell what we're doing (who's doing *what* to us) is just LAME. I got an idea. Why don't we sleep and leave our front door wide open! (SAME thing) Speaking of drugs... why are doctors FOCUSING on the disease instead of how to turn us into SUPERIOR beings? Why! So we don't get diseases in the first place! If you and I wanted to make a lot of money (all those in favor, say iiiiiiiiii) I... ☺ Would we research homeless people, find out how their life got so fucked up? Or, would we TALK to rich people? Find out how they got where we need to be? Why are doctors spending all their energy and BRAIN power, focusing on how to kill a disease? It's inside us... It's gonna hurt us too. After all, we're only human (well, some of us). ;D How did medicine, something initially good *turn* into something with so many side effects?!

The Best Medicine in the World... a Mother's hug. <3

There's so many things attacking our body today. Fake things put in our foods—like are we not real? Air pollution. Might as well pour a bag of saw dust in your room, molds, bacteria (horrible stuff) highly toxic. And what do we do? Leave bottled water in our car, in the sun keep refilling. Double dose of bacteria coming right up! Pesticides. I get they're supposed to keep the bugs OUT. But we're spraying that shit on fruits and vegetables while wearing space suits (protective gear). Then we EAT it. We've got <u>one</u> body to last our whole life—there's no recall. It's the one **tool** we've been given to experience *everything* in life. Why are we screwing it up?

An Acidic State!

INTERNAL AFFAIRS are pissed—laws have been broken. There's cesspools of bacteria and viruses used as a landing strip for other diseases. There's NO escape. Special agents Alka and Rectum are sent to the scene. They investigate, dismantle the threat. They have to go through SO MUCH shit. LOL And fat (gobs of it).

Fat is not where it's at, it's where it *stacks*. LOL An over-acidification issue where the body creates fat cells, to carry acid waste away to safer locations in the body. Attaching itself to organs for their protection (shock absorbers). LOL As we get *bigger* the acid is pushed further and *further* from our organs, so they don't disintegrate in all that acid. Acts like a barrier, keeping toxicity away from our organs. Kinda like a sumo wrestler in between me and the bully. It has a downside.

YOU get fatter—the psychological shit that comes with that. Stress on the body (weight on the organs) more cells to feed so have to eat *more*. Body gets used to that and now gotta deal with addiction and the energy it *takes* to sustain all of that. Total ABDUCTION.

FAT... has function.

It's a WARNING.

Once the body gets rid of the acidic waste through training (exercise) a healthy food plan, it doesn't need to hang on to that fat (for protection) it can let go. *Ahh...* Finally, the LAST five pounds. Other things that make our body really acidic? Alcohol. (I *know*... at least drink A LOT of water with it, to carry it out with) Sugar, fried foods, fast foods (*baaaaad*). Anger, stress, anxiety. When something upsets you (your body) it turns from a natural state of alkaline pH to acidic.

That's why they say eat your GREENS. And no, that does not include food coloring (in your drinks). Greens raise your pH levels. I put liquid chlorophyll in my water. It's refreshing! And it's green. And yeah, people will say, "Hey! Your water's green man." I'm like, "Yeah. Your PISS is yellow man. What's your point? I like green. It's the color of money. It's respectable. It's the color of TREES. Just doin' my part to keep it *green* y'all. What's with the *face?* You wanna talk vile?

I had gallbladder stones. Hospitalized for a WEEK. They told me I had no choice they needed to yank out my gallbladder. Sorry—it's MINE. Speed dial to GOD. Need another way! Tried to convince me my gall-bladder was not a 'necessary' organ. Next, they'll be telling me my boyfriend's nuts are just accessories. I research and find this plant that's supposed to dissolve stones. I get it in liquid form. Tell my boyfriend to taste it first... He chokes! He's like, "Ughh!! That's *disssgusting*. Tastes like I ate a piece of roadkill." Chlorophyll... has no taste. Chill. Besides... I dunno anyone who drank gin (first time around) and was like, "*Mmmm... yummy!*" You know you only tolerate it cuz of the feeling it gives you. LOL Wish I could video your first time having a SHOT.

K... So you practiced in front of the mirror.

The fat build up is our body's way of responding (freaking out, actually) to dealing with all that (acid). DAMAGE control! And just like a toilet bowl that's piled up with shit and *won't* flush, it explodes. OVERFLOWS. Only the mess on the floor, is nowhere near the mess inside YOU. And you can't take a mop to our insides.

K. I sooo need a shower. LOL

Can you even *imagine* all that toxic shit waste? Most of us shit, what... ONCE a day? Which means our toilet system (body) is backlogged, already. In my opinion, going to take a dump once a day is not enough. You eat three meals, you should be going three times. Fiber becomes mandatory, here. Oatmeal, lentils, rice, grains, flaxseeds (to name a few) and you gotta drink WATER. Or have nothing to take out your shit with. It becomes hard and prickly. I call it... The Pointy Kaka. Torture... to get out. We're MADE of about 60 to 70 percent water. Soda, sugary drinks are completely foreign to our body. You don't feed your plant SODA!

Actually...

The brain and heart are 73% water, the lungs 83%, skin... 64% muscles and kidneys 79% and even the bones are watery (to my surprise) 31% water. The metabolism and incomplete breakdown of foods plus the metabolic waste (produced as a by-product of cellular activity) must be BALANCED. Or removed (deported) by our body's buffering and detoxification systems (kick-ass bodyguards) through our organs, the lungs, liver, kidneys and blood (combat fighters). If it can't be expelled it builds into a toxic WASTELAND— think manyyy bullies. Water is ESSENTIAL.

K. ENOUGH of this shit. LOL

Just one thing.

Sometimes, you're so uptight you CAN'T shit. Like waaay too much homework, assignments (*pressure*). A huge fight with your girlfriend or boyfriend. So you sit there focus... TURN purple with gigantic veins popping out of the side of your neck—*squint* real hard, be practically in tears holdin' your breath (can't upset momentum) STILL... nothing. Relax... take a *deep* breath—on second thought DON'T inhale. LMFAO Pray.

When that would happen to me I'd see in my mind... *alllll* these little men working in my butthole factory—pushing (beads of sweat pouring down their faces) tryin' to get this torpedo PIECE of a shit OUT. And they'd push and *push* and I'd visualize their success—and it'd happen. Major SUBMARINE. (Sinker) My dad would always tell me to just think of *boats*...

It worked for him.

One day one of my lady farts entered the atmosphere I'm like, "Bae! It's okay. My farts don't smell." smell." He's like, "They DO. They smell like lavender and potpourri." *Awhh*... My farts smell like poopoorri. Lmaoo I had a foreign student from Ecuador read this section. He PISSED himself. He's like, "You know *eh*... right after dis *part* here, on your *eh* limination—I start eat more OATMEAL." He *looks* at his crotch, he's like... "How you say... iz more even color. Less blotchy. And my balls... they are smooth like eggs. No. More like figs... they are my fig mutants." LMAO I thanked him and started gathering my stuff. I closed my laptop, looked for my cover he's like, "K. Where iz dee condom for da' laptop? Safety first!" (Busting) He continues... "All deez derrti websites.. could be berri denjurus. Ju can get deez computer virus, dat give you DTD'S. Wheech... *eh* standz for, digitally transmitted disease. It will give you sorz on your fingers. Naasty. No longer will ju be able to sweetly caress your girlfriend, on social media messages. She will get dem too. Ju know, da' people in my country will read deez book, and dey will call it, da' pennis BIBLE. I swear... iz my oatz. My solemn oatz."

I decide to ask him about his take on guys, being from a different country he could have a completely different point of view. I'm like, "My boyfriend talks *sooo* slow. Everything he *does*... is slow. By the time he talks about his feelings it takes FOREVER. I get so impatient." He's like, "*Ahhh...* If he takes hiz time and iz slow, iz becuz of hiz DEPTH of love (for ju). He iz... how you say 'time released'." ROFL So glad I asked. He reaches for a pack of gum (awh... wants to be *fresh*) there's nothing left. I'm like, "Oops... guess you finished it all." He's like, "Iz okay I go to car, I have back up." Just *lovvve* foreign guys! They're so adorable and RAW.

My boyfriend's from Chile. His dad's always endearing about givin' him shit, makes a joke out of it. When my boyfriend was four, and learning to tie his shoes his dad tried to encourage him. He's like, "Hediondo a cocos... y todavía no sabe amarrar los cordones."

Translation: Smells of *balls*... and he still can't tie his shoes.

Course, my guy still *smells* of balls. Ten whole minutes to tie his shoes. LOL Can you imagine if our Northern American culture could adapt? Be pro-creative. We'd be like, "Mom, don't just give me shit— be creative. Talk about my ovaries n' stuff." HAAAAA!

Back to our body...

STRETCH BREAK!!

Seriously. Wherever YOU are stretch! At least, do your calves dude. Guaranteed they're tight. And make sure you press your hips forward. Just be careful if you're doin' it against a wall... (you don't look like you're screwin' it). ;D

To my girls.

Those of YOU who want to do SO MUCH in the world, I so applaud you. Clap!! Clap!! You have been primed and prepped for your position. (No doubt!) You're on top of your GAME. (*Niiice*) You're talented, focused—*driven*. But you're also wondering why you can't find a REAL guy. You ignore your feminine nature (feelings) allow more shit to come into your life (DRAMA) with friends, offer too much (exhausted) put up with *allll* this crap (from someone who doesn't really pay attention to you) so... not FUELED. And since you've been conditioned to associate *feelings* with weakness, there's no room for it (you diss 'em). Pretty stupid, since that's the part that signals when things are OFF (unhappy... feeling used). It's linked to your sense of *value* (so it tells you). What you feel inside **speaks** to you... warns you, preps you. A hell of a lot FASTER than your brain does (it sees in *advance*).

The heart always does...

Our sex hormones are high in estrogen (a feeling hormone) it would make sense then, our sense of value *comes* from how we feel (which our heart rules btw) NOT our brain. The brain's *extra* fo shur! But no matter how smart you are, if you ignore your feelings (*senses*) you'll SUFFER (just a matter of time). It's very easy for your brain to turn against you (influenced by social media, people, circumstance) tellin' you things like, "You suck... If you can't do this." Your heart can't come to your assistance, its got a 'different' teacher now... The Ego. And cuz you abandoned one for the *other*—it went straight to its head. Took CONTROL... refusing to give your heart ANY rights (when you feel like shit) so it can *slowly* destroy you or have you think everyone *wants* to destroy you. ☹ Example...

My friend Steve was tellin' me how a girl (super rich) super popular and *sooo* smart, was down a lot. Her parents couldn't figure out why (what else is new). They sent her away... To a PLACE. But she kept running away. All her friends thought she was handling it. She laughed at the whole ordeal. Thought it was one BIG joke. Her grades were high. She was hot. EVERYONE looked up to her. But in her mind... *it was hell*. Her parents tried putting her in a real hard-core facility (so she wouldn't escape). Her friends kept texting her, but she'd text back, "It's cool. I'm fine." ☺ She FOOLED everybody. She escaped...

Jumped off a bridge.

No one ever suspected she'd do THAT. ;_;

She fooled *herself*—into thinking her life wasn't worth living. As smart as you ARE if you fail to listen to your feelings, honor them (speak your truth) so it can level out any imbalance, *authenticate* what your mind's sayin' (know when it's turning against YOU) the only thing you'll hear... CRITICISM. If you plug into your heart, true harmony <u>will</u> be achieved—*after you tend to the discord.* LOL Seeing, how masculine minded girls are much more comfortable letting their brain dictate (what they should do) their feelings trail behind (at times, get lost) can't find their way back... *express* themselves. ☹

TILL THEY GET TORCHED (fucked over)

Now YOU pay attention...

But out of habit your logic continues to tell YOU where to go (*how to go*) what to pay attention to (other people's feelings/needs/opinions) which reinforces your function... what you can do for them. Which is put ahead of your feelings, what makes YOU feel good (so you <u>can</u> feel valued). You figure, you'll get to yours eventually. And cuz you ditched your feelings, they ditched YOU. Well actually, they don't really, you just don't hear 'em anymore. Cuz if you did, and they felt *valued* (you would TOO) and you wouldn't try so hard to please other people in order to FEEL good (supported)... cuz you do. You wouldn't be thinking stupid shit like, "Well, I don't wanna be *rude*... tell 'em how I feel (for real)." But it's okay to be rude to ourself (put a muzzle on it) too busy to notice—*taking orders from your brain.* Or you feel bad tellin' your boyfriend how you feel, thinking it's a waste of time. Pretty sure we're the ONLY species, that consider 'us' a waste of time. So, we take on more (as if it isn't already too much) stuff our face, which keeps our focus off stuffing our feelings (*inside*) held against their will. Become protective towards everyone *else* (though it feels like somethin's off) sadly, we don't connect it to ourself... We're *diss*-connected, remember? It's ironic how the part that isn't active (in us) will always be 'over' active towards someone ELSE.

Lookin' for a home, I guess.

For now, it's renting in another...

Where are YOU not paying attention to your feelings, right NOW?

Tell me _____

_____

_____

The healthy masculine energy in a girl, since it's all about drive, aggression and accomplishment is there to steer her ruthlessly in her sport (or career). It's like a SPEAR... It's about passion and nothin's gonna stop her! But then it mistakenly overspills into her romantic department—the manzone (boyfriend). And... She's just punctured one or *both* balls (deflating by the second) as he's whizzing around the room screaming...

"DON'T REDUCE THE TARZAN IN ME!!"

She **also** has a tough time puttin' herself first (with him). Probably cuz she's so busy acting like a guy she forgot... She's the GIRL. Ladies first. ☺ She doesn't come across like this in the beginning, oh nooo... She holds back (is a little more difficult to get). She knows once she gives in, her BIG heart will think nothin' of lettin' her do all the work. So she makes him *work for it* (in the beginning) then it's about what she can do... to prove she's 'special', worth *keeping*... !!#*%@!#*!?ck?! (COULDN'T hold it) And the reason she needs to constantly prove that? She needs to feel she *belongs*... Since she doesn't have a sense of belonging within herself (she feels different) so needs to prove she can fit in. So her relationship won't be about how she's feeling, but how productive she can be (for him). *She doesn't count.* I'm sorry... Somebody has to tell her.

I was that way... When I was human.

Signed, Your Fairy Goddess! Q:-) Graduate.

Although this type of girl is practical, highly capable, quick-witted (ingenious at times) seriously loves a challenge (since it challenges her mind) doesn't like a challenge... when it comes to her emotions. And even though she's mentally strong, not so strong when it comes to speaking about how she feels. Not so strong, in accepting she has the **right** to feel that way. THAT'S not allowed.

Gettin' *emotional*... pissed. Hit a nerve?

The core of the anger is always at the SELF...

No need to be alone... K.

Us tough bitches have to stick together!!

Guys...

For the record, this type of girl has nowhere to turn (never let you know she's hurting). She knows YOU need her to be strong. It's how she *secures* her value (to you). And that's important... cuz she has no value to *self*. So she'll never let you down, cuz she wouldn't be important (in her mind). Her connection to YOU is her connection to herself. Until she retrieves those ruby red slippers... taps three times and remembers!

There's no place like home...

(The power's inside... her)

Course, if you can read her like a BOOK (though she might fight it, at first) know and sense when she's scared—you'll be a rare find. Bring her out of the dark. And in so doing... you'll come out with *her*. Cuz she'll only truly feel protected when she feels *your* strength, which means in order for it to go through to her it'd have to go through you FIRST. She just amped your strength (FOR you). There's a REASON... you two were pulled together (parallel fears) just one's tryin' to wear a suit of armor, prove she's invincible—really heavy. Course you're wondering, "Why's she doin' that, I never asked her to?"

Important message.

Girls...

Your guy didn't just *become* insensitive (an asshole) he didn't just *change*... YOU did. You weren't like that at the beginning. Or, it was totally set up that way when he got used to the idea (you comin' after him) that he's 'priority'. *That's*... how you show him you love him. His feelings are *ahead* of yours. And naturally, you make most of the decisions between you two (you don't trust his mind). You don't even think highly of the way he *thinks*. But he respects the way YOU think. He respects your mind, which means he'll let you run the show, make all the plans (cuz he's not organized) and that makes YOU feel secure (he needs you). So you think... New JOB! Organizing my boy-friend's life. Cool. Hell no. You never end up feeling *cherished*...

Treasured.

You end up feeling **needed**. And it does act as a good buffer to keep you from focusing on your life. Oh yeah! YOU don't really have one. :P No wonder just the thought of having a boyfriend is sooo draining.

YOU do all the work *fool!!*

(Sawry, I had to) :-} Tough love.

Your guy is so used to you being on top of your game (no matter how many things you put up with or handle) when your world COLLAPSES—he's unable to be there for you, the way you want him to (he CAN'T). Those muscles are weak in *him*... he's never had practice (with you). So, like a droopy dick (cute and playful) but won't get the job done. When **he's** upset—YOU jump. Lose sleep, forfeit time with your friends (family) studies, practice, work (to be there for him). One day... You're like, "ENOUGH! I've tolerated all this shit, done all these things for you, for a year and a half." And cuz he's used to *you* doin' that (no matter what YOU say) he'll just see you as a MONSTER. Call you 'selfish'. And you suffer. But the *struggle* girl... is the war inside your own head (not so much with him). That's why you'll ask yourself, "Was I *right* to do this to him? Am I WRONG?" Any and all of these fucked-up type questions should be deleted from your memory bank. Like, immediately!

So you drop HIM.

Focus on your own stuff. NOT pick him up at 3 am (he's wasted) comfort him just cuz he asks (when you're DEAD tired). Since when did being a girl become like being a GUY? Just cuz Edward (or should I say Emily lol) needs to be breast-fed. (*Jokes*) Since when did falling in love mean to suffer? Cuz then we only bitch right after we do all this stuff for YOU. Never let you forget it! And then you REALLY hear it...

Sometimes for the silliest things.

Like right *after* sex...

You: Oh, and by the way you did this, that, these and alllll *that* wrong. Next time get it right.

Your guy: Can I get a do over?

You: No.

It's SO hard when you do like someone and you worry about *losing* them (if you don't do this or that). It's hard to know HOW to say things (without turning them off). That's why I stick to "I *feel*..." State my likes and dislikes that way. I'd be like, "No, I'm not feeling right about this." There is no REASON. You don't have to give any, you just don't feel good about it. Your feelings ARE your reasons.

It doesn't feel good—you're not doing it. You're not *comfortable* doing that. It *doesn't* feel good to you. Your guy can try to argue with you. And... What's he gonna say? "You're wrong". I'd be like, "EXCUSE me? My feelings **can't** be wrong... It's how I **feel**. My perception might be *off* but until it feels right, I'm not doin' it." It's up to HIM to make it right (for YOU). That's an investment of time and *effort* on his part. Your heart can't be fooled (if you don't just listen to his 'words') **watch** what he <u>does</u> for you, in action (*behavior*).

Hey! That's a good idea. Let's prepare a list of conditions! ;D All the non-negociables. Cuz when a guy's in love...

You're the ONLY thing on his mind.

<u>Example:</u>

I'm exhausted. My boyfriend prepares a bath for me... He turns off the lights, puts on my music, bubbles in my bath, little candles along the ledge... Takes off his shirt. He kneels down to wash my hair. *Mmmm... lovin' it!* I smell something. I turn my head—his armpits are smoky!! The flames from the candles STRETCHED allll the way into his ARMPITS! Singed his hairs. LMAO Didn't even faze him. He hadn't even noticed. And that's cuz, I was the only thing on his mind. Ta daa! LOL

If you used to be on your guy's mind (all the time) and not so much now, doesn't mean he doesn't care for YOU. It means somewhere, something <u>changed</u>. You started giving more... he started giving *less* (usually happens when a girl gives 'more'). LOL TBH if you KNOW you're a catch (you're 'it') you rarely feel like giving *more*... you'll just get happier. Which is all he needs (makes him feel successful) and he gets *happier*. For us girls (while with a guy) it's not about *doing*... it's about **being**.

I was tellin' my girl friend (in front of my boyfriend) how I *lovvve* that he does my nails, cuz he gets all serious. Starts with the coarse file, then the finer one... then the one that makes it squeak. Like he's polishing furniture. He starts perspiring on his upper lip, completely makes my heart melt. She's like, "And... What do YOU do for him?" He's like...

"She makes me HAPPY."

Girl's, if you need to address an issue and you're like... "I think that..." Where he could argue *that*... turn it into a competition (*comparison*) try n' come on top (a guy's favorite position), since guys secure themselves with their thought process (facts they know or *think* they know) 'logic' (if he's smart) he can make you see an angle you don't, then wisely make it like it'd be good for YOU (*risky*).

Top advertising firms do it all the time. lol Sucker us in... Make us buy shit we don't even need. Lawyers (most lethal) can say things in a way that messes us up. They speak a million miles an hour—fire off bullets of FACTS!! We can't even think straight. We wobble and drop—right where they want us to. The system was intended to get the truth out, with the added contrast of defense attorneys trained to show or induce doubt, so could be quite challenging as their client will be *seen* as innocent till PROVEN guilty. O:-) So words strategically placed, can make the mind go a certain way, tongue say a certain thing, emotions *react* (unfold a certain way). It doesn't mean your guy might not have your best interest at heart (when arguing a point). I'm just wondering what *pulse* he's followin' (above or below). :-\ Still, until you feel comfortable with it, means something in you doesn't understand it (feel safe with it) feel good about it.

Learning to see life through the eyes of the body...

Feelings CAN'T lie (HIPS don't either). LOL Unless they've been hijacked by the mind.

I remember this roommate. I kept asking him to put a hook on the back of the bathroom door. He'd be like, "Why do you want a hook on the back of the door?" I'm like, "Cuz that's where I put my bath robe." He's like, "I've never seen you wear your bath robe." I'm like, "Yeah. It's white with big PINK hearts. I wear it at night when you're asleep... Instead of walking naked." He's like, "I would just walk naked." I'm like... "Yeah? Well I'd have to charge you." "My NAME is crime—and crime **don't** pay." *What-everrrr.*

Speaking of bathrooms!

Why are you guys always using your dick as a TOWEL rack? Like, what's the point of that? I ask my (current) boyfriend. He's like, "You know *why* baby? It's boner fascination. But the real reason we do that? It's practical... We found another 'use' for it and it's impressive." "*Impressive*... Uh? To who, the TOWEL? K. I'm gonna put my breast in a cup. So it can hold it. Now we *both* have extra uses for them." He's like, "That'll be a cool bra—T-cups." Ugh! I'm like, "K. YOU know how you get up in the morning and you're so PROUD of it—you're practically glowing, just cuz your dick's protruding? The only reason your dick's big, is cuz you're SKINNY." He's like, "K! Straight up. One time I had a dream it was alllll the way up to my armpit. Would I still be too skinny then?" Guys and their inflated imagination. LMAO

As you can see...

No matter what we say they can *always* turn it around. LOL But they can't argue OUR feelings. Unless they're fucked (far as I'm concerned) messed up. Telling you YOU shouldn't be feeling this and you shouldn't be feeling *that*.

Well, don't *should* me asshole...

(And YOU can quote me on that) LOL

Course, then they're like, "You're so sensitive." And you're defensive. You're like, "I'm NOT sensitive." The *truth*... is like a naked girl. (Hard to ignore) Keep that in mind, here ladies. Acknowledgment is very powerful (if you're not disputing it on the inside). They WON'T expect it. When that happens to me... a guy's like, "You're so sensitive, Nichole." I'm like, "Uh... YEAH. I'm a Girl—I'm not BRICK. I feel things." And I noticed that when people tried to make me feel **stupid** (out of sync) 'bout something they were *told*... to mean one thing (mind washed, rinsed and/or recycled by media, friends, family) I'd puncture their blistered REALITY—be completely *supportive* of myself! Then they'd silently question why it was made to be so negative, in the first place. Wouldn't hassle me about it, again. *A TRAIL BLAZER* is what I am! LOL

I dare YOU... to set your own tone... step to your OWN beats. SWAY people to *your* swag.

164.

When we tell a guy how we **feel**, he can't dispute that. A smart guy who loves YOU will try to understand why... Do everything in his power to make you comfortable (even if it doesn't make sense to him). It's about YOU and your comfort zone. Girls who are accustomed to using logic (devoid of feelings) are thinkin', "I can handle this. I've handled a lot worse. I'm smart. I'll figure it out." That's *difficult*... cuz you have to be able to *trust* the guy you're with, that he's gonna be there for YOU. And that's close to impossible when you don't trust *yourself* (never listen to your feelings) don't know what TRUST feels like. Now justified, you need to let logic lead you. Sad thing is...

When LOGIC rules you...magic can't find you.

Responsibility? Oh yeah. You'll be doing allll this stuff for him, he'll be completely dependent on YOU. And like an old purse you won't be able to let it go (not feelin' good enough for anyone else) so staying...

*Magic is a **mystery**...*

It'll pull you in... when you've earned the right to see a little *more*... (of life). Something rich... something different... something **hidden**. It's where a guy goes to *discover*... And cuz he recognizes the value he'll be protective (of YOU). In order for that to happen you would have to *know* your value.

(The test)

Are YOU willing to have someone *else* give to YOU and not feel like you owe them (return it ten times over) top them?

K... me too (need a moment) :'(

Keep in mind...

Just cuz a guy can change things around (make you see them differently) DOESN'T mean he can only do it negatively. The GOOD ones, always make you see yourself in the best possible light (especially when cloaked in darkness) they're wishing they could lend you *their* eyes... see yourself the way they **see** you. The way you ARE but have so many psychological barbed wires (put by yourself or others) can't see clearly.

Example;

My boyfriend and I are studying. I'm near my period (BLOATED) my hair's in hellllville (semi-afro, curly) with chopsticks, outta control. Face... is having a PIMPLE FEST (squeezed them just before he got there) pores are inflamed and huge—coulda planted tulip bulbs in there. He's lookin' at me, he's like "You know what bae, doesn't matter HOW you look... your busted-broomstick hairdo (my whaaat?) toothpaste spots on your pimples (shittles, he noticed) lumpy bits (what he calls my cellulite) YOU'RE beautiful." *Awhh...*

Just to come clean. I use toothpaste on my butt pimples too! Only one time, I put on too much. Had peppermint flavored butt cheeks. LOL

YOU...

(How you see yourself)

You'll know somethin's off when you're thinking stuff like, self-harm, 'who would want me' type shit.

Answer...

The one searching for YOU right now.

Thinking (like you) that YOU don't exist. The one you're gonna end up with. The one, that's gonna be beyyyyond what you now think is possible. If, you cut the strings to negative hurtful bullshit thoughts and remember... *what I'm sayin' to YOU.*

The egg doesn't CHASE the sperm. LOL

Our Recipe

I was asking my boyfriend, WHY you guys never rinse and soak your dish (in water) after eating, so it's easier to *wash*... doesn't harden. So it *doesn't* stick. He's like, "Cuz it's more of a sense of accomplishment." I'm like, "K... So for you guys, a sense of accomplishment *equals* crusty dishes? So good thing we're introdushing *this* into our recipe chapter." He's like, "*Uh... Introdushing?* You might *not* want to put in that recipe. LOL" Gotta invent my own language. Just can't speak THIS one. :P

No douching HERE. xD

A Recipe...

A true remedy for cuts to our image (persona, self-esteem) bruises to our ego, broken pieces... (heart) divided... (mind) bring our soul back (to life) is what we NEED. Trying to manage our parents, studies, jobs, girlfriend, boyfriend (girl friend *drama*) is too much. Give us a BREAK! Pahleeeze. We're in desperate need of finding something we can depend on. Something SOLID.

Don't go there dude.

A Recipe...

Some kind of prescription for all the crap we're going through, would be nice. I concur. A formula that works with all variables—now that we've skidded (unknowingly) into each other's territory (masculine, feminine) aggressive now, passive later...

Typical Scenario:

Girl: "I CAN fill up my own gas tank—it's NOT the fifties anymore." Later. "I really need a hug." Then complains you don't do other things. "YOU never text me *first*. When we hang you're not really protective, you never comment on my eyes."

Guy: "Really. Like ever?"

Girl: "Well, *yeah*... Right before we have sex—you talk about my eyes lips, hips... *everrrrything*."

More messed up scenarios...

When we're pissed (silent) you ask what's *wrong*... and we're like, "I'm FINE." You leave us alone a few days, let us get 'over it' (so you think) then *act* like we've been talking the whole TIME. When we hook up, it's like nothing ever happened...

I believe the answer to all these profound complexities between us, lie in the body (*somewhere*) it can't be outside of us. LOL Something's **wrong** and we're just accepting shit cuz it seems like the norm.

Our roles have been reversed...

Guys are sayin' shit like, "You're such a COWARD. If you don't do this (that)." Where's it written that a girl's gotta be the hero? It's the classic hero's journey where a guy goes and shows bravery, fighting off evil in order to *protect* his woman... family (nation). And even today in action movies where the girl IS the hero it's a **cause** she's motivated to fight for (not a guy).

This distinction is CRITICAL.

A guy GETS his whole manhood thing... from being a hero (in some form or another) so puts most effort *there* (to win this or that), bring something to the community (necessary) be the *toughest*... smartest (singled out) *BADDEST*... (downward spiral). A leader of a gang who headlines the newspaper (to prove himself) so he can stand out (meanest, strongest, most dangerous) his MANHOOD...

With a hero there's always an element of *danger*... something he's **risking** (unknown...). Like, self esteem through theory (idea, discovery) physical injury, through sport (martial arts, wrestling, training) status... an entrepreneur, politician. Life... firefighter, policeman, astronaut, solider. It's how the hero in man is *awakened*. Going for that GIRL... that's sooo out of reach (wakes him up) sets his whole body on fire (literally).

How a guy TRIED to play that coward card on me. LOL (*Dummmb*)

I had broken up with him, so really focused on my career. He's like, "Nichole. Allll you talk about is your projects." I'm like, "Maybe, if you actually **get** a career, you'd have something to TALK about. Bean pole." Always did think he was too skinny—like, I'm sorry! Wrapping my arms around a guy that makes me feel like I'm hugging my grandmother NOT doin' it for me. K! So years later my boyfriend is skinny. See... When you make fun of someone life SAYS... Too bad! You make *fun* of him (her) you're gonna end up with just THAT. Or you say to your parents... I would NEVER do that (go into a certain career) I'm never gonna be with someone like *that*. It happens... If that's really how you feel, keep it a secret. I'm tellin' you... Life has EARS. Seriously. So my current boyfriend (with skinny arms) is readin' this, laughing his head off. I'm like, "Bae, I'm a TOTAL hypocrite. Should I write that in?" He's like, "Nahh... It's implied." Phew!!

So I get this longgg email from the guy he's like, "If you don't read *this* (shit he wrote about me) you're a COWARD." Haaa! Like, I <u>don't</u> have to prove I have balls, to a GUY. Cuz I don't. And I don't need to be brave (to make this guy happy) and prove it, mister vagina mentality. Cuz that's just how they 'trap us'. Cuz to them pussy and coward is the same thing.

"Don't be a PUSSY."

"Like hello! I AM a pussy. That's why I actually **have one**. So that would be kinda difficult, it's in direct conflict with my genetic code. You're the one with the BALLS. So why don't YOU act like you actually have some. I've got tweezers in the car—want me to go get it? And FYI when you look *down*... it'll be staring you in the face... a PUSSY."

Honestly, sometimes I think they should ONLY hand out penises to guys who've *earned* them. All the rest, pure dickless wonders. Don't know *wherrrre* you all come from. Straight up! We have to ask. When and WHY... did guys start being like that, treating us like guys? Well... We did take on some masculine tendencies... *fo shur*. Maybe we also got disconnected (un-screwed) when we got *screwed*... from our sense of value. (Pure silver, stained) ☺

Free samples anyone?!

You guys being a wiener (all authentic horn-dogs rise up) decide to go all out, take what you can (when you can, however YOU can) instead of puttin' your hard earned EFFORT into it (it's ruined so why bother). And, there's no barcode—it's **free!**

You'd think we were going out of business the way we've been handing out pussy. And you know how people get, when things are *cheap* and on SALE. They just grab—and TAKE. No concern whatsoever for the grade (merchandise) it's CHEAP, so who cares. It doesn't matter if it gets used and ends up being something we clean the carburetor with, or something the dog can sleep on (it's still somewhat cozy). And yeah... Some of you girls are like, "I don't have time and patience to play allll these games, make him wait for me."

Life's a Game...

And if you don't know how to PLAY—if you don't know the *rules* of the 'game' then although you're a talented player, it'll never be noticed. Cuz you're running in so many circles (out of bounds) lettin' the other team *slide in...* (hot guy) pissin' off your own teammates (friends) cuz they're tryin' to **tell you**—you're going the WRONG direction (picking lousy guys). You're hearing the cheers, but it's for the *other* guy who's popped your fly (cherry). Everything in life has a give and *take* (although some guys missed that rule book). LOL It has an action, for every re-action. And if **you** want him to keep *taking* keep being ignorant to the FACT that...

a) If you don't pay attention to your feelings (even when they're screaming at you) or ignore them... You'll wonder why people don't pay attention to you (*when you're in pain*). Like, no one cares! (Fine) You just keep it to yourself.

b) People will respond to you the way you respond to *yourself*. No one wants to feel their shit. But if ignored... it will lash out. In the weirdest and definitely at the **worst**... time. <u>Example</u>: Your mom, friend, someone at work FORGETS to give you the 'one' thing you ask for. YOU freak! Big TIME.

(See what I mean)

c) When there's so much **anger** piling up inside you—it fills YOU up! That's allllot of PAIN. And you wonder why you have <u>no</u> patience? Why you snap allll the time, just CAN'T take it anymore. (My bad!)

"THAT'S why, people say I get mad so quick."

d) If you a super A+ student, smart, talented, hot girl don't give yourself TIME to deal with things (bothering YOU) so plan more shit, in order not to deal with it. You'll start looking for escape routes (course you will) cuz you're heading for a CRASH landing. So you jump! Get high (stoned out of your mind, no sense being there) wasted. Yup... Totally justified. You sooo need to get DRUNK. The real message?

Telling yourself... You're NOT WORTH THE TIME.

When you feel used, sad, bad (or mad) sometimes you don't even know that you're feeling *that*. For it to pass through you (get out of your system) you'd have to first acknowledge THOSE feelings. So it's not stored, creating pressure waiting for a release. Knowing you... it'll be dealt with in *time* (translation: never). Or you'll take a jog. Go to the gym. When you do what you think is right (not <u>deal</u>) which is what you've been conditioned to *feel* is right (due to your up-bringing, life or circumstances) it makes you **believe** that you're no big deal... it's not *worth* the time (it's a part of you) it's always worth the time. No worries! I'm sure I'll have to tell you again.

We... just need to... TALK <3

Life is here for YOU... (*to guide you*)

To show you through nature (your body) signals n' reactions what works and *doesn't* (work) in a relationship. Cuz no matter what you read, who you talk to it's STILL.. messed up. Frustration builds, you're exasperated (confused) continue to go *off* course. Desperate to find the right exit you keep going round and round (making the *same* mistakes) and since you act like a guy... What do most guys hate?

STOPPING for directions...

It makes them feel stupid. (Fair)

So, they pass the same off ramp two (three) four times, **still** not stop to ASK. And stop drum driving! That shit's dangerous (and annoying). What's the SECRET recipe for us to get guys to do *things*... right? How do we let them know, without actually sounding like we're telling them what to do? So they won't *fight* it? We HYPNOTIZE them! *Nahhh*....

The simplest way...

Saying NO to what we **don't** agree with. Simple... but difficult! It's hard if we like YOU. If we *can* handle it, it'll allow you to **keep** trying (till you get it right) without feeling stupid, inferior (a dumbass). It'll help you *learn* without giving you directions (which we know you hate). Otherwise, it doesn't matter how nicely we put it, how gentle we sound, you may still feel under par. Unless you ask us. Be direct girls... so they KNOW. Am I on or off guys?

Cuz then we just get into this HUGE fight and you guy's are like, "You're always TELLING me what to do!" (Bitch) Gentlemen... YOU might want to keep this in mind. Girls work like life... When you do something in life that *doesn't* work—you don't get the desired result. Same with a US... You don't do what works... no RESULT.

It's important that we look '*up to you*'...

Getting away with telling you what to do, makes it challenging to look up to YOU. It needs to be *your* choice... we're just guiding you. Which is NOT to say you guys should be like, "Yo! It's MY decision. Like it or not." It's not about being a *dictator*. It's makin' a decision, checking with your *woman*... is she okay with it? Does it make her happy? Is she comfortable with it? At ease... does it make her feel good? Now... you're blending with her fabric (a very warm place to be). ;<>

And just cuz she's looking up to you (which *technically* you're designed to have her do) doesn't mean she's surrendering to YOU (givin' in) like it says, in all those lovey dovey songs (books) 'surrender to your man'.

The way I see it...

If I'm gonna give it. I'm gonna give it up, to the man of 'my choice'. As in... not Mr. Right (this second) Mr. Right—PERIOD. Cuz I wanna guy who can take care of me... better than I can take care of MYSELF. Who can lead me... *better* than I lead myself. So definitely sees when I'm overdoing it (taking on too much) putting up with too much shit and brings it to my attention. Who pampers me, better than I pamper *myself* (weekend trips, romantic gestures, gifts, cards) in short— *I WANT A MAN WHO'S A BETTER MAN TO ME* than I am to myself. And I'm a heck of a man! Lmao Tall order, I know.

NEED TO LOOK UP TO MY MAN.

When it comes to NOT telling a guy what to do (*how to do it*) we need to let him have his way here. "NOOOO!! *Stupid bitch...*" (You're thinking) Hear me out. Every guy has an inherited compass in his genes, (*sooo* into pointing) you didn't know? You've been using your *head* the wrong way girl. Don't think that's what they meant when they said—let's put our heads together. HAAAAA! Guys, have a finely tuned inner device directing them, or they wouldn't alllll know to dive for that *one* egg. Party time in Spermville. ☺ They'd be all over the place. Production would STALL. It'd be a mess. Every guy's organ is designed to point (the *right* way).

(Ya like that, huh dude?)

Feed the animal, keep 'em tamed... LOL

Back to your compass!

It comes to FULL alert—calibrated automatically (for fine tuning) hopefully no environmental interference (zipper JAMMED). A *wide* range (we like). G spot *sensor* (*yummm*) operates perfectly, not prematurely. Course if it's spinning out of CONTROL... that can be an issue. Waaay too much stimulus. Once your inner device is locked on target and appropriate *measures* have been confirmed. Perky. Tight. Built... just can't refuse a babe YOU follow. It makes hormones *flow*...

Girls and DIRECTIONS...

(Let's NOT even go there)

Yeah... GPS now! Not when I was a kid, driving with my dad on the freeway. He'd throw the map in my face be like, "READ!" I'm like, "Dad I CAN'T. There's too MANY lines and they're allll different colors. I don't know what to follow!" He's like, "Just follow the ROAD we're supposed to get on from the freeway." "K." We're driving sooo fast, the window's open and the MAP'S glued to my whole entire body. A map with boobs! HAAA! Then he's like, "Have you found it?" I feel sooo much PRESSURE. Like! My father's meeting and his WHOLE future hinges on whether my eye can LOCATE out of a thousand little squiggly red, green and blue **LINES** the 'exact' one, we're supposed to follow. And besides, it reminds me of the *insides* of a human body. Just like, in anatomy class allll those veins. *Grossss.*

To reiterate my point (girls and *directions* :P)

My BFF is always bitching when someone tries to give her directions over the phone. She's like, "By the time they're finished, I've already forgotten! So what's the point?" More PROOF. I was gettin' some acupuncture treatment from this Chinese lady (thick accent). I call her from the parking lot. "Hey, I'm early do you want me to come up?" "Yes! Come."

While I'm on her table she's like, "TODAY... You come on time. NO lost." "No... Today's our FOURTH week. It takes me ten times of getting lost, to know every way NOT to come. So now, I won't get lost." She's like, "Yes me too, not good with directions. My husband say, "YOU only know to go **to job... school... home...**" I'm like, "Reeeally? You too!" She's like, "Yes... Don't know why." Maybe, it's universal. LOL Acupuncture really helps when you have *tense* issues.

Which wouldn't have happened, if I hadn't STOPPED training. Major release. H<u>ad</u> a boyfriend. (Another major release) Gave myself time to do a thing called... CHILL. K, first time she punctured me those tiny needles, was scary. Then something really interesting happened. I was lying there with needles *allll* over my body, one right on top of 'it' (yup *that* spot). It starts to vibrate. Just like, when you're lyin' in bed and have your cell phone resting (there) and it's set to vibrate— SOMEONE CALLS!! Lmao That's what it felt like. I'm thinkin'... Hmm? That's interesting, my crotch is vibrating. So I'm like, "Hey... my crotch is talking to me. It's *buzzing*." She's like, "Oh... That's good. It mean your Chi is starting to circulate. Your Chi energy has been blocked." I'm like, "But HOW? There's been NO guy!" "NOT *that* kind block, funny girl. This is why... so hard for YOU to sleep. Be calm. Relax. Too much ANXIETY." And my mechanic keeps saying it's cuz I'm not gettin' laid. Whoa... My Chi's STIMULATED—I'm sooo excited!

And yeah, guys... girls get excited over *practically* everything (so this qualifies). That's why we scream and giggle when we see our friend *after* school. You'd think we hadn't seen her a whole year! Close, it was third period—and SOOO much has happened since!!

Forget it. You wouldn't understand.

Chi BTW is also known as 'vital life force', 'qi', 'prana' or 'divine essence', even though it's invisible, it's something we feel every DAY. If you can't wait to do something, your Chi is most likely strong. Can't get out of bed? It's probably weak (my issue). Angry, frustrated or depressed? It's probably stuck (my issue too). Our attitude and emotions (how we feel) are <u>all</u> influenced by our 'Chi'. In Chinese medicine a strong Chi is matched to excellent health, mental clarity and physical vitality. A weakened or blocked flow of this energy force is the beginning of allll disease. Acupuncture is effective cuz it acts on this energetic level. The needles stimulate the points in the body to reactivate *flow*—I know some friends who need it. LOL

I leave my acupuncturist sooo HAPPY. My Chi is comin' back! Yaay. I go to train my client and I'm sittin' there on a bench, she's sittin' on a matt with her back towards me, close. It *happens*... My crotch starts talking to me AGAIN. It's *vibrating* against her back. (Vag contact) She's like, "What's *that*?" I freak. I dunno what to say! I'm like, "What's WHAT?" Act like nothin's happening. She's like, "Don't you feel *that?*" "Feel what?" (Busted) My Chi is vibrating in such a HUGE way. I'm like, OMG! How do I stop it? It's drilling a hole in my client's BACK! You'd think—I have a penis. I'm trying to stay calm. Danggg, I forgot to ask my Chinese lady HOW to turn it off. Roflll Finally I'm like, "Oh that... It's just my Chi waking up. No worries." She gives me the STRANGEST look.

My conclusion:

Girls & Directions...

Directions for most girls... NOT our talent. North, south, east west, they don't come natural to us. Life, career, choices (**direction**) they don't come *easy*—just like our anatomy. LOL You guys have things come *quick* (well, some things). Why do you think we talk *allll* over the place? (No direction, man) Could be why it takes you guys so long, to figure us out. ;D

Take a second...

No really. Take a SECOND.

I'm serious, this is HIGH priority.

Don't laugh...

Lean in.

Closerrrr...

That's better.

I can FEEL you.

And what I feel I can trust.

WAKE THE FUCK UP!!

You just got a legit and *juicaaay* piece of info (guys). Absorb it. Digest it. And if you have to, swallow <u>this</u> page. Cuz I'm only going to say this ONCE.

Nothing about us follows a **path**...

(God that took a lot out of me)

K. I'm a drama queen, can we move on?

But the path thing is true. Except for the egg (who's already set on route) she *can't* get lost—hard enough when she **changes** her mind (goes off schedule) SCARES the shit out of us when that happens! Otherwise, it'd just be too easy for you guys to figure us out. No fun there! And definitely not going to happen. We're here to lead you off the straight and narrow. YOUR choice if you've driven off the edge, dude.

WE'RE HERE TO ROCK YOUR WORLD!

Test your reflexes, knock you off your feet—and into the arms of a whole new dimension. 3D CAN'T touch this! We have things poppin' out at you that you can actually **feel**. LOL It's called, the unspoken language of the *flesh*. (Yummy place to be) I'm talkin' about finding *solace* in the bosom of passion dude. Yes... A big WORD is installed here, cuz it's that important. And don't go lookin' for a big bosom in the glossary, it's solace... Stoopid. Or, you can look it up in an actual 'book' like they did in the olden times, when wizards and dragons ruled the earth.

We're talkin' about finding something **real**—YOUR woman dude. And that doesn't just get handed to you. You earn that. NGL. You get that when you decide to be brave and withstand a̲l̲l̲l̲ her (many) ways. Like, you waive the whole—WHAT KIND OF LOGIC IS THAT?! Shit... you do. And... **That makes absolutely NO sense** (routine). When we finally tell you WHY we're upset and you're like, "You're allll over the place." Cuz you don't get it. Sorry... Need to keep it real. Need to keep it personal. *We can kiss n' make up later.*

(I know you can take it)

Here's the deal!

YOU guys talk straight (good with direction) we do not. We *skate* around things, that's why you're the *animal* and we're the human. Even our language is designed to match our psyche (which is in line with *our* system). Just like your communication *style* is linked to your system. Which is WHY you always want us to get to the point. LOL *What's-a-matter...* gotta tongue typo? NOT coming out the way you want it to?

English 101 (New version)

If you look at the LAST two letters in the word *penis* (YOU guys always want us to look at it anyway) we'd get... I. S.

Infinite Source...

That's probably why you're like, "Hey baby... look how BIG my cock is." Wishin' we'd be like... "*Ooooh...* lemme put it in my mouth." I'd be like, "So, where's the *rest* of it? Oh. *That's* it? Got a magnifying glass in my car... want me to go get it?"

SUPPLY – CONTINUATION – MANKIND ☺

(True)

180.

Hold up!

In order to reach FULL potential it needs to be *drawn out*...

(Feeling warm and tingly, yet?)

YOU guys help us sift through our *thoughts* so we can actually *see* where we're going, give structure to our sentences (so it does have an ENDING) when you stop us mid way and say, "Okay. Let's go over this *one* thing first. Then we'll move on to the next one." Especially if we're PISSED. We talk about many things all at once! K. That's a talent. ;D But then we get all worked up. And you stop and say the most *perfect* thing... *Ahhh... feel so much better.* And that's SO important, cuz our entire life feels like it's *SPINNING* out of control. There's alll this shit being said about us, that are LIES!! It's a GOSSIPFEST. Social media mania! AHHHH! Texts being passed about us that's ruining our lives! (WWJT)

And YOU... just *understand* us.

We love you. oxo

Top 8 Things To Do...
When She's PISSED.

Get it right.

(Pahleeeze)

These are designed specifically for someone YOU love, not using, (trying to get in bed with) trying to get back at, trying to cancel out with someone else (hate) need to break up with. Warning...

It will be torturous

(Especially if it's been a while)

Listen: (Let her take it allll out)

And when she pauses (IF that actually happens) KEEP asking... "What *else* baby? What else is bothering (worrying, pissing you off, scaring) YOU?" Until she runs out of things to say. If you've never done this, it's gonna take some time. Cuz it does build up. Like, interest on a debt. First payment can *really* tax you. This way when she's pissed (*pmsing*) you won't have an AVALANCHE of shit thrown at you. And YOU won't be buried alive (true that). And don't *think* you can do this ten minutes before a game—we HATE that. Cuz we feel like we're on a timeline (*worst* feeling ever). It equals... NOT important. Not truly valued... caring minimal. And what does *that* mean for YOU ~~dickhead~~ I mean dude? *Aaaah...* fuck it. I meant to say dickhead. K. It means... No SEX (very long time) no kissing, no touching. Sucks... and not the way you want it to (couldn't resist). LOL

This part's IMPORTANT. We absolutely need to take out ALLLL the bad stuff (emotions). The pressure **holding it** is what's killing us. There's emotional weight attached to *those* words. Which is attached... to visual images (events). It's like having a twenty pound dumbbell around your neck (ALL day). So, when we finally **tell you** it's as if those events *left* our body (cuz that's where they're stored). And we feel lighter and more comfortable immediately! Which means, we're going to be less of a pain (for YOU) cuz it's a package deal. :P We come with our 'package'. And if you're careful you'll get a chance to unwrap it. And you guys thought you were the only ONE with a package. Lmao

Ours is hidden...

And another thing!

183.

We don't need you to *only* listen. Our plant can do that (or BFF). We need YOU to be there. Like, right *there*... So when we tell YOU what happened and it's like TWO minds there, *instead* of one. That way you can maybe *see* something we missed (ignored) totally clueless about. Then your input is valuable cuz you went *through it* with us, used your instincts, brain power and amazing perceptive skills to point things out WE WERE TOO EMOTIONAL TO CATCH. <3

Don't TOUCH her...

Don't even TRY. And if she lets you sit next to her cuz she's not seething and foaming at the mouth anymore, don't sit next to her and put your hand on her *shoulder* (thigh) knee... or low back. Unless you wanna end up with a NUB for a wrist. DON'T do it! These are *sexual* hot spots—reads as, you wanting sex or hoping you'll get some, soon after. DON'T go there. Most guys get closer through physical means (touch, kiss, taste, feel) totally pulls YOU in (can't remember why you're there, last name or what you were saying) like, you've been ABDUCTED.

(Manwhores don't apply)

Guys who sleep with anything that has a pulse, don't work the same way. They don't work PERIOD. They're ruptured... Emotional wall crumbled, feel nothing. The way to get **closer** when we're pissed, is through *words*... we're susceptible to *them*. It's our weakness. Some dick can come along, says the right **words**—OPEN season!! Guys who are skilled at saying the right words (to the right girl) will get her. Sadly. It'll never occur to her to challenge your words—UNTIL NOW. *Haaa!* For us... words are very powerful.

We fall in love... through what we HEAR.

Especially when it's for real—truthful (difficult for you to say) like, admitting you can't stop thinkin' about us. Takes us right in (if there's already an attraction). YOU guys fall in love... (first) through what you SEE. Like that was hard to figure out. LOL That's *your* starting point. Whether it sustains you or not—a whole OTHER story. The girl

184.

that holds you... is the girl that *knows* you (or how to get to YOU). It's how you guys feel connected—through your body's senses (taste, touch, smell). How we make you *feel*... when you're with us (our face when we smile) how we feel in your arms. Our scent, eyes (you can't look away). We *live* inside your mind...

Guys... physically *present* mentally ABSENT. LOL

Back to not touching us when we're *pissed*...

Let's say we had a fight. After a while, we start talkin' to you. We don't mind you sitting in our *space*. Continue to **talk** to us... But don't touch us! UNTIL we give you the OK—cuz that's not how weeee connect. It's the words YOU say... that tip-toe in our ear *float down*... plant an invisible sticky note on our heart (filling a temporary deflated being). We need to smile on the *inside* first...

Then we can smile on the *outside* (with our body). It's relaxed and content (you're not tryin' to come on to us). So we'll giggle, especially if we think what you said is cute (funny). We'll lean *towards* you... touch your arm, hand, thigh. And if you don't pay attention to our advances... cuz you're still mentally *really* engaged on our story, our seductive instincts will try to push YOU out of your mind and into our romantic orbit (your *senses*). Our love arrows are always aiming for your heart (which is in your BODY not your mind). The guy that controls his *impulses*... is the one we feel we can depend on. He's not just after our VAG. It's actually all of us he WANTS. And that's a turn on. Just so you know.

ONE more thing.

Don't make the stupid mistake of thinkin' what your friends say to do, (when we're pissed) is effective. Like, letting us cool off for a few days. Cuz girls DON'T cool off. They heat up! They're not designed to cool off (that wouldn't be practical). ;D We're designed to overflow—blow up, if we don't take things out. And then, every little thing you DO makes us wanna rip your face OFF. Cuz you have not addressed our hell. You have not eagerly pressed forward askin', (often) "Are you ready to talk? Let's TALK..." And that's cuz, in your mind you're giving us 'space'. A lazy guy's way of trying to *appear* like he's there for you (but not). So he can say, "Well, I tried. But she's so mad she just ignores me." Or "I hope it's okay when we talk next." "I hope it blows over." No brah... she'll *roast* you. The more 'space' you give her the more her mind will <u>find</u> things about YOU to be pissed off about.

Pro-tip: He who attempts *more* gets there (sooner).

Duhhh...

Don't give up so FAST. You wouldn't if it was a try-out at school. If you really want to make the team (figure out the formula, land the scholarship, whatever) you'll try AGAIN (and AGAIN). With the resolve... that whatever it takes, you're gonna get it. Plus! When you make just 'one' little attempt, we see it as you not caring (enough) even if it seems huge to YOU. Even if we *look* like we have fangs, comin' out of our pupils. Ignore. Continue to be funny, charming, witty... real. Flowers, cards, stuffed animals, helping with something we need, concert (music, more words we hear). Most important. Just get it through your head (BOTH OF THEM) we girls 'need' to talk. We're talking creatures. That shows you care. We need to see you're into what we're saying. You can't fake THAT. We need to see you need us to talk about it (cuz you need to understand where we're at).

PS If you're truly in love, you wouldn't be able to just 'give up' it would hurt you too much. You'd keep trying.

Sometimes...

We're so MAD...

We want you to *prove* how much you care, by being persistent (not forceful, gentle) but continuingly asking. The more we *refuse* (with attitude) and you come back—undeterred, undisturbed, unstoppable (very impressive) the more we feel **valued**. Look up to you (for your stamina). We need endurance (in every way). True that! LOL This is NOT for a guy, where we've made it clear—we don't want YOU. This is *reserved* for close true guy friends and or boyfriend.

186.

To YOU guys who haven't received (yet) your perfect girl, rest assured, that special blend of a GIRL is on route back to YOU. In a maze... but still searching (praying you'll find her) or healing... (from the wrong one). So don't waste time. Don't keep the one that's **right** WAITING. The **one** you won't feel awkward... dumb, under par. The **one** you won't run out of things to say to. The **one** that gives you energy, even though you're DEAD tired, the **one**... that makes you feel like you can do anyyything. The one you want to be *better* for.

Your Queen...

Distract Her: (Suggested after phase one—listening)

Your girl needs to go out and do SOMETHING (shopping, nails, hair, drive, movie). Just to name a few. And not Sex. Cuz THAT only heals everything bothering YOU. She needs to be in a totally different environment so her body will start to absorb *that* (provided she's released shit, it's not plugging up her system and there's *room*). And... DON'T say, "You're just irritable." We KNOW this!! And even though you might be thinking, "Well... If I just point it out, she'll get it." Um... We don't need to be reminded that we're **miserable**. That doesn't help. DO something about it. But for GOD'S SAKE don't touch us. You have to work your way 'up' again (or in your case *down*) LOL through our heart section. And it doesn't matter if it's at night—take her out of *that* room (where she's angry). Suggest a drive to the lake (beach) for a NIGHT picnic. Remember... Girls **equal** estrogen (a feeling *hormone*) they're processing and absorbing things allll day. That's why when things are bothering us we **can't** just brush it off (forget about it) even though we might try, it's stuck *'in our body'*. We need to talk it... OUT. So **don't** frigging try and touch us. *Touch our heart...* it's 'key' to everything (in this world).

Good practice!

That's why btw we are PROGRAMMED to talk, it makes us feel **good**. Just like, you're programmed to fuck. It makes YOU feel good, it's how you talk. I can just see a guy, be like... "Babe. We need to *talk...* hold on let me get the microphone. Speak softly. No tapping." ROFLMFAO A communicating *tool* fo shur.

Seriously, when do you guys *talk* about your feelings? When you're having sex... or we're making out (soon-to-be-sex). A spontaneous emotional eruption. LOL

One time...

I'm SO pissed. I go to the gymnasium and sit on the bleachers. Couple of guys are playing basketball, I ask if I can join in. After... I tell them how I'm really upset about this guy. They're like, "RUN. Just run till you can't feel *anything*." So I went and ran as fast as I could. Till I got pulled over by an officer cuz he thought I was distressed. LOL

That makes sense, when you guys are upset—you're action oriented! So yeah... fucking totally understandable, you wouldn't necessarily TALK about it right away (like we would). You'd play a game. Do a *contact* sport. Wrestle, do something constructive like... lose a tooth. But hey! You feel so much better after. We on the other hand, would have a *TALKATHON*...

We handle our pain differently.

We need to talk... And we also need our distractions, being in a place that stimulates other senses like, smells, sounds, sight (beautiful things) touch... soft cuddly things. So we can focus on THAT. Rejuvenate ourselves. Sometimes, depending on our connection with YOU we might *just* need to be held. (Like now) Don't say anything just go and *hold* her.

Do not underestimate the POWER OF A HUG... cuz then we just absorb YOU and your *feelings* for us (instead). It suffocates alllll the bad stuff. So we can breathe again. Like, how easy is that? But, if we're furious don't 'try' to hug us. And DON'T tell us to calm down! EITHER. Cuz we'll do the opposite. If we're ranting about all this crap between us (on the phone) and you **distract** with... "*I miss you.*" YOU will be in shock how our mood changes. No matter how upset we are at you (our world, best friend, parent).

Speaking of distractions...

Omg! There was this guy I knew for years (like a brother). He was my roommate. He was so into science and shit, he named his dog Pavlov. Always serious. I'm stressed... I decide to paint my toes. And FYI (guys) there's a lot of precision and work involved. It's not just about painting them—it's gotta look GOOD. It's gotta look clean. Then, there's always the *toe* second from the end (kinda shy) so hides behind the other one. Which totally screws up our PAINT job. And now we like, literally have to stretch allll our toes apart—HOLD them there. So it dries (or it'll smudge). A real pain. I decided to go with metallic purple, against my creamy white skin. *Wicccked...* I walk up to him... *Swaaag!* I'm like, "Hey! Whatta you think of my TOES?" He's like, "Cool. K... Back to the **real** world." I'm like, "Excuuuse me? This IS the real world, cuz the real world's about beauty... beauty *heals*... and that's from GOD. Like, honestly... every time you see something beautiful doesn't it make you feel GOOD?" I walk away. Dweeb. Later... We're watching television, he's eating a bag of chips and I put my feet up on the sofa (in front of him) wiggle my toes. I'm like, "I can't understand how you can look at my feet and not see how PRETTY and shiny they are. Like, doesn't it make you feel *gooood* lookin' at 'em?" He's like, "Well, I didn't wanna tell you... It turns me on." Uh—huh!! (Yassss!) I'm like, "That *totally* made my day. I'm gonna go put coconut oil on my legs." He's like... "K, I'm gonna go put chocolate syrup on my dick."

Don't think anyone told him chocolate is BAD for dogs. Lmao

NOT the type of distraction we're talkin' about. ;D

Don't Blow It Off: (MAJOR taboo)

If you treat it seriously... we'll feel seriously VALUED (cared for) and seriously *respond* to YOU (in other ways). I'm tellin' you right now... you know that..."Where are you? You're somewhere else..." thing we say when we're lookin' right at YOU but your mind's thinkin' about practice (a test) friend's shit? We feel that! And youuuu will come to know (oh so quickly) that you TOO will feel that (when *we're* not paying attention... and your dick's ABOUT to explode—or tryin' to.

And we don't care! We're like, "I can't. I need to stop." When you do shit like that... we feel like we're not important. Like a bag of shit. Don't blow us off. Guaranteed... you're balls are gonna blow up (like purple balloons). In other words... Just like your whole world *STOPS* when that moment *comes* (release) WE wanna be your only focus (when we're pissed). And that's the truth. Unless your world 'stops' (when we need you) we will... *make you wait n' suffer* (whether we're aware of it or not). Translated: You don't blink. You don't breathe. You don't scratch your balls (k, an itch is an itch) but *definitely* don't fart, even if you have to—HOLD IT.

I know that's hard for allll you fart enthusiasts, who like to experiment with your farts. Capture the smell in a jar and see how long it lasts. Where I come from, that's a mark against YOU—potentially damaging the ether layers. A Fairy Goddess is very sensitive to *smells*.

The urgent message here...

Not blowing us (or your orifice) off. MAKE us feel like we're the **only** girl in the world—forget that! Galaxy!!! Cuz at that moment 'we are'. It's what we're craving. We need to feel important cuz we're in pain (but most definitely *shouldn't* be just then). Your complete and UNDIVIDED attention is highly imperative. It can even be something stupid like we think we're fat. K! That's a whole other chapter. I feel for you Earth boy...

Interject:

Give her a FOOT rub, it's linked to brain *waves*. Scientifically proven. And even more than *they* understand! If it's hard (for you) just pretend it's something *else*... since you're accustomed to pleasing yourself (a lot). :=) K. Close your eyes and pretend *HARDER* (try to make it last more than seven seconds). LOL I realize that might be challenging (right now). :=) So my guy's giving me a foot massage. After he's like, "You know, the strangest thing happened. I got a *hard-on* while I was massaging your feet. (Light bulb MOMENT) ☺ It *was* your face... how you were enjoying it—it got me HOT."

A note to ALLLL guys...

You playing with our hair, massaging our head, feels AWESOME to us. Kinda like, when you're doin' your own head. We love it. Our wash that is.

(K... the head too)

Taking a comb and brushing out all our tangles *after* you've put in LOADS of conditioner is a great pampering session. Provided you don't scalp us with the *comb* cuz you're impatient. DON'T yank! If you're feelin' affectionate... WARNING. Don't let your lip ring, nose ring or eyebrow ring get caught in *our* hair—not gonna end up pretty.

6. Ask If We Need Our OWN Space:

And if we say 'yes' it means we DO. And don't feel nervous, sometimes a girl needs to *enjoy* missing you. If she's really sad and it has nothing to do with you, she'll need to feel things through (a.k.a. processing). And we do that, when we transfer our emotions to a SAD song (cry to it) or a sad movie. It feels good to us when we direct the *weight* of our emotions to a song (movie) and we're not weighed down anymore. Now, you don't have to ask why we have real sad movies in STORAGE. It's a *feeling* thing...

You don't have to get it. LOL

Girls...

Next time you're really upset and the door bells rings and you open the door, see a box of real sad movies sittin' there. He's a keeper. (He's READ the book) ;D

DON'T Multi-Task: (OVER-rated)

When we come to talk to you about something *urgent* (pressing), ~~something we're pissed off about~~ Forget that! When we come to you **period**—don't keep doin' what you're doin', glancing over from time to time sayin' shit like, "I'm listening, go ahead." That's **not** paying attention. That's cruel. MULTI-tasking on <u>our</u> time doesn't give you points (with us). It's like, when you're trying to be efficient with our boobs—a little here, little *there*. Makin' sure you've covered all the bases, THAT feels so mechanical (rushed). We hate it when you do that. It's like us... Taking your dick between our hands and rubbing it really HARD. Like, we're tryin' to start a FIRE. On second thought... you'll take what you can get (as far as your dick's concerned) bad example. So I ask my boyfriend if YOU guys would actually *like* that. He's like, "ACTUALLY... That *would* feel good. Unless a pube or two got caught in with it and the whole bush caught fire." I'm like, "*Hmm? I thought guys ONLY go up n' down, when they do themselves.*" ^.^ He's like, "You think a guy's not gonna try and find 'new' ways, after he's done it a thousand times?" Lmfao Still... Stop tryin' to do things you *think* we want and pay attention to what we do *want*. Don't work us the way you'd like to be worked. We've got our <u>own</u> equipment. Learn it. Master it... and make damn sure you haven't mishandled it. Cuz it does bite. .)

I'm *such* a bitch...

Instead of multi-tasking WATCH what we're responding to. TBH we need to be the center and **only** focus of your universe—if you're *everrrr* to enter 'our' universe (*sweet spot*). What if... you're in, and it's so *BIGGG* (SO *thick*) hard as STEEL *throbbing* like craaazy—in sync with your whole entire body, as you *slide it in and out*... she's like, "Keep going, just gotta answer this text." @_@ And if YOU stop to TEXT man—there's something <u>seriously</u> wrong with you.

I would check with your doctor.

(Maybe you expired) *Jokes*

I remember my ex. I STOPPED... mid way (had him pull out). I HAD to! I needed to PEE (so bad). It was legit. I'm freshening up, I'm rebrushing my teeth, putting perfume on my inner thigh, taking my time—he's pacing the *FUCKEN WALLS*. Walkin' in circles around the room. And I'm all happy (cuz I peed). K, I know he suffered when I did that, but it was justifiable. AND you don't know what happened next, so *hushhh*...

K... So his slam dunk is interrupted by my 'half time'. Happens. At least no one called *foul*. LOL He nails the rebound. Double dribbles allll the way to the hoop (like, both hands). Luckily, he didn't get benched, a shot to the nuts, fo shur. Definite low blow. When I come back... He's like an ANIMAL. A very *hungry* animal. He laid me *on the bed*... didn't know what to expect he seemed a little *pissed*. Ya think! After... He's like "*Aaaahh...* I came so hard. Omg... It was the longest everrr. Whoa. Incredible." *Hmm...?*

Sex 101:

INTERRUPTION...

Can be a good thing!

And don't even THINK of tryin' to reverse it on us, guys. Makin' us WAIT for it. (As if you could) It's not the same with us... cuz you'll just have to start *allll* over. See, we're even **designed** to need your full attention (or YOU lose it). So *PASS* on multi-tasking! We need all your attention. Just like your car. Only we'll run you down—fueled or empty, it's in our blood to spew. (If you piss us off) K, I guess I made my *point*. Takes us a little longer, since we're created to punctuate things a little differently. LOL

And some of us, a lot louder. *;<>*

Inspire HER...

I love it when my guy inspires me! Not, by telling me to 'not let it bother me' cuz that just tells me he's too lazy to *actually* think of a way to help me and pretty much, wants me to handle it on my own. Guys... we lovvve to see *effort* on your part, it equals 'depth' of love. And it doesn't matter if you have <u>all</u> the answers. YOU just **trying** is like water to our plant. <3 <3 <3

We grow *closer* to you... and you 'grow'. :P

This is where the listening phase is mandatory. We can't receive YOU (and your brilliance) when we're stuffed with all this suppressed crap.

Oh! And *once* you tell us all this good shit about us and inspire us—we'll need to hear it *again* (next time). We'll forget. In all fairness, you gotta understand the **next** time is like a TOTALLY new situation (even if it's the same topic). So we treat it like it's a completely new thing to be upset about. So, logically stating the FACTS (without emotion) so we can see clearly, while you reinstate our 'track record' (current shit we are dealing with and conquering) so we know **we'll win**, grounds us in our *value* (SELF worth).

THAT gives us power.

Add to that a list of our strengths (special qualities) and just like a muscle, where our focus is... izzz where our strength is. Ever notice in the gym, while you're lifting weights you will *look* at the arm that *isn't* goin' up? You may even *talk* to it. Scream at it. FOCUS on it—till it moves. Or even with wrestling... lookin' where the guy's got you pinned—gives strength to *that* area.

What we <u>focus</u> on will give 'it' more *strength.*

Crummy mood... more crumbs followin' you. Something happy, more happy feelings. Presenting a LIST... of all our wonderful abilities, will make us feel awesome. And it's NOT too much to do—you've memorized football plays much longer than this.

IMPORTANT:

1) When you focus on your **weak points**—you'll feel weak allll over.

2) When you focus on where you're **strong**—you'll feel like you can do anything.

That's why a lot of times when you're talkin' about all your shit and it's really **painful**—you feel like *helllll* (at first). Especially if you do it over and over and over again. That's *where* your focus is. Whatever you do—don't stay there! Let out the bad shit physically, too. Get your energy UP. Cuz now, there'll be actual *room* to store some good stuff in there. You just cleaned HOUSE. Once girls are **released** of their shit, you guys will be shocked (pleasantly) and surprised, when you do

it the way we *need* it, how much more quickly your *release* will be...
LOL Put her focus on what's GREAT about her! And be authentic we
don't like when it's automatic and mechanical... That way we'll really
be into it, no need to go through the 'burning bush' epic. LOL

REVIEW:

Girls, talk and talk and TALK we don't *get* to the point—we **are** the
POINT. Etch that in stone! You have your point... we have ours. ;<>
And we don't use commas in our conversation either. Which is
why, you might find yourself gasping for air... trying to swallow air
or just reaching for air (sigh a lot) when you're listening *CUZ
THERE'S NO END IN SIGHT!!* That's why it can be so exhausting—a
real test of love. :-7 I email my brother from Los Angeles, took forty
minutes to write it. When I call I'm like, "Did you get it?" He's like,
"YEAH..." "And...?" "And... I was turnin' PURPLE ten minutes into it
cuz you DON'T USE COMAS!!"

(Piss worthy)

The important thing you guys need to know

YOU...

Keep us focused and *centered* when we're distracted, going in too
many directions (HATE it when that happens). You'll be telling us
over and **over** again, "You're trying to do too many things!" You
guys... sure like repeating yourselves. LOL

K. If we're not *hearing* YOU then you're not communicating in a way
that's *effective*. Sometimes we might be a *little* stubborn... K, a lot.
You guys keep us on track. Especially when we're trying to be 'all'
things to all PEOPLE. And now we're moody (emotional) cuz on our
period, best friend just got used (extremely bitchy) or factor X. Any
and all of the above plus everything else, I haven't mentioned. You're
the moon that lights our way, with your straight forward thinking
(*logic*) so we can actually 'see' where we're going. For all you creative
types (it's in reverse) *we're* the moon that lights your way. We present
logic when it's necessary... YOU doubting yourself.

When we're MAD we just keep bringing up *everything* from A to Zeeeee. YOU help us see that we're not that far off—land is CLOSE. It's not as bad as we think. We can do it. You give us direction man (when we need it most)! You help us <u>focus</u>. You bring us in... when we're drowning in a sea of family, friends n' shit. We *need* you to ensure our way is clear... safe, protected. So we CAN get to our destination. Intact, peaceful—empowered. Have no doubt! You are ESSENTIAL. And as you put up with our shit and all the things we put **you** through, you are *transformed*... YOU become,

A SAMURAI SWORD...

You've been torched, fried, re-shaped (possibly chipped) but you did not break dude. You SO rock!

What's that?

K... in my *next* book, I'll write about... The Samurai Sword who just wanted to be a BUTTER KNIFE. Cool. Guys, I'm NOT sayin' jump when we say jump (a wuss) I'm sayin' be attentive to <u>get</u> what YOU need. Most girls **don't** want a guy they can step on. That just makes us go the other *extreme—BAD BOYS!!* We know they break our hearts but we want someone who can *lead* also. Who's strong. It's not so much that they're *bad*... that's appealing. It's that they're in charge, in control and in command of themselves (their life) or endeavor (sport, project, cause). A LEADER of the pack. They really don't care what YOU think. They'll go where most guys *don't* (dare) go, cuz they'll challenge the system, protocol, conventional wisdom. Read... a book like this. LOL They don't just *follow* other people's thoughts—they have their own (thoughts). They value who they ARE and aren't easily discouraged. They live in that *certainty*—which makes a girl feel certain of herself (and her world) cuz she picks up on it and begins to feel it come from her. Since they're a part of what's *untamed*... wild (**not** domesticated) tied to their animal *instincts* we feel safe with them. Within their animal instincts we find resilience, guts, the ability to face challenges (being with us... the **real** challenge) and are pulled to *that*...

Dude... If you **follow** your gut—not what you *think* she wants you to 'do' or say, then she'll *trust* that you say what you 'do', mean what you say. You're the MAAAAN. She'll feel calm (in her body) open in her heart... for YOU *to lead the way.* <3

We're in a new Millennium

Embarrassing... isn't it? We're *supposed* to be intelligent beings... but we're NOT advancing. There's alll these books, online tellin' us how to outdo each other, how to get him (*her*) under <u>our</u> control (sexually, emotionally, psychologically) pullin' us apart. It's meant to divide and conquer. Making it seem like having a relationship <u>equals</u> pain. So even if we wannit, it keeps us *scared*...

So we're fucking up on purpose, cuz we'd rather fuck *them* up before they fuck us up (which keeps us weak). Cuz as long as we feel incomplete (being alone) we're susceptible to other people's shit (suggestions/opinions/outlook on life) how they see guys, girls. Like, the latest fad. Which states girls should do the asking, planning, basically approach the guy (first) if we're confident. WTF? My species back home would start to lose their LIGHT if they did this shit. If YOU are truly confident you'd *know* you could bring him to you.

Like, WHO has the vagina (*crystal*) here? We DO. So why are we doin' all the work? How demoralizing for the female *spirit*. Pretty soon... since we've taken away their backbone, they'll have no need to 'man up' (we're doin' it all for them). They'll be like our pets. And let me tell you how *commanding* a dick to work is NOT the same as it **wanting** to work... for YOU.

Seduction... :*)

Is a *powerful* tool.

A *confident* girl... doesn't WORK for a guy.

Everything around us is advancing but the most **important** thing. WE'RE stuck—we're not advancing, we're having a relapse. Lmao We're losing our power... the *power of our femininity* (our magnetic sweet-spot) an ability to make things happen effortlessly. And now, the media thinks it's empowering us by telling us to get down on one knee and **propose** to a guy? *WHAT-THE-FUCK?!*

So totally act like a GUY? And you guys wonder why so many of us have turned to sluts (untrustworthy). CUZ it's turned to a numbers GAME (for us) just like it used to be for you! LOL The difference... now you value your shit (so, more picky since we're chasing you) you still wanna weed out the skanks first THEN get serious. But you *know* you won't give your heart to *that* (lack of connection) ...most of you. Meanwhile, we girls aren't paying attention to our feelings (desensitized) it's all about the SEX. We want to master it! So we put up with more (cuz we want *some*) do whatever it takes (cuz we need it) go above and beyond (blow jobs/buy you things/fight your battles/take 3 buses to see you) so we can have it (your dick). When it should be the other way around—them impressing us! Like, do I *have* to say it? Yuuup... Cuz obvious is not so OBVIOUS anymore, it's been smudged.

And YOU guys are more sensitive so you actually want a fulfilling relationship. LMFAO This whooole relationship thing needs a serious **COLONIC**. Firstly! Talking from a human point of view... If girls are the ones running after you, tellin' you they love you proposing n' shit, at some point you're gonna wonder... "Did I tell her I love her cuz I really *do*... or cuz she said it first? Did I say I wanna make it official ('marry' her) cuz I wanted to or cuz she ASKED me?"

It'll haunt you the rest of your DAYS...

Lookin' at it entirely from a Fairy Goddess perspective I have to say... it's interesting to note, that you guys immediately use your body for sex (usually without reservation) when the dick calls, your pants fall. You know you won't lose out, it's win/win for YOU. Aim – shoot - SCORE. We girls usually wait to feel *closer* (more trust) so we don't just feel *taken* from, since our investment with YOU (having sex) has to do with wanting more of that... **plus** the emotional frills. Sharing feelings is a BIG high for us. Since your body (guys) can fuck easily it'd be your *mind* that would be used to gauge (love) not your body since it doesn't discriminate. Lmao So it seems critical that your mind be involved in the final process. It MAKES the decision that you're in love. That's how you know for sure. To be deprived of using that faculty would mean you're not functioning fully and therefore WILL be questioning... On the same token, we girls hesitate to use our body (right away) cuz that is our deciding factor... that's HOW we bond... (to you) through our body. Then it's tough as hell to let you go (no matter what type of asshole you've BECOME). Knowing this... it's understandable that you guys **don't** say I love you so *fast* (unless you're a player) we girls CAN... since words are thoughts (from our mind) NOT our deciding factor. Which is very obvious when we ask ourselves three months in WHAT THE HELL WAS I THINKING? ☹ This is also why it takes you guys so long to fall in love (truly) us girls... fairly quickly.

(If we let YOU in)

SO... Sayin' *I love you* to a guy (first) and/or gettin' down on one knee (wtf) when it's crucial it comes from *him* (his mind) not YOU tellin' him, then gettin' a knee jerk response (guilt...) and/or fearing to lose or upset YOU. I mean... how complicated can it be? We've got one guy, one girl—two parts. That *reeeally* fit well together. It's not like the guy's dick is in the shape of a STAIRCASE and you have to twist it, maneuver it, bend it (hopefully not break it in the process) to make it fit. It FITS.

We're meant to fit together...

The BLUEPRINT is in the body people! And that means... that the emotional *part* (how to get along) has to be there TOO. In order for the emotions to gel (critical for bonding) the approach has to fit as well. Cuz otherwise, it's just too convoluted and confusing for BOTH of us. Bottom line! We're made of a body substance that's designed to feeeeel things. So we *know* right away if it doesn't feel right... good. Why's that OVERLOOKED? Why does our heart have to be beaten up so badly before we pay attention? Why's it put into our head that we can't be happy continually (fo shur if we keep overlookin' how we feel)?

When something comes up in our relationship that's a *contrast* (to what we want... deserve) it shows a **change** is necessary. Why's that seen as a threat? Why's it not seen as relief... (gratitude)? Cuz the moment that happens—our mind's eye goes right to what you **want**! Then it's POSSIBLE. The contrast chiseled it for us so it's CLEAR.

Remember... Before you saw *this* person you had an idea of what you wanted—so you recognized it. All that's happening now... fine tuning! YOU got the person... easy to say now (nerve wracking back then) for some... waaaay out of the question. LOL But it HAPPENED. Now that you've gotten used to having it (relationship, status, recognition) the next step is easier to fit into... MORRRE. And cuz you've eased into the first step (which at first you thought was impossible... not happening) it's easier now to ask (demand LOL) the next step... Not so foreign. All this CAN happen simply and effectively if you don't **fight** it. If you're relaxed in our approach...that what YOU want (the way you want it) is on its way... in your present situation (or new one). *Release* that whole 'it can only be this WAY (with this person, thing, scenario). The fear always hits hardest when we think we **can't**... when we're unplugged from alllll that's (already) coming. So fee l lost (hopeless, trapped) SETTLE...

YOU need only ask; What am I not seeing that I *should* be seeing? What's not here that should be *here?* And randomly OPEN the book to a **page**. Start on the left where you're thumb is... *read*. And you will see something so blatantly truuue you'll wonder why you just never admitted it (to yourself). Trust me, I've got people in exalted places... I know these things.

OMG!! It's 11:11 I'm making a wish!

That YOU share your great change with others!!

Done!

I have a serious question for you guys. Do you WANNA go through all this bullshit for another decade? Don't you get tired of walking on eggshells (more like pink landmines) every time your girl's PISSED? Doesn't that bother you off? For real... And what about when you're gone dude? It's gonna happen. *Eventually...*

What about what YOU leave behind... your 'mark' dude?

We're not talking about guys who can't *control* themselves. Lmfaoo OMG! I was at this guy's place and he's editing some photos for me.

He takes a look at *one*... tight jeans, totally lookin' at my ass. He's like, "*Whoa*... That's hot." (-_-;) I'm like, "Thanks." He starts fidgeting in his chair. I'm thinkin' ... poor guy, he's in dire need of an adjustment. He's been working on these for hourrrs. I'm like, "Get on the floor! On your stomach. I'm gonna adjust you."

Whaaat...? Guys always listen to me.

So he's lying face down on his stomach and I crouch down on top of him... crack his back. He's like, "*Ohhh*... My GOD! *That felt*... SO good." He lies there. I'm like, "K! Time to get up now." I nudge him flip him over. ***I could not believe what I saw...***

On the right side of his crotch—a HUMUNGOUS wet mark (with some other particles). Must have dried a bit. Sooo gross. He's looking at the ceiling he's like, "I'm <u>so</u> embarrassed." And to top it all off. I tell my Dentist and he gives me shit. He's like, "You're supposed to crack his back not CRACK HIS NUTS." K... So I'm multi talented. Seriously. I was just trying to help the guy release some tension. Had nooo idea there was all this lower cabin pressure (building). LOL So we're definitely NOT talking about that *kind* of mark. Honestly DISGUSTING.

We're talkin' about something that *stands* for YOU dude... Leaving your mark. (Dry) LOL And how *far* that makes it into the delivery room. Does it actually get delivered? What YOU stand for...

What **defines** YOU...

And the contribution YOU make to the world—is it *received?* Or watered down... cuz a part of you is 'incomplete'. YOU don't understand your woman (she's the *other* part of you). Which *means* you don't understand yourself (in total) man.

...a part of you is still wobbly.

Conflicted thoughts breed doubt... ☹

(And that doubt is usually about yourself)

As you keep (generation after generation) *missing* the mark... Every time you *think* you have a hole in one—you lose the game. *Daaang.* You were this *close* dude! Isn't that always the way? How frustrating for you.

(Sawry, couldn't hold it) :-}

Peace AND Understanding

It's official...

They're a COUPLE. They always go hand n' hand (never apart) constantly *together*. If one goes missing the other's LOST. No peace... can't <u>find</u> understanding. No understanding *peace*... totally absent. They tell me I always 'analyze' things. It's what us girls **DO**.

ANALYZE. And that's cuz, we need to *understand* why things happen. We need to be *peaceful*. I found, that when I'd search for angles (on what just happened) look for clues as to *why* it happened, I'd see things. Stuff would surface. I'd have a better picture and be able to move forward. Blame doesn't work... keeps you in a cage (till you're just a skeleton of your former self). Those that blame a LOT have skeletons in their closet (*fo shur*). And unfortunately that doesn't give you 'peace' cuz you're hiding something... feel like a victim of life, circumstance, person. Maybe it is fortunate. Cuz this way you can ask yourself at what point did you **know** this was dumb—BUT DID IT ANYWAY?

It's about knowing...

You may have done something (not bad) just too much, too little, (unaware) or overlooked things, when it was starin' you in the FACE. It wasn't something that just *happened*, YOU controlled the situation. YOU... knew, saw or *felt* what was about to happen. As soon as you **realize** you've contributed in some way you don't feel as pissed. There's a REASON it went down the way it did. Straight up. What stagnating bullshit belief have you been forced to digest year after year (that's NOT serving you) that you can let go of? For real. There's a need in you to know the *truth*...

The vibrations in your body respond to *that* energy.

It flows (you feel free) strong...

YOU'VE JUST ENTERED THE EMPOWERMENT ZONE.

It's how you know you're on your path...

Your body TELLS you.

It reacts. You can feel the power surge inside you. Just like you can feel your power surge inside your *woman*... Definitely, an empowered zone. :=) *What if...* YOU could be the MISSING link—you'd be responsible for leading the guys out of bondage! LOL

To all my Warriors (minus or plus boobs)

What would make *this* time around <u>any</u> different, than all the others, in your search for 'answers'? How can WE make sure *this* time, we come full circle? Achieve *THAT* mystic union...

It's our destiny.

A true *connection*...

Cuz anything less is a RIP OFF.

To succeed... First we need to realize, that it's not that we can't see the answer, it's that we can't see the PROBLEM. All dudes interested in advancing... Step up to bat!

Cuz this book's *specifically* for YOU...

Farts, Equality,
Mothers in the Dark.

Some girls... suffer needlessly.

They have sex, just cuz the guy's *there*... even if they don't want to. They stand out in the cold, talk to a guy just cuz he's taking *forever* to kiss her. They hold their fart in for like, an eternity. I did that!! Once...and *never* again. I was curled over sooo bad. Had the most unbelievable cramps. ALMOST busted my bladder. I always thought it wasn't lady-like to fart. Then again, I always thought cats were female and dogs were MALE. Lmao Girls and their cat fights, boys and their horn-dog attitude. K... So I wasn't far off. Still, I stuck to my belief about being a 'lady'. Didn't fart... *everrr*. Till about eight MONTHS into the relationship, we're in my room doin' homework at night. My fart was SO angry (felt like an *alien* inside me). Fortunately my then boyfriend is like, "Bae, it's not healthy. Just let it go." I'm like, "I CAN'T. It's not right." He's like, "Just let it go—it won't matter.

He was sooo wrong...

He's like, "OMG! The **putrefaction**... what'd you do swallow a dead MONKEY?" "I don't eat monkeys." He's like, "*Dammn*... It's getting into my lungs. Holy crap! I CAN TASTE IT!" I'm like, "It's OKAY bae... it's going away." "Smells... like nuclear fallout, our kids are gonna have birth defects." He leaves and goes sits at the furthest corner of my room (in the dark). I'm like, "Bae... It's okay, promise. You can come back." He's like, "Uh uh.... smokin' gun effect. I'll WAIT." Then I hear him chanting. He's waving his arms across his body, praying!! "...in the name of the Father, the Son and the Holy Spirit—I command you to LEAVE evil spirit!" I'm laughing SO hard. I'm like, "Bae... Are you doing an exorcism on my fart?" He's like, "Whatever it takes."He's crawling on his elbows... He's like, "*If I keep low I'll bypass the smell*. Hot air RISES." I'm like, "K... I won't eat a whole bag of Turkish figs ANYMORE. My Turkish delight farts are just too much for YOU." Honestly... it's just a puff of air. :=)

My current boyfriend's like, "Baby, was that an air bubble you just *released*?" Such a better response. Omigosh! When we first started seeing each other, I'd be over at his place studying. I'd take his hand, lead him to the sofa for our cuddlicious break. We're makin'out and he ends up on top of me. But I didn't feel his *thang*... down there. I'm like, "Can YOU press in?! He's like, "I AM." "K... I need cock form—not sock form." Then I dunno what happened... I was sooo *relaxed* I FARTED (on top of him). We laughed for a MINUTE AND A HALF straight. He's like, "I can't believe you just farted on my balls." I'm like, "K. Just so we're clear. Just cuz I farted on your balls DOESN'T mean you can fart on me." He's like, "That's what I love about you, Nichole. You're not into this **equality** shit." I'm like, "Why would I be? We have the boobs. OBVIOUSLY we're ahead.

Love being a GIRL...

Seriously. It's not about equality—relationships are never that cut and dry. LOL It's about UNITY (far more powerful) ...*closeness*. In the sports world (understandable) one team goes against another team. Equality, (level playing field) is essential in competition for guys and girls. In the workplace as well, even though it's a co-ed environment we're ALL competing for position and money. Guys and girls need to be judged equally—we're doing the SAME job! So damn straight we should be PAID equally. Somehow, this very important fact slipped through the butt cracks of society (inevitably messin' with our intimate zone) totally screwing up our relationships. Using the same rules in **relationships** we're setting ourselves up for competition, creating a rift (invisible wedge) we think we're getting *closer* (to each other) we're really only getting closer to *separation*... winning sets us APART (from others). Ma man Lau Tzu puts it this way, 'If you delight in victory, you delight in killing.' There's a time and place for killing! Relationships are NOT that. On the sports field... yeah! Fucken SLAYYY IT. I'd put it this way, 'If you delight in equality, you delight in tit for tat.' I did this... NOW you do that... OBLIGATION takes the spirit out of *giving*.

In a relationship, chivalry and equality **don't** sleep in the same bed. Thank God... It'd be side to side and we'd lose allll our positions! LOL Estrogen rules THERE. Basically... We're competing against each other when our primary focus should be *complementing* each other. In our confusion (equality leads to love) we've gone through so much heartache and disappointment. Cuz love is only found in the *right* fit... (not an equal fit). People of all different status, race, intellect, talents hook up and find their match in what may seem to others, a a very unlikely match (being so different). We've forgotten when going for love, we need not put any *effort* (to win) we win *without* effort. How fitting that we have this blind approach... Since we believe love is BLIND.

We need to put **equality** back... where it BELONGS.

(So our heart's not paralleled... but joined) <3

Back to FARTS.

After I stood up for my unequal RIGHTS (farting on my guy) I felt a lot free-er. So now, whenever I talk about something I feel strongly about, I'll punctuate it... with a *fart*. Seriously, I do. So we're hugging, talkin' about what happened at school. I'll be like, "I'm *mad*..." Fart! We'll be at the movies, get into his car I'll be like, "That... was scary." *FART*... Or, like last night he bought me a gift and he's holding me, I'm so filled with joy my entire being is glowing. I'm like, "I'm so **happy**." *Farrrrt*... He's like, "My baby, she's *sooo* emotional." "Yeah! So don't make me mad or you're gonna need a bum-shelter." Guys take notes! Just cuz we DO something, doesn't mean you can do it *back* to us. Sangu.

Girls take notes!

Farts, facts or feelings... When it comes to a girl, **release** is the best policy.

Girls... their moms (who conflict with them).

It happens all the time, you start out feelin' real close to your mom—then there's this separation. YOU butt heads on EVERTHING. Why can't she just leave you alone?! K... Stop reading. No I'm serious. Go give this part to your Mom. Tell her you wanna know what she thinks...

To Mom...

YOU love your daughter. She's exactly like you! But there's this constant rift. You're trying to steer her the right way, you see where she's heading. It's the part you struggled MOST with. You keep trying to guide her. Now... There's just constant *discomfort* living inside you, she BLOCKS you at every turn. You try not to show it's bothering you so much. Instead, the anger you feel (at yourself, really) is directed at her, tearing you two a part. Mom... you need to make *peace* with what you went through... suffered, as a result of your choice(s). It's what you *needed* to do (at the time). Ask instead... How it served YOU. It had a function. It wasn't stupid. It was necessary, given how you felt at the time (where your fears were). Once you see *that*... there won't be misplaced 'anger' at your daughter and more **importantly**, your self-love and confidence (*now*) will call to her... be felt as her *own*, not the constant feeling stirring inside you (scared, rebellious, non-trusting). She'll walk from *that* place... know she'll make the right decisions, be open, willing and able to LEARN. She feels safe.

Guys... their moms (who don't get them).

This is for YOU...

I was talking to a guy... his BIGGEST complaint?

How his mom INTRODUCES him.

He's like, "I hate it when my mom and I are out and she meets someone she knows. She's like, "This is my baby." I'm like, "Oh... My... GOD. I can't believe she said that." He's like, "It made me feel embarrassed and tiny... very, very tiny." YOU need to cut the cord mom he's SIXTEEN! When he questioned his mom (who he dwarfs) he looks down at her he's like, "WHO you callin' a baby?" She's like, "SHUT UP." (Not cool) And don't BLOW DRY HIS HAIR. He looks like he's from your era, will be picked on. New options...

Ask your son how he would like to be introduced...

208.

1. I'd like to introduce to YOU the future head of (Corporation).

2. This is my Son...

3. This is someone I'm very PROUD of (name).

4. This is my (age) year old.

I'd be like, "This is what I've produced." (I would so say that) ;D I ask my boyfriend what he thinks. He's like, "That would be cool. It's like the guy's a precision machine. A very well thought out work of art. A lady I know introduces her sons this way. She's like, 'These are the fruit of my loins.'" Lmao

I was talking to a guy, who was trying to convey to his mom what mid-terms are like for *him*. How INTENSE they are. All she kept saying... "It's okay, you'll get through it. Just focus more. You're smart." He freaks out. He's like, "Mom! I just need you to LISTEN. You have no idea how **intense** it is." Actually mom, he doesn't need you to *just* listen... he needs you to walk it *through* in his mind (with *him*). So you can FEEL what he's experiencing (so he doesn't feel alone) so his anguish is heard (pressure felt). He needs to know (deep down) he's not a wuss, dweeb... Loser (cuz it's hard for him).

He NEEDS...

a) Acknowledgment of difficulty (which gives him confirmation, it's HARD).

b) To know he's <u>not</u> weak (it's definitely tough).

Then he can rise to the challenge...

Moms if you'd like try (as an experiment).

1. "HOW THE HELL DO YOU DO IT? You amaaaaze me."

2. "What are YOU made of—it's insane the load they're giving YOU."

209.

3. "How's it possible to get allll this done—in SUCH a short amount of time?! Only YOU."

4. "You've been at it 12 **straight** hours—you're a MACHINE."

5. "Nothing short of *incredible*... YOU are."

Guys, do any of these make YOU feel better/stronger?

Stronger ☐ Waaay stronger ☐

Highlight and give to your mom. So she's empowered truly... passes it on to YOU. So she's not like, "Come love, I want you to meet somebody." The worst... "This is my ANGEL... This is *my* son." Although true, he's not looking for verification that he came from you and angels don't have mid-terms. He needs strength from *within*...

Every guy has his own texture (durability) it's up to YOU to find out what'll *tear it*... how to stretch it to the MAX—improve the quality (like only a mother can do). His reaction (refreshed/not) will let you know how effective you are. In short, a guy needs your *acknowledgment* of: Challenge - Intensity - Effort—Sacrifice. BALLS (he *has*) to do it.

Focus put *there*... gives him strength.

One thing is for sure, Moms. When you walk it through (in your mind) put yourself in his circumstance, instead of blocking his heartache, feel what he feels. That *scared*... little part inside him (where doubt lives) not only is it acknowledged—it's confirmed. So he DOESN'T feel like he's a loser (wimp). And he starts to feel his strength *return* (someone's joined his journey) he's not in the dark anymore tryin' to reach out (make someone understand). He feels TWICE as strong. And concludes, it's not all that bad. Since the doubt part of him (suffering) has been heard, can be put to rest (got its attention) a *hero* is BORN... He's armored (for opposition) recognized (mid-term's tough) fueled. It awakens the challenger in him, stimulated he feels 'capable'. And a call to the wild is *heard*...

Man or beast he's in control...

When you look up to a guy (most of the time) he really DOES try to live up to that. We love you for that! No one sees how TOUGH it is, being YOU. They will *soon...* promise. Be patient. Rome wasn't built in ONE semester. And your mom's not EVIL—she fixes you sandwiches. She puts up with YOU. Then again...

My guy's like, "I was whoored out by my mom. When she forced me to wear neon green spandex bike shorts she bought. I never wore spandex. It felt like someone was touchin' me the whole time. It didn't help that it had all these different COLOR hands on my legs and crotch, or that I was only 9 years old. She wanted me to look like the cool kid in the music video. Kids dress 'fucked up' like that, to rebel against their parents. It doesn't work if they're forced to."

Please don't force guys to wear things they DON'T like.

Then again, maybe it's a learning curve! My mom bundled me off real GOOD. Looked, like I was going to an IGLOO in the North pole—not a **summer** day camp! I had the entire left side of the bus to myself. All the kids thought I had some kind of disease. These things... give us 'image' issues.

Still... some guys have a *blind* spot to themselves. They can't see everything they're about. My boyfriend's like, "That's like a dick without his crew (balls)." Crude... yes, highly accurate though. If a guy has NO IDEA what he's capable of. Huge loss.

Hint: There's nothing STRONGER than looking into the *eyes*... of a girl you LOVE (moms INCLUDED) and have her reflect it back to you...

Allllllllllll you're capable of.

GO GIVE HER A KISS!

For those that never had or don't (right this second) wish there was a mirror and I could see YOU. I'd show you how amaaazing you ARE.

211.

Girls... Guys...
TAKE YOUR POSITIONS

In the sports world (gym, field, ring, court) is where our *true* nature shows. No joke. It's where our real colors (without restriction) are clearly displayed. With social protocol stuffed in our lockers, our genuine self (**uninhibited**) comes out (to play). And we get to *see* how we really are... Our most primal 'self'. (Maaajor grunting) ;D This is where we see our fighting **style** (how we handle life and shit). It's so apparent, as soon as we start the game...

- Do we play FAIR (when pissed).

- Do we have tolerance (what it takes, to endure)?

- Can we HANDLE it in the long run (do we bail)?

- Are we ruthless to the core (have to WIN at all costs)?

- Do we embrace our *game* (relationship) or are reluctant to give what it takes (time and time again) a.k.a lazy?

- Do we stay TOO long when we no *longer* enjoy the game (cuz people 'expect' us to)?

Being competitive all my life I knew being on the edge (at the very least) always prepped me for *anything* to come. Cuz you don't fall, you *don't* surrender... When you're pegged against the wall—YOU do the only thing you **know**...

TURN THE BALLS OF FATE YOUR WAY!!

Make 'em serve you. Raw, over easy, sunny side up—BRINGGGG IT!!

When we're physical, it's absolutely the most *honest* assessment of WHO we are (our most *basic* self) clear, raw, easy to read (there are no guards). That's why making love reveals the *silliest* fears...

AM I BIG ENOUGH FOR HER?

Commmme on!! LOL

Making love...

Seeing us for *real* as opposed to... Sex with ZERO emotions (what I call techo sex) quantifiable by rating system, total waste of time (more like a short circuit if you ask me) and you wonder why he *lasts* 7.2 seconds? Then you're like, "Doesn't that *mean* he can't contain himself cuz he's hot for me?" Uh... No. Havin' a guy really into you (into making you happy) means... you've just elevated horn-DOG to Man. :D Someone in love with YOU—*not his dick*. Sorry... not jaded gotta call a dick a DICK.

I was talking to a guy about his ex, why he figured she left. And, I have no idea where or *how* he came up with this SHIT. He's like... "Nichole, that's WHY bad boys are so appealing to girls. They're not sensitive and the good guys are. The good guys are SO highly sensitized—they come real quick." WTF (Several eye blinks)

I REPEAT...

What the fuck? He's like, "Whereas, bad boys are so insensitive they don't care about a girl, so they can HOLD IT a real long time." I'm like, "Uh... and you actually *believe* your bullshit dude?" LMAOO Maybe, bad boys are *tougher* on the inside and maybe... we find that comforting. They've been through so MUCH that our stuff, doesn't overwhelm them (like it does a regular guy). So we feel their strength, which makes us feel stronger (inside). And we feel relaxed, cuz we know we can open up about our issues, and they can take it. They don't freak out. UNLIKE... A sensitive dude. We'd have to hold it in (for him) cuz he's so 'sensitive'. Find some *other* way to deal with it (sooo much pressure). Cuz we love him and we wanna be with him, but we *secretly* feel like we're taking care of HIM. Which is why every now and then (at a party) when we've just *sooo* had it with life n' shit (possibly wasted) we mack with a bad boy. Cuz... It's the way they *talked* to us... we feel like a *girl*. We feel 'safe'. We feel like we're inside a very durable tee-pee, while this intense downpour is happening. THAT'S a turn on. It's not that bad boys are the way to go, especially if they mistreat you (their lifestyle endangers you, by association) which could be **any** guy—even a regular 'so called' sensitive guy. Messed up. If we examine what's appealing about *them*, it's that we can LEAN on them, rest, be *soft* cuz they're strong... and we feel that, it feels good. It can be a badass on the field, in the ring, group (fighting for a cause) rhymin' about it, driven by his career. Toughness means protection to us, they're used to a true challenge. So the *challenge* of being with a girl is put into proportion. Just like you like us in proper proportion—so do we. :P Then, we feel like you can handle 'us'.

Back to... Our true SELF.

When our body gets used **physically**—*SEX OFF THE BRAIN!!* For a second! I meant sports... PIG. When our body is utilized this way it LIGHTS UP (cuz we're happy)!! And people feed on that vibration... At times, too hot to handle. Hopefully, those dating have already experienced *that*. Well done! :*) When we access our body by being active, we switch ON our body's frequencies, receive *impulses* through it (most of you guys know this already). ;D That's why, it's not unusual when we're near water, mountains, nature we focus on what we see... (blueness of the sky) hear... (water, birds) feel... (grass, sand between our toes) that *thoughts* with solutions to an issue, fresh insight and people's faces... *come to us.* Then NO SHIT! Very next day—we see them. Or they call... no reason.

We were out of mind and *into* the senses. When totally absorbed by them (sight, smell, taste, sound, touch) we receive information for us *through* them. They're tied to our instincts. Our senses (current) and instincts (things *to come*...) make the path <u>clear</u> for us. Isolating all the white noise that's trying to prevent us from receiving a message... bottled for us. Challenging to understand...

(Hard to understand sometimes when the mind's NOT there) LOL

That's why when it comes to death, sometimes I think it's a whole lot simpler than most people make it out to be. For instance. Let's say someone pops up in your mind. They don't live near you... or something of *theirs* drops out of your car (locker, drawer) an old text comes up... email.

Guaranteed...

You're gonna be hearing or seeing them (soon). That day... (next) they'll contact you, connect, text... call. Or you bump into them. You're like, "Hey! I was JUST thinking of you." When people at a distance (you don't see every day) happen to contact you *after* they pop in your mind, it's as if they've already communicated with you through a *thought* or item of theirs...

You FIRST receive the message through your senses. You see their face (in your mind) without trying to think of them, something of *theirs* stumbles into view, a song (their fave) someone says something *they* always said (cute <u>or</u> annoying).

COULD THAT ALSO MEAN...

That when someone dies and you're in class, work or walking home *they* pop up in your mind (no reason) that it could be the **same** thing? They were thinking of YOU. You weren't thinking of them but they came to your head (only they DON'T have a body). So you don't meet up in a day or two (get a call). You just get to know they're *with you*...

...Deep sigh, yes.

Body responses can't be *faked.* If you're doin' something and out of the blue your grandmother comes to YOU (something she used to do with YOU or say) your brother... How he always smiled when you were *stubborn* (like, now) I believe... They're right THERE. And I do mean—right there. I don't care how weird it sounds. There's nothing to be scared of it just means... We're never truly out of touch. Honest.

Your sister is right here... <3

(She needed YOU to know that)

I COMPLETELY felt at ease... When I first realized that my mom and dad (someone I loved very much who's dead) were **around**. And it's not like they were GHOSTS sittin' on my bed. That would actually be cool. It just means, I don't get to feel alone. Cuz I know when they come to my *head*... it's their way of meeting up. What really convinced me this was true? I was wondering if all this shit was just in my HEAD. :P I met this lady, she was talking to me about this clairvoyant guy she knew and how he *sees* things. I had to meet him! The first thing he SAID... "Who's Michael?" I'm like, "He's the guy I loved but he's dead." He's like, "He's really pissed off." I'm like, "Whyyyy? Doesn't he know I love him?" "No, it's not that. Every time he tries to talk to YOU, you think it's *just* in your head."

GET THE FUCK OUTTA HERE!!

(I can't tell you how that made me feel)

It's like taking something that's really *precious* that broke... lookin' at alllll the pieces (the pain of that) and now it's like it NEVER broke! I felt SOLID... *inside*. And for all you ADULTS, intellects and shrinks, who's thinkin', "Oh... She's just in denial, it's how she copes." Think AGAIN. Cuz it's no different than being tuned into the radio. We listen to Rock but that doesn't mean that R&B *isn't* playing. It just means you're tuned into one channel (one frequency) and some people (places) can only get 'one' frequency (limited fo shur). :P When you're in touch with your **instincts** they CAN'T lie... they *only* awaken when it is real, when something's there for them to pick up on. Something stirred them. The body may contain us, but on the inside we're still *connected* (through our senses) to OTHERS.

Like, when you're at a party. Let's say you're 'used to' being loud. Like me! Well, only when I have something important to say (which is often). ;D And at this party (that you can't wait to get to) there's someone *else* that's LOUD (funny, into debates, aggressive) in fact, it's like *their* loudness is stronger (more dominant) than yours. You're like, "Omg. They're LOUD." Notice... how all of a sudden, you're quiet(er) instead of trying to be louder. It's like, the *part* of YOU that needed to be 'loud' is somehow subdued (no longer in the spotlight) yet, still connected *through* the other person's actions (your body double, stand in). LOL If you're shy, and someone at a party is uber shy, you're not as shy (anymore) cuz they're *more* shy. In a way, they've taken care of that (for you) they've helped you without even knowing it. On the flip side, when someone close to you dies... you feel them *stronger* (inside you) once they're gone. Gulp... Eyes watery is your body tellin' you it's **true**.

When that person was ALIVE there was no need to absorb them, (take in what they were trying to say, get across, what they stood for) just being there was a reminder. Which is why they were so valuable to YOU. Now, that there are no TWO physical bodies in between (separating) you two, the dominant (alive) *you* can take center stage, absorb their message (what they stood for, all you loved about them, wish you could be like) while they... are *quiet*. And since their body is no longer there (to hold them) they are free to enter (you). And the union... fulfilled (*connection* made).

(DEEP) ☺

When I'd *miss* what I didn't get a chance to do... (with my dad), I'd think about the scenarios I wanted him to be in. *Put him...* there. Like, watching me train (doing it *with* me), what he'd say, how he'd respond, how it would BE.

I realized...

All we dooo have, is memories (in the END). So why not bypass reality, now? Create awesome memory videos (of people we miss) doin' what we always *wished*... we could have done with them. We never relish (savor) things while we're doin' them... it's always after, when we're thinking of *that* time—the **memory** of it. We can have it NOW. Just go *there*... Where you wish they were, a championship, race, just before your *first* date, sweet sixteen, graduation, awards presentation, jogging with YOU... acting debut, soccer GAME. Do it with them NOW. Put on some nature sounds (sounds effects of an audience cheering lol) close your eyes and go *there*... in your mind. YOU can form memories with people—anytime (dead, busy or alive). The *tears* that fall are theirs... living through YOU.

So sleep peacefully... ☺

They're not gone. You're NOT alone. They're just connected to a different frequency (one we may not get too often). The connection's fuzzy (only one bar) too many people around. Can't tune in... (we're intoxicated, wasted). Reception garbled (nowhere quiet... can't *hear*). It doesn't mean you won't be emotional at first—you miss THEM. But for me when I acknowledged a *face*... smile, sentence (*that came*) my body would feel calm (instantly). It would *respond*... If I'd walk down the street and just *pretend* to talk to someone (I miss) without them *first* coming to me (my mind) thoughts, an item. Or if I'd be pissed—scream out to them! It WOULDN'T work. My body wouldn't change... The signal comes through our body (creepy, yes). One time I was sooo upset. Fucken frustrated. I just cried in bed... the corners of my eyes were so red and sore from rubbing them so much. I'm staring at the wall, my DAD'S face *comes* to me... I WASN'T thinking of him (too focused on my shit—requires full concentration). LOL All I hear... 'YOU *boodiful*' in my mind. His voice... (in his broken English). I just relaxed... laughed, smiled. Cried. But not cuz I was upset cuz I wasn't alone anymore (relieved).

I'm just gonna take a minute.

Let it BREATHE...

Your instincts are most powerful when they are fully engaged and you're actually *listening* to them. Only at that point, do they have permission to *enter*... (more) into your life. Hey! They're shy and sensitive too. They don't wanna be rejected anymore than YOU do. And they work the same way your body functions... so they have to be authentic.

A guy can't fake a hard-on.

K. So my dentist says he CAN. Happens first thing when he wakes up. I tell my guy... He ALMOST shit himself!! He's like, "He's saying it's **not** a real hard-on?! Are you kidding. That's the MOST real hard-on you can have, first thing in the morning. You can BREAK a door with that thing. It's like it's made of MARBLE. What the fuck is wrong with him? Probably wakes up half an hour too late when it's at half-mast."

My theory still stands...

As a girl our instincts also work the same way our body functions. Unless, you've been messing with his head (*both* ways) and you're faking it. LOL That would be an issue. It would mean you're deliberately withholding the deepest sense of pleasure from your guy. And don't think guys appreciate that. They actually wanna know if you came (or not). Asshole guys, who don't give a rat's ass are exempt. For those that don't know, that means 'excused'. Theyyyy don't fit the profile. They don't make the grade. Girls that fake it with their guy, means he has no need to learn how to work her. Skills... lacking. When a girl truly comes her uterus contracts repeatedly—MEGA suction! And lemme tell you how *that's* gonna pump you, dude.

Allllot.

Course, if the heart's not invited...

Really 'involved' it's only gonna pump *him* (jack up his register) although yours will get some action, you'll feel like he's made off with a clean get away (never paid up). He filled up and RAN (maybe even leaked in the process) O_O was in such a big hurry.

Guys...

Your instincts (if you allow them) will guide YOU to your girl going CRAAAZY (sexually speaking) what to touch... do next. It's such a powerful feeling for you as a guy to witness that.

Girls...

Don't deprive your guy—don't deprive yourself of **being** a girl (always <u>true</u> to herself). This is why, when a guy's like, "What's your problem. Why you trying to be 'hard to get'?" I'd be like, "Uh... Don't like YOU. You're not my type." Then cut to the chase, "I'm not *trying* to be hard to get. I AM... **hard to get**."

Instinct is an incredible FORCE for you—it's an inner **being**. Your inner being, that already has all the answers (for YOU). It's just waitin' for you to give it your time of day—really pissed (when you don't). So, really needs **proof** (you're listening) before it tells YOU more, a lot more *often*. Still, cuz it cares it'll always warn you, no matter what. Like, when you're at a friend's party with a bunch of people and you get this reeeal bad feeling (something's not right)

220.

somethin's gonna go down—drugs, forced sex (rape). Boyfriend or not...

NOT ALLOWED IF YOU DON'T WANT TO!

Your GUT which is felt in your solar plexus (just below your chest) soft spot in the center, when you feel *something* that's where it starts. It's not something that you can pay attention to 'sometimes' then ignore (it won't go AWAY). The solar plexus *chakra* is associated with the color yellow. Hey! I put that on this morning You'll be pulled to wearing yellow when you feel good about YOURSELF. Chakra refers to each of the centers of *spiritual* power in the human body. They're literally parts of our anatomy we can't *see*... our being. When the solar plexus is out of alignment (suppressed, blocked, constricted, messed up) certain things happen to the *body* and YOU (in your life). Since it relates directly to self esteem, healthy ego, personal power, your sense of worth—it's YOUR energy tank. It fuels you (or not). It's responsible for your energy flow (feeling happy, depressed, rejected). As well as clarity and creativity. No wonder we're always happy *doing* what we love! Like, it's never boring. Cuz of alllll this energy we get from it!!

OUR SELF ESTEEM COMPARTMENT.

And that would also explain why some of us feel good about our shit.

(Some not)

A MAP of where YOU might be... if your solar plexus suck.

Emotionally

You won't see people as they are, but how *they* want you to see them. Believing, cuz you're not strong enough to deal with who they ARE... naive (waaay too trusting). And really frustrating for everyone else who sees it—when you don't. Too weak to set boundaries (emotionally) or speak up. It's like an artery sliced...

emotionally bleeding out. So your outlook on life (self, situations) dismal at best. Not so much cuz you're negative, cuz the deepest part of you *knows...* you're choosing **not** to see (person, situation, circumstance). No inner conviction for self. Once you choose to see (cuz the constant DISAPPOINTMENT is killing you) and keep looking at it (what you've been avoiding) the bleeding will STOP. And when you *make that decision,* see it exactly as it is, WALK (speak up, change something) you'll notice right away how **differently** you react to things (used to piss you off, trip you up, upset you) it's no longer ripping a raw *wound...* bleeding. It's just a nick (no biggie). And it will surprise you, that you feel alllll this fresh new energy. Be happier, not know why. And then... you'll be rewarded. Out of the blue you'll meet someone (an unexpected email arrives) name passed, that puts you on the *path* to the 'right' person... situation, career move.

If you're on the opposite end, if **mistrust** rules you (your issue) you won't be able to see anything different cuz that's where your search engine is (looking for things you DON'T trust). You won't recognize the truth cuz you're not aligned with it (since you **don't** trust). So dismissed. Especially... with your guy (or girl) you'll see things that aren't **really** there (suspicious). You'll know if it's you cuz you'll have a need to have power over *them* (or hate them). In a relationship, you can only hate someone you *still* need... (subconsciously) fear.

Or...

You're sensitive to what other people SAY about you (starving for approval) pissed if they don't give you enough attention, indecisive... can't make up your mind. K... So that's three quarters of the WORLD. Lmao

Physically

Expect... Stomach ailments (intestinal disorders) diabetes, anorexia (bulimia) hypoglycemia, allergies, liver shit (my technical term) LOL gallstones, adrenal imbalances, lack of energy. So my boyfriend's like, "K! There's a lot of people out there who've got an acute case of 'liver shit'! LOL

Too much jager... More like *stagger*-bombs." Alki. LOL

222.

The Body

The solar plexus chakra rules the upper abdomen, gallbladder, pancreas, intestine, spleen, stomach, liver and adrenals. Since it's associated with personal power, confidence, self respect, self esteem— a strong WILL. Those of us that have our solar plexus chakra in a GOOD place will know exactly what we're capable of and where we're going. And... that we'll make it (somehow). If you wanna restore a smashed solar plexus, get your ass out of bed! Go <u>exercise</u>. Get sunlight! Eat SUNFLOWERS (*seeds*...) LOL bananas, cheese. Get essential oils or anything that smelled like grapefruit or orange flavor (lip balm, body wash, soap, bubble bath. Sing OUT LOUD... Tell your parents it's therapeutic. Focus on high notes. Like, 'Eeeee'. Belly dancing... Go to a Club! Dance... take a class with your girlfriend. Sorry dude, can't help you there. Wait! I can. Create a song for that girl! :D

Train...

The solar plexus is a warrior energy. It tells us who we ARE, our place in the world, self-care. First step. Be AWARE. The next time someone's like, "You don't have any self esteem, you need to speak up more." Although true, you need to know there's many sides to a reason. It's never just ONE reason—and don't let ANYONE tell you that. In order to really understand something, we need to look at ALL angles. Just like SEX. Can you imagine if we only did it one way? LOL Since the solar plexus is associated with the color YELLOW I decided to observe what colors I'd be pulled to, where and when.

My own scientific experiment! LOL

OBSERVATION:

When I felt open to *romance* I'd wear pink! Red... When I wanted a LOT of energy, with some girls it's like, "I'm HERE! Come and get it." But with you guys... I noticed something *else*. You wear red when you're feeling it (lovvve). Except for you guys who own a lot of reds. It's your color. You wear them like, non-stop. Or it's a uniform (that doesn't count). Before my boyfriend and I were a couple, we'd TALK...

next day he'd wear RED. Or buy somethin' in red, like cologne (a red label). I decide to TEST my theory. I approach this random guy. I'm like "Hey! You're wearing RED shorts. That tells me... there's someone you're *really* attracted to in your life. Right NOW." He's like... "How do you know she's *not* standing in front of me?" Dannng! *He's goood.*

Guys pay attention!

When you feel like wearing red (NO reason) see if it's cuz you just saw a HOT babe (girl you've had your eye on). *Psssst...* she's checking you out. Cuz something's got your heartbeats going *BA BOOM BA BOOM!* Just don't go up to *her* and be like, "I see you're wearing red. That means YOU want me."

You might get *SLAPPED*!! ROFL

Blue... I'd wear when I wanted to feel peaceful (just *coasting*) feeling good. White, I wanna stay neutral and clear (it's clean and purifying). Makes me feel refreshed. Keeps all unwanted influences AWAY. Acts like a toxic filter—*against* girls with a venom streak. Guys, who just wanna sample your goods. Orange... I'd wear when I'm happier! (Sunnier) Earth tones when I wanna blend in (not cause any shit) easy goin' (doesn't happen often) nothin' to prove. Mellow... green when I'm craving nature—I'm a nurturing soul. LOL There's got to be an intrinsic *connection* between nature and us, or we wouldn't be put in the same world. Trees have so much to give! And they never ask for a THING.

If only my brother was a tree.

We should show a little love *back*... honestly. Trees are *here* for us... When I'm **down** and there's no one to hold me, I hug a TREE. I feel sooo different. It's *proven* huggin' a tree can boost your immune system, alter your vibrational frequency, absorb your SHIT (stress) while sending it *back* to the earth (to be recycled). Leaving you open and sane (calm). Course, some of you guys may not feel that. Seein' how you piss allll over its family (in da bush) THAT tree will probably be angry. Drop a branch on your HEAD.

Where was I? Lavender! I'd wear when I'm in an uber sensual *mood* (wanna be pampered). Black, when I wanna be in the shadows or feel more POWERFUL. Cuz it keeps people away! Feeling non-descript... just wanna observe. Or... For some of you guys it's more like, "Hey... I'm dangerous. Just so you KNOW. (You noticing yet?) Don't wanna make it look like I want *you* to notice, but I do." Fine. You're the shit. There's so much to YOU. Just hoping someone reveals it to you soon.

Or...

It's a 'keep out' sign, misunderstood... too dark *inside* to see you. *Intense*. Don't wanna be known (low profile) carrying secrets.

The coolest thing about the solar plexus is that our *personality* (developed during puberty) is housed in this chakra (also known as the 'ego') way before it got corrupt (bought or traded against **you**). Those of us experiencing dysfunction of this third chakra are having major problems getting or keeping our own personal power (*space*).

Circle if it's YOU.

It's an intuitive chakra and where we get our gut **instinct** from. It signals us to do or NOT do something. A strong 'self-esteem' is an absolute <u>requirement</u> for developing intuitive skills. So get busy!!

Example:

- I CAN'T stand up to a girl (girlfriend) stepping on my face. (Used to)

- My boyfriend takes advantage. (Used to)

- Abusive parents, teacher, coach, boss, friend so feel weird... (numb) inside. (Used to)

And you're not stupid... you're not dumb. You're NOT ruined. You're not hopeless. Cuz before you can HELP a friend that's *hurting* (like you were) you'd have to know *that* pain... see it through **their** eyes.

I'm with YOU... <3

Sends YOU a feeling **ahead** of time...

Lets you *know* the excitement around the corner (puts you at ease) so you're secured. IF you know how to *listen*...

Think of a **WOLF**...

Slowly making its way through the forest... sniffing for its dinner, focused on ANY movement—then spots his target! MR. WABBIT. It's through his *body*... that the wolf senses which way his dinner will turn. AND is able to be successful. Shame...

Our body won't perform its best, cuz of a mind that **hurts** itself.

I saw this movie about vampires. The guy was trying to escape one, so he puts this huge cross—*IN HIS FACE*. The vampire's like, "This only works if you *believe*..." It's all in the mind. LOL We are the only species that has a mind that ACTUALLY turns on itself. Wtf? I dunno <u>any</u> other animal that attacks itself the way we do. Strange...

It's AWESOME how our senses work for us in our body.

And that includes... all you gamers, who can sense where your opponent's going to go next. Only, if you're feeling like shit... it can throw you off your game (a struggle). Bet if we HAD to catch our dinner, we wouldn't be thinking, "I dunno if I *deserve* to catch this. I dunno if I can DO this. What if I don't catch anything?" THEN YOU DON'T EAT.

Being athletic is one way we have to release thoughts (subconscious and conscious) that are *trapped* and stored inside our body (muscles). Like, when we're furious (just got dumped) pure helll. No worries! There's always someone just around the corner. I *know*... Sometimes that corner's real longgg. Next page, I'm gonna give an example of how we can release **stored** emotions in the body, taking up allll that extra SPACE (rent free) in a relationship.

Scenario:

So, the douche (boyfriend) goes back to his EX (go see your ex... nah, only kidding he's a loser too). The skank that cheated on YOU is on your bus sitting on some guy's dick, while he's commenting on her nipples—AND SHE'S OKAY WITH THAT. You wanna throw up. You're in shock. Which is one floor above anger—so you KNOW what's coming. Although jogging and other sports are great to work off stress, I think working out in the gym (all muscle groups) gets every last muscle fiber EXHAUSTED (nothin' is stored). And they recharge (giving you energy) instead of draining you. You're invigorated or nicely spent (anger released) feel light. Although anything to release pent up shit is GREAT. This ensures no emotional debris get filtered through *other* organs. Like, the liver. The Chinese, always knew that. *Smarrrt*. Heart problems... Result of long standing resentment, emotional problems, no JOY. Lung issues... depression, grief, fear, can't take life in fully, not feeling worthy of living. These things can eventually happen when the feelings (which are stored) are not released, ever. I'm not talking about VOICING them, only. They are volatile **charged** words... to talk them out in a regular way, although helpful doesn't remove the *residue* that lays deep in the muscle tissue, needs to be extracted.

Search your ailment (bad knee, shoulder, allergies, headaches, bulimia) *linked* to emotions.

And since acknowledged or unacknowledged anger is *stored* in the liver, that's a DOUBLE whammy. Without a release, since you think it's inappropriate (too scared, numb or painful) emotions get suppressed, internalized... STUCK. My God people! That's the ORGAN that's responsible for detoxifying the whole **entire** body! Why are we not teaching this in schools? Stored anger is TOXIC. It gets worse. An overlooked underlying cause of fat accumulation? ANGER. Hellllo! Ten pounds I can't get rid of. Like, don't make me MAD dude—you'll make me FAT!!]:<

TBH

Your organs will feel the pain... YOU refuse to deal with.

230.

Over time, this puts the body at *dis-ease* with itself (cuz it breaks down). I dunno of any other animal that does that EITHER! You know we really suck as a species. Just stating the facts. We're the most intelligent, so we turn on ourselves. Lmfaooo

Muscle Memory

We hear it all the time, coaches, trainers even people *not* into sports, say that. It's a well known 'term'. Cool. But there's so much MORE to it than that. Muscle memory (my experience) doesn't only refer to muscle, remembering what it LIFTED (last time you were in the gym) a year ago, month ago, century ago (have to include my vampires). LOL Muscle memory, I believe refers to your muscles having the ability to store MEMORIES in them. It sure explains, why when a girl gets a back massage (muscles relaxed) is made love to (especially if she's on the run, loads of pressure) *has* an emotional experience... cries (moms fo shur). And that's cuz, as the muscles get loose, are released even if she can't remember what the feeling's linked to, she'll see something (in her mind) feel something that she wasn't even thinkin' about before she had the massage (or sex) as it comes out (surfaces) she literally *feels* it.

Or you dude. You just made love (to her). You're whole body is relaxed (released) you're chokin' on your tears (watching her sleep) you can't *believe*... God sent her to YOU. You're studying her *face*... her nose, (funny way she twitches it) her *mouth*... unusual shape of her lips. *Awh*...

Once our back muscles are relaxed (released) it *allows* for more oxygen to travel through our spine. More oxygen means more emotions (that's been put on hold, blocked, no time). Especially for us girls (sensitive guys) we're lying there gettin' a massage (making love) a memory comes... (tear jerker fo shur) we CRY (unexpectedly). A scene, sentence that plays over and over in our mind (hopin' to get noticed). It's *goal*... FULL blown out **drama** (*pressure*). The ice CRACKS and we're drownin' in it (so much emotion). Now we FEEL it. We're not separate from it anymore (we're *with it*). Which is WHY it's so important to remember, if your girl's crying A LOT... ask her. "What is it that you're **seeing**?" "What's the sentence that you keep *hearing* over and over in your head?" Once seen (or heard) it won't have the same effect.

Cops and Soldiers...

Always stand up straight. Their spine is erect (muscles tight) they command attention. JOCKS, same thing, but more chilled about it. Unless they're passed out drunk after a victory, loss (sleeping or relaxing).

Then there's YOU guys...

Who rhyme, write poetry n' shit (actors) whose posture is very relaxed. Your focus... *emotions* (they're on your finger tips) you have easy access to them. LOL All this makes a lot of sense to me, cuz guys are more EMOTIONAL (for the most part) when they're having sex (spine relaxed). Then you act like a dick the next day, in front of your friends. Like, didn't we just have sex with you, numb-nuts?

Once your back muscles are soft oxygen can make its way up our spine, oxygen is needed to ignite emotion. Just like... When a baby is about to cry (girls included here) it's always (inhale) *sniff* (inhale) *sniff* (Oxygen taken in) WHAAAAAAAAA!! I first learned about this when I was studying acting in New York. As part of our exercise we were told to lie on the floor and *breathe*... in deeply (then out) so muscles could *relax* (be at ease). Making access to emotions a whole lot 'easier'. Hey! Crying on demand. That can come in handy! Haaaa! Honestly, you have no IDEA how tense you are when you're asleep. Shoulders... waaay up by your temples. LOL

This form of relaxing muscles is a crying technique—cuz it's *how* the body works. I wanted to master it! :D I put on my trench coat, went outside to practice. Thank God it was autumn. I'm lying on the sidewalk, everyone passing thinks I'm some homeless person, start tossing dollar bills at my face. Rofl But I just keep breathing *inhaling, exhaling, inhaling*... dollar bills floatin' up and down on my face.

I made so MUCH money. LOL

It's a whole other thing when oxygen is *pushed* outside. Like, you're pissed, your eyes are bulging, bottom lip's quivering—you're exhaling like a BULL (nostrils flarin'). You know you're gonna lose it! Someone just dissed your favorite BAND!

232.

Cops, soldiers and athletes find it easier NOT to show their emotions or fall prey to sob stories, cuz they stand (for the most part) really straight (muscles tight). Strong (spine <u>not</u> curved) locking air tight, so oxygen doesn't get a chance to travel so *easily* up the spine (restricted). It could be the reason they're so **intense**. They need to be, in order to jump into action! Get the bad guys. Prove their point (without being derailed). The same for athletes who compete at a dangerous sport WITHOUT any fear. Where as a computer geek (gamer) guy in the arts, appear to be more compassionate and easy going. As long as they're not in the middle of a Game (project). *Fuuuck!* They can be touchy. Their spine, is mostly *relaxed* (curved, posture not the greatest) back muscles (if any) are supple, not tight. (No offense dude) Which means oxygen is giving them LOADS of access to their emotions (sometimes too much). ☺ So 'overly' emotional. And they can get bogged down, depressed (too many unanswered questions) fear taking a stand (or lead). They work best in the background (behind the scenes) where they can be 'undisturbed' by humanness. It doesn't mean their shoulders won't *get* tense. It does mean that oxygen is freely moving. Which means they'll be MUCH more emotional (or very shy) with other people, a weird sense of humor (distinct possibility) gentle (gobs of poetic justice). And write lots of songs for YOU. And a*lllll* the stuff they've been through with you. Uber sensitive (likes to talk about their feelings a lot) gets hurt EASILY.

An ATHLETIC girl...

Whole other animal. Have you ever *seen* a competitive girl slouch? Unless, she's totally beat (maybe) wasted (oh... yeah). Otherwise it won't happen. She's got a thing called PRIDE. She walks her talk.

ATHLETIC guys...

Well... You've just got *sooo* much to prove (where your manhood's concerned) only room for ONE King of the mountain. And this is the one place (thankfully) you can lay your balls on the court—not lose them. LOL We love you guys!

A new perspective leads to new a SOLUTION.

LET'S LAY OUT OUR STRATEGY...

Study the plays (our role in it) counter attacks, tackle our adversaries (self doubt, people, circumstance) one by one, as we aim for the high ground (our place of serenity). Join forces with the mind, body, spirit(s) (for those who have more than one). TOO many shots! *_* Make the *right* choice—or you'll PAAAY.

Anything less than utilizing your full potential would be like stealing, from your guy (girl) on your 'high' way to LOVE. Since we hunt for people who balance our fouls, minimize our penalties, are victorious where we are not—highway robbery is what that is.

FOR ALL YOU GUYS AND GIRLS WHO WANT...

the very best life can offer

Attraction - Opportunity - Circumstance

(Your inherited birthright!)

It's GOT to be coded in our cells, somewhere! What if it were true... What if God's NAME was actually (literally) encoded in our body?! Kinda like, an inward tattoo. Wouldn't that be SICK? What would you do? How would you feel to **know**... God's *signature* is written inside your body? I'd feel SUPER entitled (to a lot of things). I would not feel guilty. I would not feel like I have to *suffer*... I'd feel like everything's great! And life's one big happy PARTY!! Where exciting things happen. Like, meetin' the perfect person. ☺ The perfect connection for my career! Even though I know, I'm a Child of God— that'd be *proof!* And I'd go for alllll these BIG things—I'd NEVER dream of going for. And I wouldn't wanna make it overnight. Oh... noooo. Cuz then it'd be like, no big deal. I'd make it so I'd have to work for it. I'd put some obstacles in the mix, (just to spice it up) like a hardcore gamer. I'd crank up the difficulty (make it super challenging) turn up the speed (add pressure and time limits) take on more opponents allll at once (nothin' like relationship DRAMA). LOL And cuz I want bragging rights, after I plough through the final boss I'd take on the biggest, baddest optional boss. Insanely difficult. ME... *my darkest side.*

My DOUBTS...

And every time I'd get my ass kicked. I'd laugh, grind my teeth— *VOW TO DEAL IT BACK!!* Tenfold. Knowing that each failure would **only** fuel my next victory. And this game doesn't need a reset button. I'm always being happy and excited cuz I love the game!

When I was a little girl I used to ask my mom...

"Mom... How do we **know** there's a boy for EACH girl? Like, where's it WRITTEN? How do we know, for sure?" She's like, "Every POT has a lid." I'm like, "Hey! Every pot DOES have a lid." I'm super stoked. Run upstairs to my room and look out the window. I'm thinking... I wonder what MY boy... looks like. I COULDN'T wait to meet him. Then. Terror!!! I run downstairs—jump seven steps (if I break my neck, so be it) THIS is important! I burst through the kitchen doors crying my eyes out. I'm like, "MOM!! What if there's NO lid?! What if I'm like, one of those Mexican pots with a design on it, like in the museums? They DON'T have a lid." She's like, "Go wash your hands, dinner's ready." "But what about my LID?" We're always searching for unquestionable proof.

Cuz when we feel entitled... we prefer to bypass suffering.

I don't care what's happened in your past. Don't care what you think you did (caused) made *happen*... Don't care what people *think* of you. I'm HERE to tell YOU...

YOU were *born* with a **purpose**...

You need to FIND it.

And I need YOU to come out of your hiding place. Show the WORLD what you're made of. *Phaleeeze*... WE need you. Don't ever doubt that. And all that YOU are to do, need to do... have within YOU to do, has already been set in *motion*...

YOU are on TRACK.

You've already connected to the *right* people (place) setting. Even if it's gruesome... it's there to *force* you to go where you need to go (do what YOU need to do) to find your *gift*. If it's a shitty place, I guarantee... it's gonna chisel *that* gift (even more). I love YOU... remember that. YOU will make a tremendous impact, which usually happens from the *need* to DO. You picked up this book—someone got it for you, talked about it (*it was not by chance*). All those set on being *masterful*... in Life, Love. A **true** home run—winning MATCH! Touchdown (*fo shur*). A hole in one (couldn't resist). LOL *Reeeal* magic...

Come this way!

Refuse to Be captured.

keep it Real

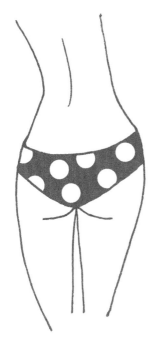

keep it Pure

Towards ANYONE including an a-hole is...

YOU... Being happy.

I know it sounds fundamentally stupid. Just hear me out. Cuz it happens to be TRUE. It's just that there's SO many layers to it, you need to understand the *mechanics* of how it 'works' (in order for it to be successful). I know, I had this *one* boyfriend (really pissed me off) my mom's like, "Just act like it **isn't** bothering you. Just be happy." I'm like, "YOU insaaane? I'm burning up inside!! I wanna go eat somebody's FACE! I *can't* pretend. But she wants me to act... like it isn't bothering me.

No. 1

It's NOT about being uncomfortable trying to pretend you're happy when you're intensely MISERABLE. You need to be truly happy (if it's to work its *reversal* powers). And it will WORK. Especially with a guy (or girl with huge ego). I broke up with this guy once, weeks of feeling like *shittttt* go by. I invite a few girls over for a sleep over. We're watching the most hysterical movie (**very** happy). He CALLS. Like... What's up with you guys, the moment we're NOT thinking of you, YOU call. Do you like, have an antenna up your ass that vibrates the *second* we're over you? Yo! Check it. She's not tripping anymore. Re-install AGONY.

I answer his call...

I'm in a super *great* mood and there's all this *laughing* and screaming in the background. I'm like, *"Hiiii!"* I'm pissin' myself, cuz we have our beauty mask on (avocado, oatmeal, eggs whites) all hangin' off our face and it's **hardened**... hanging off our chin. We look like swamp CREATURES. I remember when he and I were civil (good terms) he'd come over and I'd have coffee grinds on my face. I open the door... He's like, "Why do you have poop on your face?" You guys have nooo idea the amount of effort we put in, to stay beautiful for YOU. Omg. You should see how awesome the coffee grinds are. Especially around your eyes for dark circles or bagggs. Just mix with water to form a paste, gently smear around the eyes, let stand for 15 minutes. Rinse! And yes, you'll get called 'raccoon eyes'. I'm sure the raccoon won't mind.

So... I'm holdin' the phone very close to my ear to see if I can *hear*... a hint of a pause, sigh... deep breathing. So I know where he's at. And all he can say, "WHY are you so happy?" No reason. LOL

So my boyfriend (real time) is like, "That would *crush* me..." (Exactly)
Few days later my ex comes over to pick up something he *claims* he
left behind (by accident). *Shurrrr.* My boyfriend's like, "Maybe, he
forgot." No... he didn't forget! Naivety... never ceases to make me
wanna say. 'FUUCK NO!' Honestly. What is it with you guys, do you
like, strategically place something in our room (just in case)? Howww
James Bond of you! And definitely. A stage two clinger. It's like, you
subconsciously *know* something's gonna give... a FIGHT. So you leave
something. Cuz in your **past** life you were a girl—and you know allll
our ways (to win us over). My ex was like, "You know the one thing
I kept thinking over and over—NOT why we broke up. HOW could
she possibly be happy without ME?!" Ahahaha! It needs to be real. So
don't fake it (it won't work) cuz it acts like a magic wand, or something. When HE calls and you answer *happy* like that, the very first
thing he's gonna think...

Why's she sooo happy?

Followed by... How can she POSSIBLY be happy without me? Yeah,
you'll wanna highlight this part. Hystericallll And I didn't have to ex-
communicate my guy. I wasn't upset anymore. And it doesn't have to
be a funny movie, if you're gonna be in his class THINK... Hilarious.
Watch a video that makes you laugh your ass off, get your hair done—
feel FABULOUS! Get your energy up-up-up!! It will sting *more* than
just his ego. It must be how they're *made*... And even though they're
wired for 'ego-fficiency' (have to make her happy no one else can)
guys (or girls who think they're right all the time) can be taken by
surprise—they won't see it coming. YOU being happy (without them).
Especially guys. They'll be like, "*Fuuuck.* THAT'S not supposed to
happen. Something's **not** right. It's off." It will devastate them.
They're like, "She's SUPPOSED to be sad. I don't get it." ☺

I also think it has to do with the focus of intensity... we have on them
(our thoughts, energy). Once we STOP and are focused on something
else (that makes us happy) someone **new**, the constant energy moving
towards them... stops too. And they feel that. It'll feel like something's
'missing'. They're not as happy (not fueled). Let's hope when they
come for a refill—it's an upgrade. LOL

...Innocent till proven guilty. O:-)

240.

I think guys are made like this for a *reason*. And yeah, they can be heartless at times...

Guy: "I just tell a girl what she *wants* to hear—and I get SEX."

I knowww. A guy actually told me that! And I'll SO *deal* with that (in a second). That's just my point. They'll do what works, there's no personal feelings involved, just...

WHAT DOES IT TAKE TO GET IN YOUR PANTS?

(I'll do it...)

I also believe, that guys are <u>designed</u> in a way to bring out the best in 'us'. You're like, *Huh*... Ladies WAIT! I know it's hard to believe, cuz after you've been fucked (scarred) drained to eternity, thinking what you did was the RIGHT thing to do. Give SO MUCH.

Like...

- Putting yourself <u>second</u> (to prove you love him) his needs *ahead* of yours. Like givin' head, when you don't want to.

- Not listening to your feelings, doin' what you think is the 'right' thing to do. ☺

- Doin' things to WIN him over (buying him things) doing his homework (when you have a ton of work to do) spending all your money (allowance) to travel to see him (all the time).

- When he's upset keeping all your shit to yourself, as if to show that's how *much* you love him. Puttin' his feelings ahead of yours AGAIN. (What meds are you on?)

- Faking things to make HIM feel good. (More medication)

- Telling him how to run his life. Helping him get organized (neglecting your stuff) doing all this shit for him cuz he's useless on his own. Being like his mama. Then complaining he's LIKE a child.

- Smothering him with TEXTS, EMAILS, LUV NOTES so he *knows* you're not going anywhere... Dummmb.

- CRITICIZING how he is.

- Failing to appreciate little things he does cuz you're so tired of doing sooo much. So why bother? You feel it's owed to you—NOT to say a word.

- Protecting his feelings, watching other girl's eyeing him, confronting them. Then wondering why he says, "You act like a dude."

Then YOU change.

How he responds to you, finally hits YOU. You text him twenty times and it takes him a DAY to get back to you. He was busy. You go out with a friend (at night) take the subway, he doesn't even check in to see if you got home safely. You talk about *forever* (getting married) he starts to fidget... and changes the subject. Which then makes you feel stupid, embarrassed... a dumbass.

So... You do LESS.

You don't text him every hour. You don't text him a WHOLE TWO WEEKS. And he's sooo NICE (attentive). You care less (at least, that's how it's playing in your head) focus more on yourself, don't go out of your way (*for him*) and oddly enough, YOU learn... He prefers it this way. And you just don't get it (at first). You do less, he does *more*. Wtf? And it's actually more fulfilling for him. Who woulda thought? Even if he does *appear* to be a lazy-ass, which soon even that guy learns, that unless he wants to take up mastur-**dating** (going out with *himself*) seeing a movie by *himself,* going to a cafe by *himself,* things gotta be DIFFERENT.

And it starts with YOU girl...

STOP faking your orgasms!

242.

Seriously I'd be like, "You don't get a *moan*... unless you earn it." HOW are guys supposed to know? That's why with my guy... I always have to have things just *right*—so I draw him a MAP. I so doooo. I don't have patience for shit like that! Like *hellllo*... ZERO moisture means move *on*. Some guys just don't get it—and we get finger *burn*. Like rope burn but worse. Funny? Notttt. Or it could be real simple. Like, the way they kiss. I'd be like, "Bae, you kiss like a *bird*... I don't feel you're lips. (I squish his cheeks) You need to *pucker*." He's like... "Why don't I get lip IMPLANTS?"

We girls have always led the romance department.

ROMANCE is our game.

It's our thing... Not so much, in what we say with words, the way we *look* at you (our smile) what we *don't* say—highly magnetic. Pullin' you in... is our specialty (we know this). And a high demand list, is attached to that package. Buyers beware. Don't touch what you can't afford. LOL

YOU break it YOU pay for it... in *sooo* many ways.

It's like we've got this invisible *thread*... that's pulls YOU to us so we can inspire you to do what we need (*want*) without telling you. And doesn't come across as needy... Bossy. So, doesn't interfere (with you wanting to give). It's tricky, to tell you what we *want*... sometimes it makes you guys think we're tellin' you what to DO. Like, giving you an order. Which we are! It's complicated. And confusing (especially in the romantic, sexual arena).

All I know...

Unless a guy **asks**... it might make him feel weird (girl telling him how to 'do it'). After all, it's HIS penis. It's like, a guy giving us instructions how to use OUR vag. Annoying... He'll be like, "Relax! JUST relax! Are you coming?" *Shuuut up!* We can't focus. If it's his very **first** time, he'll take <u>any</u> directions. *Damnn*... he'll do it in a CLOSET upside down—with a baseball bat in his ear (if you say so) just cuz he wants it SO bad. Otherwise, a guy might feel stupid...

You tellin' him what how to do it. It adds pressure. Then again, some guys *like* orders—to the LEFT. Hold it! **DON'T** move. *Ahh...* right *there*. YOU MOVED!! How can you move? I ALMOST came! Now, I have to start all over might as well put an ice cube there, I'm done. I'm gonna have to masturbate. He'll be like, "Can I WATCH?" Ugh!

IF...

A guy asks you if you like *this* or that...

While he's getting to know YOU so he gets a better picture of what YOU like (*how you like it*) where you like to go, what you like to '**do**'. What makes you HAPPY. So it doesn't become like giving him a *list*... of everything you like, **don't** like (course with me, very impatient GAVE him a list—2 actually) all you girls need to do is appreciate him, when he **does** do something you like.

AND LET HIM KNOW IT...

It underlines it in his mind.

A guy really needs to know he's appreciated (**valued**) his code of 'respect'. And don't worry, it won't go to his head—that's not the head he's concerned with. :P If you tell him how much you love it when he does *this* or that. How smart he is. How you like the way he calms you down (when you're upset) the things he *does*... He NEEDS to hear these things. He needs to know what YOU admire most about him. Not just his looks—he's not your DOLL. You're the doll (remember). Let him know all the things he does that you love (he probably doesn't even know). All the things he's been doin' that make you happy. He ALWAYS makes you laugh. Says the right thing, is there (for YOU). Whatever you **emphasize** with your guy, he'll do *more* of. They're like, little golden stars added to his final term paper. YOU being the main subject. So he knows, he's the shit! He *excels* with YOU. A guy that knows he's on top of his game *cherishes* the game, its earned his respect (re-read that). He's studied long and hard for it. If you're like, "You're an ASSHOLE." Every time he makes a mistake, he will act more and **more** like that. The *reason* I say that...

244.

A GUY FALLS IN LOVE...

With how he *feels* when he's around YOU...

How YOU make him feel...

Not just BANGING you—on a *deeper* level. So he feels powerful (enough) on the *inside*. If you're just fucking, he won't be able to shake that feeling (from the other girl). He'll be thinking of *her* while he's fucking YOU.

(Time to release your demons dude) LOL

He needs to feel he has a function (**purpose**) and that he can fulfill that function... then later *other* functions. LOL When it comes to the romantic DEPT (our domain) we lead the guys by communicating *back*... how we feel about their choices. How it affects us. As in, "No... My idea of a date is <u>not</u> your basement—beaten up couch, some BEER. Unless, you want the truck driver in me who horks, farts and burps to come over (with her dreadlock hairy legs). That's NOT bringing out the diva in me." When his attempt doesn't work and you speak your *feelings* it encourages him to try (*again*) a different method, till he gets it right. So he understands, he needs to *give it*... (the right way) first. IF you don't settle for less than what you want.

Re: <u>BEER</u>

I just have to say, if you've ever smelled a hops plant, you'd see (quite quickly) its hypnotic effects—MAJOR sleepy feeling. Cannabis is used to produce hash and marijuana, they're closely related to hops. Along with other substances, one of the relaxing effect you'd get from beer *comes* from the hops ingredient hopein. Hopein is a form of morphine. AAAAAAH!! No wonder we can't stop! NOW I know why you offer beer.

Hopein you'll get some! LOL

It's also known to work as an anti-aphrodisiac, which of course... suppresses your sexual performance and drive. (NOT good) My boyfriend's like, "Really? Is that's true? Hopein is an anti-aphrodisiac?

No wonder the *sea-men* don't feel like swimmin' home... MIA. LOL When my friends have too much they can't even get it up." Guess, 'liquid courage' can't hold it up either. And! It contains the female sex hormones, daidzein and genistein (used to fatten calves, sheep n' chickens). It also has another female hormone. Estrogen...

Helllllo BITCH TITS!

Beer gut and breast growth (case, you didn't notice) is caused by these female hormones (calories have nothin' to do with it). Think about that, the next time you have your cricket pee.

Back to NOT settling...

Even if he is a **practice** run (you know you don't want him, seriously) so wtf. I'll tell you... Practice doesn't make perfect. PERFECT practice makes *perfect*. Which means, if you're used to being one way (a slut) then prince charm-the-fucken-pants-right-*off* YOU comes... And he's genuinely interested. You won't be able to just **switch** to regal mode—you'll be hand-maiden all the way.

Hope you don't have calluses.

Or, you'll pull it off (split-personality type) NOT sleep with him right away, then he's your boyfriend—YOU end up doing allll the work. Takin' care of everything. Cuz in your mind, you need to *give*... in order to get. And you never see it comin' (cuz you're used to it).

I met this guy...

We were texting back and forth. Everything's cool then one Saturday he texts... "Hey watcha doing?" I'm like, "Working on some term papers." He's like, "Why don't you come over and chill *on the couch*."

Uh... you lost me right now.

He continues to talk to me when we're with common friends. I give him generic answers (yes. no. maybe) still doesn't get it. Guys... We need to be in an *environment* that makes us happy, which tends to lend to *more* happy beginnings. Comfortable... which tend to make us comfortable with YOU. And pleasing to our senses (doesn't hurt to look at). So don't even *think* of kissing us in front of a DUMPSTER.

(Not pleasing to <u>any</u> senses)

I remember this guy couldn't *wait* to make out with me. We were on the verge of becoming 'serious'. So we're walkin' home... he stops, turns me around kisses me (*hard*). I'm like, "Whoa!! STOP." He's like, "I CAN'T I got an erection from the *tip* of my penis to the center of my spinal cord." Not MY problem (nahh... couldn't let him suffer). We kiss. I look to see if his eyes are *closed* (really into it). And yes, we wanna make sure you guys are practically DIZZY from our kiss. Plus, it's such a turn on for us, cuz you look so vulnerable (for a second). But when I opened my eyes, I saw four GARBAGE bins!! I'm like...

"Is *this* where you want me to remember our first kiss?! All I see... is TRASH." From that point on wherever we were, he'd check allll angles. Do a full turn. THEN kiss me.

That's how we feel VALUED...

Speaking of being kissed!

OMG. My first time... I was 13 and at a sleep over. My girl friend had this real *hot* brother. He was 16. I'm lying on the bed (with my eyes closed) trying to think of secrets to share. My girl friend's downstairs getting snacks. I open my eyes, her brother's sitting on my BED... I grab the magazine from the night table, open it in front of my face. Pretend to read. IT'S UPSIDE DOWN. Felt *sooo* dumb. It's right in front of my nose—like WHO reads that close. Sooo obvi. He takes the magazine out of my hands, we're staring at each other. No *words*... All I could do, is look at his mouth. Then he *leans* in.. french kisses me—don't even KNOW what I'm doing. How did this happen? It didn't make any sense. I don't even know... how to turn a guy on. I did NOTHING. I felt his lips... they were so *soft*. Then! He shoves his TONGUE down my throat. I almost GAG. Felt like two slimy snakes squishing against each other. *Yuck*. I couldn't understand why a kiss felt like *that*. He was HOT! And I read all this stuff on it—and the MOVIES!! But it felt so gross. Years later. I understood... I need to know the guy, really feel for him. A LOT. That probably makes it bypass all the mucous (secretion) part. So instead of it FLOODING my mouth (where I'm chokin' on spit) it's neutralized. I can enjoy it. Still, I couldn't think of anything but him... for days. In time, when it did happen again (with my first love) it *was* amaaazing. He went sooo slow. He didn't try to wrap his tongue around my third VERTEBRAE. It was more like, our lips were just *exploring*... feeling each other out, gettin' used to each other (our style of kissing). Molding to each other's way... till it became OUR way. Goose bumps... all over *again*.

What YOU guys need to remember...

Our mouth is the gateway to our *soul*... if done right, with all the conditions met (she's comfortable with you, both of you really like each other, wanna 'just' be with each other) acts like cementing paste. You're *one* now... She feels pain YOU feel it *twice* as bad. You're upset... She can't focus. It's like you've adopted a whole new body (to care of, watch over, make happy). If I were YOU... I'd be very careful who I let inside my pearly whites, girl... tongue twisters are hard to manage, come on suddenly (have their way). ;<> A guy will learn what turns you on, makes you happy, sad, how things affect you... If you let him know how YOU feel (about it). That way you're not coming across as domineering (when you do decide to TELL HIM how you feel) not telling him how to be, just declining what *isn't* comfortable for you. Unless he asks! You can always let him know what would make you *really* happy... (concert, movies, beach, helicopter ride, him pickin' up his socks). And, you're speaking from your feelings' point of view, a woman's prerogative (special privileges *fo sure*) **not** from your mind. Known to form an opinion and with it, an air of superiority (that sometimes follows).

Invisible price tag.

Not that YOU can't have your opinion—you DO! But when you're communicating with your guy, who you look up to (respect) it could make him feel attacked (challenged) that *his* best isn't good enough, for you. When you're telling him **what, where, how** (to do). He may see it as him NOT making the grade—can't make the right choice (a fuck up). Especially if it's in a form of a complaint, which it usually seems like to them, then they're like, "Man... my girl's always bitching about what I'm doing WRONG. Nothing's ever good enough for her."

And YOU thought you were just making it clear.

When your response (feedback) comes from the logical part of the brain (his territory far as he's concerned) it's his LOGIC—pinned against yours (or so it seems) and he CAN'T afford to lose. Then you wouldn't look UP to him. Would you? So for him it's a lose/lose. Argue with YOU and win the argument (lose YOU) don't win the argument LOSE (the ability of having you look up to him).

Tough call.

(Sucks to be YOU dude) :P

And once he feels like that (weaker) he could approach you one day be like, "It's NOT working out. I need some space." And wanna break up. He'll insist... YOU deserve someone *better*. Someone who'll spend more time with you. Cuz he's found someone who doesn't communicate the way you do (still gets her point across) so it seems *easier* (not as difficult to deal with). Especially if you're chirping on him *in front* of everyone, about what he's doing WRONG. He's gonna literally shrink in broad daylight. Not healthy, for any aspect of a man. Then again, if he's a TOTAL jerk, after he's HAD you (sexually) he'll be like, "It's not YOU... babe, it's me. I'm not right for YOU. You don't deserve someone like me." You can always say... "You know what? You're ABSOLUTELY right. Don't know *whaaat* I was thinkin." Big SMILE. (Hold) Walk... Let your body *talk* with that swag of yours—BIG MISTAKE!! (Huge) Two seconds later... he'll be like WAIT A MINUTE I thought we had something!

You'll see...

I just gotta also say, if the guy's sayin' shit like that? No doubt. You've given TOO much (TOO soon). And or, doin' things for him he hasn't *earned* yet. Just cuz, you're in shock that he's actually hanging out with you (you've been trying for sooo long). So yeah, in his mind... he'll be thinkin', talking to his buddy, sayin' stuff like, "Yeah man. She's *sooo* good to me. (Big smirk) Just don't feel like I deserve it." Like he almost feels bad, he hasn't really done anything to deserve it. So hard for him to continue. Good waiting station though! LOL

REIVEW:

If a guy truly wants to 'know' your opinion—he'll ASK. And even then, you can get your point across without destroying him in the process. If YOU speak as a woman from a feeling *platform*... Swan dive never looked so good! Lady swans...

I feel...

I'm comfortable *with*... I'm uncomfortable when you... I really like it when *you*... I *don't* feel good about... I *don't* like it when you... I'm totally lovin' *this*...

(Highly effective). LOL

A lot of you smart University girls be like... "WTF? I'll say whatever I want, the WAY I wanna say it. I'm not doin' this *shit*... I **don't** play games." I knew we'd be having this discussion. LOL So you don't play games. Huh? *Nahh*... you play your own games, ones you *invent* as time goes by (depending on what you <u>can</u> or cannot do) and then of course, get someone *else* who's foolish enough to 'play' your personal game (of power and control). So you think... You'd be the one askin', "What's your till?" STILL not registering huh? Funny thing about thinking you know *everything*... there's no invitation for something 'new'.

Doors locked *KNOWWW* everything! Sorry.

Typical.

You'll have a guy that does *this* and that (cuz he's *scared* of you). Well, let me tell you how different it *feels* to have a guy have sex with you who's afraid of YOU—and a guy who's not. A WORLD of difference...

I'm not against you.

I'm with you. What you don't know is, there's a pattern already in motion (when you're set into one way of being) ...it hurts YOU. You don't know who's steering you, you think you do. Which is why you're so opposed to trying something *different*—it feels like you're playing by someone else's rules. That's exactly what you're already doing, playing by someone else's rules—it's not your natural state (*that's* been ignored, a while now). It's ruling you... you don't even know it. Otherwise you wouldn't be so 'fixed' against trying something new (if you were not already being *played*) girl.

Omg. I even had to read that TWICE. LOL

Your mind will SPLIT...

It can work for you or against you. Your GUT cannot... It'll never call you a *loser*. It forewarns YOU. Your mind (depending on how you've interpreted your surroundings, conditions, home life, your crew) can turn on YOU (any time). Take you to the LOWEST depths of hell. It can **also** encourage YOU (when you feel good) if channeled properly. It needs *your* guidance—not the other way around. Your gut... will *only* work for YOU. It'll give you the heads up! Tell you when something *right*... no thinking involved. It knows. It also tells you—if that changes. When you're used to doing something one way, cuz you're used to thinking it's the *right* way... it feels comfortable (*fo shur*). But if you're not **really** happy—it's OFF. If then... you feel a little irritable trying to do it differently, cuz now you're going by what you feel instead of think, it's cuz you're not used to it (feelings) so it'll feel odd. You don't trust it. Get to know each other... (gut). It'll never leave you, turn its back on you. Call you bad names or think you're STUPID.

It loves you...

RECAP :

When we speak from *our* feelings (girls) it takes care of 2 problems.

1. We can be honest. Say (truthfully) how we feel without worrying about it. Yaay!

2. Not disrespect a guy, while we get our point across. Yassss!

If you're arguing with your guy, letting him know something he did **really** upset you (putting a light on your issue) and he's like, "That HURTS my feelings." He's trying to hook you in with *guilt*... turn the spotlight on him (*off* you). Conscious or not. The whole idea of shedding light is to be able to SEE (what's hurting you). Not to put it back on him, a result of his wounded self, cuz he's personalized it instead of learning from it (adjusting himself in how he handles you). He can't handle feelin' like shit so (instead) accuses you of hurting his feelings (with the whole situation). And if YOU fall for it... you'll forget what you came for in the first place, cuz spotlight's on him NOW. You place your feelings behind his (comfort him). *Grrrr!!* Quietly saying to yourself, "*Shittttt*... Can't believe how he took it so hard. I'm never gonna do *that* again. He must really care." YEAH (for his own ass). Whatever you're sniffing girl—it's doing its job (affecting allll brain CELLS at once). Man up dude!!

It's different if you're out with the girls and it's LATE (he hasn't heard from you allll night) you talk later and he's like, "I was <u>really</u> worried about YOU. I want you to text me the next time you're gonna come home waaay after you said you would. That really bothers me." Legit. I call that, genuine concern... truly gives a shit. Feels responsible.

A High card in the Game of Love.

So next time you have an ISSUE (with your guy) let him know what happened (he upset you/hurt you/disappointed you) and he's like... "**You're hurting my feelings**." You can say, "I'm NOT your mama and you're not FOUR. And if you want me to respect YOU (your mind) where I can actually look up to YOU—value my feelings. So I feel cherished... inwardly *respected*. Don't just respect me cuz I'm a coding genius. That doesn't help my heart (feel good)."

Just one of those trade-off things. ;D

Respect is a baseline. Everyone should be respected. But respect **without** being *cherished* is settling (a rip-off) incomplete. A guy can respect you (how smart you are, what you've accomplished) but how invested is he in your heart (your feelings) when you're down, in spite of how smart you are? When a guy cherishes YOU... he's inspired and so meshed in with your entire being he's not *challenged* to wait... (for sex) he's content, just being with YOU. He can't stand seeing you upset, regardless of where he is emotionally. YOU will come first.

Being cherished is like a palace BUILT on the solid rock *of* respect. YOU can't build the palace on a swamp. And a rock is very uncomfortable to live on. Respect alone is not enough. Can he *respect*... the cute way you pout your lips? How giggly and happy you get when he surprises you with something? Or the adorable sleepy penguin walk, you do in the morning going to the bathroom? If he doesn't cherish you... it's dry (alll in the mind). When a guy respects you (it's a beginning...) it doesn't 'automatically' include treasuring everything about YOU. If a guy cherishes YOU... respect, is a given.

Girls, if you seriously wanna be like, " Well, when I see him I'll see how he's feeling *first*... then I'll tell him what's going on with me." NOOOO. How's he gonna grow love calluses? You *weaken* him... that way. Actually you handicap him (TOTALLY my opinion). You're stuck in your head (where you don't wanna be) cuz you're thinking... NOT feeling (as a priority). He then learns to value his feelings **before** yours. Most importantly, you deny him the ability to make you truly happy. Do you have <u>any</u> idea how *high* he gets off, seeing you HAPPY? Firstly, he's gonna take credit for it.

Bragging rights... LOL

Secondly...

You being happy gives off a shit load of *energy*. Which overspills onto him... *all of him* (you followin'). And dude, if you want your girl to take care of your 'feelings', cool. Straight up, are you gonna feel like da' MAN *inside?* K... Pen15 you were born with. :P Manhood is a status you achieve when you <u>feel</u> like da MAN. Take care of your *woman* dude.

She wants to rely on YOU...

Think about it...

Wouldn't you rather have her think highly of YOU?

(Respect who YOU are)

What you stand for, your abilities (fine, skills). What you're *capable* of. They CANNOT design another guy like YOU... You know it, and I know it. Now she needs to know it. WALK your talk, man. Be there for your girl and her feelings. You'll be glad you did. I know... *CON - FRONT - ATIONS* can be <u>scary</u> .

(Especially with your girl). o_O

Far as I'm concerned... It's just another 'word' for getting **in front** of your *situation*. So get in front of your girl (situation)! Lead the way BOSS. The more bitchy she is... the more she needs YOU.

Girls...

No matter how many awards you get, how high your grades are (IQ), your guy knowing you're the **smartest** girl around, it won't make a difference (in your relationship) if you don't feel *treasured* inside. Special... to him. Unless you know your feelings are a **priority** it'll be a hopeless battle (you tryin' to prove how special you are in *other* ways) cuz he's not paying attention. Even though he thinks you're smart he doesn't *cherish* YOU. *I'm just sayin...*

FACTS we can't argue with.

Our body's designed a little differently, so may need to do things a little differently. And although it may seem like one mode of communicating when we're dissatisfied (*I feel...*) it's mega effective.

And besides...

It's our birthright...

We were BORN a Girl... :D

We have the *extra* chromosome. That says A LOT. We're not less than. We're twice as MUCH. Maybe that's why we have boobs and you don't. So... You can't argue about how we feel.

It's OUR feeling.

You can however, argue if we tell you that we *think* we shouldn't do it, or it isn't right. Cuz then you're like, "*Whyyy*... Don't you have feelings for me?" We just walked onto their territory girls (logic) their RULES. Which means... any and all weapons can be used to strike. So if he can outwit you (trick you) make you believe it's gonna be *this* and it turns out to be *that* (oops... *it slipped in)* you're TAKEN. And quicksand is a slow and painful way to sink (into his ways). Takes foreverrr to get out.

Giving a guy feedback is great! If you let him know how you felt on the date (liked, appreciated, felt good with, uncomfortable, too soon etc) it'll help him know how to design the next one to your liking. *DIDN'T HAVE TO SAY A THING*. Unless he's a idiot—get rid of him. Course, if it's an ultimatum you're giving... waaay too long to voice your concern. Respond, by tellin' 'em how you feel. Instead of... "K! I think that movie pretty much SUCKED. I think YOU suck. I want YOU to... and then—and DON'T forget x... y... & z." Unless he's whipped (bad) and you've already stood the test of time. LOL Guys will *learn* by what we say NO to. And those 2 *magical* words... **I feel**.

(Can't remind you too often)

And it's not about making someone do something to prove they love YOU. Don't know how all that got started. Though very tempting (have to admit). That's sadly, never someone you love only you 'use' till the right one comes along.

And YOU know it.

So... Not good practice.

Silona...

Is SEDUCTION

(A guy's favorite mating call)

A girl's power... Limitless

(Yuuup)

What Is LOVE...

What ISN'T LOVE

God designed the perfect love, thousands of years ago... it's been a while. There's been some wear n' tear. LOL We're gonna need a tune-up in relating to one another and definitely (at *this* point) high maintenance. Until things are running smoothly, in order to have something that will transport us as far as we want to go... within each other. <3

What to expect...

Love is freedom.

YOU feel free (inside) like someone came and UNLOCKED you from your silent misery. :P Sometimes, it's boredom or routine. You also feel like you can be your whole unrestricted self. And now that *more of you* have joined in... YOU feel awesome. Life's one BIG party. You have all this energy—you're never tired. It's like, you're not occupying this one little corner of the earth anymore. Your world just got BIGGER. You know *more* people too, cuz of who they know. Everything seems **brighter**. You're happier (even food tastes better). Not much bothers you. Even people who piss you off (annoy you) like siblings, fo shur parents (teachers) don't have the *same* effect on you. If Einstein was around he'd be like, "That's the **formula**!! If you feel like kaka pour LOVVVVE in your life!! It'll evaporate it. It won't be able to affect you. It's an internal drug—in house. LOL Pure. The real stuff. Putting this ONE ingredient in... makes you INVINCIBLE against anyone's pissy attitude, circumstance, result (you don't like) cuz you're like, "Who cares!" Its power to affect you is diminished to *zero*. Even your heart feels more potent, sometimes it feels like it can literally EXPLODE (out of pure joy). Everything seems to *expand...*

Your world... **Your** energy... **Your** feelings.

And yeah, your organ too dude. *Duh.*

It always seems to *rise* for the right occasion—WHERE there's an opening. LOL When you meet the *one* there's no inner conflict. It's like, your perfect OASIS with a *person* who gets you. Your purpose for *having* a relationship... to make you **happy**. Cuz that's what it DOES. You feel *awesome* just being with the person. Don't even think of tryin' to look for this, where someone's trying to get you to prove yourself to them. i.e. "If you love me... YOU'LL do it." Lame. And can we say... *old*. You're their *love* not their hostage. And hopefully not 'jailbait'.

(HEAVY fine there)

Proving you'll do something doesn't mean you love them, it means you take orders (nicely). Cuz that's the opposite of love. If love's freedom—*that's* incarceration! Even if it don't look it, it is. Your heart is not happy. It's not singing! It's not FLYING. It's not high. It's *low*... somewhere in a dungeon (dark and lonely place). Which is why you can't possibly share what you're going through with anyone else, there's no entry (YOU don't wanna make them look bad). Doing something you don't wanna do (to keep him, her) making yourself STAY out of fear (no one else would want me) guilt... (well, I did *this* to them) anger (they cheated, I'm gonna MATCH their 'every' move) **separates** you from your destiny...

2 - b HAPPY.

When you're HAPPY you can do more, feel more (be <u>more</u>) self love not excluded here. Everything *expands*... Tell me you don't *ABSO-FUCKEN-LUTELY* take a deep breath in... (lungs *expanding*) before that **first** kiss... YOU sooo do! Hopefully he's not slobbering all over you (baby wipes just in case). I was talking to this guy and he's like, "Nichole for that first *kiss*... It's gotta be JUST right. I've got it all set up. It's gonna be in a park, on a *bench*... And it's gonna be in the middle of the month cuz that's when there's a full MOON..."

My park episode was a little different.

I knew he loved me...

Even though at the time, we were still just getting to know each other (friends) I still couldn't believe, when I went to see my parents (up North) didn't tell him, he went craaaazy. Didn't answer my cell (no reception). He goes to my building (doesn't know my Floor) argues with the concierge cuz he's trying to get him to ring alllll TWO

HUNDRED apartments. Even OFFERS to give him money. Bribing the concierge! LOL But the guy threatens to call the cops my guy takes off. But he's *smart*. He returns next day (different time) talks to *another* concierge. (No luck)

I come back...

I'm *sooo* happy to see him. HE'S pissed (borderline real grumpy). I felt bad. I didn't know he cared *that* much. We had just started hooking up. After school he walked me to the subway and hugged me goodbye. Didn't let go. I can feel his *breath* on the side of my neck... he whispers, *"I want you... to be my girlfriend."* *AHHHHH!* I wasn't prepared for that! Absence *does* make the heart grow fonder (a cliché) scratch THAT.

Guys fall in love when they're away from YOU...

When they're with you... there's too many heads to deal with. Lmao

I said yes, right away...

Omg. We're official! And I can't text ANYONE. We go to the park and sit on a bench. It's so quiet, we're off the path and deep into the forest, there's no one around. Just the bees and trunks of the trees... k, one *more* trunk. LOL I straddle him... *face to face* (real close). We look at each other. Slowly... I *unbutton* my blouse, he puts his hand on my boob... *deeeep* breath. I **can't** think. I **can't** talk. But that didn't matter cuz inside... I felt amaaazing. He leans in... I pull away. He starts **breathing** heavy—pulls me in *close* our lips are about to touch... he pauses. Looks at me... *allllll of me*. And I'm *ABOUT TO FUCKEN EXPLODE.*

So TELL ME...

You don't need to take a breath.

When something like that *happens* your whole insides just keep getting bigger and bigger and BIGGER... Expanding your heart, sense of well being, everything! Especially, with my guy he's *expanding* all over the damn place. What you guys should know, is when we're in that 'state' we feel *safe* (with our heart) so we can let *ourselves* go... (body). And cuz we're surrendering to you (trust we know you love us) we're totally into that *experience*. As in, no conflicting thoughts (about ourself, shitty day, parents, drama, friends, nothing) but YOU on our mind. And when we give ourself to you, there's no *other* feeling like it, cuz at that point dude you can fully see *just* what you're about.

NOTHING CAN TOUCH YOU.

...Is how YOU feel.

Kinda makes you wanna do it right now, huh?

Excuse me! Be right BACK.

(*Muuuuuuch* better) ;D

It has to be **real**. And real's like, *baking* bread... it takes luscious, sexy *time*... to have the true flavor come out. Dunno too many guys into STALE bread (you're such picky eaters). You want it fresh, you want it wholesome.

Bake it properly!

Love *increases*... so you feel 'more' of everything. That's what it *does*. If you DON'T feel *more* you're being fooled, conned, manipulated (negotiated). And definitely settling.

*You do **this** for me (sex, hand job, blow job)*

- I'll let you ride in my NEW car.

- Introduce YOU to...

262.

- Get you back-stage PASSES.
- Do YOUR assignment.
- Protect you.
- Make you FAMOUS

Who spiked our drinks so we're not paying attention? If you don't feel *more* it means there's an ulterior motive, someone's making you <u>believe</u> that after a certain *time* (when you do this or that) if they get what they want **first** then you'll feel it... (more). Yeah... And I've got the entire FOOTBALL team twerking in my living room. That would really be something. LOL

It takes TWO to love... one to HATE

(Selfish bastard)

Need I say more? Just one thing. Love can only come when it's *invited*—it's not into forced entry. UH... THAT WOULD BE RAPE. Not so with hatred, it doesn't give a fuck who it steps on (or sleeps with). Sleazebag.

Sad thing is...

If you **fear** love (wanting but not feeling good enough) it'll shy away. It doesn't do well with rejection. That's why it's so hard, when you want something, someone (you already love them) but there's a BLOCK. Like this giant HAND is sticking out of your gut... stopping them (they can't get through). It's not that they don't want to, it's that YOU don't want them to... *even though you do*. You'll know if it's true by how you're feeling right now.

Sad ☐ Energy just dipped ☐ Deep sigh ☐

A TRUE soul connection...

YOU definitely (if for any reason have to **break up**) cannot stop *loving* them (a FACT). It's like, they have a secret compartment in your heart with their *name* on it. And most of the time (I believe) life will reconnect YOU. When it's through ROASTING you. And they're fully cooked—so you don't burp them out this time. Aftertaste can be so nasty (nothin' tastes good after). If they **die** (like mine did) then it's like... You have a *foreverrr* magical fish tank inside your heart. Beautiful, silent... they're always watching. If you're a lover, you *love*. That's what you do—it's your forte.

If you're a fighter... YOU will find a **reason** to fight.

(*Hellllo!*)

Maybe it's necessary. After all we've been told love is blind, so we gotta be on guard, right? We tell our mom we're goin' out with friends (hookin' up with a guy) she looks you straight in the eye, she's like, "Don't be naive..." Like! What does that mean?

(Exactly)

DOES ANYONE HAVE A BOOK ON THAT?

And what steps are involved to ensure that I'm not? Given that I'm young—it kinda goes with the territory. Mom keeps repeating herself. She's like, "Don't be **naive**. Don't be stupid... JUST Be yourself." ☺ Myself? I haven't even BEGUN to explore all ramifications of *myself*. I'm not even a quarter of a century old. There's four quarters to a dollar—*four* seasons to a year. I haven't even completed a whole SEASON. Give me a hint!

I'm like, "Mom. If you tell me to be *myself* there's no telling what I'll do. How can you tell me to be myself, when I don't even know WHAT that is exactly?" (So much *pressure*). It used to fuck me up so badly. Cuz she trusts me—but I get no guidelines whatsoever. Course, I suppose it's worse when they tell you a play by play—that's DATED... twenty years ago (seriously embarrassing). You're trying so hard NOT to roll your eyes. Not, that there isn't truth to what they're saying. It's just the way they explain it... it doesn't connect (makes no sense. And you wanna please 'em, not make them look stupid (same time). It's just a frustrating time. Someone give me a HANDBOOK!

Oooh. I'm sooo going to...

Personally, I wanted guidelines. I'm like, "Mom... What if he does THIS... then what do I do? Or if he says *this*... how do I answer in the best possible way, that gives me the greatest IMPACT? Catch him! And what does it mean exactly if he ***does*** do this...?" I'd even form a list of all the possibilities that could happen—never wanna miss a thing. Then I'd realize (aa-gain) what she said (although correct) was NOT for me. Cuz naturally, it's easy for moms to say 'ignore him' or, act like you're ignoring him. They don't feel for HIM, we DO! So no. Seeing a guy at a party after you KNOW he's been two timing you (with your closest friend) and you're **furious**... to *pretend* it's not bothering me—doesn't work!! I feel like a time bomb. In fact, my whole body feels like it's *TICKKKING*—gazillion miles an hour.

I took matters into my own hands...

I could tell by the way I felt in my body—it WASN'T working. Whenever I did what was *right* for me (speak up, cut someone off that was leaching off my heart valve) I'd feel *better* have more energy. Even if I was sad (*temporarily*) my body was happy. One time I really needed this guy to help me with something. All of a sudden (guess, cuz he knew how badly I needed him) he starts being such a... how shall I put it?

MAJOR prick.

He returns my calls... days after. I see him, ask why. He freaks! He's like, "I TOLD YOU. I'll call you when I'm <u>ready</u>. What part of *that* didn't YOU understand?"

(All of it... ☹)

Maybe his planets are misaligned. Hey dude. I think your Pluto is travelling up Ur-anus. Asshole. Then he apologizes on email. Lets me know he can work on it next day! Then NOTHING. I need an emoticon pulling out all his hair here. Every time he let me down he'd apologize. So I'm thinking, he just must have MORE planetary interference. *Fuuuck* that! In sheer exasperation, I over-pluck my eyebrows. Totally forgot the pluck *once*... step back routine. Looks soo uneven. BANGS it is! And if you really wanna step up your lash game, use a dark brown mascara first, let dry. Then use the blackest black, on your TIPS. As much as I didn't know what I'd do without his help, I text him... "It's not working out. I'm not comfortable with you **jarring** my system." Feel sooo much better.

HAAALP!!!

Next day, I'm standing in line wondering if I really screwed up (by my mind's standards fo shur). I open up this random magazine, what do I see?

An article...

Talking about your state of MIND. Ahahaha! Managing your energy and how it can keep you healthy or make you sick. Holyyyy crap! Someone is so talking to ME.

I knew I was taking a BIG chance getting rid of that douche (when I need him so badly). The article broke it down into watts of energy, coming and going into your body. So, let's say there's a hundred watts of energy coming to you at one time (life force) it then gets distributed into your body to maintain healthy cell tissue. How you *invest* those watts of energy can make—or BREAK you. Like! Is he totally worth it? YOU have to ask. So, if you're really pissed (relationship) in order to maintain that bullshit, your best friend's crisis (drama) that daily stress requires... twenty watts. Which leaves you with only eighty for your health maintenance. Plus, you have anxieties and feelings of inadequacy (feeling fat, stupid, not pretty enough, hips too wide, nose too big) stamped into your subliminal mind, costing you another twenty watts. Worrying about Mom, Dad (always fighting) and how the hell are you gonna pay for university (takes up another twenty watts). Add *that* to the stress of SCHOOL (fitting in, exams, bullies, dating). Abuse... God forbid *physical* that you're dealing with secretly (can't tell anyone) and you can deduct another friggin' THIRTY watts. So, if I take out my calculator...

That's only ten watts left!

To maintain our entire physical and emotional health, which is hardly enough. That's ONLY ten percent of our potential energy, cuz we've pissed off (literally) ninety percent on bullshit, worries, anxieties, (loser boyfriend, girl friend who shocks our system). And YOU wonder why you're depressed (TIRED) sick most of the time. Why you need coffee so bad, nicotine gum and energy drinks to jack up your system—when there's NOTHING to give. I never did get used to coffee... not into cheap drugs. LOL And you're wondering why you don't have energy to do things you used to DO. Why you feel down (no reason). Take inventory and see where MOST of your watts are gettin' fried, burnt to a crisp (used by a girl, guy).

FINAL ARGUMENT:

When you tolerate shit or have **unfinished** business (fail to tell someone how you feel) YOU are losing energy. My *frustration* with him tellin' me shit. He was definitely restricting (not expanding) my flow. No wonder my Chi's been frozen. Tolerating TOO much SHIT.

You never think... there's a *better* friend, boyfriend, girlfriend, job, opportunity, someone to help YOU. So you feel stuck. Once I cut him off I felt *sooo* much better. I felt happy and that gave me the confidence to tackle my project on my own! So sorry Dwight, your BULLSHIT taxes my circuits man. That's why after we scream our head off—it *feeeels* so much better. It's such a relief to get it off our chest. It's FREEING UP WATTS. Used to maintain anger and keep it in place. But we didn't *have* to scream, we didn't have to WAIT allll that time (cuz we couldn't bring ourself to say it) cuz we felt bad. We coulda said it *without* emotional coloring, which is easiest to do, when it first happens (no build up yet). Now when my mom's like "Just be yourself." I'm like. Totally! I think I found myself. LOL Or at least a guiding system, to what's fucking with me. How much that's gonna cost me. Cool...

BREAK!

I'm serious. Stop...

Waaay too many watts taking all this in. LOL Juice, protein shake, snack... Stretching (on the field or bed, your choice).

Welcome back!

Love is BLIND...

Like, who said that—some BAT?

At the risk of sounding redundant. Love is OPEN... freeee. And fine, let's cover the basics... 'sex'. Yes confirmed. Copulation... **can't** be done through the forehead—need *opening!* LOL Oh... Wait. It can. It's called a 'mind fuck'.

From the beginning!

Anything that's *open*... is in plain sight for alll of us to see. Fear... blindfolds shit from our eyes (cuz we don't want to see it). Like, the third time you go out with this guy. You're at a party, you leave to go to the bathroom, come back and he lights up a HUGE joint. YOU look at him... He's like, "I only do it, when it's offered." Shurrr. Your gut feeling is like, "What if he's LYING and he's a pothead? He could even be selling it." But you refuse to listen.

FEAR makes you blind...

I was renting a room, the owner was this creepy old man. I thought it'd be fine. His wife just left him after thirty years, felt kinda sorry for the guy. He'd wake up at seven in the morning, watch his belly dancing show. *And you gotta see...* SIXTY FIVE YEAR OLD with a big stomach and pencil legs try to jiggle his belly. Looked, like a HUMAN blender. I'd *tip toe* downstairs and watch him. He'd always say he needed to get a bell and put it around my wrist, he never heard me coming. He loved to cook... which gave me the family atmosphere I was missing. But he'd **never** put the cottage cheese back in the damn FRIDGE! It'd turn green and black. One day, he was cooking this huge POT of something... I'm like, "Mmmm... That smells good what did you put in there?" "*Ohhh...* everything, shoes, socks, underwear." "Uh... yummy. K. Gotta go. Not real hungry anymore." (Strange) I used to sit on the sofa and listen to alll his stories. How things were in the olden days. He'd tell me how whenever he lent a sweater to a girl, he'd get it back with TWO bumps in the front. LOL He could never wear it again. Walking outside when it's MINUS sixteen degrees with just shorts on, is when I realized... he's an alcoholic. Sometimes, I think as we advance into the double digits, our IQ is reduced to a single digit. It's really gross seeing an old man get drunk. I kept locking my door... In case he'd have any fantasies. Don't need a sixty five year old Don Juanna-be comin' in. *Eeeww!!!* Alcohol can do some weird shit.

One night I come home...

It's late... All the lights are on. Front door... wide OPEN. Omg! We've been ROBBED!! And they took the ol' man! Maybe his family came and took him. I couldn't SLEEP. Had no clue what was going on. First thing in the morning his wife blasts through my door. "Nichole! Have the cops contacted YOU?"

OMIGOSH! HE DIED AND THE COPS THINK I KILLED HIM!!!

She lets me know that yesterday night there were seven police cars and a ~~SQUAT~~ (I mean SWAT team) haaa... my *Englishhh*. They were all parked in front of the house. Apparently, they found weapons in the basement. O_O Cops were supposed to call me. He's arrested. Put in DETOX (few days). And still, I think it's cool. It'll be fine. Especially when he comes back cuz he's like, "You know, I told all the doctors YOU were my inspiration, Nichole. And I have to hurry home because every now and then you need a HUG." I think I just threw up in my mouth... a bit.

Whattta *CONNNNNNNNN!* Meanwhile his wife's like, "We need to sell the house—you need to MOVE. ASAP. Oh! And sorry, can't give you your deposit back." I start panicking. But when the old man assures me that although they're selling, he's moving to an apartment and he'll just get a TWO bedroom (one for me). Even offered to put it on paper, but I'm like, "Nah... It's okay." I felt sooo RELIEVED. He looks at me. He's like, "You're like the granddaughter I never had Nichole." Can we say...

TOTALLY FUCKEN STUPID...

(on my part)

Time goes by and things start feeling normal again. No drinking, thank God. He's sober. Starts being real thoughtful, makes dinner for me. I come home all upset about my day, I see a HUGE stuffed animal (in front of my door). I go thank him... give him a hug. Now it really feels like I have a grandfather. I'm hugging him thinking... Hmm? Why's my ear getting moist? Omg!! AAAAAAH!! He's trying to stick his tongue in my ear! *FUUUCK!!* Now I'm gonna have to rip it OFF—get a new one! Disssgusting. Can you even imagine if he tried... to kiss me and his dentures FELL into my cleavage?! Bite me allll over the place. Where's the steel wool? Need to go scrape my chest.

Then I thought to myself...

Maybe he's just senile (doesn't mean to). Things get REALLY weird. I come downstairs have breakfast wearin' my usual (t-shirt n' sweats) his whole face turns burning RED. Against his white hair and blood-shot blue eyes. My boobs are probably gettin' to him (on my period so really full). He starts sweating. Like literally, beads of sweat is pourin' down his face. **WHAT'D THEY FEED YOU IN DETOX— HORNY GOAT WEED?!** It's a plant, they don't know how it works (exactly) but it restores your sexual fire. Boosts your erectile function. (Shiiit) All of a sudden he's walkin' past me, he's like, *"WOOF! WOOF!"* WT... (SERIOUS)F. I'm like, "Dude why are you BARKING?" After... I'd wear my winter coat for breakfast.

TWO days before we need to move I'm like, "So! Where we moving to?" "Oh... I'm applying for welfare, you can't move with me." *WTFF?* I'm like, "What do YOU mean? WHY didn't you tell me this at the beginning of the month? How can I find another place in two days? @_@ I have no family. You know that. I have nowhere to go!" He's like, "I thought you were moving out. I was gonna get some boxes for you from the liquor store." I'm like, "How could YOU do this? Give me no WARNING. Completely endanger my life! What if I didn't *ask*...? I'd be out on the street." "Quiet! Go to your room or I'll have you OUT tonight."

Talk about... a DEAD stale being.

Fear...

Makes you <u>blind</u>. I was afraid to upset the trust I had in him (family like feeling) I shoulda had him sign an agreement, when he came back Wrinkled douche bag.

I go to the gym. Maybe, someone knew *someone*... had a spare room. I'm working out lifting like, A HUNDRED pounds. A guy from the Islands is watching me. He's like *"Whoa... YOU work 'arrrd."* I'm like, "I'm MAD!!" He's like, "Whaaa happen?" I tell him the whole story. How I wanted to tell the cops the ol' man was driving **without** a license. No insurance, and at times intoxicated. I wanted to nail his bony ass (so bad). The guy's like, "YOU... Young. You... *a lady.*" I'm like, "What does my sex have to do with this? HE mislead me! He *deceived* me. Took advantage of me." I was played by an old man. Sick fuck. He's like,

"REVENGE IS FOR THE GODS..."

Huh...?

What if they're busy? It sounded so *poetic.* Maybe, that's what they *mean* by 'poetic justice'. LOL I'm like, "I thought... God is Love. Oh! I get it. Like The Ten Commandments—with alllll the crickets and lightning bolts coming from the sky? Leave it to HIM?"

"It was locusts."

(Whatever)

Shortly after I find a PLACE. In fucking retrospect, as soon as I was out of there I chose NOT to call the cops. I felt sooo relieved and grateful, to have *found* a place. When you're happy, you really don't give a shit 'bout going back to a hole where cottage cheese infested humans, live. Still pissed...

(Piss disintegrating by the second)

They say...

The twin of the wise is always the fool..

Two sides to every coin—always the flip side, no one anticipates. Fear... doesn't just blind you to bad shit (overlooking the obvious) you don't wanna see. It also scares the shit out of YOU when something really good happens. When it's the **real** thing. Like, with love (too afraid to admit he/she is absolutely perfect for you) when it *is* real... usually CAN'T SEE IT. Till it's too late (my bad). My mom always said, "Never get rid of anyone, you can learn even from a stupid person." She wasn't *trying* to be funny. Everyone... teaches you something. You just need recognize it. Even a *bitch* like me!

(B.I.T.C.H)

BOLD IRRESISTIBLE TOTAL CRAFTY HEART-BREAKER!!

(Circle for memory) *;<>*

Another example of fear messin' with you. One day I was completely ballistically infuriated, totally freaked out on my friend (cuz of something *else* happening in my life). I TOLD her everything I felt, that pissed me off about her. She was *shocked*. She never saw it coming. She sent me a long email telling me how much she did *care*. And that I said a lot of stuff she had NO idea bothered me (about our friendship). And she could see I was in pain. She wanted to talk about it. Whoa... you guys (male homo sapiens) actually read this whole paragraph, as boring as it was for you. *Kudos!!* Kudos: Greek word meaning 'glory'. In English it stands for acclaim or praise for exceptional achievement. Well done!

Just the fact that she said *that* showed me the strength of our friendship. Allowing me to say things without JUDGING me. It taught me that it's okay (safe) to be mad at someone you love. A first for me! Cuz usually, I just write them off. Am I like... the *only* one? Course, then she gave me SHIT for holding everything in. Which I only did, cuz I thought if I'd let it all out (explode) it'd frighten her away.

Girls can be pretty intense.

272.

Fear makes YOU hold things in... *hide things* (overlook things).

And the worst, gets you scared when it's special. (Sacred) So you automatically after a certain point (when you *know* it's the 'one') do something to fuck it up. Like, get wasted, talk shit (you're not supposed to) make out with their friend. In your mind, you've been conditioned to believe *"love hurts"*. YOU can't see... love's blind remember? So gotta fight it or you'll fall... Whatta shame we don't have a BS detector built in. YOU can't fight love... it doesn't know that language.

We have it sooo *backwards...*

Our fear of someone not liking us I'm sorry to say, is nowhere *near* as scary, as our fear of someone LIKING us. That's scary. Even if our life depended on it—we could never just look them back in the eye for more than a few seconds... HOLD IT. I find it quite odd, that on planet Earth it's so much easier to say 'I hate you'... than 'I love YOU'. When one makes YOU feel waaaay better! Which btw is how you can tell if a guy's being sincere, cuz if those words slides *off* his tongue, you can bet it's gonna just slide into you WITHOUT him caring (not taking his time). Strangely we've attached weakness to love, strength to non-attached fucking. When it actually takes great BIG balls to love. It takes COURAGE. It takes guts—and creativity. (Talent) LOL Maybe that's why so many songs talk about being helplessly in love. Upside down message (and yeah, if it's one sided—not aligned) What would the gain be in having everybody *believe* that love... is weakness? When it's actually POWER.

Answer: **Total destruction**... SEPARATION.

An ass backward assessment of where our true nourishment lies. What *else* could hold us together?! Gravity holds our world—love is SO necessary to join us! Don't fight the flow man. You'll get sucked in. I just don't get it. It's difficult to accept someone loving us but it's so easy to accept guilt... @_@

(Parent)

"I've sacrificed my whole life for YOU."

Like, I never ASKED you too!

We never ask why it's not easy to *accept* love... Why's it so hard to think someone (we really like) likes us? When this whole 'guilt shit' first appeared, I was a little girl. It really pissed me off. I'd hear things like, "I did this for YOU. So why can't you do this for me?" Uh... I don't even remember asking for anything. It made NO sense. Especially with parents. My parents worked very hard, no doubt about that. And I loved them for it, but to *hear* allll the time... "I work so hard for YOU." Made me feel like my entire life would be about hell, how else could I POSSIBLY make up for all the things they were doing for me (now)? It gave me the *message*...

That life could never be about FUN or joy. I got so much to pay back!! I musta made a bargain prior to entering the WOMB based on allll the shit I did in my past life, they do all this for me and I PAY THEM BACK (with my life).

Wonder... If it was a plea bargain? LOL

DON'T BARGAIN YOUR KIDS... WITH GUILT.

(a *sincere* rip off)

Example:

- You know how HARD I work for you. (Sucks to hear)

- Do you have any IDEA what it takes to support this family? (How can I, I'm just a kid?)

- I gave up my CAREER to have YOU. (The worst)

- You were an 'accident'. (A tie for 'worst')

- I've SACRIFICED everything for YOU. (Generic favorite)

(To answer all these)

NO ONE ASKED YOU TO...

And... You had intercourse and brought me here, I didn't have a say in it. And FYI we do wanna accomplish *something*. We do want to make you proud, it's ingrained in our skull. Or as one guy put it, "I just wanna make my parents proud, so every time they ask how I'm doing, it's not a longgg story." When we receive help from family (those of us fortunate to have one) and it *comes* with an invisible boomerang that knocks us in the back of the head the rest of our life— REMINDING us we owe them, it makes us timid, hesitant to accept anything life offers. We feel we'll have so much to pay back (*later*). And that's loan sharking BTW! That's their *business*. It's run... on pay-back.

(Highly profitable)

Fear induced... not love induced. The bigger the *gift* (favor) the more severe the sacrifice to come. It's waiting for our sentence to play out, so it can have its day.

AGAIN... Loss in order to gain.

So if we do accept a break (opportunity/someone's generosity/good fortune) at some point we'll think we have to suffer for it (feel guilty). And it takes all *forms*...

DRUGS - BOOZE - ADDICTION

- Strict dieting, starving ourself, throwing up.
- Over-training.
- Over-working.
- Used for sex.
- Letting people take advantage of us.

(And you never see it coming)

Somehow we make ourselves pay for it (without knowing it) celebs, singers, famous people (I feel) go through this a lot (for *this* very reason).

On the other hand...

It's very hard to accept something GREAT unless you've been 'humbled' (in the *process*). Really, really worked for it, suffered or endured—so a by-product of your expectation. Totally earned it! LOL You're alllll MINE (got you fair n' square). And unless you're giving credit or paying gratitude to something (*someone*) outside yourself, it's hard to handle (accept inwardly). Without the 'appreciation' factor (something, someone more powerful than you) all the goodies life gives, are tough to *accept*. It just doesn't feel right. It's like, you secretly know there's something else to it, you didn't **do it** alllll on your own.

Something... Someone... Somehow...

HELPED.

It's too BIG to take in (what happened) it's too good. So you freak (quietly) and that builds momentum. YOU can't possibly contain it so you start questioning it... *enough* times till you convince yourself IT'S GOTTA BE A MISTAKE. This **can't** possibly be happening! So you FUCK it up (one way or another). Sometimes not right away but after a short while you do. Once in YOUR lifetime...

The **best** girl (guy) *everrrr* walks into your life. The problem with that... is always YOU.

That's why a lot of people who are ultra successful come from a scary past (hard past) challenging *PAST*... And that's why they seem like, they can handle anything. Most surprisingly, after all they've achieved you meet up and you're like, "Omg... They're so down-to-earth. REAL. So... nice." It's balanced now, they were fucked up before (*hardships*) we as humans are wired for struggle and restrictions (don't cherish or value things that come easy) a clue to all you skanks out there. The solution's built-in... we're meant to bust through. Like, the struggle the athlete had. A runner will always go through knee, hamstring issues, dancer... ankle problems, shot putter... shoulder. If victory would come easy—it wouldn't be a victory.

And it wouldn't feel as *good*...

And you girl wonder why he's like, "Um... This is awkward now." He didn't work for it... *sssuffer*. Since we're accustomed to struggling, feel satisfaction after a certain amount of *effort*... perhaps it's to prove to ourself how much we DO need...

SOMEONE... SOMETHING...

(Somehow)

Cuz just before we're about to *lose* our spot on the team (one too many penalties, injury) don't make the final cut for an audition, close to death in a car accident—we reach for THAT (dear God, I'll do ANYTHING, help me) so that what we need... is **demonstrated** (assistance made available) and we *know* we can have it on 'credit' (thank YOU God, Allah, Buddha, Jesus, the Universe). Then upon acceptance of goods (healed knee, made the team, asked to be a stand-in, escape death) if we're CALM overjoyed with gratitude (happy, not guilt ridden) 'bout what just happened (feel worthy) we can trust a successful transaction has taken place (you're in GOOD hands). *Ahh-men.*

There's one other way to bypass a built-in 'need' to

struggle.

Other than working really really hard at your career, puttin' in a LOT of hours, energy, training, education.

A message YOU provide...

To help people, a creative endeavor (to inform the world) like rhyming, art, poetry, fashion, a movement... start-ups, are all bulletproof when it comes to protecting your *assets* cuz you're attached to something MORE...

A great cause, change, vision, showing support and obstacles, hardships n' bullshit bounce right off you. Cuz you've got the power of largeness attached to you (helping people one by one or on a massive scale). You're like... A STRUGGLE BUSTER. And when applause, admiration, gifts, rewards come... you accept it. It also means...

YOU feeling AWESOME rubs off on other people!

The absolute best thing you can do for people, give them a taste of their *own* potential. Raise the vibration of the WORLD. Right up there with... being a Fairy Goddess! :D A Warrior of Light. Most important, when you are of value to the world, the world loves YOU (it has your back). Especially, if you have a deep, shameful secret about something that happened (to you). Writing about it, singing about it... doin' something creative gives it *direction* (out of YOU) and same time... out of millions of people. How fortunate for *you* to experience that. Back where I come from you're awarded for all those human *experiences*. It literally and emotionally makes you **rich**... YOU never see things the same way.

I Knight YOU Dude... Sir of Humanity. YOU will have the Shield of Power to make shit bounce OFF you. The Sword of Truth to cut through all the BULLSHIT.

I christen YOU Girl...

Lady of Many Worlds.

With this transparent tiara I place on your head YOU will *have* the Fairy Goddess hypnotic GLANCE... You must hold your head up high. You are joined with an ancient *strength*... (NOW). Look for a hawk to fly above you.. as a reminder.

Have you ever wondered whyyy you get pulled to look up at the sky when you're going through a lot of shit? It's callin' YOU... It's recognizing YOU. It's a part of you... waiting to be acknowledged. You've always known this, no one had to tell you. You just knew... there's tremendous *power* out there. Acknowledging that power, is acknowledging YOUR power. Cuz it's watching... you.

278.

It knows YOU. It knows what you're **becoming**. It just needs to know, that you know. And then... all kinds of evidence shows up all around YOU... Tellin' you you're CLOSE (on route). So you know... you've got something—NO ONE CAN TAKE.

So you know... you're gonna get THERE. Every time you look up at the sky you need to KNOW... it's watching. It's WAITING. To see if you recognize where **you** come from. Giving you all its *power*... through its gaze. Once you recognize that you will recognize your super POWER. Say thank you! I GOT it!!

What... is your SUPER power?

Trust me... You have one.

When I first discovered mine it was scary and cool, same time. I was like, WTF? Did I do THAT? Tell me yours and I'll tell YOU mine. :P You first!

I FRIGGIN' LOVE YOU!!

To My Knight... My Lady

BOTH of you are of tremendous value. YOU must connect to your power (now) this is no joke. You will create something very much **needed** in this world. Something no one's ever thought of. Some of you... will be seen as a tonic to all those with a weak system. Guys, girls will be *drawn* to you (share secrets) look to you for direction, advice... it's already started. They will need to TALK. No one can explain PAIN—like you. Which means... YOU can also explain the traps, snags, endless maze... that keep you there. (Escape routes) These memories are stored in your CELLS. Interesting, being physical beings that when we're hurt and in physical pain (cut, burn, sprain, torn ligament) once that stops—we forget about it. Child birth. GREAT example.

279.

But when we have emotional pain... FUCK! Can't forget about THAT.

Makes sense...

Our body's mostly made of water and water has **memory**. It always retains an imprint of what it's been exposed to. So pain... filed deep in our water is silent (immobile). Until it's STIRRED. Which is why when it's triggered (activated) has *nothing* to do with what's actually going on NOW. Once active, it carries YOU out of real TIME—back to *past* time (both can't exist simultaneously) SO it feels very real. Like it's happening now.

If water can store information...

WHAT THE HELL WOULD THE OCEAN TELL YOU? It wouldn't divide YOU anymore... but unite you, with ancient knowledge. Like! ARE there any sea creatures for **real**? Treasures!? (Take it from me— YESSSS) The REAL reason planes vanish... drop into the ocean. Are there any *other* life forms LIVING down there? And for God's sake! Is it **possible** to breathe under water—cuz that would be so COOL.

One day we'll take all these memories (knowledge) far away from here... to another PLACE. Inform *those* of what's it like to be HUMAN. And this way... Shame can't hold us anymore!

Got *lifted*—by a Higher purpose. :P

Mankind...

And YOU get spared twelve years of therapy. LOL

Once exposed, it's no longer in the dark (and scary) concealed. When LIGHT gets *on it*... nothin's there. And *nothing*... can't hurt you. Since you're **not** hiding anything anymore people don't feel like there's somethin' about you—they don't trust. If your eyes just squinted it means I'm talking (directly) to YOU.

SHAME...

THE BIGGEST TAKER OF LIFE.

It's vital to see **ourselves** as deserving. We cannot confuse our experiences with our parents with how we see ourself (*harrrd*). If for any reason they're not at their best (under qualified) absent... neglectful, WE need to realize that the World is our TRUE parent. Bit of a stretch... Not really. When we have parents who fall short, don't seem to care, we feel like there's something OFF about us. If we'd truly see the *world* as our parents... we'd know the world's gonna be there for us. <3 We tend to feel like the world's against us when we come from parents (people who raise us) that make us feel like shit (not good enough) like we don't deserve (belong) and get a total chaotic experience (environment). Problem with that... Since that's what our mind's catching DAILY—unfortunately the mind's camera is seeing the same out-dated content when we LEAVE. So we gravitate toward a crowd that's into *that* (familiar) feel close to them... like we're in the right place. And then of course, we're in that manipulated environment all over again (in the outside world).

The fact that the WORLD'S our real parent is everywhere! If the world is where WE come from... everything in this world belongs to us! CITIZEN'S OF THE WORLD that's what we are. We feel deserving of good things that come (feels natural) puts it in perspective. And that's why... we feel so good when we give *back*.

To the WORLD.

Complete... in our unique fit. Absolute ONENESS. Whether fighting for a cause, expressing our raw self artistically, workin' to keep the world safe, clean, preserving NATURE... Our real mother (for shur) although pissed at our neglect when **she** throws lightning rods at our ass—it's not cuz I didn't fold the LAUNDRY. LOL No matter what YOU go through life's source *sustains* you... cuz you're a part of something HUGE. That's where YOU come from... Everyone's like, "Where do you get the *ballzzz* to do THAT?" You're connected... *that's* how. So you've multiplied in strength. Justified...

Greatness.

For those non-believers YOU will see when you do what you LOVE... and the world gives (back) you are loved... *accepted.*

Every time a client would offer to help me get ahead, or a 'break' like, 'Wowww they actually wanna hear my TV idea!' I'd CRY... my clients were sooo annoyed, they're like... "WHY do you always cry when something GOOD happens?" Even though I'd tell them I was happy (on the inside) I *knew*... it was cuz I felt I didn't deserve it. So I didn't know 'how' to feel. So I made sure I'd take no days off (just work) no fun, just kept pushing. I felt BAD (like I *was* bad) even though I just got this gift. Makes sense. We cry (it's a function of the body to release toxins) even if it is covered in joy. Truth is... guilt at accepting something (you don't feel you deserve) is what makes it appear like tears of joy...

But joy doesn't make you CRY.

Once you feel something inside... it's hard to separate that *feeling* from who you ARE. I grew up having birthdays, typical things most teens have but the message I got... YOU can't just 'accept' things (without suffering) only then consider it *earned.* Is how I interpreted...

"I work so hard for YOU like a slave."

Not that we shouldn't appreciate that work can be hard at times, but when it's communicated *that* way, it's like there's always a stick near your ass and it's real close—ya know you're gonna get smacked (at some point).

Guilt... never teaches through inspiration...

(A parent's backward teaching tool)

I never **believed** that life could just GIVE. I always thought you needed to *suffer*... in order to get ahead. Am I the ONLY one who thinks like that? Honestly... You can tell me.

282.

It's just you and me...

Agree ☐ Disagree ☐

So I could never even say (when someone asked) 'I'm good' cuz I'd worry something bad would *happen*. Every time I did say I'm good—BOOM!! Major shit. Never failed. It was almost as if life, was sayin', "Yeah... *Really?* YOU think you can take things for granted—just cuz things are okay, now? Get lazy, not worry, be calm—not fear anymore? Well! Watch THIS. This will TEACH you." I felt so *trapped*. I had no choice but to never say things were 'good'. And for surrre 'not great' cuz then I'd be like—OMG!! They'll hear me. (*I'm not suffering*) :"|

So it did two things...

(Parents instilling guilt)

Make sure when people *would* ask, I'd hunt for shit I wasn't happy about (that wasn't perfect) talk 'bout THAT (show I was suffering). And although striving for good shit, I was AFRAID of actually getting it. In my brain if I get THERE... I'm not suffering. In **focusing** and looking for hell, to confirm I was on track and in accordance with how life 'should be' (suffering to pay parents *back*) I could only go towards stupid choices (wrong people, places, guys, girls that use me) careless with money, leave bills till the last minute. SPENDING... My dad's like, "YOU THINK MONEY GROWS ON TREES?"

No dad, our economy would be very different if it did. But wouldn't that be cool? ☺

I'd completely exhaust myself then *challenge* myself to make a lot of money *FAST*. Legally! I'd risk my safety in situations and with people. Not allow anyone to get close (no friends). Didn't rely on anyone. Train super HEAVY (no spotter) so I'd *have* to lift it. Or it'd fall on me.

Allllll to make sure I had an *intense* life...

Surely THAT would equate with what my parents *had* to go through (with me). In my head, I was being responsible by going non-stop.

283.

Having it be difficult showed me I was on top of my game—self reliant. The harder the situation the better I got... at *SURVIVAL*. I was competing *against* life. And it wasn't gonna take me DOWN. And yet, I needed it. The part that *was* beautiful. Only it seemed like it was somewhere very far away, a place I wasn't ALLOWED. It took me a long time to realize wherever I was... there were NO steel bars, (to keep me) the bars were in my head. Unless you're in JAIL... that would be an issue. But only a temporary one! Cuz in your mind you can go wherever you want. Have *that* inspire YOU... and that will MATCH the vibe that brings the opportunity to get you out of there. Cuz if you feel free... you'll attract something that gives you freedom. The hardest thing about being in a tough place is watchin' what other people *have*... that you don't. It pisses you off. It just DOES. Cuz you've temporarily forgotten WHO you are... WHAT you're connected TO... and the *power* at your disposal to **make** things HAPPEN.. I got pissed when I thought I couldn't get there. All that changed when I KNEW I could.

And oddly... Knowing and *wanting* is kinda the same to me. I WANT what I want! So it's like, I made the DECISION to have it—then decided that what I had (my abilities) was gonna get me there. THAT assured me.

Once YOU make a decision to go for something...

It's like a GIANT blade clearing the way for YOU. Honest! As long as you tell yourself **why... it's what you want**. Forget 'bout being intellectual here, it has to be about the **feeling** it'd give you. THAT'S key! Cuz you will always get... how you FEEL. And yes, that includes not making the team, being cut off from the group, the skank (asshole) who ruined your life, cuz somewhere you didn't feel entitled to *more* (heard too many stories so bought into it) it became your existence (REALITY). What determines how *soon* you'll get out of there (onto your dream) depends on one other very **important** thing.

Living (being) in the future as if you're *there* now... In other words, the reason you want (girl, guy, car, tuition, fame) is cuz of the feeling YOU'LL have when you get it. YOU can have that feeling now! Vibes unlike humans match up with their own kind (happy vibe with happy, sad with more sad) they don't like to CLASH like we do. Lmfaoo Since the world is a vibrational one... everything gives you a feeling. You like it or don't like it (even indifference is a feeling) which means, life CAN'T fuck up—it's LAW. It responds (unites YOU) with the same feeling you send out (what you're feeling inside) so actually you can't fuck up either, just slowwww down the process. i.e. not taking a break, not having fun, being hard on yourself, talking down to yourself (*hellllo*). So glad we've moved passed that. ;P You cannot afford to be careless with your thinking, think about things that piss you off, keep score (highly tempting have to admit). As a man thinketh... so he will getteth (or somethin' like that). LOL If you're already feeling great stuff (excited, happy, blessed, privileged) life *has* to match you with experiences (scenarios) like *that*. And it starts showin' up almost immediately with things comin' into your life that make YOU happier (winning something, a surprise, meeting someone, test extended, thank GOD... you weren't done, bike finally on SALE) as it takes you down *your* yellow brick road... Toto or no Toto.

You know as well as I do the second something happens to you that makes you happy—you don't give a FUCK about the idiot that never returned your video game. What this also means... your friend, parent, colleague at work who's a downer will infest your vibrational field, if you buy into their *reality* cuz honestly... it CAN change at a moment's notice. And the best thing you can do—is not buy into their shit. A lot of people feed off the attention they receive by their situation, which only makes them crave more of the same. You can remind them... they CAN create a new situation... REALITY.

WE create our own reality! Said often enough—BUT DO WE **GET IT**? What keeps us in hell is our continued focus on *that* hell, which then like a starved beggar *wants* to collect more sad shit to keep YOU focused (overwhelmed). Failing to address (acknowledge) all that is good about **where** you are, **who** you are... **what** you're capable of. What's surrounding you... that IS beautiful. Cuz that's the quickest ROUTE to your powerful DREAMS.

- Stating what you WANT... More importantly WHY you want it (forget 'bout the how and especially, when). Review daily!!!

- Making sure you match the awesome feeling (of havin' it now) by doin' things that make you excited and HAPPY constantly.

- Being **in charge** of your feelings cuz you CARE more about how you feel, than who's right and/or feelin' like shit.

YOU will see how fast life hooks you up... presents opportunities and changes all over the place—download!! It's got your back... it always does. Unfortunately you often turn YOURS (my baaad). When I realized all this, I knew that all the opportunities I saw *other* people have, everything I saw I was born for (*kept* missing) life was just saying...

Pick AGAIN! Pick AGAIN!

Don't be SAD when you see somethin' you want—be happy! Say YES to it (dumbass). Life's showin' you a taste... it wants to make sure you LIKE it. So respond the right way! It's givin' you a chance to see it up CLOSE. So you can *decide* if YOU want it.

We don't usually think of everything we feel as a vibration—we're TOO BUSY VIBRATING!! Ahaha A good feeling has a high vibration, makes you feel good (gives you energy). A bad feeling has a low vibration, makes you feel like shit. K... Someone comin' to mind? LOL Sometimes you meet someone you're like—WHOA! They have great energy. When you have a **negative** reaction (feeling angry) about something you don't have right now, or something you do have (can't stand it) it sends a negative *response*... It's like sayin', "I want something else to be this angry about." Pushes you farther *away* from what YOU wanted and/or gives you *more* of what you didn't want as per your reaction (disgust, angst, frustration). LOL

Vibrations are read as FEELINGS and/or **reactions**, not scripts (with details). LOL What's picked up is your feeling about what you're observing. Which is GREAT! ☺ Cuz we can control that. Hundo p! We can always choose not to be bothered with those lower vibrations! Vibrational SNOBBERY at its best. LOL What we need here is a vibe censor! ☺ No more lettin' people steal our thunder. Reacting to their shit only to attract MORE shit... feeling powerless. Whatever feeling WE give... Life's gonna *match* with the coming circumstance (we'll receive). It's JUST followin' instructions. LOL And the worse keeps getting *worse*... the better keeps getting BETTER (cuz that's what people are focused on). Guys... girls who focus on what they're happy about—bring more of that to them, usually popular.

Oh... That's why some guys have allll the luck. LOL Yes.

There is ALWAYS something we can think of to feel good about. It doesn't matter if it's a hundred episodes of you and your cat, a video, a song, reliving how you two met—it'll WORK. And if you can't find anything just look out in the world—**look at everything possible!** And know you can have it, when you feel good *enough*... to accept it (allow it).

And... just so you know. Worrying, doubting, hating, blocks allowing the good comin' to YOU, cuz it's an exact contradiction to everything you have going for YOU (a whole other vibration). If I were you I'd start focusing on what's unique about YOU. What makes you REALLY happy (what you have to look forward to) like NOW. Feel it... cuz if you think about it, if you had it *now* there'd be so much JOY in your heart. Connect to the delivery process... a **feeling** of JOY. The *better* you feel... the more you'll allow (YOU are *more* than worthy).

Technically speaking...

It's like, you salivating when a warm apple pie is *about* to come out of the oven. Your body wouldn't be able to produce **joy** (thinkin' about somethin' you want) if it wasn't cookin' for YOU (right now) getting ready to give it. You're just happily expecting it, preoccupied doing somethin' else. Till it finishes baking... blissfully waiting. EMOTION is key.

OMG!! I'm SO excited for YOU.

YOU need only remember...

Where you are is temporary—where you're *heading* permanent. People who make it BIG in the world, have thought, dreamt, ate and shit... their DREAM (for a long time). It's all they think *about*... even if they don't speak about it. Put your eyes (daily) on your dream (even if it's just in your mind) and whatever ELSE that makes you feel good... cuz *that's* the conveyor belt gettin' you there. If there's a bad thought (vibe) flip it. SQUISH THE MOFO!

YOU dictate how life's gonna be...

(Not the other way around)

So watch what you're responding to. If it isn't worth your attention IGNORE it. And think about what would be *perrrfect...* right NOW. Feeeel it. And when you do SEE good shit you want. Fucken celebrate!! Cuz it's comin'! First clue... It reached YOU. It gave you a glimpse to see if you like it. Enjoy the peak-a-boo! Don't shut your eyes to it.

Example

People makin' out right in front of YOU. Be happy! It's close. Some-one going away on vacation, someone getting backstage passes... it wouldn't be around you (now) if you weren't aligned with *that* (vibe). Like a ripple in a lake, your boat's coming. It just needs your approval (before it docks). It's asking you if you LIKE. Confirm... (broader shoulders, six-pack). Thanks (longer legs... bigger boobs). :D Copy that! Don't block it and mutilate it with a random bad thought that has no business taking over your mind without your consent. MASTER this...

I'll show you how to bring your SOUL MATE to YOU.

(I'm not kidding)

When you see someone—and you *know* it's LOVE. You're not like, "Oh... Wish I *had* that." You go for *that*—with the intention of gettin' it. Maybe there's an obstacle. She's with *someone*... your insides just turned to goop. Or... He's stuck in a two year (live-in) ship. *Fuuuck...* They didn't accept you at the University (of your choice). No opening at the most *perfect* job. No way you can afford to go to *that* school (specializing in your talent). All YOU know is, you want it! So you keep thinking about it (while you pursue other things, take steps). Then, no shit! YOU bump into *that* guy (girl) who's no longer in a relationship. You get into 'another' University, find your dream girl! Someone quits... you're HIRED. There's an opening to audition for **that** school. Something... *happens.* YOU brought it to you.

288.

With your focus...

Once you see something you **want** and you feel (love at first sight) YOU need to *have* it (you deserve it) you're gonna get it. It's yours—cuz YOU love it. Inside you... (belongs to YOU).

Like love... it draws YOU to it and it to YOU.

The ONLY thing that stops good things from happening?

Something inside you telling you... YOU *aren't* entitled. Fear (I'm not allowed that) there's something bad about ME. Which means, when you see good stuff happening (to *other* people) you get jealous—cuz there's nothing about you saying, "YOU want *that...?* Go get it! Cuz you *can* have it." When you're hesitant, cuz in your mind *having* it means a lot more pressure (responsibility) like being with the most POPULAR person (everyone wants) there's jealousy to deal with. How do you cope? Getting that BIG opportunity... What if you can't keep up? Cuz they *really* see something in YOU. What if they believe you can do it BUT you let everyone down? There's soo many expectations. Losing all that weight and getting so much ATTENTION (when you're **not** used to it). You're mostly shy and reserved (*haaard*). Your fear... even though it's like a *hissing* sound is loud enough, to influence you. You need to get over the fear and just deal with your GREATNESS gurl (dude). <3

And you <u>can</u> handle it.

Cuz you'll have allll these amazing people around you, supporting YOU. You won't be alone, like you are now. Life is NOT your enemy. It's your Butler! Giving you selections every day. Just friggin' choose! And if you **love it** you'll feel like you *deserve* it. You'll HAVE to have it! Lovvvve it...

JUST be careful...

You could be dealing with your family's 'under-wrappings' (scarcity conditioning/unworthy stumbling blocks) WORST type of sabotage.

Every time I landed a scholarship for dance (something I lovvvve) secured a spot on the cheerleading team for the CITY, role for a film, pageant finalist, my mom and dad would FIGHT. Actually, when they were both mad at me (even if I didn't do anything wrong) I was *relieved* (they weren't fighting with each other). So there was never a time of being ecstatic, that wasn't ALSO accompanied with anxiety, pain, fear (sadness). It was a package deal.

What I got used to...

Sadly what you're used to, shows up again and again and AGAIN. It's like there's this secret chip installed inside you, that connects you to a chain of events the *moment* good shit happens—that RUINS everything. So now you interpret (learn) understand (mistakenly) that JOY is accompanied with PAIN. :'(

To gain...

There must be loss (discomfort) struggle.

And sure enough THAT'S what happened.

Till finally I couldn't take it anymore I just asked... (more like demanded) 'WHAT is it I'm NOT learning?!' They say... you keep making the **same** mistake till you *learn*—but there's no fucken tutor! If you don't get it, too bad. :P YOU just don't learn. Which equals pain and then of course, you've got grown-ups all around you saying...

- She (he) just doesn't wanna LEARN. (Not true)

- They just wanna get in TROUBLE. (A LIE)

- They're just ASKING for it. (Yeah for 'help' only you're too dumb to see) ☹

- They just wanna be ALONE. (No one wants to be *alone* they want to be understood)

Every time things would be progressing in life—DRAMA alll over the place. The day I demanded an answer from LIFE I was waiting in line, for a drink. I hear a random person talk on their phone. They're like, "If you're intense with life, you'll attract **intense** things... to your *life*."

Fuuuck...

FREAKED ME OUT!!

THAT was it. My whole life was *intense*...

In fact when people asked how I was I'd say, "INTENSE." I was just being honest *and* it didn't threaten my 'suffering' criteria. From the time I ran away from home... brutal. So FORGET enjoy myself—I had to be on guard. Who knows what's out there (if shit like this can happen at home)? The very thing I was preventing myself from doing (fun, chillin' with friends, self care) was the <u>very</u> thing I was craving, woulda made my life less scary, woulda made it more fun and beautiful. But I couldn't... in my mind, I wasn't allowed. I 'owed' life... Right there and then I decided.

FUN! FUN! FUN!

(Would be on my agenda)

But that's SUCH a waste of time... When you're working on your CAREER, a project you're passionate about. Especially with all this pent up shit inside me, it'll totally ruin my FUN. Nooo—ope! Is how I saw it back then, before I realized I *could*...

If you're super responsible, never allow yourself 'certain' things (usually a first born) or have parents *leave*... (older sibling getting into trouble) your perspective of what's natural... the 'norm' is skewed. You most likely, will have a hard time having fun (it doesn't feel natural). It won't feel comfortable. You've been punishing yourself for a long time babe...

You're DONE!

(Needed to hear that!) LOL

When I completed this first draft, it took *foreverrr*. The next phase of everyone's like, "Go write outside. Get some sun! It's **such** a nice day," But I'm like, "Nooo! Then it feels like I'm not WORKING. Like, I'm enjoying myself havin' fun, cuz I'm outside. I must stay indoors. It's a serious book!" Once I completed *that* (yearrrs later) everyone's like, "Let's CELEBRATE! Go OUT! I can't believe you're finally DONE." High school girls and guys are now in University, everyone's SOOO stoked, but I'm like "Nooo. You know I don't drink. So getting *wasted*... with my head stuck in a toilet seat NOT—doin' it for me. I don't like frothing at the mouth." "K. Let's go for ice cream!" "Are YOU kidding? Do you know how <u>much</u> work I have on the *next* phase? I'm going to sleep so I can get up early and start."

DUMMMMB...

Everyone was SO let down. Cuz apparently I have problems, climaxing (enjoying ma' best moment). It wasn't till weeks later... I realized I had *ruined* a great feeling of accomplishment. Not just for them, but for me TOO. I didn't 'acknowledge' the work I did (at all).

<u>CONCLUSION:</u>

Even if we do try to enjoy a promotion, journey, accomplishment (*person*) cuz we feel guilty, we didn't suffer to get it (nothing was asked of us) it's just *given*... we FUCK it up. To justify the suffering we're accustomed to. So cycle is complete (in our minds) we don't deserve anything coming to us (as a gift). We could be talented, great with people, at the right place, right time—all that WON'T matter. We'll over do drugs, booze (fucking) be careless, hang around bad people—to complete a *secret* code of ethics planted in our BRAIN.

WE CANNOT GAIN...

WITHOUT LOSING

That's why getting someone to do something for YOU... making them feel guilty also never works (in terms of you being free). YOU know what you DID (somewhere you feel guilty too). And you just chained your ass to them. YOU can't escape what you 'do'... it's attached you. Even if the guy (girl) doesn't know—you'll act as if they **do**. Over-compensate somewhere, under compensate somewhere by trying to act too *natural* or disinterested, as if to say... nothin's different. But it's so obvi (so it stands out). It's kinda like, when you go to a garage sale or buy something off someone. As soon as you hear them say, "Look. I'm not trying to cheat you or anything." You know... they are. Or someone's like...

"I would never take advantage of YOU."

Yeah, you would.

"It's not like I say this all the time." (Yeah you do) The only reason you're speaking about what you *don't* do... is cuz in your mind it's echoing (LOUDLY) allll you **would** do. So you have a *need* to say you don't cuz you're answering yourself subliminally. You'd never have a need to say what you'd never do (if you weren't already thinkin' of it) it wouldn't occur to you.

*LISTEN to what people say they'd **never** do... (to YOU)*

"I'd *never* hurt you..." (Hmm...?) They've hurt someone before. Doesn't mean they'll hurt you (necessarily) just be aware they have a *pattern*. Parents, if you're trying to get us to appreciate YOU teach *that*... by appreciating 'us'. Don't be a meany-go-beany. Point out special things you see in us (we so need to hear it). We'll tune in to what *you* see...be *that* way. And don't let us WALK all over you (either). That's not helping—that's *enabling* us to be that way and teaches it's okay... expected. Then we have a rude awakening that CRUSHES us (eventually). When life's like, 'I DON'T think so....' I remember being so frustrated hearing the same thing day in day out, with my parents. Till finally, after hearing it so much I'm like...

"I didn't ask to be BORN."

Now, that I've advanced in time...

I know in my heart I did *ask* to be born. My soul <u>did</u> wanna do something unique. A GIRL. Haha! So I was born with skills I needed to have in order deal (*hardships*) while strengthening my resolve to get what I WANT (one way or another) without compromising (integrity) myself. Which chiseled my weapon of choice—to be launched into this WORLD...

Nichole...

Firing ONE!! <3 <3 <3 <3 <3 <3 <3

Not allowing myself to be lured into my parents way of thinking ALSO freed me from blaming *them* for what they did (didn't do) correctly. To me, guilt's a close cousin to blame—they're related (kissing cousins *fo shur*). An incestuous TRAP. You can't have one without the other (it's in the genes). No matter what happens, no matter how *severe* (it's... just... something that happened) if I blame them, I'd feel worse. Like, I'm a *victim*. Like maybe... I deserved it. So yup it happened... and I'm still AWESOME. <3

Ever notice victims...

Before they speak 'bout what happened (or even after) they feel like it's **their** fault. Even if intellectually they understand it's not, they feel BAD. Hard feeling to rip off you. There's no real understanding of WHY it happened, nor is there minimizing it—it falls on someone's head. Yours... (theirs). Here's the thing! YOU can't suffer if you don't see yourself as suffering—too busy focusing on what you WANT. LOL What you want to accomplish. It excites you! It's almost as if, all the other shit is just background noise. Cuz in the room of your MIND you've got the best song playing...

Youuuuu...

And what you wanna DO.

294.

I met this incredibly talented actress. Her brows were seriously on fleek. She gave me a call one cold winter night, let me how she LANDED this big opportunity in Los Angeles. I'm ecstatic for her! But then she's like, "I'm gonna move out! When a guy or girl says that... It's SERIOUS. It had to do with her step dad. She couldn't fucken take it anymore. She never lost her cool before—this time she DID. I was so scared for her cuz I didn't know where she'd move to. How safe she'd be.

The only thing I said...

"Linzy, you've got allll this great stuff happening. Focus on **that**. Go there... Make it HUGE (in your mind) think about all the things that's gonna happen! Each morning in your trailer, when you're gettin' ready with your makeup lady, going over your lines, end of the day when it's a WRAP—how amazing you feel! All the people you MEET. Doin' what you love DOING. And you'll see this shit with your step dad, is gonna be like a *little* cloud. That's gonna go POOF!! All gone. Cuz you have so much sun around you, so it's gonna be like this little speck. And cuz you're stoked about everything it's gonna act like an invisible barrier. He'll STOP trippin' cuz he'll see it bounce off you. There'll be nothing to feed his fire—severe anger management ISSUES. And the fact that you're half anticipating it... is NOT helping. It eggs him on, he can smell that. Just like an animal who smells fear —*he'll goes in that direction*. So when you focus on all your stuff it'll be like love... And when you're in LOVVVE does <u>anything</u> bother you?" Hell no.

YOU'RE IN LOVVVVE!!

So I say this to YOU...

Whatever unfair treatment is goin' on... which tends to make YOU feel like shit (hate the world). Even though in your mind it's NOT fair, the fact that it's happening may make you believe *somewhere*... you deserve it. Your focus CAN'T be there. And the only way that's gonna happen, is if what you're thinking about you're totally craaaazy about! For me (regardless) it never stopped me from going after what I wanted, only made me focus *harder*. Cuz I wanted something fierce. High powered ammo—no one can match my bullets! Spirit driven...

Ever since I was a little girl I HAD to ask...

If God is all powerful, I bet HE doesn't feel guilty 'bout ANYTHING. I'm supposed to be made in His image, so I'm not buying into this whole guilt CRAP. I'm like Him, a Child of God. Maybe, that's why it's so easy to feel guilty—WE CREATED it! Damn(ed) fools. We didn't create love. *It's always been there...* And what's a *part* of us is always toughest to tap in to. Reach... *Love.* We come to ourself LAST.

(Deeeep)

We ask friends, parents, people, what they think... Only after they confirm our choices (give us a hard time) we finally say, "Fuck it."

I'M GOING FOR IT.

Come to ourself *last...* but we do arrive. Lmfaoo

And can we *just* get rid of the middleman ALREADY? First, we get influenced by what someone *else* thinks, our feelings on mute (we don't hear them) we figure this person MUST know. They're the only voice we **hear**!! Years later, we realize we didn't enjoy it that much (choice sucked) it wasn't AWESOME. Now what? We... realize that our destiny is *supposed* to be what we're going after—THAT'S why it's playin' on our heart strings. We feeeel it. And that's why... we were born a *certain* way (certain mind-set) with a certain *gift* brought on... perhaps, by a need to *block* out things around you. Like a welder— it burned your core... *as it shaped you.* And now you're something unique—STAND OUT. And if you don't know what that is, take fucken inventory! So no one can tell YOU what you can or cannot do. As it says in the oldest book in the world...

Know Thyself... *there's a reason.*

And while we're on the TOPIC. How come flowers never feel guilty? It doesn't matter if *their* petals are open or closed. Ya think, one flower is gonna feel guilty (pressured) cuz the flower beside it *isn't* open? So the big FAT bumblebee is gonna come to the flower that's open. It's not gonna think less of the flower that's not open, it'll just go there later (at the right time).

To know, out of forty million to two BILLION sperms—YOU were the *only* one that made it. Can you even imagine the pressure? Everyone chasing that one little egg! YOU were the *FASTEST,* *s*trongest (k, *sneakiest*) that got through!!

It wasn't random you *come* with **PURPOSE**. Lmaoo

(And yeah, pretty much all you guys come with purpose) HAD to!

YOU know... Even if you don't know, you know (you still know) that your destiny is waiting to connect with you. **Don't** keep it waiting. It'll be pissed. And so will I. It's not nice to piss off your Fairy Goddess!

You have no idea what I'm capable of (hee hee).

You'll know it's your destiny, by how you're feeling... how happy YOU are when you're doin' what you **wanna** do. Mind you, it <u>is</u> human nature to ignore what's right in front of us (SO is). How many people visit the *ocean*—when it's actually right in their BACKYARD? We want things **only** once we're far away from them (never have them) or miss them.

We're weird...

How Love OPERATES...

It must flow... (*back n' forth*)

Kinda like our bodies! LOL

It needs to *circulate*... It doesn't work if we love *them* and they kinda like us (but we're not sure).

My girl friend's like, "When guys have sex they have it **without** their heart." Yeah... That's cuz they have a *heart-on*... Must have gotten lost in the translation somewhere. In all seriousness, even if love's a religious thing. Like, God, Jesus, Buddha, Allah, the Universe we feel the love *back*... THAT'S how we know it's there. Something confirms it for us. It's personal. We're lovin' something and we feel love *back*. It's given... *received*... given back (like a circle). A ring.

(*Bling! Bling!*)

A ring is a symbol of love...

(So smarrrt)

Love can't be contained (put in storage) though sometimes we wish we COULD. Haaaa Everything has a shelf life, before it needs to be cooked... *Hotttt!* Sometimes the shelf breaks—load's too HEAVY (weighs you down) tainted (tampered with) so need to get rid of it. Guess, that's what they mean when they say... 'If you let them go and they come back they're YOURS. If not, they never were.' Another cliché (eyes rolling to the back of the skull). Like, I'm gonna wait! Have him attract alllll kinds of shit (possible infections, diseases) bring it *back* to me. Don't think so. How 'bout...

'Since when does a Goddess run after a mere MORTAL'?

Never did like clichés, they're like chewed gum (passed from one person to another to *another*. There's like, no flavor LEFT. It's not juicy. So NOT retaining our interest. Why doesn't it dawn on anybody that you can't teach anything WITHOUT conviction. And conviction comes from inside of you—your **experience**. It's nothin' outside of you. So words heard (over and over) read... passed on, turn *mute* (in our ears) are not *received*... haven't paid their dues. So don't get to be owned, digested. experience comes with a price! LOL

So love... can't be controlled, limited, restricted or trapped.

YOU can't <u>force</u> someone to be with you. OR think, I know they want me, it's just a matter of time. On a rare occurrence, it could happen (it's possible). NOT usually, by a cocky acknowledgement on your part dude. "She wants me I can SO tell." Talk to the HAND... foot... butt. You should know anything done through active manipulation (on your part) will *reverse* and you'll find yourself manipulated by the <u>need</u> to control the situation AT ALL TIMES. Your Fairy Goddess has spoken!

Stings like a bitch...

When I first dated this guy he was like... "I'm gonna make you *come* so bad, you're gonna want me allll the time." Cute. He wanted to show me how much I would need him (want him).

What ends up happening...

He goes *crazzzzy* over my body. He's like, "I CAN'T believe I came three times!" Honestly guys... What's the big deal? It seems like such a monumental event for YOU. So I ask a male species, he's like, "Nichole, if a guy comes **three** times—it means you're hot." *Ya baa da baa doooo me...* Like NOW. This guy (once we were official) was so into how my body responded... *he was controlled* by his need to be in **control** of my body—like an ADDICT. Allll the time. He needed to see it *respond* over and over and OVER again. It made him *craaazy.* It's all he thought about. I'll never forget this one time...

It's really late at night and we just finished doin' it. He's like, "*Whoa... all that power with these four fingers.*" Hysterical... Well, not at that moment kinda preoccupied (but after fo shur). We're making out I direct him to my boob... he puts it in his mouth. He's SO into it (such a turn on). Then he does what allll you guys do *when you have your mouth full...* Looks right AT ME. Like, 'Am I doin' well?' I'm like, "*AHAHAHA!!* Bae, I can't stop laughing when you look at me like that, while you're sucking my boob. YOU take away my erotica jones. He's like, "You mean erogenous zones."

Same thing.

Guys don't try to look or be a *certain* way—just be into it. Oh! And when you get out of bed for God's sake, be CAREFUL. Watch where you're puttin' your hand. Especially, if we're lying on our front and our boob's peeking out of the side. Like, when my guy got off me... didn't pay attention. I'm like, "*Ooouch!* You stepped on my BOOB." He's like, "Is it *okay*?" I'm like, "It's cool... I'm gonna step on your nuts." "Just one right?" I'm like, "A boob for a nut." It pays to be a ballerina... nutcracker is always ready to perform. :P

Later on...

You know how you are when you start off sleeping with your guy, you're allll tangled up, come middle of the night you've drifted *farrr* off to the other side (of the bed). YOU start to crave his warmth, so *slowly* you edge your way back to him (to be *close*). He's lying on his back but I really need to go to the bathroom. I come back. Can't wait to snuggle with my bae. I JUMP into bed. He's like...

"*AAAAHH!* YOU just hip-checked my dick." o_O "Oops! Sorry... is he OKAY?" He's like, "Don't worry he can take it. KNOCKED the wind outta my left nut." (Casualties of Love) I felt bad. Gave him space. He starts to doze off but I start to miss him. And you girls know how you get when you just gotta feel like he's allll YOURS? I lift my thunder thigh—slam it down! FASTEN HIM to the bed. My hand goes down *there*... He wakes up (no surprise) he's like, "Ya know... if you squeeze my left testicle—my right EYE will pop out." I'm like, "OMG!! Reeeally?!" He's like, "NO. Only kidding." He turns me over on my back... looks at my boobs (aaa-gain). Seriously, don't you guys ever get tired of lookin' at 'em? *Nooo-pe.* They were full (close to my period) so fall to the side. Carefully, he scoops one up... then lets it fall. He's like, "I love how your boobs go panoramic when you lie down." I'm like, "What do you mean?" He's like, "Just like those photos you take, when you can see the whole view." K... My boobs have now reached scenic proportions.

He got me SO hot...

I went all Nosferatu on him—gave him a hickey on his neck. He's like, "You suck so *harrrrd*... Whatta you got a turbo diaphragm—just like a vacuum cleaner. I think you sucked in my lymph node! It's gonna be BLACK."

CERTIFIED BY NICHOLE. LOL :-E

The next night we're at the movies standing in line, he cops a feel... but I up him one. We're at the Chinese buffet, surrounded by tons of people pickin' their food. He picks up a spring roll and squeezes it... I put my hand on his crotch squeeze *my* spring roll! He stands there. He's like, "It's NOT a bike horn." Squeeze! squeeze! :D

So love... can't be manipulated. And that includes any spells you girls *think* brings him back to YOU. *You'll be under the spell...* thinkin' it can happen. True magic is born *part*... 'right mix', part chemistry, **part**... somethin' you can't explain. So it CAN'T be forced (for shur) and it can't be transferred. It's a *love* thing... We get penalized for shit like that in my orbit, our degree of power *drops*... (for good).

Other examples...

I'll do him (for now) cuz I don't have anyone else right this second, and it's my ex's best friend—it'll make him jealous. Besides, he's really into me, so it's okay... I *suppose*. Or, I'm gonna show *her* that I can get ANYONE. I'm gonna fuck as many girls as I WANT—starting with her best friend. I know she's hot for me. She's gonna realize that she's missin' out. Then she'll want me. (*I hope*)

Too bad there's only one way of spelling...

<u>NO</u>

Wait!

Nada, nie, jo, non, ne, nono, zákaz, nej, hindi, nein, ekki, tak ada, nem, nil aon, не, geen, nē, ebda, nei, não, nr, ne, nej; inte, Hi, không, dim... a couple more from around the WORLD. Practice!

I remember when I *did it*...

It was purely to try and cancel out *another* guy (who was insanely tuned into me) it was ridiculous how we clicked. Like, I love it when a guy notices my shoe laces are untied and thinks I might trip, so kneels down to tie them for me. Right in front of EVERYBODY. And he did this, the first time we talked. So hard to resist. The *comfort* level... unreal. It freaked me out! Even though I didn't sleep with him (yet) I had to get him out of my system. This was dangerous—couldn't stop thinking about the guy... drove me crazzzy. So I hook up with this *other* guy (I had stopped seeing) used to call me non-stop and invite me over. Now, I'm like, "Hey! I'm coming over!" And even though I did feel comfortable with mister 'substitute' when we did it (slept together) it DIDN'T feel right. Cuz it only made me want and think of the other one even more (SO screwed). Guys TAKE notes!

To be clear... fucking someone to try and CANCEL out your feelings (sexercism lol) regardless of reason (guaranteed) you'll feel worse. It only makes you want the one you *want* even more. Now you're gonna COMPARE. Game over... What's the sense of playin'?

Girls...

Let's not even *start*... when it comes to us and love (more notes guys) how crippling it can be, crying non-stop for THREE days in a fetal position—just for starters. So your parent's like, "Are you sick?" They want you to go get a blood test. You're like, "Mom. I'm in HELL now. Can you leave me alone?" (Wishful thinking) Ditching your friends, they don't know what to do with YOU. Unreachable... (tough place to be) All kinds of thoughts are gobblin' your brain. Result. PURE mush. And this is what I mean. Love *has* to be circulating... It's not just about the guy you love—it's about YOU (too). The part of you that's doin' something YOU love (**to do**). So love can *continue* circulating in your life—act like a wicked armor. Against allll those bad thoughts you get about him (her) friends, feeling like shit... hopelessness. Cuz when you're focused on what you *love* you feel *loved*. Simple I know... yet so missed. And that... will accomplish a great buffer.

JOY.

Something you're stoked about in your life (something you love to do) in order to attract love *back* to YOU. Cuz love's a *growing* energy... it expands (likes to *reach out and touch*). LOL Fear withdraws... it's scared (figures) so it won't be reaching out any time soon.

YOU have ugly thoughts, you'll get *more* of that (situations, people) that draw your attention. You have awesome thoughts (what you can BE... DO) you'll receive opportunities to get you THERE. You have doubt... you'll receive *pleeenty* of situations where you have reason to doubt (did he/she cheat) cuz that's where your focus is.

SO THAT'S ALL YOU SEE.

Sadly...

And you miss *other* things—they'll FLY right by you. You won't even notice them, they'll be under your radar (way too much friction in your cosmic storm). Then one day, you'll be like, "You're kidding? SHE liked me? But I never saw that." Take a look at how you're feeling (most of the time). YOU scared you'll be tricked (fooled)? It'll happen. Fearful *thoughts*... It'll produce more of the same—*TRUST* me on this one. The most intense thing you're scared of—brings it right to YOU. If that's allll you're thinkin' about. You keep running the same thoughts so no choice—till your mind BELIEVES it's real, actively pursues situations (people) that get you *there*...

1. Getting caught in a lie.
2. Getting pregnant.
3. Having your secret... out.
4. Being taken advantage of.
5. Your best friend fucking you over.
6. Your boyfriend (girlfriend) CHEATING.

So that your mind can finally say, "TOLD YOU SO." So, you'll believe it next time (more often). And... It can control your life. What can we do right now, to get us out of that?

MAKE A LIST OF <u>EVERYTHING</u> THAT MAKES YOU HAPPY!

304.

And I don't mean... like, you're reciting it to a priest (God, rabbi, pet rock). I mean... putting your focus on what's really exciting! That's happening to you NOW bringing more of that—to YOU. Take what you know you can <u>do</u>, amp it!

Like, if in the past you landed a job (real easy) and you're looking. You can be like, "I'm so grateful that I can land ANY job real easily!!" If your mother, friend (some other source) gave you A LOT of money (last minute) when you really needed it and you need it now, you can be like, "I'm so grateful I ALWAYS get large sums of money out of the blue! Right when I need it." If you had an audition and you killed it. And you're going to the second one, you could write... "I'm so grateful I'm gonna SLAY this audition!! Get hired on the SPOT. Impress the shit out of the director." If you and your boyfriend (girlfriend) have been FIGHTING you *could* write... "I'm so grateful that I have the most incredible guy/girl in my life, who constantly (remembering times they did) shows me how MUCH they love me and <u>only</u> me." WATCH how your mind *goes* there...

You need only search for a *morsel* of truth in a situation you're aiming for (memory) that happened. Shoot for the MOON. Blow it up! Elaborate the fuck out of it. It doesn't matter if it was something you did when you were a kid. Use it NOW. Like, if you talked to a girl effortlessly when you were seven, remember *that* and write... "I ALWAYS talk to girls easily and they lovvvve being around me! They always wanna get to know me."

IF...

You're bummed (life sucks) write things that make you *happy* (you're grateful to have). And if you can't think of anything—think of something awesome you would **lovvve** to have (be truly grateful for) cuz that's where it starts! Think about *that*... give it three days. And watch your world turn AROUND. The key is, to write about what you want *more* of. So hunt and keep hunting. Like a true warrior (princess) and I <u>promise</u> right after you write, you'll be in a TOTAL different head space! To actually GO make things happen—don't waste that energy. Pick up your phone, go knock on a door, talk to someone—ANYONE! Just go after what you want. Cuz you wouldn't be reading *this* book... if you weren't already be aligned with it. And expect, the unexpected. I'm talking HAPPINESS coming, almost instantly. Course knowing you, you'll be saying shit like, "Whoa... Whatta coincidence." LOL It may not even be the actual thing you're aiming for, it <u>will</u> be something that will prep you for THAT. I can just see you saying, "Hmm? Wonder what happy 'unexpected' good shit is comin' my way?" Go ahead. Ask...

Then video yourself and let me know what happens!

It's important to structure it this way cuz when you feel like CRAP you think (decide n' act) with the expectation of it NOT happening. Cuz you don't think it's something that will happen for you. When you write a bunch of things you're *excited* about forthcoming (exactly the way you want it) cuz it's covered in a 'grateful' overcoat, it protects you from yourself (downpour of shit your mind's tryin' to give you) thinks you deserve. You will be SO happy. Your energy will go UP. Attract *other* happy things that glue their (nice) asses to yours. This is not a lengthy process. ONE page.

A note to all manwhores...

Writing; "I'm grateful she's sucking my dick." is not what I'm talking about. It's about more than *that*... And when you actually think you deserve more (not afraid to go for it) you'll get a *whole lot more*...

One dream Girl... Guy who's SO boss.

ORDERING:

Before any of this can happen... **You** need to feel awesome about yourself (truly) cuz you'll attract what you 'are' right now (deep down). The grateful list puts you in your inherited *birthright*... a place where you feel and sense <u>allll</u> you deserve. From there, you pave the way for your SOUL MATE (to come). And you thought I forgot...

Just be forewarned...

You WILL bring them to you. And it will be scary, that a person for you 'actually' exists. LOL It doesn't matter where you are right now. If you have braces with a full headgear (like my boyfriend did) pimples (like I do) live in the projects. The sun shines on everyone and everything (not a select few). So... they will find YOU. Bottom line everything is ENERGY. And energy *goes* to find its own... energy. Ready to start?

Cuz there's no turning back...

GO somewhere quiet, a private place. Write on a PAGE (or two) what **exactly** your soul mate (most perfect person for you) looks like, mood, what you love about them, what they do, how they act or behave (accent) what they wear, what they love about YOU... how they make you laugh (make love... when it's time) all the non-negotiables. Give yourself a MONTH.

And a month is NOT long to prepare at all for the *perfect* guy (girl).

With my guy... He told me he went on a mission with his friend (to find the *perfect* girl) together. They went to his room and took a white piece of paper and began writing. The whole idea was to write it and release it to the universe. My boyfriend's very thorough, specific and CLEAR about what he wants. He's like, "She <u>has</u> to have a magical quality to her... like a Queen. She has to have high morals, no skanks." It took forever for him, to complete his PAGE. His friend's like, "It doesn't have to be perfect." My guy's like, "*Really*..." He knew it had to be <u>exact</u>. Or he'd only get what he wrote (not what he wanted). So I asked him if he wrote how I'd be *sexually*... He's like, "Well... I didn't write that part cuz he woulda seen it. But there was all this intensity boiling up INSIDE me! Like a laser beam shot outta my forehead—etched it on the paper." I'm like, "Yeah? Well... How did you want me?" (Smile) "Like an ANIMAL... *like me*." "AM I like an *animal*...?" "You're my sexy little *beast*." He continues..."It's two in the morning in the middle of winter, when we went to complete our task. I took my lighter and we walked across the street into an empty field, with our papers. The plan was to burn the lists and deliver them to the universe. It's crazy windy, minus twenty five degrees Celsius and I'm out there with my *lighter*. LOL The only thing the little flame could do was turn the corner of the paper brown. It wouldn't catch— like, fireproof. I probably would have gone through the whole lighter fluid, trying to burn that one *piece* of paper, but my fingers were stinging from the cold. I'm like *'FUCK THIS!'* I go back to the garage come back with a BLOW TORCH. I hold the paper with the tongs, but it blows away. I'm chasing the paper in the wind!! LAUGHING the whole time. I catch it. Pin it to the ground—torch it. Alright! Done. Then ran my ass back into the house cuz it was so fucken cold."

I couldn't believe he went through all that. LMAO

Plot twist...

Less than a month later after he did that, I'm lookin' to rent a place. I see an ad. It's HIS. I call, agree to check it out next morning. After I see it he's like, "You know, when you called... I was so depressed. I heard you say, "Hiiiii!" And snapped—right out of it! I kept thinking. What is it about her *voice*? I've never experienced anything like that. Soon as I hung up with you, I drove to the house and spent the ENTIRE night cleaning. The doorbell rings, I go downstairs, throw the broom in the closet and open the door (sweaty as hell). When I saw YOU... I literally took the first deep *breath* since we talked the night before. So many questions were going through my head, I had no time to process. I couldn't speak. I just stood there... like an idiot." True that. Thought he was in a coma with his eyes open. That's when I'm like... "Can I come IN?" Followed by. "YOU smell. Bad. That's no way to sell a house." (Omg. Can't believe I said THAT) Although we talked for a while, told him about the book I was starting, I never ended up taking the place. Didn't like the other roommate, told him she'd be trouble—which she was! And that I'd feel a lot better if he lived there. He offers to move back in (still didn't believe him). I left him my name and email—he lost it.

Tried for months (yearrrs) to figure out the SOUND of my last name (all variables of it) so he could find me and message me. FIVE years later, he finds the (now mangled) piece of paper with my name and email on it. He emails me... "Hey! It is you!" I see it... think 'creep'. Don't reply. Meanwhile he goes back to school, starts doing heavy introspection about himself, his life... a very severe past.

Somehow he finds me on social media (don't even *remember* accepting his friend request). LOL Two years later... He's popping up all over my feed. Who... is this guy? I like what he's posting but need to know *more*." Can't be too careful. I'm a safety GIRL! I message him...

"WHO are you?" He's like, "You answered an ad and came to my place... seven years ago." "I DID *whaaat...?*"

(Still no memory)

He's like, "At the time you were starting a book, it seemed very significant." OMG!! He remembers my book! It's gotta be true or he wouldn't have known about the book. K, so I remember discussing the book... not *him*. We meet up. Still... no memory.

I let him know I'm looking for someone to help design my book cover. He lets me know he just finished design school. (*Sahweet*) From the first night of working together... we were **attached** to each other. I thought it was sooo thoughtful when I was tired and leaned on his shoulder, that he put a cushion *there*. He's like, "Here, that way you don't have to feel my bony shoulder." Then he's like, "You know... When we first met, even though you didn't end up renting and we just ended up talking... I was awestruck the whole time. It was literally like a UNICORN had wandered into my backyard. I didn't want to flinch and scare it away. After you left I was like—*who was that...* that caused such a reaction in me? I've had people come and see my place before. That never happened. I was LIT up. And I was so down, at the time I was completely fascinated. All I could do, was watch you... And I was curious about the book and wanted to know *more*. It's like... I wanted to be part of it somehow. (Now he is) I wanted to be there to see it do what it was *supposed* to do. Once you left I was like, ohh... God. I couldn't **stop** thinking of you." :- ~~~~

This is WHY...

It's critical to do the two steps 1) grateful list 2) precise list of guy (girl) and in THAT order. Cuz, like my boyfriend... most of the time we say we really want to find *someone*... deep down we're scared of *having* 'em... so we fuck it up! HOW COULD HE LOSE MY NUMBER?! Or, we're scared of them finding out how **fucked** our family is. Scared, they won't want us if they know our *secret*... our SCAR. Our defect (to us) how messed up we are. These two steps will intercept your Tasmanian devil—stop him (for good). Leave him toothless.

309.

A message from my boyfriend...

When you finally DO meet her... you're gonna mess up. It's inevitable. But it's OKAY... she'll think it's cute. You're gonna be nervous, forget what you're saying, act like a IDIOT. If she's really the one, she'll love you even *more*... for your 'humanness' (as Nichole calls it). And when you're writing her character traits out, you need to *feeeel it* when you're doin' it. I mean... you need to have a BONER. It needs to be real (*to you*). You need to see her face, how she makes you feel when your with HER etc. And if you do it *right*... once you hook up with her she may get weirded out by the whole extreme comfort level thing (and act STRANGE) like Nichole did. LOL It wasn't until three months after we got together (lying on the sofa) she's like, "OH... MY... GOD! I remember YOU!" And jumps up!! LANDS on my stomach, throws her arms around my neck bursting with joy! What's a misplaced rib in the name of love? The WHOLE time she didn't even know who I was. Lmao

Amaaazing things will happen...

If we can get out of our OWN WAY.

I never understood that (at first) till I took acting lessons! People think acting is about *pretending*. It's about **doing**... and if you're doing—you're BEING. More penis wisdom! LOL And you can just TELL when an actor sucks cuz that's what he does... gets in his own way. Cuz he's sayin' his lines while in his head, he's rating himself. Sayin' shit like... "I wonder how I look? Do I look STUPID? Do they think I'm good? Can they tell I'm star material?"

Too much self awareness... leads to fear.

(YOU holding back)

When your eyes are mostly focused inward... they're not working (can't see in front of you). When your ears are listening MOSTLY

310.

inward... they're not working (can't hear what's being said) REACTING to your head. The actor's supposed to be talkin' to his scene partner, but you can tell somethin's off. When you're talkin' to someone your focus is on *what* you're saying (to them) not how you're sayin' it. Unless you're nervous, your butt hole's doin' like, 500 contractions per minute. When you're talkin' to a babe AND yourself, so you're like, "Hmm...? Wonder how I'm doin'. Wonder if she thinks I'm an idiot. (Probably) DON'T stare at her boobs! Omg. Her nipples just got hard. Wonder if that means she's into me."

Why do you guys ALWAYS think that? There are other things like... wind chill factor, period factor, irritating bra factor—you're NOT the only factor. Now it's understandable why YOU look so lame and sound stupid talkin' to her. Cuz in your mind you ARE. In order to get out of your own way YOU must be focused on where you're *goin'*... It's like tryin' to walk... but you keep lookin' at your feet, so you keep trippin' up. You CAN'T split your focus and expect to get somewhere—your focus is half or *more* on shit that don't serve you. When an arrow's split down the middle, it doesn't have the power to get where it's heading. It's too delicate. The air'll take it wherever the fuck it wants. Exhausted... It'll just fall to the ground, probably land on some tossed condom (used). Like, what is it with everybody—put those things in the garbage! Poor chipmunk. Starts chewing on one and chokes or dies of suffocation. Out of alllll the degrees of YUCKITUDE that's the WORST. Too bad about that arrow... it coulda gone places.

Thank God Robin Hood's arrow was mint. He'd never let his mind wander from what he's aiming at. He HAS focus. Think, he's saying shit like, "No one's ever tried this before. What if I FAIL? What are the *chances* of me succeeding, anyway? What if I look dumb? My dad never gave me any direction. Mom paid more attention to the chickens than me." You think he gave a shit about where he was from or WHO he was competing *against?* He wanted what he **wanted**— that's it.

The rest...

Many... many arrows.

Soooo when your focus is on your frustration you're like, "Fuck it— I'm DONE." You feel really hopeless (just like I did). I COULDN'T take it anymore. The load, the obstacles (year after year, after YEAR) no one to turn to. No one to *hold*... pressures, circumstances just too friggin' much. I'd go to the lake, climb on a rock tired AF collapse... listen to the water. Cry my eyes out. This old, lady comes by. She's wearing bright CORAL lipstick—almost blinded me! She's walking her dog with her cane. Actually... I think the dog was walking her. She stops. Sits down on a small rock (next to me) she's like, "Tell me.... allll about yourself." I'm like, "Whooo sent YOU?" Cuz there's **no way** she coulda seen me crying.

I tell her all my frustrations. People telling me I can't write this book, it's too raw— *JUST WANNA TELL IT LIKE IT IS!* Crying so hard I can hardly breathe (hiccupping at the same time) sounds like I have a speech impediment. Hate it when that happens. I tell her I have to STOP (writing). It's like putting a knife in my stomach—murdering my baby (book). ;_; It's a Boy... It has a penis. LOL

She stands UP!

Waves her cane in the air she's like, "YOU will **NOT** stop this book! and no one will make YOU stop this book!" Go! Grandma Moses! Lmfaooo

Re-Cap!

- Feel like shit (overwhelmed, tired... hopeless feeling).

- Went to cry by the lake (refreshing, beautiful... peaceful).

- Met Grandma (being good to myself, rewarded).

When you start paying attention to yourself (SELF-care) start doin' things that make you feel good (even if you're crying in the process) see a movie, buy yourself a new dress, go to a concert, play music LOUD, sing even louder! Sit in the rain (*kiss in the rain*) eat a cup cake—but *only* the icing part. Take your grandmother out, tell her about your guy (girl). The world sees *that*... gives you allll that good stuff *back*...

An example of that...

I broke up with my (*current*) boyfriend, he was acting like a dick. Sooo done. Every night, I'd go to bed and think how gooood it *feels* to have his arms around me (as if he's still with me) his love, all the different ways he'd show it. How safe... I feel. And I'd fall asleep with a big smile on my face. I **refused** to let the feelings of over-with-ness enter my body. WOULDN'T EVEN LET... a single thought of '*he's not with me anymore...*' come in. End of the week... Sunday morning. I'm reading my bible. He CALLS.

"Nichole...

Every single night this week I had a dream telling me NOT to let you go. And that I **had** to make up with YOU. First day, two, three days... I thought was just a spillover, cuz we broke up. But by day FOUR I already decided—I'm gonna do it. I'm gonna find a way. I start brainstorming on how I'm gonna fix this. Day five, six, seven— SAME dream!! How many times is this sign gonna flash over my head? I'm calling!! WE have to be together... This is so *fated*. I sat on my bed and designed a 'plan'. I wrote out plan A plan B, C and D. If it came to plan D I'd work on plan E. Fortunately, plan A worked." ;) We met up took a long drive, talked. He was sooo serious. He's like, "You know, for seven days in a row I woke up with such an *intense* feeling. Like, I was being told sternly 'HEY smarten up!! YOU gotta get her back.' It was like a harpoon pulling me—a HARPOON with a chain. By the 7th night... I had seven of them all pulling me. It unbelievable."

Then he told me his secret (fear).

His dad, only other person in the world he really, really loved, died. Completely fucked him up. Got into drugs... worst pit of hell ever. Took him foreverrr to get out. He was scared that one day... I'd die. (No kidding) So it made sense that just as we were getting *close*... he'd act all weird n' shit not even understand why. Automatic asshole BUTTON activated... as soon as I'd land on his heart. Then I'd with-draw, then come close...withdraw. Finally ended it. Sometimes guys girls act fucked up (not their usual way with you) cuz they're really scared of gettin' **attached** to you. It doesn't mean that you tolerate it. You need to cut the ties so it'll jar them awake.... From their bad dream. I told him right there. "Do not continue to think this way or you'll invite it—we're connected!" That's when he declared me... His White Magic Woman.

His mermaid...

When you **still** feel strongly about your guy (girl) in spite of their distance, something may be controlling THEM. Like I said, it doesn't mean you put up with it, that would tell them it's no biggie. Being separated from them, will allow their true feelings to surface (override the *fear* controlling them) while experiencing life WITHOUT you. If you don't push for their emotions (to surface) they will... just from sheer absence (voids need to be filled). And all things eventually rise... to surface. It's a Law of the Universe.

Often I've asked myself...

Did I *make* him have alll those dreams... by refusing to let go of the love I felt for him (act as if nothing was wrong)? Just cuz I didn't wanna feel pain? Maybe... You know mermaids, they can move into different realities. ;<>I only allowed thoughts that made me feel *good* about him (without expecting anything) I felt like I still had him, like nothing changed. Which is why like *magic* everything changed. Without me having to call HIM. Or the worst... I just wanna hear his voice—hang up.

When we're young we make a vow to be 'something'. Super hero, astronaut, president, movie star. BREATHE under water! Imagination gone wild. Then in our teens we make a vow not be abused (taken for granted, used, bullied, criticized) takes us right out of MAKING anything-happen mode (permanently). Like attracts like, when it comes to how you *think* and what comes to you. I gave love... I GOT love. Pure and simple. Ever notice those types...

They complain about *everyyything*.

314.

I mean they like, got a MASTER'S degree in complaining. Course if it's someone you've known for a long time, you might take it, make an excuse as to why you can't sometimes (when you REALLY need a break). But you'll see that these people, are polluting your atmosphere. You start seeing things like they DO (just cuz they've had a bad experience) it's like, they've hijacked your emotions, recycled them through their garbage incinerator—everything looks like SHIT. And that usually ends the friendship (can't take it anymore). And you're always tired after you've seen them. Although you listened, gave advice (obvious thing to do) drop the person creating hell, change something about the situation, they DIDN'T listen (nothing changed). And you don't wanna abandon them or anything, but it's sucking you dry. Tough situation. But was it a friendship or did they just get used to YOU soaking up their shit? In the end after seeing you, they feel better (their load lighter) you feel drained (yours heavier). I used to work on a farm. The farmer's like, "Nichole remember, if you hang around *shit* you're gonna start smellin' like it." I get it. Course... he never did explain why his cow almost LICKED MY FACE OFF whenever I'd milk her.

Guess I found her G spot. LOL

People who complain usually *continue* to complain. And are they the only one with crap happening? NOOO. Attitude is like a *muscle*... YOU rebound from shit when you're pumped (stoked) which comes from your attachment to something that you *love* (sport, project, cause, hobby, career) it feeeeds you. Brings this awesome feeling so you're like, full speed happiness. All the time. Self-loathing (hating on yourself) attracts bad shit. It's just answering its call (what you're sending out). And that is...

I DON'T GIVE A FUCK I WANNA FIGHT!

Cuz somewhere you were *mis*-informed.

That you're not worth much. That what you wanna do is <u>not</u> *worth* much (so heart shuts down, dies) so you don't care what happens to you (now).

I *know*... I felt it many times.

My Dad never had time for me, no matter how many awards I'd WIN. He'd never pay attention to me... Except when I was little girl and he'd claim bragging rights on how much he spent at the dentist, on my cavities. Like! You're the one feeding me chocolates! So embarrassing. I made myself not sleep for THREE whole nights. Just to get back at him. Like it worked. All the fights my parents had just before a dance recital—screaming alllll the way there. I was the only one who needed extra make-up. When I got home I didn't eat for TWO days. I wanted to hurt them! Show that when YOU hurt me. *I will hurt me more...* Brilliant logic. ANYONE relate? What did you do, or are doing NOW to punish someone? (Mom, Dad, boyfriend, girlfriend)

For your eyes only...

Whatever you wanna do—and I don't give a fuck how **difficult** or impossible they say it is. It's POSSIBLE.

Pop Quiz:

What man looked at the auto industry is like, "Maybe... everyone's fucked." created the first inexpensive mass-produced automobile? Ford. What man looked at time and space is like, "Maybe... everyone's WACKED." redefined how we see time and space? Einstein. Columbus looks at the horizon is like, "Is everyone... DUMMMB?" K. They didn't all say that but I'm sure they must have thought it. Do you have any idea how big Columbus's balls had to be to pull off that journey— no GPS? He didn't know what would happen to him (and his men) his heart just said GO!! *It knows things...*

(In advance)

Just like when you meet someone and you *know* you want 'em in your life (foreverrr). You become best friends (or more). But how did you know? When you first saw them, you didn't know much about them...

You saw them across the room.

316.

Each of those men challenged society, by looking into something their heart *pulled* them to do. Look up the first man that made a helicopter fly (when no one else could). Guess what? The very first helicopter ALREADY existed… centuries ago, in ancient Egypt. For real. Strange hieroglyphics show these highly developed crafts, we're talking planes, submarines, helicopters—even flying saucers! WTH So, some Pharaoh had the plans designed already. Probably sittin' on a plate of locusts.

(It coulda been a delicacy) LOL

There are sites you can go to that TRANSLATE your name… into hieroglyphs. Mine has a vulture in it—so be careful. I might circle above when you feel like shit—pick your brain! Haaa!

Meee…

It doesn't matter how big what the challenge seems to be, if it's in your heart **'to do'** it means it's tapped into *something* from another time (another *place*) born or not yet born… in this world. It's bringing you a hint of acknowledgement… it **exists**. And YOU have been selected to bring it to the World.

There are singers and composers who actually have melodies come to them in their sleep! They have notebooks and recorders on hand. At any given moment a line for a song or tune could come. They've tapped into something not *here* yet… and they're smart enough to know to LISTEN. Do not undervalue the **unique** (at times, more like weird) qualities you've been born with… to do whatever you've been chosen for (branded a certain way by you). Your next step… Find your strengths (talent) idiosyncrasies, quirks or peculiarities (that should be fun). ASK your friends! It's your duty cuz *baby*—that'll highlight it! It's your first clue, you're on track. And since it's coded in your heart it'll be *triggered*… when all of a sudden you're TOTALLY stoked over something. Inside YOU you'll already have the plans to make it happen! Just like helicopter man. And you *will* be connected to the right people, be in the right situation (even if it is annoying and or, hard to deal with) in order to make it **happen**. Become…

The FIRST _____ everrr.

Write it damn it!

You need only **decide** and life WILL do everything in its *power*—
to *MOVE* shit out of your way. Make it appear. It's already been
ordained.

That's why there's an imprint in your heart... xo

Just decide!!!!

<u>Example</u>

When I first met this girl (who really supports me) I was writing at
the library. Although her friends teased her about this book, she kept
telling them she thought it had a lot of insight... (inspiring). I had no
idea at the time, she was mostly into hanging out with her guy friends,
(she called 'her boys') not really into her *own* kind. Don't blame her
with the bunch I saw her with, I'd ditch them too. She had *one* close
girl friend.

She reminded me of me... I usually only had one close friend. An
aversion to my own tribe. LOL I knew I could help her in terms of
seeing **why** she was the way she was. She was attractive (little heavy)
but I knew she didn't feel comfortable like that. I could tell she
was miserable. Reserved... didn't talk much. Unless she was drunk,
then she could be herself. She was usually distant. But lovvved
children! She'd babysit them alll the time. I'd see her with like, SIX
kids in her car. I'm like, "THAT'S alllot of kids." She loved being
with them, teaching them life *skills*... ways out of conflict, giving
them belief in themselves. I started training her. We got close. One
day, she lets me know she got into this HUGE fight at a party, night
before. Like! Ten losers pile on top of her, cuz when she's drunk her
mouth SOBERS up! She starts sayin' shit (she could never say) so
no longer distant—more like IN YOUR FACE. Even though, what
she said to this one guy he had coming (fo shur), she was so angry
inside she wanted to fight—take it allll out (held it in for sooo long).
So she PUSHES the guy in the pool. I should mention it's November.
Everyone went CRAAAZY!! Cops were involved and everything...

318.

When I saw her the next day... She's like, "You know, those bicep curls we do REALLY help! I can tell, my punch is much stronger. HOLY CRAP! And I *feel* better too. Even though, I did get a little beat up n' stuff. I took it all out!" Her face was swollen (bruised) her eyes were *puffy* (purple, green) the bridge of her nose was sooo wide, she looked like a KOALA. Too bad she didn't look like a WET koala!!. Seriously. Look up the image—they would have allll ran away. LMAO Luckily, she didn't lose a tooth. She's trying to become a dental hygienist.

GUYS beating up on a... *girl*?

Like! What is WRONG with YOU?

In her life...

She *brought in* bad shit. She also brought in weak guys (she had to take care of, rescue) she'd sneak them into her bedroom, when they were in trouble. Or speak on their behalf (protective). At times, they complained they felt like they were her children. Even when they wanted to pump her gas, she'd be like... "It's MY car. I'll pump my own gas." Since these guys were passive, not really driven and her actions made them <u>more</u> like that (looking out for them, taking care of them) it put her masculine energy into overdrive. Then one day, she tells me she got hired in a dental office. I was sooo happy for her! She was like, dental hygienist by DAY... Koala Fighter by night. LOL But it wasn't till one day when I received a call from her, that it was **clear**... why we connected. Even though at the time, she nor I saw her specific connection to the book, her voicemail made it clear...

"Omigosh! Nichole, I've got this IDEA! We have to do a book like *this* for children—ABOUT their issues and struggles." She was so stoked! It was her 'calling'. And I let her know it was already on my list. We'll probably call it; *The Wisdom of the Kiwi*. LOL And yes, she could run with it...

It's her baby.

- She was connected to something her friends **didn't** agree with (she felt for in her heart).

- She was a *certain* way... so the book <u>spoke</u> to HER. She was heavy, which created a path for us to get *closer* (training) and our friendship grew. She was in trouble (bad shit) which showed me (and later her) she had 'little' value for herself in comparison to the others she cared for.

- She had a passion for kids, which led to something she was BORN to do.

DESIGN a book! That helps CHILDREN have life skills! So they can be the absolute best they can BE!!

So again, if YOU have a vision of something you wanna do, it's not insane (ridiculous) it's *ahead* of time. And don't let **anyone** tell YOU what you can or cannot do, cuz *clearly* those rules have been broken (many times) by men who didn't even finish school. Like, Abraham Lincoln. He barely went to school. He was a self-made man who educated *himself* reading at home. If you get your butt in gear, allow whatever's ticking in YOU to ring LOUD (proud) guaranteed, it'll summon a *vibration* to connect you to alll the things needed, to bring YOU there. Another reason it's important to do what you *love*...

Especially for us girls.

It keeps US afloat...

When our love boat's shaky (sinking) hits a ROCK—explodes.

<u>Example</u>:

"I can't **believe** he just cut me off—after alllll we've been through."

Not only will you stay afloat, you'll be *revived*. Cuz you've returned to your home base, something you love. And when a guy senses you *don't* need him. You can be HAPPY (without him). It makes him wanna find a way to make you happy... *with him* (a challenge). Then he feels SPECIAL.

So yes, maybe our mermaid needed to get out of *that* boat—it's not her true environment anyway. She gets her nourishment from a place *unknown* to man... a place secret to her heart (only).

Her *passion*...

It's what makes her untouchable (immune to heartache).

She's self-contained, in need of *nothing* (k... almost). And this way... when there's an issue it's no longer, "Is he gonna hate me now? Will he leave me and find someone ELSE?" It's more like... "How *exactly* is this guy contributing to my life again?" Only the **real** thing has a chance in hell of reaching YOU cuz you're already 'high'. It's the only thing capable of putting you on top of the MOON.

Love... ;<>

When you choose to hook up with a guy and share that *passion* (that you love) since you're stoked about it—it's HIGH voltage. It ignites him (if he truly cares for you) and he feels that off of YOU. So he gets **charged**.

Ohhh... That's why he said, "*I CAN'T BELIEVE I CAME THREE TIMES!*"

(I get it) :D

If you're pissed, hardened (dead inside)...

YOU haven't found your passion (yet) so have confused it for *him*—(being 'all that') and he lets you down. A feeling, I don't wish for anybody. It's worse than death... you're alive, but you feel dead (no one interests you) and love... sees it (your attitude) as a CLOSED for the Season sign. Meanwhile your heart's trapped in the cellar screaming—hey! I'm down HERE! Can't you hear me? Trouble is... No one can hear you. Most people can't interpret indifference as a 'cry' for love.

A tear is like a diamond...

If it falls from your eye I will catch it.

If love's not flowing, cuz there's restricted access, **no one** will be able to get in. Cuz what *can't* enter... eliminates all other entries as well. There's a lock. And a self-imposed prison can't lock the world out *without* also locking YOU in. And that hurts (you feel unwanted) When there's a *block* from love it can't continue—and separation doesn't feel good. That's why we feel PAIN when we hold love back. Like, when we're mad at our best friend (parent, boyfriend, girlfriend) it feels like we're keeping it for *ourself* (love) but we're actually keeping it from ourself...

Even the body's designed in a way that's like a circle!

When we look at the body (if we look carefully) we'll see an *entrance*... It's there to greet something. Alright! I'll say it. Penis. (Happy?) This ensures that the circle of energy is continued—a constant pouring, absorbing (k, pulsing) throbbing, *THRUSTING*... did I miss anything? LOL As well, emotionally there's a *flow*... a yin, yang (aggressive, passive energy) calm/excitable persona, shy/extravert personality. And that's so, they don't obstruct each other's course... just harmonize (creating balance) as one feeds *into* the other...

Cementing a union.

Like a catcher and a pitcher, it's a solid team.

Opposite *energies*... ATTRACT

YOU thought it meant somethin' else. Haaa!

I've been asked *so* many times—how do you *HOLD* it? Especially when there's SO many guys around. You're like, surrounded by allll these (guy) friends that make you feel so comfortable (only they're NOT boyfriend material) it can be difficult. Seriously, it's an issue.

K. To answer the first one. There's NO WAY I'd let some guy **'do me'**, fill up on unleaded gas. Like! That would totally mess up my engine. Cuz my engine's finely tuned, it can't be with some dip-shit dippin' his wick (*cheapest* way possible) not to mention, it damages the quality of performance (fo shur) decreases significantly. *FORGET* endurance! It gets used up so quickly. So when you're goin' uphill (bound to happen) 'hard times', you start hearing *knocks* (HIM banging you against the headboard) you wondering when it'll stop, sure indicator you've used a real cheap brand of oil. NOT the best, cleanest you *could* be having. Sometimes it's challenging... you're wasted and there's some cheap dumb fuck and noooo supreme octane in sight! You know it's not a MATCH. And there's low grade bad shit everyyywhere. Do I need this shit in me? But you're sooo low... Whadda ya do? Personally I can only say two things.

NOT interested in having my exhaust spit out toxic shit *(grosssss)* I want real sparks! I wanna ROCK. (Like, literally) I want my engine *purrrrring* the whole time. I want my gears *stripped* by someone who knows what the fuck he's doin'. Cuz he's familiar with how to run me properly, cuz he's the right FIT. He's not a part-time mechanic he's a formula one specialist. I'm gonna tell YOU one more time...

Refuse to be CAPTURED.

Keep it wild. Keep it Real. Keep it PURE.

So you guys are like, "But don't girls WANT sex?" Those that are ready... Yes! Double, triple, quadruple times YES. But depending on how the situation plays out (if she gets used) she could try to convince herself SHE fucked you. Yeah. Like, she just sprouted a cock out of her head—so now she's screwing YOU. Or, she'll wait... make sure her heart's <u>not</u> sitting on the sidelines (wishin' it was <u>its</u> turn) it's included.

SINCERE SEX FLYS!!

(*Smarrrt*)

In order to love a girl you must reach and penetrate her **mind** (as well as her *organ*). The half way point is where her heart lies... always, if you're a MAN.

If you're a worm...

I'm sure you'll wiggle your way into a different territory. Just watch out for TRAPS. You never know what swarm of crabs you're about to walk into... And secondly. Like! I'm *gonna* 'give it' to a friend—who's NOT what I want (or *who* I want) which only makes me want the one I **want** (even more). So... dumb. And since in his mind, it's just a favor-type thing, casual (nothing serious) all the other amenities (that come with it) *gone*. So after you've done it with him and all of a sudden he's NOT so available (like he used to be) or the girl he's been talking to (which you completely know about) looks like DRACULA to you. And she's about to suck allll the life out of your friend—his time, energy and his affection! Or the TOUGHEST. He's so in love with YOU (now) it threatens to *destroy* your friendship and or super annoys you—cuz he's NOT what you want! The other way I see this...

A bottle of perfume...

(Stays potent)

A tiny bit attracts from a *distance*...

If you mix it with water it (something casual) what happens? It becomes diluted... *weaker* in scent (not as alluring). When you *hold it* cuz you don't need to prove shit... guys can sense you haven't been dipped *into*... your scent is STRONG (unfucken diluted). When you walk you reek of potency—and they *know it*. Bottle <u>hasn't</u> been opened. They want it. Nowww you get your pick of the litter, hopefully you'll pick a *genuine* breed. A lot of un-evolved specimens out there (diseased, faulty, nasty shit). When you need to **refuel** (especially when you're used to a lot of pit stops) your fuel tank's low and you're nowhere *near...* it.

YOU have 2 hands (alternate).

Let me re-phrase that.

Guys, don't want you less when you hold out—they're wondering what'll it take to make you BUST. They want you *more...* It's a given. A powerful place to be.

My boyfriend's reading this, he's like... "Omg. That's soo true. When I held out, I couldn't believe what was happening." "WAIT a minute... YOU... held out?" He's like, "Yeah. My friend and I decided to do this competition. How long can we can hold out—NOT ejaculate. No sex." I'm like, "But guys masturbate—like every *other* minute. Is that a myth?" (Big grin) "We held it for a month." I'm like, "Really?!" He's like, "And we didn't see each other all that time, cuz it was summer, we lived far from each other. But holy crap! When we got back, compared notes we couldn't believe it. It wasn't **only** the girls that were pulled. *It was everybody.* People were being so nice—inviting us to places." "Get out!" LOL He's like, We never stood in line. We were so lucky! It was dope. All these opportunities presented themselves to both of us."

Whoa... It's NOT just girls.

It works for guys TOO. That makes total sense, cuz that *area* is such a powerful energy. If you don't use it and it's STORED—you're gonna be a **powerhouse**. Cuz you have this intensity about YOU. You're gonna stick out. Just look at all those countries, that are impoverished and guys have like, seven wives NOT a lot of tall buildings, cosmopolitan activity. Countries with only one wife allowed—*A TON OF BUILDINGS!!*

(Something's gotta be erect) Lmao

Key point!!

Sexual energy (*stored*) is a powerful launching pad... *for?* YOU decide. For now it'll show in the way you WALK, TALK... *look*. And that will pull them in...

ANY TIME - ANY PLACE - ANYWHERE.

It's your choice.

And sure, they can call you a tease. It means you're not STUPID. Just like this one guy, I was working with him when I was a waitress. He had mad steeze. I was *so* into him (he was older) always asked me if I needed a ride home. Sure beats taking the bus! I felt so free in my world JUST cuz I was in his car. He was in control. And I liked that.

Then I dunno know what happened...

It just got *known* that I was his girl, cuz he'd take me home every night. On the weekend when everyone's like, "Nichole YOU coming? There's this new Club opening." :D I'd look over at *him*... He'd be like, "I'm taking you home." And that was that. Brain shut down (temporarily). I know... something felt off, but there wasn't ANY guide books on 'how to be', what to look for. I didn't *know* what to do. I didn't know how to think. I just knew, it said A LOT... that I attracted this *older* guy (while I was just a teenager). I mean, he was a MAN. I couldn't believe he was interested in me! (I was still a virgin) I felt so *protected* when I was with him. He looked so confident. He'd always wear a black leather jacket. Didn't talk much, but I trusted him.

(So *I thought*...)

When he'd drop me off, he kissed me so softly. Not like MOST guys. Pointer! LESS tongue. Even though, I wanted much more that's all he did. Hate waiting for what I want. *(Pouting)* But I wasn't gonna show him how badly I wanted him, that woulda been my downfall fo shurrre. Then one day (after work) he's driving me to what I *thought* was my home, only he tells me he wants to go to a HOTEL. Omg!! YOU'RE kidding. :D I'm going to an actual hotel with a 'man'. I was stoked, cuz I thought we were going to mack in a BIG way! I just *lovved* it when I felt his HUMUNGOUS arms around me and I couldn't break free. I'm not joking. He's strong. He would look at me smile... my eyelids would be low (shy) but I'd peek through my lashes. His cologne drove me *insaaanne*. Just the smell alone, put me in the mood... cuz it wasn't OVERKILL. Like most of YOU do. Whatta you do... BATHE with it? It's supposed to attract—**not** be some kind of insect repellent. Singe the hairs right outta my nostrils! Seriously. A bit goes a long way.

I FELT like a woman...

He was aloof (an untold story) no one knew much about him. He looked a little scary (didn't smile much) serious. But that didn't scare me. In fact, that's how we met! He was outside at night on a smoke break. Had a hoodie on, underneath a lamp post. His face was in the shadow. All I could see were his lips... they were stern. I walk up to him. I'm like, "You look... SCARY. I feel safe with you." He showed some teeth! Smiled. I really liked his friend, which told me he was decent. His friend seemed nice (lot more talkative though). K. His friend was cute (just acknowledging the obvious) he'd *never* talk to me while we were together but stared a lot... He'd be drinking his beer looking over when he thought I wasn't looking. Guys we HAVE an eyeball lodged in *both* ears **at all times**.

(We see you)

Still, I think you guys must have this silent code that READS:

YOU talk to her YOU die—still friends though!!

That night...

In the hotel I was *nervous*... but mentally prepared to be with him. It was so good to see something OTHER than my room. I already prepped my girl friend (just in case my mom calls) I was with *her*. I take my shower put *allll* my lotions on, brush my teeth, my tongue, my lips—no kidding. Omg! Your lips are *sooo* much softer after. And my tongue! OMG. It felt like I took five pounds off my tongue. Ohh shit! Gotta tell you something.

Call it intermission.

So my (*current*) boyfriend and I, were hugging after soccer practice. It was so cute... you know how you're standing *face to face* and your guy puts his forehead on yours (real close)? My guy's like, "You're *still* pretty. Even with just one eye... my beautiful CYCLOPS." But his breath! *Baaaad.* I don't care! It ruins it for us. Then we gotta pretend we enjoy it (which we do) but it's *gross.* So we can't really enjoy the MOMENT. I'm like, "Bae, you need to drink more water AND you can't go to morning practice—not brush, cuz you're lazy. I don't wanna a guy with GUM disease."

(My dentist taught me well)

He stays overnight. He's walking me to my bed, I redirect him to the BATHROOM. I'm like, "Kkkk... YOU need to brush your teeth, gums, tongue, esophagus... lungs." And I go sit on my bed. He's yells! He's like, "CAN YOU BRING THE LUNG BRUSH BABY?!" Girls, we need to be honest with our guy at all times (if we're bothered) about breath, (not fresh) dirty nails (including flesh-eating guys who nibble away at their cuticles) texting.. while they're with YOU. Like, WTH? Why are you with me if you're texting someone else! If you don't talk about things that make you uncomfortable, he won't know. And that's not fair.

Back to my first MAN experience!

I put on sweats, a big white shirt and lie down on the carpet in front of the bed... to do my leg raises! I wanted my stomach to be really flat for him. I'm on sixty three and he starts to get impatient. He's like, "Come to bed." I'm like, "I will... right after I'm done. I have to do a hundred." I end up doing *more*... cuz now I have to warm up my flexibility! I always stretch before bed. So I'm on my back, with one leg up by my EAR (ballerina's forté) he's leaning over the bed, with such a *sad* face. He's like, *"Are you comin' to bed any time **sooon**?"*

330.

I'm like, "Yeah. Just gotta do my OTHER leg!" (I was stallin') Why? I dunno... I needed a PLAN. I didn't have a plan! Cuz what if he decides to 'do it'? O_O So I figure, wait till he's *really* sleepy then slip into bed (he'll be too tired to do it) and we could just cuddle. Or, would it turn into an x-rated cuddle? Not sure...

What happened...

He woke up! Like, in a BIG way (I'm talking all over *bigggg*...). He got right on top of me! He had *such* a great assss. He was tanned... wearing his white underwear (*sooo hot*). And I loved it when he pinned me down... pressed into me. But I was waiting for him to kiss me—allll he wanted to do was THAT! So I said no. Stupid. Had you kissed me like you were supposed to (for as long as it took) there's no telling what *might* have happened...

(Thank GOD he was impatient)

I had a smile on my face next morning—he did NOT. He drops me off. And I might as well have had my NAME allllll over the FRONT page of the newspaper, cuz by the end of the day everyone's like,

NICHOLE'S A TEASE!

K! Prick tease... LOL

(That's a matter of perspective)

Royal prick tease it is!

Cuz I didn't give him what he *wanted*. Cuz I don't give... *unless* I'm comfortable—on my terms and in my way. And love's full term not a part-time night course. Already got my GED thanks. He stops talking to me. But his *friend* starts. :D So my girl friend's like, "Good for YOU." Helps, when you choose smart girl friends. Then I was speaking to this *other* girl... She's like, "Nichole I'm a virgin by choice. Whenever a guy asks me if I'm a virgin I'm like, yeah... but it feels soo negative. Cuz allll my friends have sex like, on their **'to do'** LIST." I'm like, "K... The next time a guy asks if you're a virgin, first of all... It's NONE of his business. And like, WHO the fuck is he? Your Priest? I'd be like, "Yeah... I haven't been tampered with—I'm like a *live* wire. *Tsssk...* way too hot for you." Then... "Sorry NOT open for the general public. My lips are reserved." He'll be like, "Reserved for who?" I'd be like, "Reserved, for the one who can afford it (*whole* package)." He'll be like, "I CAN afford it." Invest in the meal, then you can taste... (*sniff*).

Maybe.

And I love it when they're like, "Well, how do you *know* if you've never TRIED?" Same way I *know*... I don't have to TRY a spoonful of dog shit to know it don't taste good. And for those that have a need to ask...

SO when's the last time YOU got laid?

Do I look like a DUCK? (:V) Quack! K. Maybe first thing in the morning with my big bunny slippers. I walk with my toes turned out (dancer). Omg! I was leaving ballet class (late for school) I run into this guy, who I've had a crush on for 3 grades worth and he asks me out! I guess... his balls finally GREW. We go to the movies and start to *mack*.

AND THIS IS A MESSAGE FOR ALLLL YOU GUYS!!!

Maybe even... tattoo it on your **forehead** where you won't forget. When you take us out on a date... don't take our hand and force it down *there*... We know where your dick's located, we don't need directions. Unless YOU don't know where it is and need confirmation. Now it's gonna take TWICE as long. Oh. And that *hand... on-the-head* thing you do? We CAN'T breathe. That should be illegal!

A guy really into you (boyfriend material) makes sure you're happy (in a safe environment) before any of that 'ever' happens. He'd never force YOU. During my mid-terms my (*current*) boyfriend tries to help me relax. Exams... *such a bitch*. Turns my MIND to fried beans. I'm in his arms cuddling, trying to revive my brain, which is pure mush at this time. For the LIFE of me! I don't know *howww* we ever got talking 'bout earthworms, but we did. He's like, "Did you know that worms don't have arms?" I'm like, "Really? They don't have tiny little arms?" He's like, "No, they tunnel their way with their mouth... they eat their way to the other side. And they can go in *reverse*—their asshole becomes their **mouth**." *"Whaaat?"* He's like, "And they don't have eyes *either*. But they can sense vibrations... That's how they know what's around them." I'm like, "WHOA... Wait a minute. I'm still hung up on the fact, that their *mouth* and ass can be interchangeable." He's like, "Actually their poop provides nutrients to the soil, turns it into a natural fertilizer. There'd be no flowers if there were no worms." I'm like, "For real?" He's like, "Yeah. When they eat the soil and it gets into their gut, the enzymes n' stuff get into it and they poo it out the other end. Unless they get confused and eat their shit." "Omigosh! That's *grossss*."

He's like, "Regardless the soil gets uber healthy. For thousands of years, they were the best fertilizers. Then synthetic fertilizer hit the scene. MONEY fiends." I'm like, "You're so smart bae." He's like, "You know, they really don't need anybody they're asexual—they fuck themselves." "Woww... How independent can you get." He's like, "And they're shaped like *both* sexual organs." I'm like, "K... How's it shaped like a vagina?" "On the *inside* there's a vag-like tunnel and on the outside it's shaped like a dick." "Hmm..." "And they can replace or replicate lost segments. If you cut them in half they'll just grow back." Hmm....

Next day I look up allll this worm stuff... (online). Yup. Everything's true. EXCEPT one thing. I'm like... "Bae. Worms are hermaphroditic. Which means, each has both male and female reproductive cells but they can't self reproduce, so they gotta hook up. So you're *wrongggg*." He's like, "But... They have *both* organs? WHO'S having the kid this time? LOL And still, they choose not to be alone. Fascinating." I'm like, "Actually, they have a very complex fertilization process, which keeps them from fucking themselves. So hate to repeat myself (but I'll make an exception) you're WRONG. They reach sexual maturity in four weeks, thought WE started young. And they come up (*above* ground) to leave their home to have sex. Yup... Keeps getting tougher and tougher to find privacy these days. They shut off all outside stimuli, so they can focus (hard to stay in the moment if you're thinkin' about shit). They don't like the light. Just like me!! I hate when it's dark... we're in the middle of it—LIGHT'S ON!! You lovvvve lights *on*. Why do guys like the lights on it's SO unromantic? I feel like... a scientific experiment." He's like, "Cuz we like to see you." "Why, afraid you won't find it?" "No, I know where it is." "But it makes me feeeel, like I'm on display. Like... I'm an OBJECT and you're examinating me on a slide. *Like...* I'm some *thing*. Can you see how that's NOT turnin' me on—and I don't need to further your education." He's like, "Well, at least that explains why I make you *simmer*... LMAO" "Yeah... Well I MAKE you explode. LOL Like, the other day when I was sittin' next to YOU and I put my hand on your pants. You're like, "You just gave me a tingle sack..." AHAHAHA!!

Interestingly...

It takes worms up to an hour to do it (same, minus the 13 seconds it takes most of you guys to come—max). When the mood hits they lie together with their heads pointing in *opposite* directions. We can do THAT. Mucous is then released as they're pressing *closely* to one another (*feelin' it*...) sperm transaction takes place. Deposit guaranteed. The worms separate... probably due to the fact that there's so little courtship to begin with. Lucky, you're not a worm." He's like, "Not most of me... anyway." LOL "I feel like worms have a message for us." He's like, "Yeah...?" Even though at times we're swallowing SO MUCH SHIT in our relationships (going backwards) regurgitating the past, we're **processing**! Now I know why you park your car and kneel underneath the wheels when it's raining. YOU wanna see if they're doin' it.

My lips are sealed. :#

BOOBIE - TRAP

(Proceed with Caution)

(a.k.a. Pinch Hazard!)

When We Give Our Guy SHIT

What REALLY happens...

Girls... trash-talking guys, blaming them for things that aren't their FAULT. Like, I was in a girls' change room. This girl's like, "I can't believe he can be that STUPID." I'm like, "What happened?" She's like, "He didn't get the **right** one." (Item) I'm like, "Did YOU tell him, what kind?" She's like, "No... If he LOVED me he would know." I'm like, "WHY would he know? I'm curious. Like... *Whaaat's* with all this telepathic SHIT?" Girls... Friggin' tell your guy what you want, he'll get it. All guys second the motion, pound desk. TWICE.

Seriously, I almost slapped this bitch.

Girl: Guys are so ANNOYING.

Nichole: Why do you say that?

Girl: I offer this guy some help on his assignment. I told him to call me on Friday—he texts me WEDNESDAY. Ugh! So I ignore it. He text me sooo many times I finally put my cell on, call REJECT. LOL What's his problem? I told him I'd have it done by Friday. What a fuck up.

Nichole: Hmmm... He probably wanted to check cuz his project is real important to him.

Girl: Yeah, whatever. He calls me on Friday and I tell him I don't have it done. Like, why are you CALLING me before the date? Did I not say, I'd talk to you on Friday? Did I not say it in English?

Talk about abusing LANGUAGE!

Those aren't even real questions—that require an answer. They're designed to reinstate a point of view (hers). Wish I could represent *him*...

K! I'M REPRESENTING ALLLL YOU... GUYS.

It's hilarious how most of the time we don't even ask a question, to find out. We ask to make the other person *question* themselves. Same with listening. We don't listen to *understand*... we listen to reply. LOL Does it ever occur to anybody, that we're made with two ears and one mouth for a REASON?

337.

MANIPULATION TACTICS 101

(catch it)

1. Do you **really** wanna do this, when all the odds are against you?

2. Are you sure you wanna go, when chances are you'll NEVER get in?

This tactic is also used by people trying to sell you something you have NO interest in or don't need.

Man: Nichole, do you think with all the money you'll be making at this job in 5 years, that it would benefit you by giving you the freedom to pursue your own career?

Nichole: YOU just set up a win-win question for YOU not me.

And that's NOT even a real question. It asks and *answers* at same time. Loser. Like, I'm gonna make a guy millions get pennies for it. If I CAN make it for him, I can make it for myself! And why would I invest my energy to help some guy build *his* company, LOSE five years—start from scratch on my own life? Lame. If it does nothing for YOU don't do it. If it gives you something blast through it, give yourself a timeline and don't let them suck you in. Your FIRST loyalty, is to yourself. NOT... securing points so your boss is happy and buys you pizza. YOU need to be happy.

When you're happy *amaaazing* things happen. And it doesn't matter how many jobs are out there (or NOT) if you have experience or NOT. Go!! To where it excites YOU to be. Knock on **that** door. Fuck! Tell them a book made you to do it. And *expect* to be offered something—cuz that something is *expecting* YOU. Just don't tell 'em the title. You'll need to break 'em in first.

IT'S GOTTA MAKE YOU HAPPY

The right one... will accept YOU.

This mind-set is NOT a usual one. And definitely a 'red flag' to the average adult. So I got a bit concerned that parents would be thinking...

WHAT ARE YOU DOING TO OUR KIDS?

Do you know what the economy is like?

I'm helping their balls grow.

I go check in with a neighbor (adult) get his take on it. He's like, "But Nichole... If all the positions are filled in a company, they won't be accepted." Noooo! If you're **excited** going to a company, you don't care WHERE they put you (at first). You just want to be a part of it. And when you're stoked—people NOTICE." It's an irresistible energy.

Like a PUPPY. You come home and see this excitable little ball of energy. Can YOU resist picking it up? No matter how BUSY. It makes you... Cuz it makes *time* (and you) stand STILL. It's gonna take you... By force (if necessary). Your resistance will melt. That same energy inspires doors... to open. It's hard to refuse someone who BELIEVES they're of value to you. Everyone wants some of THAT. You don't have to be stuck working in a mundane job with an anal boss (in an environment that sucks). Then you get used to that (mistreatment) and later... Think you deserve it. Then it's hard to have the confidence to leave (go after what you really want) what's waiting for YOU... Where you're *truly* directed. Where it'll be FUN and you're happy. Plus...

It's the era for entrepreneurs... Start-ups!

It's all over the place. There's sooo much global communication available, that if we mix our traits and strengths together it'll point us in the right *direction*... where there's a need. Give us the initiative, drive and energy to DO start ups! Consulting firms, services, awareness ventures, artistic creations, whatever. Helping the community, country, world... is where it's at. We have a message, we feel bigger (more important) on this mission. We merge with something meaningful—a marriage of creativity. Loads of sparks, excitement, highs, almost-made-its. We expect and accept (sub-consciously) good stuff happening (all the time) cuz it's *not* just about us. Even obstacles are fun—cuz we're BREAKING them!! Telling all those (who didn't think we'd make it) where to go, is always fun. The *advantage* of having this kind of life (mentality) comes into play especially when we don't realize our parent's sense of 'littleness' has taken over. Although they meant well it's rubbed off. So we get used to 'settling' or become fiercely driven—then fuck up. Deep down, a part of us doesn't feel like we should be there (top of the world). There's shame linked to a parent (family, sibling) since we're attached to them it makes us feel like *that* (without knowing). Giving off the signal that we SUCK... so just send a bit of good stuff (to keep us going) don't really give anything awesome. And since we constantly feel a sense of lack (get desperate) we overdo (to please) kiss ass (not trust) attract what we *don't* want (cuz it's the **only** thing on our mind). Fucked up cycle to be part of. When what you're doing becomes of GREAT value cuz it involves doing things for people (your community) your mind becomes <u>clear</u> (clean) like before it got polluted with bad seeds growing there. Restoring a winning attitude towards yourself and *others* (no imprint of loss). No bigger thrill   than being known for something YOU thought of. Like... Where would we alllll be without TEXTING? We'd actually make eye contact. Lmfao

My neighbor grumbles to himself. I can see he totally disagrees with me. And now I'm not so sure (anymore). Just cuz MY balls are SUPER size—maybe I shouldn't reinforce that? Maybe it's wrong. In fact, maybe this whole book's off?! #!!@*?#?!!*#

That same night... I'm PISSED so ready to pull out ALLLL my hair, I go online and see an advertisement for a fashion Magazine. Hmm... Wonder what my horoscope says for THIS month? I start reading and it says that I should look up this *book*. I find it online and select a random page. And WHAT do I see? A blank page that says *only* this...

YOUR work is important! Do NOT give up.

Right there!

340.

In BIG letters. K! I'm NOT giving up.

Next day I'm drivin' (still disturbed) I have no idea if I'm leading you guys the right way. I pull into a bookstore, get the book. They have one copy left.I buy it. Go to the very *last* paragraph of the LAST page... I couldn't believe it!! It talks how this whole generation is starting to realize that there's gotta be a better way than working ourself through alllll these degrees of BOREDOM (socially accepted misery). Yaaasss! It said 'exactly' what I said. So many people are being laid off (retiring) and looking for something—an opportunity! New IDEA. Something that'll makes them feel ALIVE. Feed their *hunger*... doin' something they've always wanted to do. Super size BALLS it is! LMAO

K. Back to guy bashing.

Ladies slicing a guy's morale (especially behind his back) causes *us* to lose ground (not them). We know we've *trashed* them... stench stays on us not *them*. And I CAN'T believe all this cyber bullying. One thirteen year old boy sitting with two girls next to me, overhears me talkin' 'bout the book. He's like, What's the book about? I'm like, "It deals with young adults and their issues." He's like, "Well I got a MAJOR one! (Points *right* at his friend) Sheeeee threatened to chop off my manly parts if I didn't make up with her. And she was the one who broke up with me. Said, I was just her TEST SUBJECT." I'm like, "Next time a girl gives you a demeaning remark—repeat it back! Be like, "OMG! I was just going to tell YOU the same thing! You were MY test subject." He's like, "EPIC comeback." LOL Course, then you go to your buddy and let it all hang out. Once you've **spoken it** out of your system, you'll be like, brand NEW.

It is SO important to be a Man these days, especially in a time when *most* girls are acting like it. Which throws off the whole species! We're like... WHAT'S a Man...? Does it have boobs? I'm not sure anymore. YOU dude... are 100% authentic MALE material. All hairs, smells and' habits. Like leaving all food packages 'open' (after you use them). Your ears *will* continue to GROW. *Just so you know.*

You're an **original**.

There's NOTHING like you. You're the reeeeal thing. That's SO exciting. You were *born* a MAN. That STANDS for something. Honor... is *extended* to YOU. That's why you were given a part that stands at attention (just to remind you). It does however salute us as we walk by. LOL

But being CHASED by a fourteen year old hulkette down the hall, then scared she'll confiscate your *goods*. Like, wherrre did this threatening to cut off a guy's dick come from?

I did some research...

Apparently...

One of the oldest tales of penile rage dates back to early mythology with Osiris (Egyptian god of the afterlife and underworld) and his sister, who also becomes his wife (Isis, goddess of motherhood and magic). Like, incest is NOT best people! Anyhoo... turns out their brother Seth freaks out (guess he felt left out) in a jealous fit, kills Osiris. Cuts him into fourteen PIECES and throws him all over Egypt. Isis... is beside herself. But she does not give up! She goes out there and is able to collect and assemble thirteen pieces... but she can't find the penis. And that's cuz a fish ATE it.

Being the goddess of magic she makes him one out of GOLD. (Resourceful girl) And brings him back to life. Now, we know why they 'em... the 'family jewels'. Rofl

TBH...

When we give our guy shit sometimes we don't even have the WHOLE story—and we react. In our mind we're re-enacting the scenario in a way that makes us look like an IDIOT. Of course, there's always the exception to the rule. YOU guys know who you are (this book's not about assholes). SO... Complaining, bitching, spazzing in our guy's face. What we're not seeing... before you can *attack* (scream your head off) you'd have to see yourself as *weak*. Or the need to do that wouldn't be there. You'd WALK.

Screamers, accusers, blamers… all fall into this category.

When you spaz (freak out) it's cuz you're feeling helpless 'bout something. Which is not to be confused with having a bitchfest (collective complaining). Still… Guys don't respond to us bitching— they're not into words. They're *action* oriented. They respond to something like,

THE DOOR SLAMMING!!

YOU leaving…

Creative sensitive-types excluded. They'd wanna talk about it at all times. Unless… YOU girl remove yourself from his TOTAL being… he'll **know** you're not going anywhere. If we're still bitching, we're nowhere *nearrr* the vicinity of LEAVING. Dude—*etch this part in your brain.*

We're invested…

(Emotionally)

When we bitch it's like, throwing manure on our shrub. (YOU) Yes, smelly at times (allll our crap) but for your own good (most times) cuz it helps you and your *shrub* grow. LOL

As long as we're bitching we're invested…

Course, we are looking for a return. And believe me when I say… your whole stock market will CRASH if we don't get it. Love stock down! Even if you try and trade it for something else, you'll only get cheap stock (no one wants it). So your stock has diminished (in value) fo shur.

Given, you guys don't respond to words it makes sense that when you're stoked—you're still MONOTONE. You see this hot babe, ask her out. She says yes. You're like, "K…" Lmao

I was hired at a gym, they never had anyone with television exposure. My boss is like, "I'm REALLY excited to have you here." I'm like, "Really? Your whole face stayed the same the whole time you said that." YOU guys don't have an excitement *bone* in your whole body. K... Except for *that* one—that's why it's called a *bone-rrr*. It's the only thing that gets excited. Unless you're on the field, your whole body goes craaazy. Then you win and do real cool things like—smash into one another. But there's *another* strange thing...

YOU seem to have this weird pact... with our anger.

You use it to gauge (estimate/measure/test/determine) where we are... (*with you*). Busted! We can be on the staircase at school, talking to our best friend. YOU (our ex) will show up and make FUN of our best friend. Just to get a rise out of us! And it always does. And we always fall for it.

(I had to tell them, guys)

Can we kiss and make up now?

K, be like that. Are you pms-ing? Cuz   I was talking to this guy and he was telling me, guys pms like—nobody's business! It's just more subtle, they don't have a period." NO kidding! They have an EXCLAMATION point! (Couldn't resist) I know some of you might be offended.

Guess you're pmsing now.

Back to this thing you guys do with anger... and US.

I had this client who kept screwing up on his diet. I spent like—a hundred plus hours on it. Royally pissed me off. To make matters worse, he waits till the end of the WEEK—to let me know. I'm like, "Why don't you just <u>tell me</u> at the beginning of the week? We could fix it. And we could have **avoided** allll this, me giving you shit." He's like, "But... I like to see your eyes when you're *angry*. It shows you care." "It shows I WHAAAT??" *Grrrr*... THAT did it. It reminded me of a time when a boy teased me in grade three. All the time. I got so

344.

MAD I cried almost every day. Then I asked my mom, WHY. She's like, *"He likes you..."* Why can't people be NORMAL?

EXPLANATION...

Many lifetimes later (didn't get it first time round). LOL I figured it out. Since we girls don't really show our feelings, cuz we don't really wanna hurt anyone's feelings OR we don't wanna show *too* much, you guys have no way of telling how we feel. It's the one way you can TELL (that's why). Course, this doesn't include all the mean girls who tell you guys to your face—you're an idiot.

When **we're** angry we're invested...

Back to my client!

So I continue training him, only I take it up a notch. He's now thrown up for the THIRD time. I'm like—"EAT IT!!! *Nahhh*... only kidding. But I'm <u>not</u> cleaning!" Virgins at the gym. HBIC

(Head bitch in charge)

To sum it up.

Screaming (spazzing) at our guy, freaking out in public, in ultra high decibel. Sets us back every time (not to mention) throws us off our game... Throne. It shows them they're the shit. And no matter how much we 'suffer' we'll still put up with it.

How I first saw this...

I'd go to the gym, walk into the girls' change room—they'd be having a guy ROAST. Sharp piercing remarks (*cutting*) slicing guys to bits... Talk about bad karma shwarma! Then feel bad afterwards (privately to themselves). Here's why... We're forgetting one thing. Those **same** words (we use on them) that we say so easily (mentally in our mind) we use on ourselves... We so do (just not aware of it). We'd have to cuz it's sitting there (held in storage) ready to aim (them, us, whoever). It's just under the wire—so you can't tell. But it's there, every time you hear silently...

"You're such an IDIOT."

"YOU keep fucking up."

"What's the matter with YOU?

CAN'T YOU DO ANYTHING RIGHT?!

(...Remember now?)

I had this one rich lady client... with a certain *AT-TI-TUDE*. I guess, cuz she had so much money she thought she could do whatever she wants. Wronggg. It didn't matter what she did. She could get up in the middle of a CONCERT they'd have to stop the show, escort her out. At least that's what I was told. On the first day, I get there... I'm like, "Lie down on the mat, I'm going to stretch you." She's like, "MAKE... me."

The *worst* thing to say to a trainer...

(Who knows judo)

I take her over my shoulder—FLIP her. She's laughing! So glad she took it well. :P I'm stretching her... all of a sudden she looks right at me, she's like... "You're a MORON." I'm like... "*Excuuuuse* me?" I'm lookin' at her... thinkin', **I CAN'T BELIEVE YOU JUST CALLED ME A MORON.** And it occurs to me... That word, that's so easy for her to say, is a word she's *also* accustomed to hearin' a lot. In her mind... *to herself.* I'm like, "Omg... I can't believe how hard you are on you **yourself**." She's like, "What do you mean?" I'm like, "There's no way you would have said <u>that</u> word... if you weren't already used to sayin' it to yourself, in your head. It was on standby, ready to go." I kept looking at her... Couldn't even imagine how many times a DAY whenever she felt stupid (a dumbass) she'd called herself that (MORON).

346.

Her eyes get watery...

My Dentist keeps reading this part over and over. He's like, "HOW did you know that?" I'm like, "What... they don't teach you this in Dentistry School?" He's like, "I just received the Dentist of the Year Award." I'm like, "Do they know that you dropped my retainer?" Silence...

(Didn't think so)

MY CONCLUSION:

We can only say things we're familiar with (closest to *home)* as in, it takes up space in our brain. We wouldn't say something that's not **already** there. And if it's in our mind... it's *there*. So it can aim outwards, inwards and right between the eyes. LOL If it wants. If YOU let it. And THAT hurts cuz you never see it coming. It's undercover (aimed at someone else).

Invisible boomerangs are hard to see...

How come we're the only ones that do stupid shit like that? I dunno any other animal that does that. You'll know when you've uncovered the *truth* of a situation... someone being mean (what's truly going on) cuz you'll feel relaxed (anger gets deported instantly). You're *calm*... no longer affected. Content. You know it has nothing (CLEARLY) to do with you. Maybe that's what they mean, when they say the truth shall set YOU free. :D

Tid-bit

If you don't crowd your mind and form opinions (so *fast*), suspend judgment (for just a bit) *coast*... (easy for me, I was in SHOCK with Ms. Moron) you'll leave *room* for the truth to enter...

There's a very old secret...

Planted in every human.

You will always think that someone else is doing to you... what you're doin' to *them*. Keeping secrets from YOU (you've kept a hidden agenda). Suspect *them* of flirting (you're checking people out). Think they've lied or don't trust them (you've lied at some point). Which is why to make sure this seed doesn't sprout (*up your ass*) at the most inconvenient time, you must communicate your authentic thoughts, between each other (don't be afraid). You will have the most sacred bond.

Be willing and happy to WALK (if you need to) cuz the one you ARE meant to be with who fulfills every dream and fantasy (beyyyond what you now think is possible) is on *their* way. And close.

(It's WHY you opened to this page)

There is no... by *chance* 'coincidences'. Everything's strategically placed, depending on your readiness (primed with good vibes) expectations (*worth* intact) mission (drive). Otherwise you wouldn't have connected to *this* one... an almost perfect match. It's the nature of humans to fiddle with something till it *fits*... so it's near. Enjoy your fiddling! And if it's not a snug fit, it almost *is*...

With the next ONE.

Course, if you fiddle *waaay* too long you could lose precious time (tryin' to *make it fit*). A relationship is the most perfect GIFT to ourselves. It's where we get to join with the rest of us... <3 Since there's absolute trust, emotions... old issues (deep shit) surface and breathe in their safety harbor. Shielded...

Your guy or girl **will say, do or act** in a way that will trigger an imprint (you thought was long forgotten). A situation... unfair (un-finished) unjustified. To give... what was never given (extract what shoulda never happened) stamp out what continues to scare YOU. And cuz there's nothing but lovvve in every inch of your being, there's no bad **feelings**. Whatever you went through you talk about it with non-attached ease (as if it happened to someone else).

348.

The whole purpose of a relationship is to make YOU happy.

(Selfish with intent) LOL

That's its function. If you're not happy it's failed its mission. Not necessarily the other person's fault (a lot at play here) but definitely an eye-opener! A simple test... If you and your girl (guy) are tight and you're feeling a lot more love... appreciation, gratitude in your life, than anger (criticism, depression, negativity) mission accomplished. If it sucks and you're feeling (giving) more criticism, blame, hate, complaints (negativity) than you are loving feelings THAT'S a clue. If you're going through a difficult time it can all turn around if (in spite of it all) you focus on how you first met. Alllll the times you had (with them) what you *never* believed they'd do (for YOU). They will feel the intensity of love... a strong tug (if it's a pure connection). If you're glued at the core. Inseparable type.

<u>Example</u>:

My guy and I were at the cottage. We had the place allll to ourselves. We're lying in bed... I can't believe he's wearing his socks! Like, *where's he going?* LOL I'm like, "Cuddle RULE. No socks!" We hate that guys. *Just so you know...* He completely took me off guard when grabbed me *close*... his eyes bubbling with I love you brightness. I see a tear fall quickly down. He doesn't even wipe it he's so deep in thought.... He let me know how he **never** DREAMED he could be *this* happy. Awhh... When a guy cries like that, it's not boo hoo-type shit. Like some guys... YOU wanna slap 'em. It's... an *escaped* emotion that caught him by surprise. It's like, they're so torn their words *barely* make it out of their mouth (gulps are plentiful). I don't remember whaaat he said, or <u>did</u> that set me off!! I was SO pissed. I was like—A VOLCANO WITH BOOBS!

It was over.

I declared 'us' broken-up. All that rage... from where? I had no clue. But it was too late. And I was stuck cuz I couldn't leave the cottage. Two hours away from the city no bears to piggy back. I had no choice but to face the wall... *pretend* to be asleep. Each minute... is like an

HOUR my mind's like, 'This is WAR.' But then, something inside me is like... *'reach for him.'* I will NOT!!

I'm way on my side of the bed (hoping not to fall off the edge) makin' sure he *can't* touch me, or see my boobs in my night gown. I face the window. Thank God I had the moon to keep me company. Felt so alone. Tried to figure out what type of face the moon had on tonight. Most likely... A pissed off face! Then a voice inside me is like, *'take his hand.'* NO WAAAY! He pissed me OFF. Few minutes go by and I'm literally fighting my thoughts... which is really hard to do, given they're invisible. Kept flippin' towards him, towards the MOON— towards him! Moon... I felt like a human shishka boobie!

Then something faint on my back... takes my attention, the tips of his fingers... *reaching* for me. It had been there the whole time (speaking finger language) makin' little hearts. Even though I didn't know it... *I felt it.* That's why my thoughts... were like that. OMG! He totally imprinted on me. I slide *close* to him... I take his hand, put it in a warm place... near my heart. Stayed like that the whole night. My guy... He's my SUPER glue (can't part from him). Except. When he farts. Omg!!!! It like, came from NOWHERE. We were sleeping and I heard something really LOUD. I'm like, "What's THAT?" He's like, "Science..." I'm like, "That's NOT science, that's a cascade of *ROCKS* fallin' from a mountain with poison gas residue. You guys declare everything *gross*... a scientific experiment. Like, WHO takes a lighter to their ass—when they're about to FART? Just so they can see a stream of blue-green flame!!

EACH relationship...

Makes you see your (*true*) self. With each button (sensitive spot) he or she activates YOU get to see more of yourself, uncovered (too scared to come out, till now). So be thrilled... You're close. YOU'VE almost revealed your whole complete self (entirely). And as soon as you do... it'll mean you're with your *other* half. And they will see the parts they need to be *gentle* with (cuz it's no longer concealed). Till... not one scary thought (he'll leave me/she'll fuck me over) remains. When what you fear has no hold on you—it's like a bad dream. Has no POWER... once lights are on.

People...

Whether it's about relationships, career choices or direction, love to tell you what you CAN and CANNOT do. What you are... will never be (*have*) in your career... life, guy or girl. When you hear something right for you, energy will rise in the body (an indication it's in agreement). When you meet the **'one'** or hear of an opportunity, get an idea (you're totally stoked about) YOU'LL feel *lighter* (inside) like you can fly!! As opposed to hearing a friend (parent/stranger) tell you something about you that's NOT TRUE or tell you what you **should** do... you'll start feeling *heavier* inside.

(Opposite of light)

And if you're used to livin' in your brain (rationalizing n' shit) like, they're smart (I should listen) they know better (they're OLDER), you'll be in conflict cuz your stomach will continue to sink. Your body will always light up with EXCITEMENT the **moment** it recognizes that you're *close* to something that will make you happy. And yeah, you guys have *another* device that does that too...

TRUST me...

Your body (dick) will feel dead (just hang there) if it's not what you REALLY want. (Awkward) Not doin' it for you. Something happens in your career (at work) or you meet THAT guy (girl), you'll feel *lighter*... high (more powerful). You own it. Your receipt is in the body. You can't lose it, just misplace it.

(When you don't pay attention)

Truth is... being en**light**ened.

(There's a *reason*... the word light is in there)

RULES OF ENDEARMENT:

When someone's telling you something that isn't true (for you) it'll weigh you down. Pay attention to that feeling, it means something's off. Immediate places it happens. A hair salon. LOL You get your hair colored, a cut. You have five people around you (the whole staff) tellin' YOU it looks great. You pay, go home, you HATE it. There was no excitement *inside* you (no WOW) when it's perfect... you're like, "Omg! I LOVE it!" You're energetic (cuz it's right for YOU) same thing with buying clothes. The sales people are over your shoulder tellin' you what they think. I'm like, "Uh... When you're all over me like this, talking I CAN'T hear my own thoughts." What I **really** feel.

Your Coach... "I **don't** think you're ready." There's a whole shit load of energy exploding inside YOU—I'm READY! I'm readddddy. Or he's like, "I'm going to put you in a regional gymnastic meet. I just want you to learn this ONE move. You've got three weeks. You can do it." You feel like you're sinking through the FLOOR. You're NOT ready. Sometimes people will talk you up (or down) without meaning to.

Your Mom... "I've made arrangements for you to go to this AMAZING camp. You'll learn all about Modeling and Art. It's where all the elite go." YOU feel dead inside (self-explanatory). Sometimes a parent may want you to do something they wished *they* could have done. It's not that you can't learn from the experience—you can. That you DIDN'T like it. And you shoulda listened to yourself. This works (mostly) when you do have a choice to accept (or not accept) the advice or suggestion of people involved. It's different when you have no CHOICE—you're being **re-routed**. To connect, find... establish your next step. So no matter how disappointing it might seem, look around YOU, see who you bump into. What that leads to. Due to the fact that you HAD to move, leave (cut someone off). I promise, it will be an incredible **reason**.

CHANGE IS GOOD.

(Don't be afraid)

I hand the final draft of this book to a manager of one of the top book stores in Toronto. He's pumped. Loves the concept and offers to edit it it. For free. AND he's a history teacher! I'm STOKED. Weeks later I schedule a meeting.

Even though I know he's only a quarter of the way through, I'm sitting there listening to him, tell me a seventeen year old would NEVER get it. Like, kiss my butt? (_*_) They WILL too get it. Just cuz YOU wouldn't have gotten it when you were seventeen—stop projecting man! Then he tells me it needs to be structured more. That I should make my point *first* then tell the story—that's how *other* books do it. And my stomach's DROWNING IN ITS OWN ACIDIC BILE). Had I not been aware that when things are in sync (hearin' what's right for you) your body responds in a great way, I woulda been in TOTAL agony (majorly fucked up). I would of stopped. In my gut, I felt alllll this energy (excitement) writing it *this* way! I would have never known that what he's saying was not right... for me (*this* book).

And besides...

Structure and I don't get along. If I want structure I'll go build a building! If it doesn't make you high (naturally) like you can float (you're sooo light) it's off. Doing what your **heart** wants YOU to do will always... guarantee a GREAT response in the body.

It's how it TALKS to you.

Answer... by being stoked! ☺

There's always a MAP to get you where you want to go in life.

If you don't READ this...

You'll be reading self-help books forever MISS the whole point... Says the guy who read this chapter.

Blame doesn't work. First of all its PREHISTORIC (our ancestors did that). LOL Sadly, it keeps trickling down like a *broken* water pipe. Like... When we blame our guy, which keeps us hooked into blaming ourselves (later). "Like, whyyyyy did I take him BACK?!" LOL

We forget, inside each and every one of us lies everything we *need* to create a miracle... God called it MAN. LOL And the exact kind of guy... love (relationship) we want—we've always had within our grasp. (K... *grip*) Lmao It's in our genes, quite literally (our *jeans*). If, for any reason the PLAN (what we're *meant* to have) remains uncovered (us unaware) we'll be taken by the undercurrents of *doubt* (one **mean** mother-fu--ker) thinking we can't leave, feeling like we can't have it all (that would be too perfect) until we SNAP.

Our tolerance 'marker' has been extended indefinitely...

We can't take it ANYMORE!

Not to mention drives our guys craaazy, cuz they don't have a clue, what's going on. My mechanic circled this part in **RED**. Wrote YES!! Across the WHOLE page. It's almost like we've advanced, but we still got this dinosaurus mentality—*BITING OUR GUY'S HEAD OFF!* The second he pisses us off. And there's all this stuff online telling us what to do (giving us 'options') informing us, telling us so much confusing shit.

One advice from a guy...

He's like... 'Guys, when you're talking to a girl, say something nice about HER. Comment on her eyes, lips—some *other* part belonging to her.'

Everything sounds so artificial (fake). You guys, might as well walk up to a girl, be like... "Yo! I like your properties. Wanna hang out?" All the info read online doesn't work (TOTALLY my opinion). Firstly, you guys **aren't** into self-help books. Especially when it comes to *your* girl. I mean, you can be encouraged (forced) to look into it. Deep down... you're gonna feel like shit (under par). So the whole thing FAILS for 2 reasons.

REASON number one...

It's either written by a guy and *his* experience. HOW the hell does that help YOU and *your* girl? So he gives you his experience—he's not YOU. Unless what he's talking about is a universal truth, registers as valid (it won't work in the long run).

REASON number two.

The **reason** a lot of books and info out there tell you how to be won't work, is *cuz*...

Like a little kid who tries on mommy's (daddy's) clothes, hats, shoes—it WON'T fit. That's *not* where you're at. And you'll trip, fall or bang into a wall. Cuz YOU can't *see*. You need to **fit** *into* the clothes. You need to *own* them—not have them own YOU (so uneven) makes you look stupid. YOU make the label, cuz you're hot, smart, sassy, totally confident (not the other way around). You buying something cool, tryin' to make up for the fact *you're* not (cuz that's what YOU see). So it's nice that you can get all these pointers (self-help books, articles, online stuff) but they fail to *connect* the dots... leaving you incomplete, unclear (without a frame).

You're frame of reference IS you. That's where it starts and that's where it ENDS (outside fillers don't solidify you). Once intact, you won't drop. Secured... you'll hang nicely.

(K. That was tempting)

I was driving home one night...

Wondering if what I had to say (the way I was sayin' it... 'stories') would be good. If it would truly help you guys. Just when I was askin' I turn on the radio, to a channel I *never* usually listen to. A Talk Show in progress. It had a Rabbi on it. Now a Rabbi to me... seems like a 'know-it-all'. But this time, what the Rabbi was saying **seemed** to be meant especially for me.

A BLESSING. ☺

356.

He was talking about... If you could tell a good STORY bring some *wisdom* to it (important lessons intertwined with the story) it would be ABSORBED... Words alone are static. He also talked about how every generation says the <u>same</u> thing (in their own way, style). Only, telling a story gives us the ability to get into the deeper layers (we like... deep) It touches the soul in a way the literal can't. Can you imagine asking a question while you're driving, turning on the radio and someone like—*confirms* it? Freaky!

A story... is how we connect to human beings.

Only usually—it's a sob story! We're VENTING. LOL No one wants to hear that. It's tiring to listen to, no uplift whatsoever (best friend, boyfriends excluded, you have no choice). It's pointless to mention girlfriends... we know when you need us we're there. We've got plenty of venting stamina. LOL

What I lovvved is how he talked about cavemen! :D

That part was *SICK*.

He talked about how cavemen would go hunting, come *back*... sit around the fire and talk about their quest. They told a STORY. Omg. I could just *see* it happening! It'd be awesome cuz they'd get into all the juicy details. Like... How they were about to be EATEN!!! *AHHH!* It's like you're *right* there! I can't even imagine the suspense. Even if they were limited in 'words' they still made sounds... what they *saw*. "*Ugh! Grrr... Crunch, crunch—bones breaking!* What I never thought about... was how he said if we had a room filled with students, who *wouldn't* normally talk to each other, tell them to tell a STORY—it would have the *power* to break ALL cultural barriers (bring us all together). Awesome. We should do THAT.

By telling a story we're allowing others to relate to it in their *own* way (their pace). And allll kinds of amazing things can happen. I think that's why singers and rappers do so well, it's sooo relatable... Alllll that pain. Love ya all, WHO TELL IT LIKE IT IS. Inside... a good story, there is meaning for *everyone*. A great 'story teller' leaves it open to *interpretation*.

There was this 24 year old girl, named Sharon. She worked at this cafe. It was a long day of writing (fucken speculating) brain totally absent. I asked Sharon if she could read ONE paragraph (an analogy). I wanted to see if anyone could even RELATE to it. Did it make <u>any</u> sense? Would it do anything for her? She reads... stares at it for like, a good few minutes says NOTHING. Then...

"OMG! If I HAD this book when I was fourteen my whole life would be so **different**. That TOTALLY spoke to me!" EXHALING... (good fifteen seconds). It was like she was standing *there*... looking at all the **hows** and **whys** of everything that happened in her life. I couldn't *believe* from my perspective, it directly related to HER. *Whoa*... think I levitated from my chair man (intense). It was confirmed to me that day, storytelling glues us humans together. Stories INSPIRE. Not just cuz they teach us lessons without being preachy, cuz on some level everyone's *stirred*... so they question, reflect, act (are awakened). And like he said the best stories, are the ones that help widen people's perception—*our book?* Yaaaass! <3 <3 <3

(Brain and I, reunited)

BACK to b-lame...

People we don't like (butt heads with) school, work, neighbor (that pisses us off) parents... could all have a special gift for us. It's just wrapped in LOADS of attitude, camouflaged in situations we hate (never just handed to you—more like SHOVED in your face). Just like the Rabbi. I COULDN'T stand Rabbis... since I was a little girl. Like I said, they always came across like they knew everrrything.

And guess who else *thought* she knew everything? (Moiiii) It seems like we automatically *don't* like the people who are exactly *like us* in some way (usually a trait). The bigger the hang up (**something we DON'T like about ourselves**) the more they'll piss us off. LOL Since we're not aware that we have that trait, we'll only recognize that we HATE IT—not the fact that we're exactly like *that*. So we'll only see it outside of us (on someone else) hysterical... Too little self awareness means we're led by an invisible string that yanks us every time we're forced to *stop*... and recognize (*this*). Which is why we trip up so much (we don't see it's *us*). As a result *blame* the other person. Here we don't see inward *enough* since our eyes are planted outwards.

358.

Make a List!

See what really pisses you off about a guy or girl (you hardly know). You'll see... it's the *exact* same trait YOU have (somewhere). Or they'll appear to be a way you *won't* allow yourself to be, see it as weak disgusting, nauseating) and you resent them for it. Truly... You resent yourself, cuz deep inside you are *that* way—so PISSES you off when you see it.

One of my girl friends CAN'T stand girly *gurls*.

(Guess, I was the exception)

My *balls* appear as needed. LOL So she likes to hang out with strong (tough) girls and like *them* she too ignores her feelings (just like they do). If she's lying on the sofa with a guy friend and he acts like a jerk, she'll be like, "What the hell... we're here, I'm naked. Let's do it." (Rather than speak up) Like, "You're acting like an idiot. I'm leaving." She doesn't like acting like a girl cuz she *thinks* being a girl is weak, (cuz inside that's how she *feels*). When you have a need to be strong (tough) on the outside, chances are you're 'not' (on the inside). I think this is why when you meet a really TOUGH lookin' guy inside... he'll be the *sweetest* thing... My point. With this strong tough girl (who's really like melted toffee inside) this would explain why it's so hard for her to say how she feels... with a guy. Cuz THAT takes balls. When I asked her why she didn't say anything she was like, "Way too much trouble. Not worth it." As in... *she's* not worth it.

She didn't like girls, cuz she thought they were weak. Which is exactly how she is. But didn't recognize it in herself. So I'm like, "You should get to KNOW the girl inside you—introduce yourself" And that way she won't be in the dark (with a muzzle on her mouth) 'silent'. She'll stand up for YOU. Refuse to put up with SHIT. And then, maybe you won't confuse a 'girl' with being weak, cuz inside you'll be strong. And not totally *lose* yourself to a guy (like you do).

WOMAN UP!!

Girls, make peace with your issue.

Give it permission to 'be' or just coast with it... cuz you need to be like that for now (so needing attention) insecure (saying what you don't mean) wanna be *liked*... (doing things you don't like) favors... you force yourself to do.

The TEST.

If you're okay with it (*issue*) you won't pick on it (in someone *else*). It won't bother you (you'll be gentler). You'll understand first hand, why they're doing it. It's a SIGNAL... When you see someone that irks YOU. *Pssst!* You ARE exactly like your mom (dad) on the inside... that's why you CLASH. Lmfao

Pay attention...

When your friend complains (*to you*) about someone else—that's your <u>first</u> clue! THEY'RE exactly the same way (somewhere). I was doin' my cardio and this girl sits next to me, starts bitching about this *other* girl, who's flirting with a guy (not *even* her guy). She's like, "She's always flirting with that guy. She's allll over him. *Disgusting*..." I look over, doesn't affect me. Then she leaves (thank God). She goes over to meet her guy—and what's she doing? Draped herself allll over him, like a wet towel. She's doing everything the *other* girl's doing... to *her* guy. Getting him water, setting up his weights, fixing his hair (like he's her CHILD). Honestly, she's like his personal manager. So remember, next time you're pointing the finger at someone, there's a *reason* there's **one** finger pointing at them THREE at you. Thumb's a neutral party. Examples...

1. **"He thinks he's hot shit!"** Where do YOU think you're hot shit? What are YOU *proud* of?

2. **"She flirts like crazy with every guy!"** Where or how have YOU appeared 'desperate' with guys (...or *guy*)?

3. **"She needs SO much attention."** Where can't YOU stand to be <u>ignored</u> (not be the main focus)?

360.

4. **"He's so self-centered**." What GOAL are you pursuing that's *excluding* everything and everyone? Ultra important to you.

(Worth repeating)

It's a 'signal' when you see someone that irks you (it TELLS you about yourself).

If you've HURT your girl...

Blame = pain (mild to severe).

If you've accidentally hurt her (set off a trigger) first thing you guys (understandably) do, is try to get off the hook (explain it away). Make a comparison, how it never affected her *before* (another time). Go to your past (blame your father, mother, politics) WORST thing to do. Cuz as soon as you begin to defend yourself, you've lost her... (emotionally speaking) and yourself (actually). Cuz the only person who needs defending are those who feel guilty (*somewhere*) which then makes them feel like a victim (*in their mind*). So explaining it away, givin' reasons as to why you did what you did (blaming her) tellin' her she shouldn't be upset over something so small (although maybe true) she *feels* strongly about it. The more you go *AWAY* from her (not trying to understand WHY it hurts her) the more it separates YOU from her, cuz you're *competing* with her pain by justifying yours (didn't mean to, feel bad) the more... you **drive** her thorn IN.

When all you were tryin' to do was prove how much you loved *her*, by trying to EXPLAIN you didn't mean to.

Course...

YOU don't realize you're doing this.

If you don't defend yourself, know it's OKAY you made a mistake, (stepped on a landmine, in her psyche) dive *instead*... further into her self-perceived pain (ask her to describe what she's feeling) YOU will lose the need to *defend* yourself and won't feel guilty... due to your experiences (mom/dad's effect on you). Most important, you'll be *there* for your girl, in her time of need... *take the thorn out.*

When you don't put the spotlight on yourself, which continues to show *your* flaws and defeats the whole purpose (givin' her relief) you and her **both** will recognize that her anger has *nothing* to do with YOU (directly) except that you tripped a wire, got allll tangled up in it.

(Fool)

Cuz when your lioness is hurtin' even though you're tryin' to help, her anger will overspill to YOU. A fact... So it's best to not tangle yourself in her trap, get her out without makin' her feel bad in the process. And be very CLEAR about the one common denominator your built on... And that is, even IF you fucked up—you're still MAGNIFICIENT. For real. Help her see that. By keeping the focus on her... so *she* can keep the focus on what she loves... you. (not her pain).

PS This only works when you didn't actually do something to HURT her (like fuck on her). Get what I'm saying?

INTERMISSION...

(...So brain can rest)

Seriously. Go workout! I'll wait.

Jog, swim, play basketball. Rollerblade! K. Grunt... sweat...

Endorphin high REQUIRED.

CLASS IN SESSION!

Reading and researching how to get a girl... is **unnatural**. (To me) You miss out on all that *cosmic* energy (between you TWO) cuz it's trying to TALK! But you're up there in your BRAIN (trying to remember shit to say) not in your gut (and if permitted) getting to know *her*... via her vibe.

Guy: Uh. Hold on... there's something I'm supposed to say *right* now to get you interested. Just can't remember it. I'll be right back.

Girl: ☹ :S :<

Remembering techniques, especially when you see girls in groups. Like allll those 'can-openers' (conversation designed to get you in) processed *fo shur*. LOL

TECHNIQUE:

Rule #1   Girls will always be in groups, so you have to engage each one in a specific way. (Like you're gonna remember)

Rule #2   Say this to No. 1 this to No. 2 And DON'T get it confused. (How 'bout just be real dude)

Rule #3   Make sure to *win* over No. 3. She's a loner. The odd one in the group, highly critical She's got a chip on her shoulder so all guys are dicks to her. (Maybe she has a REASON)

One guy explains it further...

"The whole theory is that you target the HOTTEST girl (girl you want) and from there you run a *routine* to create higher 'value' for yourself, in *front* of your target. While befriending all your obstacles (her friends) also the line backers—usually the fat chick in the group." I can't **believe** you guys call a girl that's overweight—*A LINE BACKER!!* That's so mean. That's like, calling a guy who *doesn't* know how to kiss—A SAINT BERNARD. He just slobbers allll over you (FAIR). Even the guy proofreading this chapter is like, "True!! Omg! Me and my friend have LITERALLY done that. Can't believe I just read that. When I see a group of girls together... somehow the level of intimidation rises. I'm like, 'What the FUCK do I do?' So here, agreed. As for the rest of it, just sad. One day... I just wanna be able to WALK up to one I like."

Soon... Real SOON.

Let's examine how YOU guys work.

You guys *like* natural...

That's why you're always like, "You don't need make-up. You look good without it." *Right...* and we just shopped for allll these different shades and colors just for you (EXTRA thick mascara). We put it on you're like, "*Whoa...* I didn't know you could *LOOK* like *that.*" In terms of researching shit (personally) I feel the most damage on these 'How To' books are—it CHANGES. (So often) Depending on what's in... OUT. Fad of the month. What celebrity starts *what*? So now we're *allll* doin' it. I mean, we're like a bunch of domestic animals TOLD where to go. Only we're left to deal with our own crap. Not fun.

WHERE ARE MY LIONS?

(...Lionesses)

Who stay true to their heart! Who wouldn't take an easy catch—even if it was the *only* catch. They're not scavengers, they don't like used shit. They wouldn't touch something dead (in soul...). Not if it was the last fucken thing on earth. They have pride. The lion only protects the lioness HE chooses. So you might wanna rethink that, "Oh, he's so CUTE... I'm gonna go after *him*." thought pattern of yours. And now you know why, no matter what you do, he's not protective (with you). Doesn't care where you go, who you're with, when you come home...

And YOU thought he was letting you be independent.

LMFAO

A Lion Rules His Jungle...

The jungle doesn't rule HIM.

364.

It's *natural* for him, what to do (or not do). He listens to his **instincts**, he's not scared of taking chances. He leaps, he roars (quietly licks his wounds) THEN leaps again. Do you think a lion is gonna sit there think... "*Hmm*? CAN'T figure out that lion. Let me go ask ANOTHER lion, see if they know. I got a better idea! I'll do a search online what a lion feels and thinks. Take instructions from there (memorize it) practice on *another* lion. Then wait... Once my lioness comes I'll try it." So he waits (balls shrink by the minute). If your balls would shrink every time you hesitated, we'd have a lot of peas walking around with hairy legs.

Fear makes you do... dumb shit.

Guys you have the instincts to know what to DO. Stop listening to the internet n' bullshit! Then you act too fast, not fast enough. You're touching her boobs thinking... "K. What direction? Does it MATTER? Clockwise... counter clockwise?" If you're touchin' her and she's thinking about her ex... the fight she had with her girl friend, latest movie, what she has to do that day—you're not on point! Cuz when YOU are ... *all thoughts stop for us.*

So you start makin' out, your hand's going up and down her body. She stops YOU. You're like, "*Huhh?* Party pooper." Like... fuck off! (Is what she's thinking) Guys, when you search 'how to get a girl...' stuff, part of you feels uninformed (YOU don't know). You accept that. And somewhere you feel immature (not man enough) lacking... Unless it's how to get LAID. Moral code not assigned.

(Needs to be activated)

AND FOR THOSE OF YOU WHO DON'T KNOW...

You need to cuddle first before *anythinggg* happens.

Ammmateurs!!! Alllll of you. So you receive instructions, you now need to remember (added pressure) then quietly admit defeat to the deepest stratum of your being (YOU don't understand your girl). That's gotta hurt. Even if she seems to like the idea of you learning, have no doubt (on some level) it will make you question yourself. Plus. Most of you HATE to read. I swear...

(on BOTH ovaries)

I will do my very *bestest* to make <u>sure</u> you NEVER have to read another self-help book again (pinky swear). My boyfriend's like, "That's SO funny. You swear on your ovaries. Guys are gonna be like, 'That's golden. I can't believe, I've never heard that. I gotta use that, cuz I value my balls. I SWEAR... On my balls!' Epic. Actually... I wouldn't use that. I'd be more like... I SWEAR on my girlfriend's ASS." LOL True.

K, the second reason you guys won't benefit from this method is... information OVERLOAD. Not only is it tedious to read—it's like your **last** chance! If you don't figure a way to make up with her—she'll BREAK UP with you. And you're gonna be thinkin' about the way her ass looked in those shorts, the times she gave you a big hug and you felt her soft boobs pressing into your chest as she smiled, the way she took a deep breath when you put your hands on her— and you can just *feeeel* it gettin' stiff—*IT'S GONNA CRACK AND BREAK!* So you're studying all this shit, talking to your best friend (dad) whoever's at your disposal... a stranger in the stall next to you. Only he's so into answering—HE just peed all over your shoe. Next time you go in you LOOK AT THE WALL... some guy comes in you're like, "Don't talk to me!"

That reminds me!!

One night, my boyfriend and I are at the lake and I had to pee (BAD). It's dark, I'm squatting and my boyfriend's standin' there, in front of me, tryin' to make sure no one's passing. It's challenging. People keep walkin' by. An old man on his bike *AND HE'S LOOKIN' BACK!!* WTF?

I hate peeing mid-way.

It's not like, we have somethin' to *hold*... (squeeze tighter so it stops). You guys are so lucky! My boyfriend and I climb on this giant rock. He needs to take a piss. No one sees *him* cuz it's over real quick. There's no squatting feat he has to master. Especially the part, of not pissin' on your shoes. So now, I'm frustrated as hell. I wish I had a dick! It'd be so easy. If I HAD a dick—I'd be making designs with it, I'd use it, like a GIANT pen. I tell my guy... he's like, "It gets old bae. Maybe in the future there'll be plug n' play genitalia and you'll get to have a dick. See how it feels to take a piss." If I had a dick now, I'd piss on his LEG.

Back to what doesn't work for *most* guys...

Say to a guy, "Bae we need to *talk*."

WATCH HIM SPROUT WINGS OUT OF HIS ASS!

Ghosted!

That's cuz, that 'word' will always tell a guy something's WRONG. It spells one thing and one thing **only** to a guy's psyche. A very long, lengthy go round and round—*never* really get anywhere 'type' conversation. My guy friend is like, "Beyond truth... Nichole. When this happens to me I'm like... WHY am I here? Why am I alive... I wish I HAD ear muffs."

Draining... Exhausting. And mostly TAXING.

Tell me about it?

I AM... tellin' you about it. Why do you guys always say the OBVIOUS? Never did get that. We'd be like, "Where were you last night?" You'd be like, "Where *was* I last night?" K, using a question to represent an 'answer' is false misrepresentation. Or you're like, "Are you sure you wanna break up with me? Cuz chances are... finding someone like *me* are pretty slim." If my eyes were revolving doors they'd be goin' NON-STOP.

And that's, leading the witness!

OVER-RULED.

You state the obvious, mislead the witness... *right to the couch* (bed) repeating things! Maybe, that's why it seems like we talk *more*... cuz you say less—repeat everything BACK. Lmao Love givin' you guys a hard time (makes up for alllll the easy ones). ;D

Another thing that *doesn't* work for you guys.

Anything that requires MEMORIZATION. Think. Guys and shopping list! (*For-get-it*)

It's not PRACTICAL.

I was speaking to a guy. He's like, "Omg. A guy and shopping LISTS. I fall prey to the shopping lists. Even if it's five items for my mom (MAX) I'll remember two to three (maybe)." A guy's attention span, very, very SHORT (for girl stuff). A hundred page instruction book (in very tiny print) he'll read, it's specific. It directs guys and shows them *how* it works. They know once they put it together, all that effort—it's gonna work! Unless it's defective. So if they're putting their effort into reading something longgg, they're gonna expect it to work. Or they'll just go to the STORE get *another* one.

WE don't come with a guarantee, warranty or rebate.

Guys! It's not about getting books out there that tell you how to SCORE, fuck, double-fuck, inside, outside, upside down (mind games) it's about...

KNOWING...

1. Your self-perceived notion of helplessness is a trick. All misery comes from the ridiculous notion that you are powerless. The requirement that being depressed *demands*... YOU **ARE** LIFE.

   It can't touch you!!

2. Thoughts about hurting someone (teaches that you *too* can be hurt). It's how bullying got started. (I believe) If a bully's been hurt, he'll make sure he hurts you before you hurt him.

368.

3. All thoughts make you feel good or bad—direct your thoughts accordingly. Don't let them pull in random shit (hurting you). Remind yourself (*often*) and look at a list of 7 things that are awesome about YOU. Have your best friend recite it weekly!

4. Every thought you have *gives* evidence to what you see. (An eye witness) LOL It shows you what you're thinking. And what you think of, you will hold *close* (value). Envy, jealousy, hate, fear, joy... lovvve (seeing the best or worse in anyone). When you're mad—count the SECONDS that you're losing (in life).

1. Closing the heart valve (talking metaphorically, don't actually try it) regulating allll love thumps *closes* off all access to 'knowing'. If you acknowledge what you see (not make excuses for it) act on it, then like a CHILD you won't be fooled. Cuz like a child... your heart will **warn** you when it's about to be dropped (*smashed*) into a billion pieces.

2. Unlocking the secret compartment of your girl... so she's no longer concealed (from YOU). So she's not stuck (fighting you, past experience, fears) and you can't move past it. So you can learn *her* puzzle... see her clearly (secure your place) retrieve your access code.

A *perfect* union.

We're talking about something that *isn't* common knowledge.

Vault's open dude!

It's YOURS for the taking... A *formula*.

To the world of your *choosing* (cuz you'll see how it's wired) understand how it works... (where the fuse box is) how to prevent a blow out. LOL So you can embrace your enigma (*crazy bitch*) study her wonders (*often*) cuz she'll TOTALLY inspire YOU. When you least expect it. When you've run out of options. When you're ready to give up...

Guys love 3 THINGS...

Seriously.

To Explore... (*every inch of our body*).

To conquer... (**the *BADDEST* bitch in town**).

(And their most vital navigating tool)

Their **Penis**...

(That's why they're always holding on to it) LOL

(Any objections?)

Didn't think so.

I used to ask my mom tons of questions about GUYS. She'd be like, "The answer is in the *question*..." I'm like, "Mom, don't be the riddler now. I need to know." It used to infuriate me. Now, I see it is true. The answer is *embedded* in the question (especially with us). LOL True dat. Both literally and metaphorically, cuz guys will ask...

WHY ARE GIRLS LIKE THAT?

Answer:

(*...in a poetic sense*)

A tiny seed plants itself in your brain during puberty (some waaay earlier) and it grows and *grows* each year... till you find yourself wedged between a rock and a *soft* spot (hopefully). LOL Just praying the integrity of the **rock** can sustain itself. ;D You wrestle with your impulses (touch her, don't touch her) somehow get alll caught up... budding plant *chokes* you at times—captivates you at others. Like she'll go from a double A to a C CUP hot babe—in one summer!! She's a woman (total blue jean vixen). Efforts to escape are futile (heart's in isolation) you shouldn't have looked. Booked. It gets worse. Confusing passes (smiles, then no smiles) giving you... 'Who ARE you?' *looks*...

Making your life a living hell. Exasperating attempts, being judged, and your dick wanting to pop out say Hiiiii... marks your time. You need the biggest binder (just to cover it). How do you even **know** when she's flirting or just being friendly? Bound to a term of uncertainty a long awaited trial becomes your foundation. Ahhh... THAT'S why the handcuffs.

It's familiar... Lmao

Is it any wonder by the age of five a subliminal trigger is directing your first impulse—*WHO CAN PISS THE FARTHEST!!* The ultimate challenge. To prove yourself (temporary release). LOL Come high school you're allll pissing down a slope—buddy's in the lead yellin', "*Haaa!* Bitches!" A definite prelude to a lifelong tour *packed* with LANDMINES to surmount (positioning crucial) maneuvers to master, (intellect, tomboy, girly or combination... which ONE is she) drills... best way to approach her. *CHASING* becomes synonymous with breathing—she's always watching. Do *this*... Don't do that. Oops! TOO late. *Why did I just say that?*

PRESSURE...

To WIN...

Is built on structure (it's tangible) but when you're forced to deal in a different *sphere*... one that doesn't specify clear-cut instructions of just how to PROCEED it not only challenges you, it frustrates the hell out of you. I hear you...

You guys aren't supplied with utensils needed to fine-tune a girl's *diffused* way of thinking (not focused, allll over the place). Havin' a convo—great deal of time to make a very small point, who's prepped for *this*? ADMISSION fees!

One way or another it's gonna cost you.

At some point (depending on your pain threshold) you may have no other choice, but to bury yourself in school, work (projects) something that is RESOLVABLE. Escaping through friends, enjoying a beer unanimously agreeing that allll girls are fucked serves as a powerful laxative. Pissed off, confused and fed up, some of you dive into a new pair of TITS. Drowning your sorrows in bootyism becomes a well-sought out diversion.

And yes IMPORTED GOODS welcome (fake boobs).

Sadly, a few of you go completely over the *edge*. Never come *back*. Drugs have that effect. Can't tell you how much we miss YOU guys. In all your messed up attempts (to please your girl) it's amazing YOU don't stand in the middle of the street, head hung low (*both* of them) drop to your knees and beg to be ABDUCTED. To a place... Where they **don't** change their mind TWELVE times an hour.

TRUUUUUUUUUUUUUUUUUUUUUUUUUUUUUUE.

Yeah... most definitely highlight and give to your girl.

Girls (brace yourself for what I'm about to say) GUYS... are rulers of this world (hypothetically speaking) their strength, like their organ is on the *outside*. WE are rulers of *another* world... our strength like our organ is on the *inside*... for only we can take you home (*sucker*). It's almost like... We're the spiritual tide and guys are dependent on us to *deliver* their souls (talk about a burden). My dentist is like, "I don't get this PART." Seriously dude... YOU need to spend *less* time in people's mouths and more time somewhere 'else.' LOL

K. So guys have muscles so they can LIFT things (be efficient). What's that girl? Yes... I know YOU can lift things too. I know you're capable—that's not the point! The point is... Chances are you're not letting your guy assist you. And cuz he's ACCUSTOMED to *that* he won't offer (now). And that extends to *other* areas. Like, when he comes to pick you up and he's texting you from the driveway—I'm here. Yeah... Well my VAGINA'S *here*—so if you want it come and get it. Meanwhile... You're running around like a rooster on ACID, "Omg! Omg! He's HERE!!" Zippin' around in a million directions getting ready for him. YOU peek outside... Half *wishing* a magic carpet would come and take you out there. Why can't your guy carry you to his *car*?

Come to my DOOR—make me feel **WORTHWHILE!!**

(I'd start squatting if I were you)

Soon, guys'll be tossing their dick through your front DOOR. Since it has a remote, it'll guide *itself* directly to your room. He'll text you... "Start without me. Gotta finish this ONE game." And you're sitting there, with a limp dick in your hand (dysfunctional). Sadly. Your mind wanders *elsewhere*—to *allll* the other fun things you **could** be doing— as he YELLS from the car. "I murked that game! Killed it." ☺ Then one day he CAN'T even get it up (naturally) so YOU have to do all the work (*alll* the time). Like... life's not tough enough. Cuz once he does less and *less* girl, you will start to do <u>more</u> and *more* (in **every** aspect of your life). And you wonder why he's so much *work*? You approached *him* remember? YOU went over to **him** and introduced yourself.

(Great BALLS on your part)

Did you borrow his, try 'em on for size, get your *own* custom made? YOU set the precedent (in terms of who puts out the effort) which tells him you *don't* mind, and you LIKE him (**want** him). He doesn't even have to TRY. No need on his part to man up. YOU already did it for him. Good job GI Jody!

So, expect less and less from *this* type (as time goes by).

THE LAW OF DIMINISHING RETURNS

(Economics 101)

FYI It takes great balls of STEEL to look a guy in the eye (that you <u>like</u>) HOLD IT (least) FIVE seconds. Then... smile. Toughest thing you'll ever do. Silence... is seduction.

(Know it, own it. And *occasionally* shove it in their faces)

Like, I'm drivin' to the movies with this guy and I'm lookin' at *him*... Could JUST TELL he was busting. Wanted to know why I was staring, but didn't say a word. The more I *looked*... the more he got super hyped (freaked out in a good way). And that's cuz, I had this smile on my face. Like, I knew what he was *thinking*... The more I stared, *smiled* (said nothing) the more he got worked up. Finally, he's like, "The way you're *lookin'* at me—I'd do ANYTHING to find out what you're thinking." Like, ZIPPO! Was on my mind. I was gettin' off on him freakin' out *thinking*... I was thinking about him. When all I was doin' was being... silent.

A *powerful* girl is magnetic... pulls a guy to **her**.

She has the most dangerous kind of balls... *Invisible*.

Ya think Mona Lisa's smile was all hype? Lasted centuries... She had the *LOOK*. Sometimes when things are so easy to DO they get overlooked. Like, why bother? Then we actually (bother) DO sooo much. Get zero results.

Human mentality. LOL

Help guys evolve girls!

Make 'em carry YOU to their car!

Cuz when YOU feel special...

His dick will feel special.

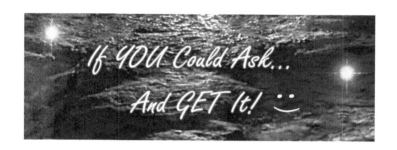

Not *that*... LOL

(K, just for a second)

1 sec. ;P

I was listening to my music, pacing back and forth in between my sets at the gym thinking... *"Why would the *book* I'm writing be **really** important? And *poof!!* I got my answer. Just like in the bible, man! ASK and you shall receive. Maybe, I shoulda *asked* for a yacht? My guy's like, "Nichole, in the bible there are two statements. One is... 'Seek and you shall find.' And, 'Ask and you shall receive.' You've combined them *both*... in your question." Hmm... I guess, that's why I GOT an actual answer. It's challenging sometimes.

HOW to ask...

YOU have to figure that part for yourself.

If it were simple, everyone be doin' it—havin' a happy LIFE. What most people don't get is that your brain will *answer* (bring to YOU) whatever question you **ask** it. So don't ask it dumb shit, messed up questions like, "Why did he (she) leave me?" Cuz it <u>will</u> give you like, a thousand and one different *reasons* as to why. Like... all the stupid things you do. Also, when a lottt of bad SHIT happens (some of us) are like, "K. What's next?! Just give it to me. I can take it." Or... "What other fucked up thing are gonna happen to me now?" When you 'ask' your brain's not gonna *ignore* the question. It's good like that. The question begs to be answered... it *looks* to see the answer. And it **will** FIND it. Problem is we've set up the *wrong* question. :P So we're gonna get the **wrong** answer. Ask! How asshole (*skank*...) leaving YOU right now, is gonna be advantageous to you. Or, what's gonna happen next—that's gonna blow your mind. Make you forget allll this shit? That's... a good question.

Example:

How will (*name*) leaving me right now (losing my job, not being able to compete, having to move away) be so LUCKY for me? Why's it the BEST thing that can ever happen for me?

THIS is sooo gonna serve me!

I *know*... (it's not easy).

When you're like, "How's this gonna help me in a way I NEVER thought possible? Your brain *has* to answer. Which means it won't *miss* the mark (answer) it gets into **focus** (for you). Just like a sniper! Emitting a red laser beam putting it right in FRONT of you (so you can see it).

I had a client *think* he could dick me around with my money. Ahaha! Even though he's loaded, instead of givin' it to me on time he tells me he'll pay me *next* week. And what'll ya tell me next week? Your canary has hemorrhoids? *Nooope*... want my money NOW. I call him. Explain that his checks are out of State, takes an extra ten days to clear (almost three WEEKS before I get paid) need it on time. I'm NOT waiting for my money (kept that part to myself). LOL Sometimes I'm a scaredy cat. So he decides if I can't wait he can go get *another* trainer. Like! Does HE like to wait for his money??? I'm like...

THIS IS GONNA BE THE BEST THING

THAT EVER HAPPENED TO ME!!

I'd say it over and over in my mind. It's not that I was being *positive*—I was being DETERMINED. Hell of a lot stronger, far as I'm concerned. Never understood that... People be like, "Just be positive!" While I'm sooo fucked up (friggin' annoying). Honestly... I'd see *nothing* in my mind, what am I supposed to focus on? It was so vague. I'd be like, "There's nothing to hang on to except a word." Or sometimes you think about the word (positive) but your <u>gut</u> doesn't match it. Cuz you don't feel that way! And that's why sometimes you PRAY and PRAY and PRAY... You think it's not answered. But you just don't **hear** the answer. And the answer is...

It didn't happen, cuz you're **afraid**.

Deep down you actually don't want it cuz you're scared of it, even though in your **mind** you know it's good. Some reason you fear it. You fear *accepting* it... Cuz of what it might mean to you, what you tell yourself you are if you accept it (selfish, need too much attention, didn't do what mom or dad wanted) it's your *mind* that actually needs the PRAYER. LOL

378.

So YOU receive what you need.

Unless your MIND accepts... it's truly what you deserve, no amount of prayer is gonna bring it to you (while you *fear* it). It's answering your deepest wish... your **fear**. Unless someone's prayin' for YOU it will compete for attention. Hopefully grandmother's got connections in high places. LOL

When you believe in yourself...

ABSOLUTE love (suspending judgment... no blind spots) permission given to experience allll these things, is granted. You understand each one of *them* (awful scenarios, unfortunate mistakes, setbacks, being lame trusting someone you *knew* was gonna fuck you over) brought you HERE... Where you are NOW. What you have to *offer*... (cuz of it). And cuz you now have something to offer—you <u>feel</u> more deserving of good shit happening. In fact, some of you even EXPECT it. *Aaahlllo!!* The two tie in together. All the bad shit that happened and what it made you <u>into</u> TODAY.

A Juggernaut...

The manliest state of existence. Basically being able to do any of the following: sawing wood with your penis, eating cement for lunch shitting out gravel, chest bumping your garage door open, causing it to dent like tinfoil, jumping off a building and breaking your fall with your ass, power sanding your car with your morning stubble, pinning down a whale for a 3 second count—from inside his stomach etc. And YOU girl...

An irresistible SIREN...

The ultra in feminine prowess. Basically being able to do any of the following: blowing a kiss causing it to rain in the Sahara creating an oasis, batting your eyelashes making all guys around you GROW full beards, flipping your hair causing ALL fire hydrants to erupt, fastening your shoe strap making the satellite fall from the sky, when you smile you create a gridlock across the city, when you stare at a guy he turns allll WOLVERINE on you.

When you're totally smug with yourself expect wonderful things to happen (cuz that's what you FEEL is coming) what you *want*... it's usually played out in your mind (detailed) <u>exactly</u> what you want (to happen). Intend to happen... Make HAPPEN.

When someone says, 'keep the faith—THINK positive' unless it's attached to you (what you're capable of) it **won't** be consistent—and yes, totally my opinion. Cuz the second something happens that knocks you *off* guard—your won't be in positive mode. If it's not coming from your GUT (what you're made of) gone through. And when you feel... something bad 'might' happen and people 'round you are like, stay positive, don't think negative. YOU can tell them... "I'm NOT thinking, I'm feeling—and something's off. And I'm gonna honor my body communicating to me. I'm gonna stay aware. I'm not gonna cancel it with my mind, I'm gonna see where it's taking me." *And that way...* when the coast is clear and your body's CALM (happy) and people around you have their doubts YOU will have none (about what you can do). And YOU'LL go for it.

Cuz you've learned to trust your body—it's **never** off.

When I said, "This is gonna be the BEST thing that's ever happened to me!" and my client decided to go to another trainer I was being precise. I wasn't like, "K. I'm gonna THINK positive. Hopefully things will work out (somehow)." I was being **factual**... givin' an order to my brain. Still a scaredy cat, but more determined to have my way than scared. That helps. If there was money in my account and I didn't really *need* his money, it woulda been a totally different situation. I coulda waited an extra week. I had forty three DOLLARS to my name. I was about... to receive two thousand, four hundred dollars but I don't let ANYONE insult me. Just cuz I'm not a big establishment, you have to make me WAIT? After I hung up... before I could even REALIZE what I had done. I'm like, "What the fuck were YOU thinking? How will you survive? None of your other clients are due for payment." And then I *felt*...

The MOST incredible surge of '**energy**' inside me.

(Every part of me was totally stoked)

I told him off—stood up for MYSELF. So then I thought. K, I really need this one vitamin (I'm out) need to keep up my strength. LOL I'm going to the health food store, spend half of what I have on that. I go there buy it, chat up the sales girl (who's gained a lot weight) give her a few tips. Leave.

Just as I'm walkin' out the door... Owner RUNS after me!! She's like, "Heyyy! Excuse me. I saw you talking to our cashier about training. Are YOU a trainer?" I'm like, "Yup." She's like, "I have four telephone numbers for YOU. These customers came to me really needing a trainer." I walk outside... Stop. LOOK at the numbers. Everything inside me is ABOUT TO EXPLODE. Energy just keeps building and building! Like—I can't believe what just happened! That... And many many more, instances *like* that.

ONLY REINFORCE THAT...

a) When your body (inside) is HAPPY your world will be happy.

b) Life rewards COURAGE—straight up!

Check this out.

Three weeks later...

Four thousand, two hundred dollars richer! I'm driving to a client, I get a call from that health food store. The vitamins I ordered for a *certain* individual (that's no longer with me) Mister stinge bucket, is there ready for pick up. I call him. I'm like, "Hey David it's me. The vitamins you *need* are at the health food store. And I don't care that you're not with me anymore—YOU better go get them. Or your ASS is sooo grass." He's like, "Nichole! I've missed YOU. I'm heading home with my wife, we just came back from a funeral so I can't talk. Do you think we can start up again? I can have a check ready for you TOMORROW." I'm like, "Hmm... (Count to 5 to add suspense) Okay." I hang up. Coulda done a BACK FLIP in my car. It's not easy... what I pulled off with my client (and yeah, back flips are hard too). ;D

It's working with the *unknown*... its ways are always secret.

Doo do doo do doo do doo do...

Divulged only to *those* who take the LEAP. They *learn*... once they LAND (same goes for the flip). LOL

Especially in challenging times, a lot of lip service preaching have faith (so, not that it's *new*). Like this one guy... He's always sayin' "Keep the faith Nichole." In the same tired voice, when I'd have like an EPIC to deal with—fourth one of the MONTH. And I'm *thinking*... K, how LONG? Is there a time limit on this thing? How long... do I keep the faith? I *feel* like a DUCK (a sitting duck) *waiting* for shit to happen—how come I *don't* feel inspired? WHERE art thou swan lake? >.<

Waiting and anticipating WITHOUT action (justifying faith) is an incomplete equation. Being motivated to DO... ACT... MOVE **comes** from being inspired. And that comes from... what you TELL yourself, (*command* yourself) it means. Like! I'm GONNA DO THIS! I don't care how it looks—I'll FIND a way. That works cuz you *know* it to be true (inside). And self has to *listen* cuz body will go where it's directed. So MAKE good things **happen**!

It's your spiritual duty!

Just like when YOU cry.

Most humans here don't know YOU have to give yourself permission to cry (in your head) so it happens. You have to say... this means *this* THAT qualifies crying. Or it does not happen. Like, when you're so overwhelmed you're crying, then all of a sudden you're like, "This is STUPID. I don't wanna cry anymore cuz of *him*... her." But you're unaware moments before everything that OVERWHELMED you to cry, was caused by somethin' you said (to yourself) in your head... that broke YOU.

Example:

"When will this *everrr* STOP? Mom and dad <u>always</u> fight. I can't take it anymore! This is so fucked—I'm TIRED of all this shit." "She (he) <u>never</u> listens to me. Like! Do I EVEN matter? I feel sooo taken advantage of—I always put my family first. My brother gets away with *everrrrything*." THEN... You cry. YOU get the final say of what these actions 'mean' to you. How you see them in your HEAD behind your forehead (where the powerful Oz sits). LOL What it tells YOU you are (or not). You *can* turn it around by asking. "How will THIS... (whatever made you so mad, injustice, manipulation, bad choice) work to my advantage? What skills am I developing (in this very fucked up scenario) that will benefit me now? What am I *forced* to learn that otherwise I WOULDN'T? How does this put me **ahead**? How does it HELP me?"

Actually... You hand out permission slips DAILY (to guys n' girls) that say or do something to YOU... then certify it (declare it valid) by telling yourself... YOU deserve it. You're a loser (hopeless). You had it coming. No one will ever want you (something's wrong with you). And any *other* facsimile of bullshit you can think of to authorize a release of tears. Only at that point do you CRY. Most of the time the permission slips are so outdated. We're talkin' two SUMMERS ago. And we're givin' clearance every time (feelin' like shit) just cuz he's being a DICK or she's the biggest Bitch in the world.

It's how they lock you in... go on vacation, leave your permission slips at home!

One more time before lock up!

YOU give the <u>final</u> command babe. YOU tell your mind what just happened... and what it means to you (how you see it) interpret it. You're the material witness! Whatever YOU say goes. Don't serve time (*trapped in your mind*) let time serve YOU.

And DON'T waste any of it on them!

Yes. Re-read (worth it).

I've bookmarked the last page with a heart so you can read it again. When you need to (or upset). And ask yourself...DOES it even qualify?

Case Study:

YOU and your Guy (Girl).

How you act... signals another person to be (or do something).

Cross Eggsemination: LOL

If he's (she's) doin' something that hurts... (ongoing) somewhere YOU didn't stand up for yourself (you gave in). You gave too *much* (out of fear you'd lose 'em) so not being 'real' (not the real YOU). You didn't break it off when your GUT told you to, insincere to yourself is insincere towards *them*... You acted in contrary to what you *wanted* (just so it looked like you were tight, in sync with each other) or thought it'd make them happy.

Damages:

You're shocked THEY broke off with you.

Verdict:

Deception breeds more deception...

(It has to, it can't give birth to anything but what it is...)

Case closed...

I was talkin' to my friend who's studying Law. I'm like, "Pete, if I say 'without prejudice' in the beginning of my book will it protect me? I know most people write it in as a means of protecting themselves, in case of a dispute (legal jargon). ANYONE can misinterpret a book. He's like, "Nichole. You can say... *without prejudice* in your book, but it has no meaning and no protection. It's like a guy saying... without prejudice—just before he puts his dick in. There's no protection." I getttt it. Lmao

384.

Be truthful to the other person without emotional coloring... that tends to happen when you let it build. At first, the situation's annoying. Then WORSE. You freak, spaz, snap, separate... Now you're resentful (you've put up with so *much* shit) you're hurt. **DO NOT BE AFRAID** to tell someone it's not what you want (to do). Like, "I just wanna be upfront with YOU, you deserve that." Tale signs he's regal (top quality) and unknowingly upset you.

Number 1. He'll have a very serious face (borderline mad) that he may have hurt YOU.

Number 2. He'll be like, "Thank you for telling me. I don't want you to do anything you're not ready to DO."

Tell it like it is.

K. I know what you're thinking.

Last two pages... are scary—CUZ THAT'S WHAT YOU DO. And you're like, "Omg. If I don't change **this**... *this* is gonna happen. But that's just my natural instinct... to be like this." FYI It's not an *instinct* it's a safety mechanism, that you developed (due to fear) to protect yourself cuz of your experience, circumstance and/or inherited it... by observation.

Instincts...

(Always lead the right way)

Especially, if it's got the mind's blessing. :P There's no fear, dread or doubt. And life starts dropping 'unexpected' things in front of YOU to confirm... *that* instinct (is solid). Like... you know this. It's happened a dozen times (you just never told anyone). For instance. You bump into someone you haven't seen in a long time, a person who sits next to you starts talkin' to you, you're in line and you overhear something that TELLS YOU you're so right (to do this).

Instincts shut down... when YOU deceive yourself.

Since they tell the *truth* they don't like to mix with liars. (Sorry) When you deceive yourself (not admit what you know) you deceive *others*... You *think* you got fucked, feel like shit (want revenge) which keeps you hating and no matter what, you can't escape that feeling... (ANGER) they did it to YOU. As long as you 'see' it that way, you feel like a victim (loser). You never saw your 'part' in it. You assumed it was out of your control. Listen up!

(Stop chewing gum for a SECOND)

When you really need someone (and hide it) cuz you don't feel strong inside so make *THEM* your whole life's focus (don't feel good enough unless they're with you) they're gonna smell that. It won't happen at first, it'll happen *later* once your guard is down. They'll start acting different, taking advantage of you (take you for granted). It's not that they wanna be mean and step on your face. It's just human nature to pull *back* (not call right away, snap, take advantage, grumpy) when they feel you need them *that* much. It won't matter if you hide it, cuz what you don't say... you'll act out (in behavior). And that's always stronger—IT'S TRYING TO SPEAK. LOL If you can't feel comfortable to say it (*I need you*) your behavior will over-emphasize it. It doesn't have a mouth—needs to be loud. And always an overkill...

That's WHY guys can't stand girls that are 'needy'.

(And yet, they want to be **needed**)

It might start off okay, then unaware... he'll be thinking something's OFF. He's not turned on anymore (like he was in the beginning). He's not trying to be an ass—the chain's just too heavy. At least, that's what it feels like to him. He might not even know why.

(YOU owe me dude)

It's totally different if we're open about it. Like, "I *really* need you to listen, I need you to come over. I need your help with *this*..." It's not muddled in deception. We tend to NOT respect a guy (girl) who doesn't respect themselves (high sense of value). It tempts us to *step* on them (here n' there) cuz they're just taking it. So it starts out small, then escalates. It's not always malicious, it can be very innocent. Like, you coming in five, ten, fifteen minutes late. Your BOSS saying nothing about it. You figure it doesn't matter. Or, you change plans *last* minute (a few times) and your best friend's like, "K..." Till one day she's like—"We're DONE. I've had it." Or your boss... "DON'T come back." *Fuuuck!!!*

Responses...

TELL YOU WHERE YOU'RE AT WITH PEOPLE.

Your response to what's happening can also turn your life AROUND. You make life *happen*—life doesn't just happen to you. Your *response* to what's happening dictates what *type* of life you will have. Are you responding from your *past*... or in real time. LOL You're leading, by your *response* (how YOU see things). What you tell yourself it means. Like, that job you thought you LANDED. They gave to someone else. Response: *Greeeat!!* Cuz YOU won't need it!

Promise...

They said they'd give you a chance (play the lead, in at half time, first dibs on beta test) THEY changed their mind. Response: Awesome! You get a call next day and land a commercial, you're recruited to a winning team, you get *hired* as a game tester!! ☺ *SICK*... You're also leading your life by being 'specific' and clear about what you want to *happen*—at the beginning (NOT the end). You're listing exactly what you want to happen. First thing when you get up!

- School ACCEPTS me!

- I'm BUYING that 'new' video game.

- My girl and I re-unite at tonight's party!

- My parents allow me to go—TOTALLY trust me.

- I killlll my AUDITION!

You carve out a *trail* for you to follow, get where you wanna go (love, job, career, money) so you don't get **derailed** by bullshit. Things people tell you (attempts to be helpful) *PAHLEEEZE*.

FEAR...

Is an **uniformed** gut, that doesn't recognize the constant energy going into the body (like happy feelings) as a signal to proceed (with choice, decision, thought) towards a gut-induced goal. Cuz once that happens, mistakes you'd normally make don't *attract* you (anymore) no pull. That's cuz when you have a MAP you can't get lost (*be mislead*). There's NO doubt (you'll get there) your eyes only *see* and look for ways (through people/conversation/things you hear/read/impulse decisions) that get YOU there.

Example:

You're saving for something BIG. So you accept anything... (job). You start off small, even though you know you're worth more, cuz you know they'll notice how awesome you are. Soon... they acknowledge how good you're doing and tell you you're getting a raise (next month). Next month comes, you're having lunch and they tell you it's not *that* busy, they're not making that much money. TOOOO BAD! You're still calling them on it. (Raise!) And if not... YOU leave. Cuz they're not sidetracking you with their crap. You're still giving them prime service—they've already acknowledged YOU'RE worth more.

And YOU will see... when you take this **courageous** (till you get used to it) 'step'...

LIFE WILL REWARD YOU!

Like, next few days.

(With something great)

If you keep pushing forward, it will acknowledge your choice (not putting up with shit) deliver YOU to a golden opportunity (you didn't see coming). Cuz inside YOU feel like a million bucks, cuz you didn't

388.

put up with shit (settle). And people will hear *that* in your voice. Respond… in kind.

When YOU know what you want, you make sure to overlook any and alllll bullshit attempts, that could knock you off center. So that only something that truly **helps** enters your space. All the rest, your eye won't catch—it's locked on to *just* what it wants. It's already been prepped *exactly* to what you want to happen. And since you did that, your mind reads that with an *expectation* of it happening.

So it leads you to it.

As opposed to…

Not being clear about what you want—so leaving it up to the DAY.

Something I call…

The WAIT-and-SEE syndrome. Being at everybody's beck 'n call (just a random day). Let's see… if I wait long enough, will the 'day' notice me—give me what I want? So you're waiting on people's time, availability, economy, holidays, your horoscope (was it good today) whether you pissed dead center in the toilet (or not). All the games you play (with your mind) in hopes of changing your 'luck' (day).

I ask my mom how my brother's doing while I'm in L.A. She's like, "Well. You *know*… it's winter everything's slow." Really? I'm like, "Money… doesn't *know* seasons. Tell him to find a 'need' in the neighborhood. Since he wants to be a hair dresser he can *offer* a Christmas Special!" My boyfriend was on his way to his new job. I text him… "Let me know what *interesting* new person YOU meet." He QUITS (same day) job sucked. Next day I'm at his place, I see this business card on the table. I'm like, "What's *this?*" He's like, "Oh… I met someone really interesting. He offered me a job." "Annnd… You were gonna to tell me… When?" LOL Most people allow a situation to dictate what the outcome will be. TOTALLY backwards. And then when it's fucked they're like—"*Whaaaat* happened? That's NOT what I wanted." And they try to figure out what went wrong. But they can't, cuz they have zero idea of what *shoulda* happened—there was never an AIM. No direction (no want, no desire). If it's not set up *ahead*…

you will doubt your ability to make it happen. Cuz you can't 'see it' happening (for starters). So you can't assess it properly. There's no certainty. Just like a guy getting ready to run a race. Tell me, he's NOT thinking of the finish line! (Before he starts) Or a knock out—before entering the ring.

So get outta bed!

And be like! "TODAY something soo in-cred-ible is gonna HAPPEN!" I'm finding the perfect JOB! The most amaaazing GIRL is gonna walk right up to me!!" Then... some hot babe steps out of a car, has a flat. You're the *only* guy standing there... waiting for the bus *(saweeeet)*. You're thinking, "She won't want me cuz I don't have a CAR."

Oh... She'll want YOU.

You are important (with or without a car). **WE** make cars... not the other way around (cars *don't* make us). There's always something a girl needs (in her life) that YOU can assist her with (contribute) be there for. She might not even be aware of it. Till YOU bring it to her attention. Find it! Find out what she *needs...* emotional support (big one) mechanic savvy, tech genius, etc. etc. YOU brought her here with your STATEMENT. Now, unlock the secret code that'll release her (for YOU).

MAKE a statement! Every time you get out of bed (I triple dare you). It can be different **each** day—just JUMP out of bed and let *the world know...* You're not messing around anymore!! YOU want what you want! And say what's gonna happen. Not in a droll... I don't-really-give-a-fuck type way. Like THIS is what I WANT. Order!

Cuz if for one day...

YOU got to be... GOD

Could create **any** day (for yourself). What would it be? No limit man! It's God we're talking about. YOU would have *no doubt...* it would happen. Yaaaasss. Before I go to sleep or first thing in the morning, I write the day of the week top of the page and whatever comes to me...

390.

that I want to happen. I'm like, "K! Monday. What an unexpected AWESOME day!" *It happens...*

Just play with it!

When I first started writing I SO needed a laptop.

Every day in the gym, I'd see a random guy I'd be like, "Hi! I need a laptop." One by one they'd start greeting me each day. A guy walks by he's like, "Hey, how are you?" I'm like, "I need a laptop." :D He's like, Uh... I asked you how you are." (*Duhhh*) I'm like, "I got it. And the way I AM... is I need a laptop." This went on for thirty days. Every day same ol' thing. "How are you?" "<u>STILL</u> need a laptop." One day this lady overhears me comes to talk to me. She's like, "You shouldn't let guys *know* you need them dear... (K, ANTELOPE) then they'll see you as being 'needy'." I'm like, "Uh... you're the one that's needy. You're the one tryin' to hide how much you *need* them... (Typical) I can tell a guy what I 'need' cuz I *know* I can WALK (any time)." At that exact moment—couldn't time it better if I wanted to! A guy comes over... He's like, "Hey Nichole, I..." I'm like, "NOT now. Not in the mood." Lady got me annoyed. He's like, "Noooo. I GOT it." ☺ I'm like, "You got... *what*?" He's like, "I got YOU a laptop. One of my client's getting a new one. So I told him I know someone who really needs one. I'll make sure it's set up for YOU." AAAAAAAAAAAAAAAAH!!!!!

Every time someone tries to explain why I CAN'T do something the exact opposite happens. And... just to be clear, I have no trouble lettin' a guy know what I **need,** cuz I know my value (on the market) unmarked bills. LOL Not a lot of hands—touchin' this.

No guilt here.

When you're not honest with yourself (lettin' a guy know what you need) like I said, it's not like you don't communicate it. (YOU do) It's in your behavior (sometimes hot/sometimes cold). So comes off louder, than if you said something. Then you appear needy. Whenever anything **isn't** expressed when it first happens (continues to be ignored) it needs to be over the top to get your attention, so gets convoluted, cuz it wasn't voiced. So TALKS without words. LOL Just like talking to a foreigner. You're all animated, jumping up and down, using big arm gestures. You'd think you were trying to land a PLANE. That's why a lot of girls who see being vulnerable as weak, will work very hard (overcompensate) to be resourceful (strong) not speak of needs, make sure they don't need anyone.

Truth be told...

If they let their guy see their vulnerability (the way they really ARE) that they're not at ease with (don't feel they have the right to be) NOT used to, it'll go into OVERDRIVE. Their biggest fear...

(So, best kept at bay)

One of my friends was tellin' me how when she slept with this guy... he did all this weird shit (she didn't like) I'm like, "Did YOU tell him you **didn't** like this n' that, so he'd stop?" She's like, "*Nahh*... I wasn't connected to him. So I didn't say anything." *WHAAAT?!*

She wasn't connected to *herself*...

So her body became a weigh-in station... he loaded, finished, took off. And cuz she wasn't *connected* to herself it felt odd to tell him. When you're honest about who you are, cuz you're not scared to 'be', as soon as somethin's NOT aligned (with **that**) you get this jab—YOU feel it. And you speak up. Leave—WAKE the fuck up. They're NOT the way you thought. It happens really quickly. We just usually overlook it.

Being authentic *breaks* deception in half, even if you're with someone who's not real (a fake), it *forces* them to be real. The only way you can be real—is when you know you're the shit. Or where I come from... YOU shine! Your value (to *yourself*) has to be as TALL as a mountain. Kinda ensures that nothing *except* something strong, durable, with stamina—ever reaches YOU (it wouldn't have the stamina). And there's no bragging necessary... mountains know how awesome they ARE.

Back to the FAITH thing!

392.

When it comes to establishing that WORD **faith** (knowing something before it happens) it comes from a *place*... no one sees **but** YOU. That's why you need to bring it out—for the WORLD to see. LOL Like, why would we even ask someone else to confirm what we *know* when WE see it? Course, it's different when someone has faith in us (we can't see it yet) the challenge there, they need to make us SEE IT. And usually, it's by their intensity (alone) the vibe we feel through them (not just their words) that fuels us. Till our blurry vision of what we're capable of... comes into focus.

How many times does it happen?

We get pissed... someone beats us in track. Next year we're like... There's NOOO WAY they're beating me *this* year! YOU kill it. When you take <u>action</u> you don't just *believe*... YOU know. Cuz you want it. And you know you deserve it. So you don't *just* keep the faith— the faith *keeps YOU*... Maybe it just got lost in the translation somewhere. You're not striving for something while in doubt, your action confirms—*IT'S GOT YOUR BACK!*

I was tryin' to explain this to a guy. He looked at me for a long time, like he was frozen. OMG! Maybe he was abducted 'momentarily'? Cuz they say... if that happens you like, have no memory whatsoever. Then he's like, "Nichole you're so COMPLICATED." I'm like, "Uh... I'm supposed to be complicated, I'm a WOMAN. If you're not complicated you don't qualify." On second thought... he couldn't have been with more advanced beings, he'd see the obvious. I tell my boyfriend he's like, "A woman's <u>not</u> complicated. She's complex." Omg... I think *he's* been abducted. Makes sense, he has such large hands with E.T. finger tips. Only an advanced man would get that. Put it in perspective. All you wannabes just bitch about it. ;P

When it comes to a lot of **pain**... ASK!!

Your brain has to *look* for what you **ask it**. It's like a camera... it needs to SEE what you're aiming at, so it has to be *real* (what it's looking for) summoned by YOU. So it has to bring it. It WOULDN'T be able to focus on a tree, if the tree is not *there*. The question needs to be set up *properly*. Making sure it's designed to give YOU a way out of your shit (predicament, pain). Structured to relieve you of your pain. Highlight this. It does NOT matter how bleak your situation is... just 'ask' babe. And *expect* to get an answer. *Hugssss!*

Examples:

- This is the <u>luckiest</u> thing happening to me! How is this the LUCKIEST thing for me?

- How is this gonna bring us even *closer*? (After a big fight)

- Why is it best I leave NOW? Why am I <u>so</u> needed where I'm going?

- What's *about* to HAPPEN that's gonna make me <u>so</u> **happy**?

- How is breaking off with him/her now, gonna be the BEST thing for me? (Us)

- Why is it important I change jobs/career/schools NOW? Who am I about to meet, that will **change** my life?

- How is the money I need for THIS... gonna come to me?

- How is being fired now... gonna bring me so much MORE money?

It won't make sense... till YOU see the turn around.

(It's a vibe thing)

It's not educated—it's soul related.

So much so that I SWEAR to you, even if you just broke up, see them as if they're on *vacation*. See it... as some time for yourself to enjoy away from them. See it, as them just going away—nothing happened (but that). Wait 3 days. Expect a call. IF... you hold that thought (vacation) and be happy. They need a chance to miss YOU. It doesn't matter what they said, what happened, how fed up they are—it CAN all change. Just like that! Magic Fairy Goddess STYLE.

Back to the Gym...

SO I asked... pacing the gym floor in between my sets, I'm like, "Why is THIS book I'm writing gonna be so **important**?" And BOOM! I get my answer. I'm lookin' up and there's a day time Talk Show on the monitor and it's pullin' me like craaazy. I take out my ear buds... 'Due to the rise in teen pregnancies, they're going to be implementing masturbation in schools.'

(Think you guys'll *score* high there) LOL

K. So what does that mean exactly? Teaching us... we can do ourselves once a day—like a vitamin? Twice a day (for extra strength) THREE times, for extreme deficiencies (extra temptations). Showin' us we're entitled to touch ourselves—cool. Puttin' our focus there so young?

What happened to a thing called... C H I L D H O O D?

So now we're not just hyper, we're hyper-sexualized! Taking away our first time is pure robbery. No pun intended. Cuz when we *discover* that on our own... it's very **special** to us. It's like... we've opened up this secret chamber leading to an amazing place. Now, instead of learning about it in the privacy of our own ROOM—it's associated with the public (and other adults). Like, I wanna be thinkin' of my teacher when I'm doin' it. *Grosss.*

My boyfriend's like, "They've ALREADY taken away our first time, with a person. Cuz I went into it thinkin' I gotta do this... I gotta do *that*. Messed me up. Now they want to take away the first time with *ourself*? They wanna make it mandatory with workshops n' shit?" I'm like, "I know. It's masturbation, not probation. Why are we being supervised (exposed) sharing something so private?" Definition of bation: A thing or person regarded as upholding or defending an attitude, principle.

Hard to do... when our rights are taken. When I saw my very first sex video in school I was MORTIFIED. And I was 12! I'm like, "There's no way that HAIRY WORM is ever going anywhere *nearrr* me." Telling us masturbation is a natural part of life. Cool—but doing a whole program about it? Forcing us to go *there*... on a school schedule (not our own natural spontaneous timing) totally ruins it. And why's **nobody** talking about the POWER of love... biochemistry of *that*. How COOL that is. An actual high (without breaking any laws). :P We're not talking a buzz, we're talking a true drug illicit HIGH. One emotion that can make you do ANYTHING. Make you lovvve cooked eggplant (when you hate it) or an equivalent, just cuz you *love* the person. Make you go for days without sleep—STILL have energy. Make you crave healthy food, when you're a junk fiend. Drop a bad habit in a millisecond. Be so psychically attuned—it FREAKS YOU OUT. Like, finishing his/her sentence (reading their mind) feeling their pain, even though they're not in front of YOU. Or if you're real tight like my boyfriend and I... He hurts his knee, next day my knee hurts (his feels better). I have a headache, he gets it (mine leaves). Can't say it's always fair. He gets injured so much more, but it works out in the end. I have my period... He has stomach cramps. (Yaaay!)

Why is THAT not taught in schools—guys and period CRAMPS! ROFL

In my opinion, we don't reduce teen sex (pregnancies) by focusing on a sex act—by ourselves (masturbation). LMFAO We do it by focusing on the person we ARE. Our self-esteem... so we're not pulled to go to sex (*to find it*) define who we are by what we DO or who we're with. We focus on the *magic* of that one emotion that's SO strong everyone sings about it! We focus on the integrity we have with ourself and the *certainty* in life we feel cuz of it, the unbelievable feeling of that. We focus on self RESPECT. How to keep it, make sure we don't lose it, misplace it (with things). Besides, it's not like we wouldn't eventually find out about it (touching ourselves). LOL True...

Some girls *can't* cuz they don't know how. Like me! I didn't have a clue, unless I was in the *bath*... I BONDED to that tub, man. Wanted to buy a necklace with a faucet on it. Show my devotion. LOL Omg... I'll never forget when my brother casually is like, "I remember when I walked in on YOU..." I'm like, "Um... Walked in on *what*?" "When you were masturbating in the bathtub." "Youuu did not." "Yup. I DID. I saw you... and your whole kit 'n caboodle." "You did NOT see my kitten caboodle!" "I did. I walked in... You didn't stop—and Dad's screaming about the water bill!! Better than a Bar-Mitzvah! Rofl" OMG! Erasing from memory, emptying recycle bin. o_O

396.

Since I grew up spending alotttt of time in my tub, you can ONLY imagine how I freaked out, when one summer I'm house sitting this lady's cottage and I notice—NO TUBS anywhere!! Omg. I'll DIE. I'll LOSE my mind. I need a tub! I go to the kitchen—FRANTICALLY whip the fridge door open!! Maybe a tub'll spring out?! I'm staring inside the fridge, the cucumbers are hiding *behind* the tomatoes. *Nahh...* I can't. I decided to try n' chill. Watch a movie. I put on a DVD. I'm lying in bed trying NOT to think about it. Hmm!? *That's weird...* There's just women in the movie... and they're alllll NAKED. Omg! You're kidding. O_O I look at all the other movies—she's a full fledged lesbian. So I watch! Maybe we'll learn something. :D

They're all in a circle... never saw so many breasts in one time. There's huge breasts, small ballerina-type breasts, wiiiide... like the Grand Canyon type-breasts, micro nibblets. Omigosh!! Elephant tusk-type breasts. It's a BREAST FARM!! And sure enough it's a LESSON on doin' yourself—*perfect!!* So I'm watching, one hand down my pants *workin' it...* I see her rub herself up and down—so I do it. But I'm a little impatient. So I start going *really* fast—really hard!! And I start talking to myself too. "Come on!! :D YOU can do it! *That's it...* gooood. Go! Go! Go!" Holy fuck! I sound like a guy. ☺ Now I know why you guys say DUMB shit. Someone gave you the wrong INSTRUCTIONS. That's how you work a penis! Not a vagina. *That's* a specialty. *;<>* My hand's going *UP AND DOWN* sooo fast—it feels like I'm using myself! (Almost cried) Seriously. It was emotional. It felt like I was *fucking* myself. I was disgusted with myself. Same time, it was hard to stop. How am I going to face myself tomorrow? Douche bag ho. Then I just *slowed* down... really got to know 'her'. Told her it was okay—just take your time. "Ahhh... *that's it*. Gawd you feel *amazing*." And something started to happen. First... my thighs were quivering, my butt's pushing up so *hard* it cramped YOU'D THINK I WAS FUCKING A GHOST. The more intense I got... the *slower* my hand went.

(GRAB a pen guys!)

Finally. I POP. I'm like, "Again!! Again!!" I *sooo* need to sleep. ☺

Still, to have it be a part of school is just weird. Going through an awkward time like that in CLASS... very unsettling. It's so important the first time happens in a private place, where your parent can turn a blind eye, smile inside knowing... my kids JERKING OFF. LOL

When the outside world punctures your safety bubble... a once in a life time magical experience—ruined *forever*. It's about you learning 'bout yourself... not someone else teaching you about yourself.

So now the *whole* world knows I'm masturbating Monday through Friday. Not in the MOOD... I get a C (major assignment). Oh! And watch out for the masturbation PATROL. If they catch YOU fakin' it— you'll have to stay after school... till you get it RIGHT. Could take *hourrrs*. More pressure on *coming*. NOT good for the female species. It's not a race guys! (As I found out) :P

It's *about* giving in... receiving (*pleasure*) and that's not gonna happen BTW if you think you're there to please HIM girls (while he's touching you). It's about YOU... all you. So you're not *trying* to make anything happen. He is. And that can only work, if YOU trust him. He loves you...

He communicates his love *for you* (in touch).

Course if that's not there don't expect to have FIREWORKS exploding in every direction possible (inside of you). And if on the rare occasion he's *skilled*... expect those cheap little fireworks. Fizzle out in like, TWO MINUTES. Cuz it happened technically, not in your heart. She has the final say.

(Hopefully, a lot of high notes)

And when our pleasure monitor reaches its peak—YOU reach yours dude (orgasm). And when you've *worked* your girl (manual labor, so has its charms) it's YOUR turn... to feel (the now fo shur) *heat* of your woman. And yeah, some guys may be real good mechanics, mess with your head (makin' you think it's better **you** do them 'first') or alter your monitor (give you too much to drink) so your body's more *receptive* to their skills (or LACK of). Sad. And it may feel good down *there*. But if it doesn't in your *head*—it'll only feel like HALF of you is satisfied. The other half, you sent away (past her bedtime) locked up (cuz she would so TELL) or just plain ignored (you don't wanna deal with her now) you're wasted. It's too bad your body doesn't ALTER (change) depending on how happy it really is.

Cuz right now, you'd be walking around with *half* a body—head totally missing (heart dropped, in the sewer somewhere) crotch shot *fo shur*.

Cam-toe or not, still pathetic.

–I'M NOT SAYIN' IT WON'T FEEL AMAAAZING at times, but it **usually** does when you 'think' he really likes you (cares for YOU). Or you try to *fool* yourself into thinking that, so it can feel amazing. Or... You're so cool and together you don't give a shit—far as YOU'RE concerned *you're* fucking him. Really? Cuz although you can change your mentality, you still have the vagina. And *that* comes with an emotional package. You'll need (after continually fucking your big bad wolf) to see, feel or hear from HIM (sooner). Like, much more often.

But that's NOT what you signed up for!

(And he's knows it)

So what now? Another guy... And another one after *that* and another one after that. To make up for the one that **didn't** CALL. Cuz you're gonna show you don't care. So your heart continues to go into debt—even though it's in overdraft (more like OVER-daft) you overextending yourself. You don't *feel* bankrupt (vaginarupt) you're taking it out on other guys—by fucking THEM.

K. My theory...

Re: Masturbation

When something natural (masturbation/sex) becomes a focus or is mandatory (*forced*) it's not the same. Something *dies*... you *have* to do it. You're being TOLD to do it. It's necessary to DO it.

I can see why parents freak out, they can't see a way out. They're concerned, but they can't *reach* you. Never really *knowin'* if you're tellin' them everything. Fuuuck no. What's weird... In their era sex was never really TALKED about (much). In fear they'd actually find out they <u>can</u> get pregnant (ostrich in the sand technique, way to go) guys that talked to their dad were mostly told to be 'careful', but go ahead and enjoy yourself. ☺

GOD HELP YOU IF YOU GET A GIRL PREGNANT

We've gone from not talking about sex, in fear of the consequences (baby) to having condoms *thrown* at our face. As one teen puts it, she's like, "My Aunt just says—GO! Have sex. Have fun! Just be safe. Like, 'fuck' it's okay. As long as I don't get pregnant." She's 15. So not inspired to find love... inspired to FUCK. So, let's find a way to kill those sperms. Lose...

THE MOST INCREDIBLE FEELING IN THE WORLD

Re-cap!

First half of the twentieth century—condoms TABOO (can't talk about it) second half of the century, condoms pushed. Turn of the century... MASSIVE masturbation!! *Hmm...* What are we missing?

A little thing called... **Love**

(Doesn't take much room)

Reserved for 2 'usually'. <3

THAT'S WHY THIS BOOK IS SO IMPORTANT.

Had my first meeting with a bunch of girls to sample some chapters! One girl's SCREAMING—pointing to a page! She's like, "Right here!! Here!! You're so feeling me. This *part*—truuue." It was about mistreatment (understatement) but to say ABUSED I personally... would feel like a victim. Again... hard to feel you have a *right* to conquer and be victorious when you feel guilty about something. Cuz even if it was done to YOU (in your head) you're to blame.

(Even more depressing)

One girl who had multiple sclerosis was like, "The first day I go to my counselor she SO pissed me off. I'm like, 'I'm telling YOU my story as a Survivor and you wanna turn it around, 'call me' a VICTIM? Take any hope I have LEFT? How am I supposed to have any kind of life—without feeling like it's been taken from me?' *Shuuuuut up.* I'd rather eat drywall than see her again." Agreed. Another girl jumps off her seat! She's like, "*I will NEVER just fuck again.* Unless, I'm truly in love." I know what you guys are thinking.

Bulllll-shit...

But it's just like YOU guys when you're *inspired* to play a sport. At first, you play for the love of the game. Then you notice *people* don't play fair. Coaches (refs) have their faves, your body gets slammed... nose gets knocked off center, they call foul (unfairly). You're hurting. So you say fuck it—*screw the game.* (See, it happens) :P You start cheating. You start playin' to see where it can take you, who you can get back at—fuck over. (That's always fun) Everyone's doing it, so why not you? You decide to be like everyone else, cuz you feel *ripped* off.

Until one day you **realize** you just love the game. ☺

So you PLAY. YOU play hard and you play rough. But you play clean—you play true. It's the real deal for you. Well SHE'S looking for the real deal (too). If a girl can be **inspired** (for real) she will change *BACK* to her original nature, before she was persuaded *off* her game. Welcome back Little Red Riding Hood—Wolf can go fuck *himself* (they're into masturbation these days). LOL

Which brings me to my next point.

I ALSO needed to show some chapters to you guys (get you to READ). *HAAAAAA!* Didn't know *what* to expect—you guys hate to read! But YOU sooo surprised me. Allll kinds came. There were computer wizards, musicians, high IQ types, low IQ types, jocks. One guy came in shorts... JUST shorts. And OH... MY... GOD abs frigging RIPPED. Like, does EVERYONE have to look like they've had a digital make-over? Dannng... an eight pack. Buffed bastard. *Yumm...* we're talking strawberry cheesecake *yum.*

(Salivating as we speak)

I compose myself. Hand out all the chapters and sit down. I'm watching you guys read... literally (technically) almost peeing in my pants. Cuz you read so friggin' SLOW!! And with zero facial expression. And I'm thinkin' K. It's *funny*... WHY is nobody laughing? All your faces are buried in the PAGE—well it *izzz* 'bout **woman**. You're soo serious. It's UN-believable. Maybe, we just underestimated them ladies.

They <u>do</u> take love SERIOUSLY.

It's just gotta be the right one.

They've only got ONE heart and they're **logical**. They're not gonna hand it over to butcherella (or skankatella for that matter). They're kinda scared to show—*just how important it is for them*. They're secretly wishing... we *wouldn't* GIVE IN (so fast)—it'd mean we're the ONE. They need to know we're stronger than the one-eyed-beast, slicker than the JOY stick, more important than 'mini me'. (YOU named your dick mini me?) *HAAAA!*

And *why* are you guys always like, "Ya wanna see the SNAKE?" You think we wanna have a snake anywhere *near* our vag, seriously. It would be helpful if you used a metaphor, that's more appealing. Plox. You're SO proud of it. Probably... cuz you're hoping it'll make up for all the emotional shit you'll be messin' up on. The one thing you can depend on to do the job (your extended self). LMAOO

I remember gettin' a call from my boyfriend, my phone was screwed so couldn't answer. I text him... "Did u text me?" He's like, "Must have pocket dialed you—shame on YOU (his name for his little buddy). Oops! I mean BIG buddy. :-} Question. Why do you guys name your dick but not your balls? Talk about neglect. They're kinda important. I ask my boyfriend. I'm like, "Bae. What do you wanna name your balls... 'silent investors'?" He's like, "I named *one* of them." I'm like, "Yeah... What'd ya name him?" "I named him Bally-ball..." "You're kidding." It's so valuable they give it a name (like a pet). Which is why they need to know and trust—YOU'RE the best. You've conquered everything... Their bullshit, smooth talk, *promises*... you're totally worth it (their heart). What they *attach* themselves to has to be say *A LOT* about them. So it needs to make them 'more' (calculative sons of bitches). They don't just give it out like that. They're not STUPID. They wanna *know* it's a **love** thing... They wanna *know* you can <u>match</u> their strength with *inner strength* (they don't have that) that's why they can fuck so easily—just like a sneeze. Isn't that how you GUYS put it? (Quick release) LOL

It's all out in the open now—just deal with it.

Back to the chapter reading.

I sat there for a good HOUR. Like I said, you guys read slow—but you fuck fast! If only we could *switch* those two chromosomes. I sat there re-evaluating my whole entire life. I had no idea what you guys were thinking. It was EXCRUCIATING. Like, having a massive headache just looking into open space... *numb*. I had to **wait**.

I HATE waiting.

I reach into my bag and pull out a bag of chocolate. I rip it open. WTF? The bag's only half full—when I need my fix! So unfair. I'm eating you allll at once! *Withdrawals*... (feeling like shit). So no one's sayin' a word. There's not even eye CONTACT (couldn't detect a thing). My whole life's tumbling down! If I farted would it even matter? Maybe, you know how us girls can be when we release a *silencer*. (Deadly) Cuz we'd be on the sofa (with you) watching a movie and this green *mist*... would start fillin' the room. At first, you wouldn't know what to think. Then your eyes would *sting*... the paint would start peeling off the walls. It would hit YOU.

The SMELL...

I DECIDED not to fart.

One guy jumps up! *SLAMS THE CHAPTER* on the table. He's like, "Pure GENIUS. It's hilarrrious. You write SO raw. It's like. A giant cock smacks you on the forehead. Irresistible." (What a visual) THAT... was worth waiting for.

The next guy finishes, springs UP!! Looks like he CAN'T hold it all in—anymore!! His cheeks are so FULLLLL—like he's got somethin' in his mouth. LOL Hey! I don't discriminate. LMAO He's all bright red! He's like, *"YOU TELL IT LIKE IT IS!!* We bag 'em and tag 'em. It's what we do! And you tell it like it is. It's about TIME." *Hmm...?* Bag 'em and tag 'em. In other words... *garrbaaaje.*

(Take out, once done)

A lot of work ahead of us girls.

I get ready to leave and there's one last guy... He's stoked! He's like, "Nichole! You think OUT LOUD. Most girls don't say what they *think.* This book is gonna be a guy's equivalent to HAVING a vagina."

Glad I asked. :-}

SUMMARY:

A GIRL will respond to inspiration. It's *her* calling... she's made of the stuff <3 so it'll register. Just like when someone tells YOU, you <u>can do</u> something. You feel it... When tit's true. Oops... typo I swear! LOL It was a slip. Where was I? Oh yeah. When you're inspired, it jump-starts your motor and you *SOAR!!* Trouble is... Not all of us have *that* person around. K! I'm THAT person for YOU.

<3 <3 <3 <3 <3

Girls...

YOU keep yourself lethal (powerful) when you dance, stretch, work out, cuz you're doin' something with a sensual (sexual) energy. Which ensures that *your* bottle of perfume... is not broken into (*stolen*) thought he cared (used) sprayed... (just randoms) no real interest, spilled... come on too strong (turn off). I say work out, cuz I notice while training (especially with music) it affects your *walk...* facial expression, attitude (mood). And I notice, that no matter what exercise it's kinda real *primitive.* You're bending over on a bench... ass hiked up in the air—like a BABOON IN HEAT. Especially when a

404.

guy (you like) is watching. You finish that... walk over to a machine, *plennnty* of swag... Guys are adjusting their dick... to the left, right, up (down) 'Ahh... I'll just tuck him behind—don't want no trouble.' That's another thing we don't have to deal with... cumbersome nut sack. LOL There's times where you guys are like, "*Shiieeet* I'm sittin' on my nuts. NEED to adjust." Only you can't freely adjust your junk when you're with a girl. Then later... YOU take her home she's like, "Uh... Back there at your place you had this *LOOK*." "Oh yeah... I was sittin' on my nuts."

GO AHEAD ADJUST YOUR NUTS.

(No one's looking) LOL

When that happens to my boyfriend he has this *look* then soon after, he's like, "Excuse me babe, I have to straighten my vas deferens." I'm like, "Uh... Is it crooked?" He's like, "There's *two* of them, actually. And basically it's the load canon—they're tubes covered in muscle that assemble the troops. Suck in allll those sperms, from my balls. Then *contract!!* Fire 'em off." And to think... I used to think biology was boring. That's sooo involved. My guy's such a brain. 8-} Now I know when he's having a vas deferens MOMENT.

Back to summary!

Why... we girls <u>are</u> powerful.

When we work out (especially in the gym) every machine is set up, so we can sit comfortably – arch – stretch, be totally uninhibited. We could be sitting in a vertical machine with our back straight and our boobs are four feet in front of us. (Requires arching) LOL Course... if you're flatter than the Plains of Abraham it's only two feet. I'm cool being like that, don't like *anything* in between me and my man. Like to keep it *close*... For all you big busted girls—no effort to get anyone's attention. (Legit) So we're sitting in our machine, with our legs spread wide (for grounding) have this *uber* serious face on (concentrating) and all guys see?

What a true sex-machine YOU are.

It's just how they see us. LOL When we work out hard, it's a turn on for them. They take that intense *effort*... put it elsewhere. LOL It's sooo automatic, it's like... they see us in 3 (sexual) D. And we know what we look like (even if we act like we don't care, or real serious) we know... It's a safe environment for us to be TOTALLY animal. And we will have fun with it. For the appropriate guy (someone we're pulled to) sometimes, just to test it. It doesn't happen often (especially for us serious-types) but when it DOES, we know *exactly* how to stretch... what exercise to do (in which way) if we're attracted to YOU. It'll just happen... We'll bend a little more, arch a *little* more, stick our butt out (a little 'more') put TOTAL drive into what we're doing. Just so you know...

It's the Law of the Kingdom...

When a male **pea**cock (*haaaad* to) struts his stuff, he attracts a female. It's the LAW... (she's pulled). With us what's particularly appealing is the environment, it's a sport (it's technique) over-emphasized or not we're not trying to be sexy... we just ARE. In our jungle! Rofl I remember this one great song came on, I start jammin' movin' to the beat, totally into it. Everyone starts to smile. Some BIG guy goes to complain to the manager. WTF?

Apparently my moves are too distracting for him. Guess his body's *strength* can't protect him from a *girl's ways*... LOL Can you imagine if we moved like that... bent over, stretched at our job (library) class, café? Especially if we're flexible. I wonder, how a guy working at a café is gonna respond to me ordering a latte with my leg up by my ear?

G-R-A-N-D... slam latte. Haaaa!

K. I'm not held responsible for your body's responses. :P

It's just liberating for us girls. And yeah, I know it bothers you guys, when we wear our tna pants to the gym. Talk about being blindsided! You never see it coming. YOU go to the gym, in the mood for a real serious workout, some girl walks by you're like, "Uh... Did you see THAT?!" And you get knocked off your center—JUST like a sucker punch.

406.

(What a bitch move) :D

Consider it a warrior's *initiation* (into the jungle of Pussy).

How much can you resist? How much can you block and keep **A)** your composure **B)** your aim (steady and unwavering) cuz that's the secret combo to getting you **in** not responding to the obvious (she doesn't feel that's ALL you *want*). She feels you're interested in 'her'.

And where sex comes into play...

Resist (coming too soon) block (just fucking her) keep 'self control' (she needs to feel you're in charge) so she can dis-*charge* (herself) mind n' body.

Mmmm... I smell creation.

To the extent you do NOT focus on her (*in her pants*) is what will determine how *much* you'll be able to ONLY focus on her... when she's with YOU... (Sex)

(Great PRACTISE)

THE BOSS...

While you're in the gym it's good to remember, girls can also be *playful*... there'll be times when she'll be girly, times when she'll be serious (so her clothes will change) she'll be in sweats—it's JUST about the training. There'll be days when she'll be down, she'll need bright colors (or solid black) a splash of mascara, gloss—or just a baseball cap. She'll need her *music*... so she can cry it all out. (Cardio) She always feels better after she cries it allll out. Depending on what phase you come in, she may be still going through her rinse cycle.

(Always a hell of a lot *lighter* once done)

Then there are those days... *when she's on the hunt.* ;<>

407.

You'll recognize her by the scent... *alluring* in every which way, from the way she attacks her sport (weights, basketball, volleyball, hockey, cheerleading, gymnastics) to the I - don't - give - a - shit 'bout YOU (vibe) she sends out (cuz it's just the opposite). Especially, if you two have been eyeing each other (a lot). Or she'll be wearing no make-up—just fresh clean outta the shower (hair a little damp) loose 'look'. She's a jungle cat and she's raw. Just the way you like it, dude.

Wait for it...

If YOU could ASK... And GET It!!

Name 5 things in your life YOU feel happy (grateful) about.

408.

I'll go first...

I'm SO grateful... ☺

1. ___God brought YOU to me. ♡___

2. ___I can make you see things you never saw.___

3. ___My words REACH you.___

4. ___I have a chance to affect your Life. ♡___

5. ___My connection to YOU... UNBELIEVABLE.___

Your turn... ☺

1. _____

2. _____

3. _____

4. _____

5. _____

Master others and you'll get ahead...

Master YOURSELF... You'll be <3 <3 <3

Unstoppable

How a girl's built, guy designed—
people (manufactured)

412.

When a guy sees a girl that's *not* afraid to speak her mind, doesn't seem like she needs *anyone*... the challenge to *prove* her wrong is irresistible, she's highly magnetic (not a weak minded dude btw who gets intimidated a leader type). Some of you girls are like, "I'm not magnetic." You ARE. You sooo are!! You just haven't learned **how** to turn it on yet.

(YOU will) ☺

So fundamentally speaking guys have muscles (tougher skin) not just so they can be helpful and survive the elements—five o'clock shadow—MAJOR sunscreen protection. It's so when we give 'em shit they're over it in like, TWO seconds. LOL How long do we hold a grudge? It's a *foreverrrr* thing (most of the time).

Someone giving us SHIT—we don't get over so *fast*. We're too busy justifying the assholeness of their accusations (hundred times a day). Guys are simple. They're *linear* thinkers, they think from point A to point B—*BANG* away! LOL They balance our complex nature. They **don't** do gymnastics with their thoughts (like we do) take it backwards and forwards, upside down. Try n' make sense of it, from every direction. They don't do alll that work. What do we have going for ourselves? Markers out!

THEY'RE WHIPPPED. LOL

(Yup sometimes the truth hurts)

Our sex... is our most 'powerful' thing. Which is not to be confused with giving it away. It's a party, I'm drunk (won't remember a thing) BFD type thing. It's about keeping it exclusive (*private* club). Like, why the fuck would we just hand it over... now that we know (we got the *power*). WHY the hell would we?

I was talkin' to this guy and guess he thought it was cool confiding in me, since I know his girlfriend. Like, I know she likes being in *charge* alllll the time. So we're talking he's like, "I feel like the GIRL in the relationship." I'm like, "You ARE!!" LOL He's like, "YESSSSS!" I'm like, "Dude... I wouldn't brag about that if I were you." He's like, "They're the RULING CLASS."

413.

Truuue... ☺

Still, I felt bad for him. He'll never get a chance to live up to his full potential (being a GUY) she's being a Guy for *him*. Depriving herself, (and him) of allll the gifts being a girl brings. A loaded woman...

Dangerously delicious. ;D

Similar to a fighter. When you're training for a championship, SEX... is never part of the protocol (not usually allowed). Your energy needs to be concentrated, intense—explosive. And people wonder, why I lift TWO times my body weight. LOL That sexual energy in you is so powerful... YOU have no frigging idea. Let it build... It will draw a lot to YOU. It infuses everything you do, with a thing called, 'intensity'. And YOU become intensely passionate in allll you do—YOU stick out, man! It's a serious kick-ass 'energy'.

Again. Why would I waste all THAT on some cock? They're like, dandelions. Allll over the damn place. I prefer... a rose (with *thick* thorns) my twin flame. Much more sturdy than all those dandelions, (all messed up, need to hang all over each other) too weak to stand up for themselves) don't last, gets old *fast*... soft n' gooey.

Gross. >,,<

A rose has always been a 'symbol' of love...

What's a dandelion a symbol of?

Our soil's infected. LOL

Bring out something strong, cuz those mother-fuckers are hard to get rid of. What makes them so difficult? They enjoy the best of *both* worlds. Their seeds ride the wind currents... (clubs, schools, gyms, concerts, parties) poised to drop into the slightest opening (your *bush)* propagate the species (pollute the field). And below ground... they strike hard n' deep. Pullin' them out of your life can be problematic. Thick headed (more ways than one) they easily fracture (prematurely)

414.

so a fraction of them remain to regenerate (cause disruption) MAJOR issue. You will attract powerfully as a rose cuz you're a *different* scent... No one can match YOU.

And you know it.

So this guy who has a girlfriend I *know*... keeps trying to get close to me—she's my friend! Hate it when that happens. SO awkward. Cuz if I TELL.... She'll be like, "Whore. I thought we were friends!" Just don't need allll that drama. If she was my best friend—I'd be SO screwed. Naturally... I'm like, forget it. But he keeps sayin' things like, "There's this fire *in your eyes*... Where's all that intensity comin' from?" I'm like... "There's all this smoke *up your ass*...

I KNOW where that's coming from."

Besides...

A rose doesn't speak... ;D

(Like, I'm gonna let that worm crawl through *my* petals) LOL

Once I was invited to a party, my mains weren't there so was by myself. Everyone's wasted. It's late... I'm sittin' there wondering *why* I'm still there. Bored AF. I got swim practice in the morning. Like, are the bags under my eyes even worth this? Everyone's on the floor... puking their guts, makin' out, acting like a douche. One guy's shagging a girl on the sofa (doggy style). Like. Will you laser that shit! Why do my eyes have to suffer—look at your disgusting ass. I felt so alone. There was no one to talk to... since they were all 'busy'. A guy passes me a *joint*... He's like, "Heyyy... try this shit. It's really good." Guess he needed my approval. I'm like, "Ya know what? I'm already high. YOU... Catch up to me.

Like, YOU think you say **do this**—and I'm gonna run and do it? Do I *look* like your intern?" Said it a bit loud...

Everyone... one by one starts puttin' their shit *down*. I swear. And I'm thinking... HOLY CRAP! One person has the *balls* to say, "Eh... Not doin' it for me, I have plans for my brain." And everybody starts feeling stupid, embarrassed. Alone... *That's* hilarious. Cuz one person didn't fit into the *wheel* it upset the whole apple cart. And they all fell tumbling down (not high anymore). LOL Finally Humpty Dumpty can have some company. And I don't CARE if it seemed stupid or whatever, I took a chance sayin' that. I didn't know if they'd force me or whatever. But *sheeet*... one person rejects it and they ALLLL reject it. Power in numbers does NOT apply here. LOL And **nobody** tells me what to do.

And what's all this hating on you cuz you're not givin' it? Cuz you don't casually fuck (some decrepit loser). And who started this shit anyway? The lowlifes who got HAD—that's who. And you're telling me...

WE...

CAN'T allll get together say, "FUCK THIS! I'll <u>do</u> what I wanna do when I wanna do it—cuz I wanna do it. Not, cuz I'm being forced to. Asshole."

So your best friend ends his LIFE cuz these losers spread an email, text, put up shit on social media (they heard or saw). Cuz they couldn't face him. Hey LOSER!! Lemme know when your *balls* wanna come out and play. Dirt bag. Cuz I'm not letting ANYONE destroy their fucken life cuz of YOU... Parasite. And that includes 'any' parasite that wants to emerge. If you can find the courage to drop the disease— you're with us.

ENOUGH ALREADY!!

There are so many guys and girls... who die in *silence*. (No one hears **their** pain)

They don't have *strength*... to get out of their cocoon. They don't wanna rat on anybody so they have nowhere to turn for support (they hold it all in). Till one day they explode. Misplaced anger always gets YOU in trouble. It's stored—like a loaded gun.

Once the trigger's *pulled* it can hit ANYBODY in view. Misguided power is like a nuclear bomb. Innocent people get hurt. Bruises inside and out (heart... face) cuts (body n' soul) hurts so deep (things they said) swollen (all over) especially your pride. And you're still just trying to say—

WHAT YOU DID WAS WRONG MAN.

(WHY won't anyone hear me?)

Cuz... it's too muffled by anger, too long contained (so forgotten) too muddled by current situation (so faded). I *know*... I've been there. Sucks real bad. After a physical **fight** you're like, "Whoa... That was such an adrenaline rush!" Course it was. Your ANGER finally got a chance to escape—it's been confined to an air-tight place (you never speakin' about it) so yeah, it's fucken ecstatic.

Only with some... it's more like an *execution*.

On the day of his 16th birthday a student took a gun and blew his brains out (in school) He writes in his suicide letter to his mom the reason he took his life was cuz of school.

Zero tolerance – What HAPPENED?

He tried repeatedly to get help from school counselors. He was picked on, cuz he didn't wanna have sex with just ANYBODY. Since, when if a guy wants to remain true and not fuck a ho, is that grounds for hating him? TOTALLY fucked. He was targeted for being *true* (to himself) regardless of what that may be, is nobody's business. They pegged him as gay. And... WHAT?! Whether you're gay or straight being true to yourself means, never needing to be put on the stand. You are the only **true** judge—don't need anybody else's say so.

And can we just STOP hating already!

A final note...

Your mind *will* fuck with YOU if you don't have an outside voice (*to assure*) an inside voice... to console YOU. I'm here to reinforce. You are of value. <3

I need YOU... babe

(Alllll of you)

Repeat:

Once you feel bad about something, you'll feel guilty (especially if, no one's there to TELL YOU different). It doesn't matter if you did something or someone did something to YOU. Secretly, you'll feel like it's your fault, like you did something (caused it). Even if it isn't true, it always feels that way (inside). So you expect bad shit (tolerate and accept it) welcome it... Like the student, cuz you have no inner strength to fight it (so do the worst to yourself) ...*murder your soul.*

Deep down YOU feel you deserve it.

In relationships where we're being mistreated, everyone *knows* it's nothing you did. But you feel it musta been something you did or it wouldn't have happened. Which is why so many of us *never* leave fucked up relationships. K. just WALK.

When you feel bad you (subconsciously) look for ways to *punish* yourself—so don't care if you fail, are isolated (no friends) too busy to make time, let people use you, take advantage of you (fuck you over) do TOO much, while you slowly die *inside*... darkness (alone). So you get in trouble with the cops. Big FUCKEN deal. I shouldn't care about myself (***I don't deserve it***) I need to be punished. Bring it! Is what's driving YOU...

GUILT MAKES YOU ITS BITCH...

418.

It has a way of making sure you're *stuck* in a place you don't wanna be, your past and future (same time). YOU feel bad (so expect the worst) and you're scared of the *future* cuz again... MORE shit. Can't move forward cuz although some days you feel great (you can do **anything**) next day... BURIED in doubt. So you pass it off as a bad mood. Next day... Feel good again! Then NOT. Then yes—so YOU go for it! Then not. You're like, "*Just*... fuck it! WHAT THE HELL WAS I THINKING?" And you wanna give up.

It doesn't matter what people say, how much they encourage you. As long as you feel **bad** you'll think (even if it's something done to YOU) I musta brought it on, something's wronggg with me. I'm stupid for lettin' this happen.

I don't deserve good things to happen...

(So hard to get rid of)

So you do stupid shit like... Study or work NON-STOP (till you fucken drop) tell yourself once it's all over you'll take a break. So for now, let's take alllll these uppers to keep you AWAKE. Or pot to *relax*... Especially YOU adults. You're supposed to be a friggin' example! You postpone gettin' your car looked at, when it's driving funny (blow a tire on the highway, lose your breaks) almost get into an accident. You get this pain in your stomach, can't get rid of it—OD on antacids. Till it's absolutely fucking killing YOU and you find out you have a hernia. Or your appendix is two minutes from BUSTING. You have acid reflux so bad cuz your diet is TOTAL shit. Your knee is acting up again. So is your back—NO TIME. You'll just take some pain killers for NOW. Then you're so hooked, you can't get off them.

There will ALWAYS be things in the way of other things, that need to be done. Always 'more' to do. But you need to fulfill your quota of pain. So you overdo (under do) cuz you fear the future. Cuz you feel (and you may not even know it) you need to be punished. It's goin' over and *over* in your mind. And you wonder why there's so much bad shit happening? YOU check your horoscopes every day, just so you can be prepared. Just to make sure the coast is clear—maybe something GOOD is gonna happen?! (Finally) Cuz you're *always* paranoid (but you can't tell anyone). And no matter what anybody says YOU know (for you) it's true... bad shit happens!

- My Mom was so MAD she stabbed my leg with a pencil and *smashed* my knee cap with the hair dryer. **My mind** said... YOU made her do it. She had to stab you with a pencil, smash your knee cap. YOU drive her crazy.

- My Dad was so angry when I asked why I had to leave the kitchen table, while studying for an exam. He whipped a spoon at my face and cut my head open (warm blood pours over the table). **My mind** said... YOU made him so mad questioning HIM. What's wrong with you? He had to do that, he works so hard. You're BAD.

- My Mom left me alone with my gymnastic coach after I pleaded her not to, he's sexually attracted to me. **My mind** said... You're a BIG girl. Don't be such a cry baby, Mom's busy.

- My Mom and dad FIGHT all the time. **My mind** said... They have so many expenses YOU are the reason they fight. Why were you even BORN?

- My Dad never spent time with me, no matter how many sports awards and good grades I got. **My mind** said... There's NOTHING important about you (can't you get that). YOU need to suffer, didn't make the grade (IN HIS EYES). Not good enough.

Proof this is <u>still</u> in effect...

- My Dad never held me, too busy watching the news about his country. **My mind** said... If I create a PROJECT for the world, that's truly valuable—*then he'll want me...*

It took me a long time... to be able to stand up for *myself.* Cuz even if other people were pickin' on me, at least everyone *else* was happy. A direct **parallel** to what I went through at home with my mom and dad... Whenever I'd be isolated in my room I'd talk to my sister through the vent, with a morse code I designed just for us. We'd plan our getaway. That's when I heard my parents talking about me and realized as long as they were *both* mad (at me) they **weren't** fighting.

420.

Fighting against me <u>equaled</u> peace *between* them. So I learned other people being mad at me served a purpose. THEY GET TO BE HAPPY. It became my function.

And it never left me...

It didn't matter when I was continually asked why I kept reconnecting with someone who hurt me. It drew me in... fulfilling my function. Every time I'd get deeply hurt it'd take days, weeks to get over it. Wouldn't hear from him for months... Then, all over again. Making him happy was paramount since he was like family. His happiness BECAME mine... no surprise, I needed *him* to feel my own. YOU will take that *sentence* you said to yourself (death sentence) into every new situation, even though it's no longer *that* situation. It's like being fitted with the wrong bra. It doesn't fit... you're popping out (embarrassing) digging (*painful*) restricting (can barely breathe) but you're STILL wearing it.

K... *wrong* jock strap for YOU guys. :P

WHAT HAVE YOU NEVER BEEN ABLE TO GET OVER?

If it makes YOU sad you've discovered its hiding place.

My _____

My mind says _____

My_____

My mind says _____

My_____

My mind says _____

This ISN'T for the faint hearted. It's not easy to stab fear in the eyes (you'll cry) it'll hurt... for a bit. It has to, you just punctured the fucker! It takes a real strong soul to look at what's *secretly* following it... influencing all its moves (decisions). But I promise YOU after you apprehend the villain, he won't be able to do what he's doing. And you won't feel like a stranger to *yourself*. Cuz if you do... you don't feel at home in 'any' situation. And since you're at odds with yourself... you'll be at odds with everyone around you (cuz you don't fit in) *inside*...

(*Ohhh*... that's why) :P

Which is why I wanted to quit writing *this* book (at least) a million times. In spite of daily reinforcement by my team, random people, guys, girls (clients) and they weren't just like, "Hey. Good luck with it." They were more like, "OMG!! Where can I get this BOOK?! I need it like, yesterday!"

It still didn't matter...

I'd be like, "K! Almost done." then CHANGE my mind. Stop. Not write anymore. And it annoy everyone. All the guys and girls would be like, "I'm WAAAITING." ☺ ☺ ☺ I'll never forget Mark...

He was one of the guys who jumped on board way in the beginning. Met him where I was working part time in sandwich shop. He was so excited! He couldn't stop talkin' about it. He couldn't wait for it to be DONE. All the adults around me were pressuring me to finish, fast. They kept sayin' you guys wouldn't wait—you'd lose interest. You're hyped now but have a very small attention span. Yeah, to shit you're bored with. I felt sooo much anxiety. I couldn't sit on the toilet... without writing. I'd have little scraps of paper all round me and just sit there. Not realizing... I had a fat red horseshoe on my ass. At night, I'd go to sleep thinking about a chapter—wake up reciting it. It was weird. I told Mark how all this adult *peer* pressure was gettin' to me. He's like, "DON'T rush it Nichole. Creating takes 'time'." Even one girl's like, "Nichole, I've waited twenty one years to lose my virginity—do you think I CAN'T wait one or two more years, for a book?" Omigosh! I better finish. Before she turns into one of those ladies with twelve cats.

One day I just decided to quit... and although I had gone through *enough* shit, to qualify a quit button, when I told Mark he had tears in his eyes. He's like, **"IF YOU DON'T WRITE THIS BOOK SO MANY PEOPLE ARE GOING TO BE ANGRY WITH YOU!!"** His voice *cracked*... Took me by complete surprise to see so much *pain*... He totally believed in me (the book). What it stood for—YOUR voice. And yet, I couldn't justify my doubts (really). Yes it taxed me, all the stuff I went through but that would *never* stop an athlete from reaching his (her) 'gold'.

YOU holding my book...

It was at that moment, I realized what happened to me in New York *didn't* stay in New York. It followed me... TOO afraid to tell my mom I hit bottom (school) that I needed twenty bucks (for food) but even *more* terrified to hear... "I'm busy now." (*Drunk*) Or overwhelmed to deal with me now. I call... "*Hello?*"

"Hi Mom... Just wanted to hear your voice. K, bye."

It's hard to *think* they're not gonna refuse you, when it's happened SO many times (before). When a parent is an alcoholic you go through that A LOT. But it doesn't matter (to you). To allll my fellow brothers and sisters *realize* how fucken stronggg you are to get through this drunken minefield! At this point you like, have 8 tentacles on all your feeling receptors. You can sense any one's mood before *they* do. Connect... like no one can. See details, most people miss... YOU will never be average. *You are the seers of this **time**..* You will protect the *heart* of humans—like an army of angels. *FEARLESS* is what you are.

When an alcoholic parent vomits on the carpet, looks down sees you cleaning says,

"YOU... *Are my Heart.*"

You learn the love is real... just you can't touch it *everrrr*.

I hang up.

She has no idea of the state I'm in. But again, the thought of her KNOWING and still refusing, would make me want to kill myself. I couldn't chance that. It's a hard pain to explain. As I dealt with what I needed to... fear n' all I'd remember the constant *feeling* attached to me...

YOU'RE REALLY NOT THAT IMPORTANT (TRULY).

(No one would miss me if I left) ☹

And up to this *very* moment... I still feel that feeling. Only less and less frequent. And no one understands *behind* your eyes is a hidden compartment to your hellll. They just look at you and think, she's (he's) SO 'gifted'. Everyone loves them. They're SO popular. How can someone like *that* have any doubt?

...That's why.

On a positive note my home life made me stand up for *myself...* (in the outside world) wouldn't BUDGE. I remember my Dad laughing sayin' I was stubborn. I'm like, "Dad I'm not stubborn—I'm **determined**." I spoke up at that party, cuz no one's gonna make me do what I don't wanna do. Cuz at that very moment—I felt good about my shit. It was one of the most *powerful* experiences ever...

After that, I felt like I could do ANYTHING. ☺

Thank God my balls don't clank when I walk.

(Hate to forewarn the enemy)

When you're striving for something cuz it's in your blood, even if it's brought on by a negative event (don't mean shit) it GOT YOU THERE. Be grateful. Be happy there's something ONLY you can do. So whether it's singing a certain way (you feel soo deeply) art (really abstract cuz your family's *ABSTRACT*) acting (need to express your pain) a powerful business idea (you were dirt poor) a book on value... cuz you feel you have none. YOU will *sooo succeed* it's gonna be sick.

424.

Cuz you won't stop, till you get there.

It won't let you...

And, you will see that YOUR place in the world (in spite of everything) is not only guaranteed—it's calling YOU. Nowww. That's why you can't shake the feeling (no matter what). It can't be fulfilled by 'anyone' but YOU.   ·

It's YOUR creation...

Without YOU the world would have an empty *space*... Some Alien's checking us out, is gonna think we have a CAVITY. Cuz you're NOT there. Don't think they're into root canals. We can't have a missing piece! It'll be off. DON'T let that happen.

I beg you...

And I DON'T beg.

Pretty *pleeeeaz*...

(with an **extra** cherry on top)

Fine.

You can have *your* cherry underneath, dude. LOL

Ten things that PISS me off.

Check off if you AGREE.

- ☐ People telling you your dreams are out of reach.
- ☐ People telling you, you can't achieve something cuz you're too young.
- ☐ People telling you, you can't achieve something cuz it's too late.
- ☐ People telling you, you'll never make it cuz of this or that.
- ☐ People telling you to try drugs, only then you'll know how it is.
- ☐ People telling you if you do this, then you'll get that (only way).
- ☐ People telling you, you don't know what you're doing.
- ☐ People telling you the odds of winning are slim to none.
- ☐ People telling you it's never been done—don't bother.
- ☐ People glorifying death... as if it's some stardom thing.
- ☐ People telling you alllll guys (girls) are this and *that*.

426.

Are you READY to change your WORLD?!

Course I'm not gonna forget! LMAO

Being a Girl... IS your strength.

(Sometimes the obvi is *sooo* missed)

Our sex...

Is our power. And yeah, yeah... I know what they say. It's a man's WORLD. True. But it's a woman's *universe*. And we own it! Haaaa!

We run the cosmos...

(That's why we named a magazine after it) LOL

It's our territory. We're connected to the unexplained... LOL Your Fairy Goddess has spoken! (*Aaagain*) Maybe that's why we need to be the *center* of things. It's our home base. No wonder, you guys are always tryin' to slide into it. First base, second base. *Ahhh* just friggin' walk ALREADY. We like it, when you take your time. My brother's always like, "Nichole, the world doesn't REVOLVE around you." "But I feel like it does." ☺

We have the spiritual advantage...

Maybe that's why most of the spiritual leaders are men—searching to find what we already KNOW (inside). We're born with enormous spiritual strength... whereas you have to *earn* yours. LOL That's why *weeee* have the vagina—make you earn it! Makes sense. Cuz YOU guys'll go into the wild, think about life's secrets n' shit... When it's right *there* in front of you. YOU climb the highest mountain, challenge mother nature and her elements—so you can *find* truth. When it's been staring you in the FACE. Your *greatest* challenge... US babe.

Assumed **name**: LOVE

What is it they say? You wanna HELP the world—start with your OWN backyard! Pick up all that trash (you don't need). Give some shit *AWAY*!! Clean your ROOM. You wanna spread love, peace n' all that— start with your <u>own</u> family. Pay attention to your 'girl'. Wife, kids (if applicable) dog, fish, cat. Your neighbor.

Never know when you're gonna need that douche bag. LOL

Condensed VERSION:

YOU guys travel to the ends of the earth. Feel your isolation... associate *that* with power, then have trouble connecting (*back*) cuz you link <u>that</u> to weakness. Maybe cuz you ran *AWAY* from yourself dude and now facing a human, kinda reminds you that YOU are (actually) one. Lmao The defects you see (cuz trust me no one sees them the way you do) are little trinkets that help distinguish us. I mean, how many red rubies can there possibly, be? K! I'm a blue pearl. Shotgun! I called it—car or no car. What's YOUR gem?

(Name it babe)

I'M A _____

Write it!

My point is...

You can't give yourself... and not feel like a gem (valued when shared). Unless ripped off (said he wasn't sleeping with anyone) theft (virginity given on a dare) snatched (preserved in ointment in case of rough handling) YOU *drunk* out of your mind while he tries to fuck you in the car (bathroom stall) friend's party—so clueless where you are. The price of giving is 'receiving'.

When you give cheaply... YOU feel it.

430.

Getting them back...

Even if you think it's a good idea to *scare* them (fuck somebody) they did it to you, so now YOU show them—you put **fear** into *them* (like they did with you). You make 'em think you could be doing it with someone else. Maybe, even get involved with some weird shit, like groups. You want them scared—they need to know you're capable.

Trouble is, you're acting on the *defense* (they did it <u>first</u>) that comes from feeling like a victim (place of weakness) and that's where your decision is coming from (so fear *remains* and always will). Cuz fear is darkness... you're scared cuz you don't know what's happening next. When you *match* that (do things you don't really wanna do) YOU continue to live in a cave.

ALONE... SCARED... TRAPPED.

Whenever you act out of FEAR it bites you up the ass—you won't even know it's back there. It's waiting to catch you off guard (keep you dependent on being 'fearful'). Always checking on your guy (girl) cuz you just did something that wasn't you (to get back at them) so you no longer trust *yourself*... so can't trust them. IF YOU CAN DO IT—THEY CAN TOO! And you were just trying to teach them a lesson. But you FAILED. Cuz you followed a weak teacher. You have to feel it, in order to give it (love/hate), you have to 'be it' in order to *have* it (strength or weakness YOUR choice). Hopefully, strength so your gem won't crack, split open (*under pressure*) break off (lose yourself) fragment (go to pieces). ☹ Love... when it's true, needs no defense.

Cuz when you LOVE you feel strong.

And if that's not what YOU feel. That's not what it is (cuz it doesn't change, it's FLAWLESS). It shines whether you look at it or not, paying attention to it or not. It's just waiting to be *valued*... (connected) just like a gem. ;<> Every day we're connected is a **good** DAY. If you hear a high pitch sound in your ears... it's just me (connecting). <3

If your dog could TALK and says, "What's a Girl?"

How would YOU describe a girl?

Cry easily). Feels incredible! Girls are difficult & don't have a moustache

Get excited over EVERYTHING and confusing.

Girls are COMPLICATED

BITCHY!

They TALK They obsess over things

They get a PERIOD!

Girls are always doing

A girl is a clothing & money grabbing machine that never stands up for 'sexy'

over - reacts (nothing) but also sensitive

She can

They have Boobs

An (All sizes)

unpredictable ocean of turmoil, emotion and power.

Girls gossip & make fun of you when they're drunk & they're even more

THEY HOLD GRUDGES.

They tell you to do something — then CHANGE their mind

THEY

They have a VAGINA,

Girls are difficult

Girls are curvy :)

They like to keep you waiting

They constantly nag

A girl is good looking can be crazy and cause you as much pain as pleasure.

They scream when they see a spider.

They Coke bottle width

They have soft lips.

A girl is beautiful, sexy, smart, attractive, seductive, my motivation (at times my transportation) a Goddess in her own mind...

At first all we know — they're sexy and we wanna fuck them.

sweet

everything else doesn't matter.

EMOTIONAL

They admit when they're wrong (guys rarely do) and they always remind you when you're wrong

Girls get jealous alot.

They smell nice

girls are very dramatic then gossip + make fun of you :(

then like to attach dead hair to their own (known as extensions)

GIRLS NEVER SAY WHAT THEY'RE THINKING THEY USE THEIR BODY TO EXPRESS THIER FEELINGS. WHEN YOU TRY TO MAKE OUT WITH THEM THEY DON'T SAY NO, THEY PUSH YOUR HAND AWAY!

433.

A Girl (in a guy's mind)

- Has a vagina.

- Gets a period.

- Is dramatic and over-reacts.

- Tells you to do something... then CHANGES her mind.

- Is COMPLICATED.

- At first sight, the only thing you KNOW she's sexy and you wanna fuck her.

- She's one of two genders that can RE-PRODUCE.

- She's bitchy.

- She holds grudges.

- She has 'boobs' (in all sizes).

- She screams when she sees a spider.

- She obsesses over things and constantly worries.

- She's CURVY.

- She smells nice.

- She likes to paint her nails.

- She likes to attach dead hair to hers (known as extensions).

- She TALKS a lot.

- She cries easily.

- She's emotional.

- She admits when she's wrong (guys rarely do) and reminds YOU when you're wrong.

- She's like the underdog. You never expect her to win but she DOES.

- She keeps you waiting.

- She's a clothing obsessed money grabbing human, that never shuts up.

- She's beautiful... sexy, smart, attractive, seductive, my motivation (at times my transportation) a goddess in her own mind, everything else doesn't matter.

K. We've established the fact...

YOU guys don't know... (everything). Except for what you learn in school. Observing, watching us in the hallway... your *imagination* while jerking off. LOL

We girls, need to look at how we're affecting our guys (what's working, what's NOT). And we need to be very <u>clear</u> on the message we're sending out (so you're not confused) and we don't get screwed. So, do YOU girl wanna be mostly masculine/feminine in your relationship?

Here's your first clue...

Do you need to be *right*?

Or...

Do you need to be *happy*?

And you CAN'T pick both.

(Pick the ONE that <u>matters</u> to YOU most)

Have no clue...

What guys want girls to know...

1) Don't expect us to say nice flowery things during movies, that's A LOT of planning. Then we worry it'll be all wrong anyways.

2) Calling you on the phone doesn't mean we want you to be our 'girlfriend'. It means we're seeing if we like you. Try not to get it confused.

3) When you jump up and down and scream and giggle, it's seriously embarrassing. You get excited over everything. You see each other and SCREAM.

4) PMSing is no excuse for us. Being rude if we don't do something perfect while you're pmsing is boyfriend abuse.

5) Talking about your 'big' butt is BORING. And don't ask us if you look fat we don't know! Accept who you are or DO something about it. But stop tormenting us cuz we never say the right thing anyways.

6) If you want to show off your boobs don't complain everyone's looking. That makes no sense.

7) Most guys are looking for the 'right' girl. We're just trying to weed out all the sluts first.

8) We cannot READ your mind. Get it ALREADY.

9) We really appreciate when you tell us we did something RIGHT (for a change). Instead of just complaining when we do things wrong all the time.

10) We want you to like but not love our friends. We are secretly jealous when any guy looks at YOU (but we'd never show it).

11) We worry that you will dump us.

Enlightening... Lol

What guys don't know...
(but wish they did)

What girls want you to know...

1) Don't think just cuz you didn't tell us, we're never going to FIND OUT—we will. Half the time it's written all over your face.

2) It absolutely floors us when you know certain things. Like, our shoe size, favorite ice cream, TV show (movie) singer. See, we're not that hard to please.

3) No matter what we say, we hate your ex-girlfriend (for sure). So <u>NEVER</u> bring her up.

4) We check our phones *every* hour to see if you have replied to our texts (then worry if you haven't).

5) The fact you might leave us for another girl, keeps us up at night. And <u>every</u> night until the relationship ends.

6) When we act sad, we secretly want you to hug us. And that's also btw why we like SAD movies (we cry it all out to them). They have a purpose.

7) Our favorite part of texting is at the end when you say good-bye cuz that's the part you say you love us (you're scared shitless to say it in person).

8) If you go through our purse you will get SLAPPED. Fo shur. Depending on our cycle (period) it might be a lot of worse.

9) Yes. You might be the reason we failed our History test (most likely).

10) We don't care about what we talk about, just as long as we have your attention TOTALLY. It makes us feel special, even if we act like it doesn't matter.

11) We love wearing your hoodies cuz even though you're not around, it makes us feel like you are. We know this sounds weird.

(Re-reading is helpful)

441.

Process...

Dude...

Do you wanna be the MAN? ☐

      Do you wanna have your very own **dream girl**? ☐

Do you wanna look out for your GIRL? ☐

      All 3 checked off indicates YOU'RE ready.

No worries...

She'll be as gentle with you as you've been with others.

Tale signs they're in LOVE...

- They don't wanna sleep, if it'd mean missing 'time' with YOU.

- They cook for both of you and put it on ONE plate, don't like being separate from YOU.

- When you use their toilet, almost fall in it, leave a sticky note that reads; LEAVE THE TOILET SEAT DOWN! Underline it five times. They look at it... claim it a work of ART. Take a picture n' post it on social media. Or, let you use their expensive shaver.

- They send you a text. "Bae, my heart hurts... What's upsetting YOU?"

- After work they go to THREE different supermarkets to find your favorite TYPE of yogurt cuz you're coming over.

- They call you their heavenly pita (or appetizing equivalent) you nourish their soul...

- You blow a fart while cuddling. They're like, "You know in those old videos where they show atomic bomb testing, how it flattens the TREES? That's what my leg hairs just did." Laughs.

- If they need to wake up early and you're over, they'll set the alarm a bit earlier just to cuddle (hold you).

- They see you with pimples (scars) say... "You're so beautiful."

- They're at the bank and tell the teller it's your ONE year anniversary. She's like "What do YOU have planned?" They're like, "*Shhh...* I gotta be *careful* can't speak too loudly." She's like, "Why? Are they here..." They're like, "They *live* in my mind..."

- They offer to do your nails (or toes) even though they have no CLUE what they're doing. When you come out of the shower, they wanna dry your hair, so you don't catch cold.

(Tell me YOURS I'll post it)

444.

Zero moisture...

MEANS move on!

How life talks to YOU...
—(Part 1)

I rented this room from a single mother. She was weird AF. When I first went inside her house, the incense candles were so strong it made my eyes water. When we talked she's like... "I don't expect you to be like ME... I just want you to keep things neat and tidy." Cool. But she kept *repeating* that like... ten times. She's like, "I don't expect you to be like ME..." (over and over again). I needed the place so I took it. (Warning: GUT overlooked)

A few days later I move in. It's a NIGHTMARE. I'm studying in my room, she pulls into the garage, then there's a knock on my door... She's like, "I noticed your lights are on." I'm like, "Uh... yeah. I'm studying." She's like, "Well I only use my night light and *both my* teenagers never use the main light." Yeah... Well *both* your teenagers aren't paying you FIVE HUNDRED DOLLARS A MONTH for a room, I thought to myself. Next day it's Saturday I redo my WHOLE schedule, so I can study in the day (sunlight) not use the light. Curtain's wide open and I'm sittin' near the window, I can see her sweeping the leaves outside. At least, now she won't complain.

There's a knock on my door...

"I noticed you were sittin' by the window, all the neighbors can see you." I'm like, "And...? I'm doin' my homework." She's like, "Well I would never sit in front of the window where *everyone* can see me." She was so adamant about sayin' how she **didn't** expect anyone to be like her, when in fact that's EXACTLY what she expected! That's why she kept saying it. It's like, she's was having a conversation with herself (in her head). 'I don't expect you to be like me' answering the part that whispered... YOU better be like me. Or she wouldn't have had the <u>need</u> to say it (so often). Now I understood. She didn't even let ANY random drops of water drop in her kitchen sink. Had to be bone dry. At allllll times. Her kids would put all their dishes (dirt n' all) in the dishwasher (not to deal with it). MAJOR OCD. That evening, I walk up to her I'm like, "Just giving you the heads up. I'll be leaving at the end of the month. Please have my last month's deposit ready." Later, I hear her discussing it with her kids... she DOESN'T have the money. I cut my losses, tell her to keep it (probably needs it more than I do). She's UP in my face—tonsils full vision and all *SCREAMING*...

"You're the DEVILLLLL!!"

OMG! Why's she saying that? I call my friend and she's so nervous for me. ☺ For a minute felt kinda powerful... her naming me after Lord of the Underworld. Never had that before. Next day there's music friggin' blasting in MORNING!! Whole house is **vibrating**. O_O It's playing the *same* lyrics over and over again...

'I will not let the devil take me.'

WTF? There's banging outside my door—*SHE'S NAILING A CROSS ON THE WALL!!* And she's hanging a garlic vine! I'm freaking out. There's this uber intense smell from incense lit all over the house. She's ripped Bible passages and put them on <u>every</u> step. It's *Carrie*... alllll over again! I RAN. Almost wiped out goin' down stairs. The fumes are SO thick I start feeling *dizzy*. The music's so loud the entire house is SHAKING.

I feel like I need to go get **baptized**!

And I'm Jewish. I drive to the lake and even though it's apparent she's not all there, I felt bad (I upset her). I felt hurt... confused. Like, AM I not a GOOD person? How could she call me that? I always get things like, "You're an *angel*..." Seriously. It was very disturbing. I'm sitting on a boulder, near the water and I notice a *letter*... folded in half, right next to me (with a rock on it). Someone left a love LETTER... for a guy (or girl). The wind picks up and it starts flapping. Omg! It's gonna blow AWAY. They'll *never* know how much they love each other!" So I get a bigger rock and put it on top. To my *surprise* I see something I TOTALLY didn't expect.

448.

A Letter...

To Whoever This
May Find.

I open it...

Hello,

This letter is intended to give you a piece of a great message that I know if accepted will bring you love, joy and peace.

This letter is from God.

I don't know what road you come from friend. I don't know the scars your heart, and perhaps body, may carry. I don't know the person who has broken you or the trials you face. However, I do know that whatever wounds you embrace, whatever burdens you carry, that all can be healed through Christ.

Look around you friend, there is indeed something more.

"Come to me, all you who are weary and broken and I will give you rest. Take my yoke upon you and learn from me, for I am gentle and humble in heart, and you will find rest for your souls. For my yoke is easy and my burden light" Matthew 11:28

Your things will get old ... you want more, you want better
Your relationships grow stale ... you want more, you want better
Your appearance and youth is quickly escaping your tightly clenched fist ... you want more, you want better.

Find the source that never changes nor erodes, His name is Jesus Christ. "For God so loved the world that He gave His only begotten Son, that whoever believeth in Him should not perish but have everlasting life!" Holy Bible - John 3:16

This message was very much meant for you dear stranger for God makes no mistakes.

May you walk with the Lord. Peace and love will follow.

Life TALKS to me!

NEVER doubt that life is ALWAYS talking

To YOU.

Reminding you how POWERFUL it is...

(How taken care of YOU are)

Understood... <3

Virtual hug. :*)

YOU... **TALK** to me <3

WJPTube

From around the World!

POST CARD

Fuckman, this shit is so informative, thanks! Anthony Ball

It was purely awesome don't let nobody hate! OrangeRebel13

YOU buddy, need more recognition for sure! You're so funny speaker :) Augusta Strong

nicely said! I love your channel so much :) Agatha Willow

Repeat button is getting raped! Laura Beck

It doesn't get any better than this. Superbly done. Thomas Fitt

That is something special... Dremora Chillbuddy

The Wisdom of the Penis
888 Bloor St. East
Suite 101
Toronto, On L4J

This is the reason why there are words in English dictionary like spectacular :\ Zoe Flint

hahahahaha!!!!!!!!!! yoswa1992videos epic!!!!!

She is so funny :D elenaobt45channel

Your videos are like crack... I NEED MORE every god damned time ;D far62tube

FIRST CLASS

FRANCE
TOUR EIFFEL · PARIS

The new way...

SEE what your senses are showin' YOU (gives you the EDGE)

LISTEN to your senses (takes you where you're most HAPPY)

SPEAK UP when your senses tell you to (giving you POWER)

A Message in a bottle...

I find it odd...

That the first draft of The Wisdom of the Penis was completed at 4:00am Dec. 21, 2012. The day they predicted the world to end.

Enter...

A new world!

The Wisdom of the Penis.

An era where darkness, greed, manipulation and brainwashing are left behind. A time where truth... true LOVE and a whole new way of relating is born.

Refuse to be Captured...

Keep it Real. Keep it Pure.

Your Fairy Goddess

In the course of writing this book a few things happened...

YOU became MY family.

I cried A LOT.

I realized, in trying to reach YOU... show you (*teach you*)
I taught myself, showed myself. Reached... myself.

(I owe you) LOL

I have come full circle to *know*... when it comes from love

YOU CANNOT FAIL.

Come take my hand...

YOUR FEEDBACK

On Sat, Aug 21 2016 Kay wrote:

Since I've known you Nichole, my life has drastically changed. My perspective, my goals, the way I have learned to interpret life, my relationships, and myself belief. At the point in my life before we got to know each other, I was lonely and felt like so many things in life were just NOT worth it. I had no one that truly understood me, and I couldn't relate to any of my other friends. I knew how smart I was, and what I was capable of, but it just seemed completely pointless to go through school MEMORIZING everything, and following a structure of a lifestyle I didn't fit in with. I KNEW drugs would alter me in a bad way, I knew it was a waste of myself... to just waste away because I felt aware and alone. I didn't know what to do! I didn't know what profession I wanted to go into, I didn't know where I was going to end up! I had decided... I'd be a gypsy. I'll move away, somewhere in the wilderness, with nature, somewhere secluded, and not obstructed by pollution... with the one I love. And that's what I'd do with my life. I completely felt you from the moment we met, I knew you'd be the only one I could really talk to. Your book's concept **changed** me. I'd come home to my mom and I'd be like, "MOM, TODAY IM MAKING $500.00!! OKAY." You helped me realize the value of pursuing something that made me happy, and why it was so important TO ME to take care of myself. And that I couldn't do it as a gypsy in a trailer park. As a woman, there are things I need, to be healthy, to be *happy*... and vice versa.

You helped me discover that I wanted to help people, I learned that I could. And that is why this book is so fucking important! It helps people! ACTUALLY though, it's not like a self-help book type thing that's BORING. Nichole your book has helped teens quit DRUGS, leave ABUSIVE UNFAITHFUL boyfriends, girlfriends, STOP drinking, RE-INSTILL SELF-WORTH so teens aren't having casual sex, PURSUE their DREAMS because they believe in themselves! My friends have changed, I've changed, everyone that comes into contact with your life altering concepts, CHANGE.

On Sun, Feb 3, 2017 Tony wrote:

Nichole did what others couldn't... listen. She could listen to more than just problems, she could hear the tone in my voice. The amount of weight I carried with each story as one progressed darker, she could visualize the pain I had. It was incredible, simply because she gave me power to see where to go, to lead me on the right path. She's a life mentor, a guardian. She's a special person with a gift to give people, the courage to walk away from shadows, to back away from dark tunnels. She gave me the courage to turn away from those who did me wrong, she gave me a lantern, a special lantern that lit up the dark. I have no desire to do drugs.

I knew I needed to see her because I couldn't take it anymore. I had no strength to fight my demons, to cast aside my temptations. She showed me courage, she showed me a plan... A plan to jump to an opportunity of a lifetime. My life. I cried in front of Nichole nor did I care if anyone saw. The only thing was, I loved how she still listened and knew. Just KNEW what to say, how I felt, where I was coming from. You know, if it wasn't for January 29th 2013, 9:05pm when I saw her, my life would be out of control... Spiraling down into a world of addiction, no sense of love and feeling, just temptation... winding and winding. Nichole is and will always be more than a treasure or an asset, she is a gift. She is inspiration, she is a message in a bottle, cast upon an open sea, reaching out to anyone whose interest is to read what this message in a bottle is. She's more than advice, she's an artisan whose only objective is to shape our world alive. To build an empire of our own, to fill it with knowledge, wonder and love.

Side note: Nichole, ever since that day I have no desire for pot nor those who I surround myself with. You have honestly altered my life once again. I remember the first time I cried on the phone with you, you gave me the strength to turn away from the girl who hurt me, the vultures picking at my dead Tony, to lift him up and nurture him.

P.S. I fully extend an invitation to my wedding. I don't know where she is but you're invited and it's happening. lol!!

On Fri, June 26, 2014 Sandra wrote:

Hug Nichole you are inspiring, contagious, stunningly beautiful, imaginative, young, vibrant, intelligent, a role model, a leader, an out-of-the-box forward thinker, innovative, and so many other things! And I have barely met you! You are awesome, truly. Nichole, if "we are the future", we need people like YOU to share with us, guide us, help show us so we can be ourselves and to help show us so we can step outside of what is comfortable (routine, tradition, or safe in a possibly unhealthy way) if we want to. And I think we NEED to! YOU and what you have to share are a big part of the future too! And you so have something HUGE and shaking to share, so be loud girl!

On May 27, 2017 Marianna wrote:

I was ready to walk out the door. I knew Nichole would be the only one who would get to him. I couldn't believe how she 'knew' what I was feeling. And would tell my husband in our session without me telling her. That got me to trust her. Her insight, about how my parents are, freaked me out. How would she even know my mother doesn't throw the scraps of vegetables out, but throws it back into the soup? The assignments she left us put us on track. She brought to my awareness... me, my needs, my voice (which I never released). She made it fun. She made me laugh so much with her analogies. She made it simple and it was 'clear' what was off. Her concepts were right on and made sense. I felt completely safe with her. I could NOT believe when my husband started doing the laundry, picking up his clothes—asking me if he could help me around the house. I WAS IN SHOCK. If you go to Nichole you too will be surprised, relieved (laugh a lot) see yourself, your life and your guy (girl) in a TOTAL different way. As a newlywed I had a very hard time adjusting to the changes in my life. A final conflict between my husband and I made me realize I needed some help. Calling Nichole was the best thing I could have done for myself and my marriage. She was able to make us see each other's sides, she taught us valuable lessons that will help us in the long run and she restored my hope.

On Mon, Jun 21, 2015 Steven wrote:

Nichole, thank you so much! Your insight has proved invaluable! :D With what happened twice I thought I was going to lose it. I couldn't stand that whore of an ex that was giving lap dances to some guy that I hated at the bus stop. I thought that I was going to kill them all, I felt pissed at both the guy and my ex. Moreover, I felt stupid about myself, because I asked her out before. I saw someone beautiful, not a slut. But this is where you showed me how different you were from everyone else. You didn't say 'ignore it', you showed me a way to not just stop her actions—that really hurt me, but to change how she behaved towards me. And as I did what you said when she was trying to be a slut, she never did it again. It worked flawlessly! She never waited for me to come to the bus stop, and she never did it again. She's out of my life now and all because of some simple, but golden advice that I would've never been able to fathom. When you gave me a chapter to read I could not believe what I was reading. Finally!!! Someone who understands us! I want to go scream at the top of my lungs about The Wisdom of the Penis! It is so NEEDED!!!! Nichole, thank you sooo much! :DDDDD.

On Jul 13, 2015 Karen wrote:

Nichole I don't know where to begin with the way it made me feel... after realizing. The past few days I've been fucked up... like 'muddled' and completely distant and out of it. And now that I feel like myself... and actually **feel**... now, that I'm back on my feet and grounded, I realized how you built this kind of haven around me while I gave myself a chance to come back together.

I just wanted to tell you how much I love you <3 it was just like an instinctive thing. You just went into this mode, that recognized what I needed to recover. And I felt safe under your wing, while you were out in the world creating miracles, I was recouping in my mini-bubble incubator. And even when we spoke it was like, different. You knew I was cut off somewhere, trying to bridge... It just made me feel really safe while I was weak. It reminded me how much I love you. And how I'd do ANYTHING for you. No one has that. No one would recognize it... because people don't blanket each other the way you do. I say blanket cause it's not like a single action! It's like a way of being.

I love you

On July 5, 2015 Anthony wrote:

Nichole I feel so comfortable talking to you about my problems cuz it's not like you just have knowledge but also the understanding that not even parents understand. It's like you took Anatomy and Psychology at the highest of levels and just made it seem like a joke.

Nichole you're not just the person I just want to run away to for my problems, you're more than that and everyone knows that. You help me with problems I didn't even think were rational and realistic. I can pretty much say your work is 'ludicrous' but by far the best damn thing. You're not an average adult, the kind that's either, snobby, horny, vile or pathetic. You've got funk and soul. Since when do you see adults like that these days? Sometimes it's better to be different and far from the norm. It's what you're best at Nichole. You're what's needed in this world.

Nichole you're the shit! You're like the Modern Prophet Isaiah!

On Dec. 18, 2016 Mariah wrote:

"Hey! First thing first, I adore your writing. You may be an adult but you are the true voice of the teenagers. It's unbelievable how you capture the things we can't say because we are stuck in this awkward age of being in adolescence. We are expected to act like grown-ups but have all these restrictions and things that we aren't allowed to do yet. Like everyone else we wake up, go to a place where we don't really want to be, get judged, fall in and out of love more times then we dye our hair during our rebellious phases and yet we can all relate to 'The Wisdom of the Penis'. The way it is written is almost like this generation's version of the relationship bible. It deals with all relationships; it deals with the issues we all have experienced. Nichole Kolman you are someone I am proud and feel very honored to know because of how honest, kind and intelligent you are. Not only has your writing helped me but you, yourself has helped to make me the young woman I am today. 'The Wisdom of the Penis' is going to help young ladies around the world, but that's the thing... You don't have to be in your teens to read and understand the true meaning. I will be giving this book to my Mom and my friends so they can understand we are not alone in our feelings of insecurity and confusion about modern day relationships.

Although this book is written in what people my parents age would say, as 'confusing' we just call it "instant messaging lingo" you feel as if you are reading your own youth. Nichole is someone who is going to change the world, whether it be by one alarming, eye-catching title at a time, whatever. The title of the book may seem shocking, but the real boner is the content. Thank you on behalf of all the girls you have helped, whether it was before, during or even too late, we all realize how lucky we are to have you as a friend. A real inspiration.

- Mariah

On May 3, 2015 Kim wrote:

This book is more than unique Nichole it's the Bible that Jesus would use. I mean this in the sort of humorous, non-offending way of course, ha! But this overall gives a genuine tone of honesty. You like what you do and people like what you do too. You know we all got the questions and uncertainties, and that at the very least, you have the guidance that shall direct us to the right answer. Soft-core poet. I like.

On September 24 2016, 2015 Darren wrote:

It was a complete surprise when you just came and sat next to me at the gym. I had only seen you there on a few different occasions. What you did was different than what anyone else had ever done. I've never had anyone be so 'exact' about who I am, what I've been through, where I'm going. That's RARE. You feel me, you know where my strength is. That's extremely comforting. You hit the nail on the head. And I knew you knew me inside cuz I had never talked to you. You reinforced the things I wanted, needed on the way, doing. Moving in circles, you walked with me until I could move ahead—now instead of circles my focus is <u>clear</u>. Again, very comforting and <u>very</u> rare— I mean WHO DOES THAT? After you talked to me Nichole... I began to question myself less. I am not influenced by others but I was **affected** by you. I know now that the circle has stopped... I'm focused, I strive for people to understand me, but they don't. You do...

Thank you.

On Apr. 4, 2017 Kristina wrote:

I have known Nichole for six years now. I met her while she was writing her book. Instantly, I was intrigued. Once I read a sample chapter I was excited to see that the way she writes reminds me of Maria Montessori and her principles in regards to the way she developed the Montessori School System. It felt so right. The life lessons, inner tools, self value principles, connection with nature and your own instincts all matched, were sound and inspiring. It's about time a book like this came out. Most of the information seems like 'common sense' however, most people are missing this knowledge. This book is meant to offer inspiration, support, wisdom, and knowledge to teens and young adults who have always wanted 'more', but didn't know how to get it, didn't fit in, felt lost, scared, pressured, hurt, or are oblivious to the mistakes they are making. This book is like the key answer to the biggest exam (life). As a Montessori teacher, I see the huge need and value in this book for our students, parents, as well as us adults, who don't feel threatened when knowledge is presented in a way that's designed for the generation preceding us. Since the book deals with a time when we, most likely didn't have a book to make sense of things, it gives us closure on some things, establishes a healthy, inspired reconnection to ourselves and has the innocence, newness and energy of first-time love within sight.

Nichole presents her ideas through personal stories and metaphors, in a language young adults understand and makes it interactive. Sadly we, as well as our girls use the media as a reference on how to act and look. The media is sending incorrect and destructive messages. She addresses this on all fronts, from media control, to self image, forced peer pressure (work, school, relationships) and going against the pack. In today's world, when watching a show or movie the female characters are usually having casual sex. This is how sex is portrayed. They almost always sleep with the guy on the first or second night, or leave that one and find someone else. Is this the message you want to be sending to your teens? Or even to adult women?

In overcoming her obstacles and during her ten year run writing this book, she's never stopped writing, no matter what loss she incurred, health challenge or emotional pain. This enables her to reach every single person from every corner of the world. I'm always amazed by her strength and determination. Those are awesome qualities that she possesses. Anyone reading this book will feel like she's right there. They'll feel like they can get through anything. Nichole breaks it down and shows them how to respect themselves. This book is not only amazing it is a <u>must</u> for anyone, especially young adults.

On Dec. 18, 2016 Melissa wrote:

I'd seen her before, two or three times actually. My first sight of her, I was automatically intrigued by her. Something about her told me I needed to meet her and when she approached my friend and I at a café asking for a 'word' (slang) for the book, I knew it was supposed to be like that. Nichole has guided my thoughts and actions positively, helping me to better understand how things worked and how my opinions on things were not what I wanted them to be. We talked about things I'd never told anyone in my life about. Nichole had an amazing glow, a positive and inspiring shimmer to her. She is my role model. My friend and I both had our eyes opened to the world that day, the minute we talked to Nichole we knew our lives would change for the better. We ended up staying about 6 hours talking and laughing, which isn't something I'm used to as it usually takes a while for me to open up. With Nichole, everything was different. She said I needed a man who could take care of me for a change, in comparison to the others with whom I had been with (taking care of them). My second time meeting with her I brought up a guy that had caught my interest and Nichole had talked to him as well, a few months earlier. I felt that was another act of fate. She told him, he needed a girlfriend who he could take care of, and who would do the same in return. He and I had talked about it, and it essentially brought us closer and closer. With Nichole's gentle guidance, I ended up dating him, never have been happier, both him and I owe our happiness to Nichole. We have had our disagreements and every time Nichole has been there with me, to assist me in re-evaluating the situations.

I pay great gratitude to Nichole Kolman

Actually... It is I who am privileged to write for YOU.

My blood line...

(vibe)

soul connectors...

And I won't STOP till adults listen... hear YOU.

So that you learn to feel respected, valued. Parents and adults need to know that when they abuse YOU you will abuse society. The anger needs to seek an exit—it's looking for a way OUT. It will find it. Once we are accustomed to being valued, inspired, there's no telling how GREAT our nation will become! We can bring in... the new **AGE**. A word meant to be attached to newness (elevation) hope.

I GOT your back.

I dedicate *this* page...

To my BOYFRIEND. Who brought
me back to life, found me at my
weakest moment...

STILL made it magical.

Who said, "Nichole... It's like God
put a *piece* of the sun in YOU.
Darkness HAS to go. Unstoppable."

Who makes lying next to *him* so
complete... There's nothing else I
need in this world (except YOU). <3

Who calls me...

His White Magic Woman, the man
I love...

      Christian

Who confirms daily, that if you keep
reaching no mater what... There'll be
a HAND extended to you. It has to...
You're meant to be embraced.

Loved...

It will come. It's trying to find YOU
right now. <3

Nichole Kolman
Your Fairy Goddess

The One meant to be with YOU...

Has the POWER to unlock you from your demons (relentless blood-suckers) tryin' to take you under... dragons (assholes tearin' at your heart) mind slayers (thoughts that haunt you) and that's cuz... They **touch** your spirit. They're key to illuminating your shadows...

They show you HOW and WHY you work the way you do. They can do this cuz they're the *closest* to you. They'll trigger all kinds of shit (you didn't even know bothered you). They'll free you from all this, cuz they're NOT afraid of the *beast* inside YOU (you... at your worst). They know the **real** you.

Signed,

Daughter of Darkness (Transformed)

The Fairy Goddess!

You'll know you found the real thing...

When it feels *unreal.* LOL

Just so you know...

DON'T MESS WITH ME!

I'm OVULATING

The wisdom of the penis?

(blannnk)

HAAAA! Only kidding.

Whaaat...? You don't think there's a *wisdom* to the penis?

YOU think it just gets lucky or somethin'? Oh... I *assure* you. There's a wisdom to the penis.

It's coming...

Seriously.

WILL the battle of the sexes ever end? I dunno...

There's always somethin' rising up in the middle of it. Ahahaha! But maybe we can get to the root of it... *follow* the lead, trace it back to the seed, discover the wisdom of the penis.

So *hang on...*

Not to it!

Do that on your own time. .)

The Wisdom of the Penis

Graduated...

BIG balls. LOL

A shout out to allll my Youtubers!

TALK to me (if it hit home). <3

Nichole

Mwwwahhh!

SUMMARY

What IF a book had a magical element to it? For real. What if it could be used as your OWN private oracle? What if... It could talk to YOU? Respond to you *live*... as you're responding to it?

It would have to be written by an author who has 'unexplainable' psychic experiences with her body's *impulses*... and yours (while she's writing). An author who has her finger on the *pulse* of the public (issues, pressure, bullying, shame, highs n' lows) who's tight with YOU. Like she's right *there*. As creepy as it sounds YOU trust her. She makes too much sense. You're excited when you read it—cuz now you know *fo shur* you're right (always have been right). And your *hunch*... feeling was—BANG ON. It'll gives you enormous strength HOW she explains it. And now you see the many sides (angles) of a guy's or girl's MIND. How they view things, what's going on in their head (*true* fears). Once you see a situation... you'll see all situations with parents, teachers, coach, boss. Sad thing is, you'll wish you had it last year, last month, LAST week. LOL You have it NOW.

This book breaks all TABOOS. It jump starts critical issues circling YOUR life, hunger for knowledge (shit you put up with) the hope that drives you... *the dream inside of YOU*. Written as if she's a young adult of today, it's as if she's been transported to the FUTURE, experiences allll these relationships, drama n' life shit, then comes back... to tell all the girls, why guys DO the dumb shit they do (feed her heart before you feed your hard-on). Tells all the guys, why we girls do the crazy-ass-bitch things WE do. I mean... There are reasons why we do what we do. Still, enough of them 'expected' to read OUR mind. And the life signals we miss... till (sadly) it's too late. Written in slang, it's raw like our music—with emoticons (for true emotion)! Text messaging and fast one-liners for real communication. Totally piss worthy. It's emotional... Powerful.

Personal... <3

It'll create a paradigm shift...

A radical change in your underlying beliefs and/or theories.

Made in the USA
Middletown, DE
12 September 2023

38376588R00295